Jane Coverdale worked as a scenic artist in theatre, television and film and as Art Director and graphic artist on television commercials, music videos and series TV Drama in her home country of Australia.

The Jasmine Wife is Jane's first historical novel and was influenced by her time living in Chennai, working with renowned Indian actor and director Kamal Hasaan.

f www.facebook.com/authorjanecoverdale

The Jasmine Wife

Jane Coverdale

A division of HarperCollins*Publishers*
www.harpercollins.co.uk

Harper*Impulse* an imprint of
HarperCollins*Publishers*
The News Building
1 London Bridge Street
London SE1 9GF

www.harpercollins.co.uk

This paperback edition 2019

First published in Great Britain in ebook format by
HarperCollins*Publishers* 2019

A catalogue record for this book
is available from the British Library

ISBN: 9780008336301

Set in Birka by Palimpsest Book Production Ltd, Falkirk
Stirlingshire

Printed and bound in Great Britain by
CPI Group (UK) Ltd, Croydon CR0 4YY

For my family

Chapter 1

Sara could hardly believe they were there at last. She had been on deck since dawn, not being able to endure the agony of waiting any longer.

At first she was unmoved by her earliest glimpse of India, except for a deep sense of relief at having survived the journey, and the curious feeling of being inside a picture book.

She stood transfixed, as parched of life as a dried flower pressed between the pages, till, all at once the breeze shifted, and carried towards her the elusive tang of the distant shore.

Her past returned with an almost magical clarity, and memories, long forgotten, crept out of the shadows to taunt and provoke her.

She remembered the sickly-sweet smell of flowers turning brown in the sun, trampled offerings, scattered and rotting on the steps of forbidding temples dedicated to fantastic and unlikely gods. The stench of open drains fused with the heady and seductive scents of sandalwood and patchouli. Patchouli! She mouthed the word almost with reverence as she breathed in a hint of the musky, ancient fragrance. There was no other perfume that spoke the essence of India with as much power.

She could almost feel the touch of a thin dry hand, grasping her own, as she followed behind the hurrying figure, tottering along on her little legs, her starched muslin skirts rustling through laneways crowded with stalls and people, her eyes fixed on the bright sari as it swayed ahead of her. Her mouth watered with the memory of forgotten tastes. Mango, thick, creamy yoghurt and freshly ground nutmeg, sweet sticky rice on a banana leaf, a dish made as a special treat by her ayah, Malika.

Sara hadn't thought about Malika for years; now all at once she was flooded with sensations threatening to unbalance her, and unravel her tightly held self-control.

Malika! Sara strained to remember her face but could recall nothing of her features, only her cool touch, deft and reassuring, her fine wrists and arms encircled with a hundred shivering and tinkling bangles, and when she walked a cloud of patchouli followed in her wake.

Malika! Who had slept at the foot of her bed, and had wailed inconsolably in her grief when she had been taken away, tearing at her thick black hair and rubbing the oil from it onto Sara's bright curls, as though giving something of herself: a talisman, to protect her.

Sara reached for her handkerchief but could not stop the tears. All those years in England and she hadn't cried. But the tears came fast now, choking her with deep silent sobs. Soon they subsided into a sniffle and then, with a flush of shame, she remembered where she was. She looked around and was relieved no one had seen her outburst except a dusty seagull with one leg taking a rest on the ship's rail.

A new smell separated itself from the others, but this time Sara pressed her handkerchief, now a damp and salty rag, to her nose, though it was not possible to stifle the horror. There was the stench of death nearby.

She shaded her eyes against the rising sun and, there on the hills in the distance, she could see the skeletal outline of the Towers of Silence, tall sticks of rotting bamboo where the Parsee dead lay, on beds open to the elements and to the mercy of the scavenging birds. Against the white sky, the ragged shapes of vultures floated on the air current, too lazy and well fed to hunt for live prey.

She closed her eyes, and relived again the peculiar sensation of being inside a child's skin and chattering to her dolls in the garden of her childhood home in Madras.

Everything there had been cool, lush and fragrant. The only sound birdsong and the soft laughter of the servants as they moved on silent feet over the marble floors of the faded mansion sheltering amongst the trees.

Within the compound of her old home, the giant figs and magnolias had hung like canopies, protecting the delicate English flowers from the burning sun. At times, even roses and lavender were coaxed into bloom and, for a moment, it was possible to imagine it was England after all.

She recalled looking up, shading her eyes against the hazy sky, distracted by the sound of fighting vultures above her head. Then, as wild as the imaginings of a nightmare, the remains of a human arm had dropped with a sickening soft thud on the ground near her feet.

They should have known it wasn't possible to keep India out, despite the high walls surrounding the house.

Sometimes, a band of diseased monkeys, as savage and merciless as pirates, would appear without warning to swing down out of the magnolia trees to upset the table and steal the tablecloth, before retreating to the garden wall to jeer at the servants with bared teeth.

Then, again, they would be reminded that, outside their ordered and tranquil oasis, there was India: the real India, desperate, hungry and passionate.

Her mother's face rose before her, the features hazy but idealised to perfection, an image fixed forever in her mind, as no picture of her survived to tell the truth of her loveliness.

She recalled the sensation of being lifted to sit on her mother's lap, the rustling of silk, the fleeting fragrance of Attar of Roses rising from her clothes at her every movement, her high gay laugh, childlike still, as she ran barefoot across the lawn to join her little daughter in play.

To Sara she seemed to have always been a wraith, a fairy, with no more substance to her than a dream. Her father was a stronger memory, as she wore a miniature of his likeness in a locket around her neck.

The shape of his face was like her own, the full mouth and thick chestnut hair, but more real to her than his image was the faint memory of a pleasant aroma of sandalwood and tobacco, and how he had read his newspaper to her, and encouraged her to read books well above her age. It was he

4

who'd encouraged her to speak Hindi, and to play with the village children so she could learn their ways.

He was kind to everyone, especially the servants, and spoke to her often, even as a tiny child, on the need to remember that all humans were created equal, at least in his home. And, even from the distance of time, she could recall a hint of bitterness in his voice as he spoke those words.

It was a message that had stayed with her throughout her life, and she had clung to it, as a gift he had left her, even though she was often reprimanded by her aunt for being too familiar with the servants.

Then, without warning, there were dim shadows and pain, a blurred image of a crouching figure by her bed, forcing bitter liquid through her clenched teeth. The hallucination intensified with the sounds of strange indistinct chanting, a fierce brown face close to her own, rising and falling through the mist.

Then, later, only six years old and an orphan now, dazed and frail still, being led away from the prostrate and weeping Malika.

Then a long sea voyage to England with an unknown English nanny, who held her hand in a tight grip as she waited on the doorstep of her Aunt Maria's home, till the door opened, and she was brought inside to be taken care of.

No one knew how painful it had been to be uprooted from everything she had loved, to be left to find her way in a cold country, in the cold house of indifferent people.

There was rarely any discussion about her dead parents or the home she had left behind. It seemed there was an unspoken decision to put the whole episode out of her mind, and all memories must die with her parents. She recalled her aunt's words whenever she dared to broach the subject. "Your father had a wild side ... somewhat like you at times ..." she would say with a reproving sniff, "and it was hoped India would bring him to heel. But things went from bad to worse ... We knew little of your mother, only that he said she had some Spanish blood, which would explain those eyebrows of yours, and your father was determined to have her."

She didn't say, 'in spite of the objections of the family', though it was clearly implied.

"He broke with us as you know, and the first we knew of you was a letter telling us both your parents were dead. They found you in the servants' quarters with an Indian woman and some barbarian priest. That's how you came to be here, and that's all we know of the unfortunate episode."

Even her name had been considered too pagan for this new world. She'd been christened Sarianna as an affectionate salute to the country of her birth and had known nothing else. When it was dropped in favour of Sara, "a respectable English name", she had been too young to protest. She'd become Sara Archer, though somewhere in the back of her mind was a vague recollection of another name, a name she couldn't remember.

It wasn't Archer, she was certain of that, and her aunt had no intention of enlightening her.

The subject was dropped, and it was unwise to attempt to raise it again, but Sara could see she knew more than she was prepared to tell. She just wasn't going to, and now that she'd died after her long illness the name had died with her.

The mystery of her parentage didn't seem to matter compared to the enormity of her loss. As a child, numb with shock, she went through the motions of living; of attending boarding school; of strict rules and petty punishments; of eating lukewarm, tasteless food, and learning how to stifle any show of ill-bred passion.

It was hoped she had been well and truly immunised against the more fervent emotions, though they hadn't been entirely successful.

Her small rebellions showed in the letters of complaint sometimes sent home to her aunt.

"Sara is at times sullen and unruly. She runs when she might walk and seems to have no interest in the feminine arts. She has also been found reading a book of a nature we find unsuitable for a girl of her years and written by a Frenchman no less! She has been duly reprimanded, and the book confiscated. Her most serious misdemeanour is of riding a horse bareback outside of the usual riding lessons. You know what irreparable damage that may do to a young girl. Perhaps even blight her chances of a respectable marriage. Need I say more ..."

7

Sara Archer, a good plain name for a good plain girl, though with her unusual colouring and high cheekbones she should have been a beauty, but, after years of stodgy boarding school food, she was overweight and cursed with sallow, dull skin made worse by the long English winters.

Her aunt despaired of the girl's appearance, using every remedy short of powder and rouge, though, even with the daily doses of castor oil and cream of tartar to whiten her complexion, her skin remained lacklustre and dull. Her hair though had always been admired. In a plait it was as thick as a man's fist, and even her aunt admitted grudgingly the colour was lovely, despite being more red than brown, and too heavy to crimp successfully with curling irons.

Though the cold weather was her chief enemy to beauty, it seemed her nose was always pink and swollen, her eyes constantly watering and her body stiff and ungainly.

She felt she was almost always shivering, except for the few brief, warm luxurious moments spent in bed in the morning before hastily dressing in her icy room then rushing downstairs for breakfast, where she sat as close to the meagre fire as she could, her hands clutched around her teacup, desperately trying to warm her chilblained fingers.

Sometimes at night when she lay in bed rigid with cold, her life in India came back to her in strange little bursts of disconnected memory, flooding her with longing, and enveloping her with warmth.

In a candlelit room with dark wooden floors, she lay in a small white bed under a billowing tent of mosquito netting, while she listened, wide-eyed and sleepless, to the sounds of the night invading the room on a warm perfumed breeze.

Sometimes, she shivered at the sudden scream of a cornered animal, and the horror of the whimpering that came soon after, then an ominous lingering silence. Or, the most terrifying of all sounds, the haunting chant from a nearby temple, where the worshippers were known to practise the forbidden rites of the goddess Kali, who wore a belt of human skulls around her waist and brandished a bloody knife above a decapitated head.

She knew about Kali, all the children did, but, despite her terror, she relished the bloodthirsty image with a curious delight.

Then, a suspicious rustle in the bushes beneath her window: a bandit perhaps, come to rob the house, or a python, gliding its way across the terrace to eat one of the hens.

Though to chase away her fears, in the corner of the room came the peaceful breathing of a sleeping figure, ever present and comforting, her beloved ayah, Malika, and she would fall back to sleep at last.

Then, more happily with daylight, the screech of her pet peacock, who followed her everywhere. The feel of cool fabric on her warm face as she ran laughing through sheets of luminous silks as they hung floating from between two coconut palms; the sounds of laughter, and music; a band of musicians wearing brilliant blue turbans, the plaintive wail of a sitar, and food, always food, of every kind, aromatic and delicious, spread on a long table placed under a shady arbour, surrounded by people, their faces blurring into each other, but all of them, it seemed, were happy and caring. It felt too she was the centre of their care, and she felt safe and, most of all, loved.

A young sailor coiling a rope looked up and gave her a curious stare, bringing her back to the present. Sara straightened her spine and began to pace the deck again; the waiting had become almost unbearable. A trickle of perspiration ran from beneath her wide straw hat, down her throat and into the neck of her white muslin blouse. Her skin beneath her bodice was slippery with sweat, so she would have to keep her arms firmly pressed against her sides in fear of the dreaded stains under her armpits flooding into even wider crescents. She thought how much cooler she'd be if she hadn't been wearing a corset, and it was tempting to throw it overboard as she had done with the huge cane bustle her aunt's maid had packed with her luggage. It would have been more sensible to just have given the bustle away, but she'd thought as a symbol of her new freedom it deserved a much more dramatic send-off.

She'd thrown it overboard at dawn, and watched it hover for a long moment on the waves, refusing to sink, and taunting her for her mutinous behaviour, till it floated almost out of sight and sank at last.

The young sailor smiled at her now in an admiring way, then strode along the deck, his wide baggy pants flapping lightly in the breeze, his linen shirt open at the neck, and Sara thought how pleasant it would be to wear such clothes. Her own long legs were encased in cotton bloomers and hidden by the thinnest layer possible of petticoats. She gave a furious little kick of protest under her skirts, but she knew to throw away her petticoat as well would be a step too far.

She recalled her aunt's constant refrain over the years beating into her brain like a mantra. "Whatever you do or wherever you are, do not let your standards drop for a moment. People will judge you by how you maintain your appearance. A slovenly exterior shows a slovenly will."

Sara laughed to herself. She had already let her standards slip and was surprised by how little she cared. Clearly it was other people who seemed to mind.

The hated curling irons too were abandoned almost as soon as the ship had been out of view of the shore, and her hair had improved dramatically ever since, shining with a new life and colour now it was allowed to be as it was meant to be.

She reached up to smooth the heavy chignon held in a wide tortoiseshell comb and tucked a few loose strands under her hat. It was difficult to be neat in such weather, but she consoled herself with the thought that perhaps Charles wouldn't notice ... Men usually didn't notice such things, but then, he was always so immaculate himself and he couldn't abide untidiness in others.

Dear, dear Charles ... Her face took on a faraway look as she cupped her face in her hands, her elbows on the rail. She hadn't seen him for over a year, not since their hasty marriage on the day he'd left to return to India.

They had planned to have their honeymoon on board the

ship, but when Sara's aunt became gravely ill on the day of her marriage, Sara had no choice but to stay to nurse her till she died. But, even after her aunt being long buried, Charles wrote asking his bride to wait a little longer before joining him. His letters told of typhoons and outbreaks of hostilities amongst the natives, or cholera amongst his staff, then, finally, the need to wait till the end of the monsoon.

She'd decided she wouldn't wait a moment longer, regardless of disease or bad weather, when at last, when more than a year had passed, Charles's letter arrived and freed her from the home where she'd begun to feel she would never escape.

"You must take a passage on the *Charlotte*, leaving Liverpool on 22nd October. My friends Lady Palmer and her daughter Cynthia will accompany you. Unfortunately, Lord Palmer must stay in England for a few months longer, which means I am in charge here ... a very good sign for my career. They've been in Paris shopping for Cynthia's trousseau, after having become engaged to a young man who will be in time, a Baronet."

He was clearly impressed with Miss Palmer, and he proved it with the following lines.

"I cannot stress enough the importance of you becoming friends with them both, my future may depend on it, and the long voyage will give you that opportunity ..."

Sara's thoughts drifted back to the world she'd left behind. The solid two-storey, red brick house near Hampstead Heath, set securely amongst pleasant oaks and a garden full of snowdrops and bluebells: a safe world of middle-class respectability, where no hint of worldly passions would ever be likely to enter.

After visiting on a regular basis for some weeks, Charles had come to the house to say goodbye before returning to India, and everyone assumed he'd come to ask for her hand. When he suggested a moment alone with her in the conservatory, her aunt could barely contain her excitement and rushed forward, taking both his hands in hers in a way to show he was already a member of the family. "Of course, my dear boy," She smirked and winked till Sara thought she would die of shame. Though even she fully expected he'd ask her to marry him then.

But it came to nothing. He took her hand and held it for a moment, then said something about how he'd miss their amusing chats, and how he'd hoped she'd find time to write to him in India.

A terrible attack of panic overtook her. He was going to leave without asking her to marry him!

She thought of India, and how much she longed to go there, so she defied convention and took matters in her own hands. She swallowed her pride and prepared to lie.

She blurted out, "I'm sorry, I won't be able to."

He was clearly taken aback.

"I may be married soon, and it wouldn't be appropriate to write to a single man."

His face showed no emotion, though he flexed his hands behind his back as he paced amongst the potted begonias.

"Do I know the fellow?"

"No, he's someone I've known for a long time." She stared at her feet so he wouldn't see her eyes.

"I promised him my answer within the week."

"Does this mean you'll accept him?"

"The family is very fond of him, and so am I really ..." but here she hesitated, then sighed, hoping to plant a little seed of doubt in his mind.

"But he's a highly respectable man with a bright future ... so ..."

She had almost begun to believe in her fictitious fiancé herself.

Charles left the house deep in thought, and Sara was convinced she'd never see him again.

"Well?" Her aunt met her at the door, her uncle standing behind with a foolish smile on his lips.

She tried to speak but no sounds came out. Her humiliation was too great. She rushed to her bedroom, her face averted, her aunt's bitter words following her up the stairs.

"Whatever did you do wrong this time?"

Later, when she emerged, her face red and swollen with shame, her relations scarcely bothered to hide the fact they thought she was nothing more than a liability.

She thought back to that evening's long, silent, unendurable meal, the air thick with disapproval. Her uncle's furious tight-lipped sawing of the roast, his resentful way of handing her the plate without looking at her, and how he gave her less meat than usual.

Now there was no escaping the endless censure and, with the departure of Charles, there was nothing and no one to look forward to, just endless days of boredom or visiting her aunt's stuffy friends and walking the pekes. She'd developed a hatred of the poor things.

The next morning, in an attempt to recapture her lost pride, she put forward the idea of going to India by herself.

"Hundreds of girls do it." She raised her chin and glared, even though she knew she might have gone too far. "Why should I have to wait for a husband to take me ...?"

Her uncle was moved enough by her outburst to put down his newspaper in a way calculated to increase her fear of him. "So, you would join a shipload of common shopgirls, to trawl amongst the rabble of India for a husband? Simply because you can't find one here ... or won't," he added, referring to the time when she had refused what was seen as a perfectly good offer from a country parson with a generous living because she couldn't bear the way he blew his nose then examined the contents of his handkerchief.

For almost a week she was hardly spoken to; the outrage was too deep.

It was while she sat, frozen with humiliation, staring down at her untouched breakfast, that the maid had entered and announced Mr Charles Fitzroy was waiting in the library.

"Perhaps he forgot his hat?" her uncle remarked cattily as she flew out of the room. In the hallway she took a moment to tidy her hair and compose her face into what she thought was an expression of pleasant unconcern before she opened the door to face him once more. Even so, her voice came out husky and cracked. "Mr Fitzroy? I didn't expect to see you again."

He was standing by the window staring out at the garden, still covered in a thin layer of morning frost, then, with what seemed an enormous effort of will, he turned to face her.

"I've been thinking ..." He took a deep breath and swallowed hard, unable to look at her while rolling his hat around in his hands. "Look, I can't accept you'll marry this other fellow. I had it in mind that you might marry me."

She held onto the back of a chair for support. "You didn't mention this before," she answered at last, her voice shaking.

"It didn't seem fair to ask you to give up your life here, but it seems if I wait any longer you are lost to me. Though if you love this other fellow ..."

"No, I don't love him," she managed to blurt out, "I never have. I was going to refuse him."

He took a step closer. "Are you going to refuse me?"

She had just enough self-control to pause for a respectable time before answering, then to allow him to take her in his arms and clumsily brush their lips together.

Then the relief, the blessed relief, to be able to announce she'd received a proposal of marriage from Charles Fitzroy, and that she'd accepted him.

It was decided to arrange a special licence so they could be married almost at once, then sail for India together on the same day of the marriage, therefore saving the cost of a honeymoon.

Later, when the first throes of excitement had died down, Sara examined her reasons for accepting him. She was fairly sure she loved him, of course, although it had taken her some time to realise it. He'd been lured to the house by her ever-hopeful aunt, as had many other young men before him, and placed as an offering at her feet. Knowing she was expected to encourage him, she'd felt a stubborn resentment, telling herself he was no different from all the others.

Then, while they'd been playing tennis in the garden and he'd paused to take a breath, he was, without warning, suddenly illuminated. He stood with his shoulders back, his chest heaving from the pace of play, one hand on his hip and the other holding his racquet nobly by his side in the attitude of a Greek god. In the soft afternoon light, with the sun shining on his bright blond hair, he appeared almost unbearably heroic.

For a few moments it was as though the world had stopped spinning, and she remembered the flash of realisation.

I love him! I'm in love!

With that insight everything changed, and she couldn't be easy around him any more. Just brushing her hand by accident on his caused such an intense mingling of pleasure and fear, she felt sure he must know. Even her laughter became forced and unnatural, and she couldn't look into his eyes without blushing and turning away.

He was different to the other men in her narrow circle.

He was on leave from India for only a few weeks and

brought with him into the stuffy air of parsons and bank clerks a lingering atmosphere of adventure and glamour. He told of cobras found asleep in the billiard room at the club, of tiger shoots and playing polo in the shadow of faded pink palaces. But, most of all, he intrigued her with his tales of the Indian people, their strange customs and powerful beliefs, transporting her back to her childhood and the world she so longed to recapture.

As a child she'd gone to bed each night hungrily devouring library books written by yet another female traveller, either fictitious or factual, braving it alone in foreign climes. The women she admired rode disguised in flowing robes on testy camels over vast deserts, or roamed the South Pacific in search of their tropical destiny.

She'd wanted to be one of those women, but how she would go about it was uncertain until Charles had appeared.

For Charles, it was a revelation to watch her shining eyes and rapt expression every time he spoke. It occurred to him it would be very pleasant to come home every night to such an infatuated creature. Though he couldn't know it, it was not so much his masculine charm that caused her face to light up whenever he spoke of India. It was India itself and the prospect of adventure, or perhaps discovering something of her past, that held her spellbound.

He almost visibly shuddered when he thought about some of the girls he'd met in India. Like the other men in his crowd, he cast a calculating eye over the cargo of English girls, the so-called "fishing fleet", who arrived every October and stayed till the beginning of the hot season in the hope they'd find suitable husbands. He found the idea of choosing from amongst them impossible, as even the plainest and poorest of them showed an unbecoming haughtiness. For the first time in their lives, these girls found themselves in demand, and were going to make the most of it, despite the fact most of them, in his eyes, were only just passable.

After a few years of rejecting all those put before him, he decided to return to England on his next leave and find a wife for himself.

Sara Archer was not exactly beautiful, though certainly far from plain; she was what was called attractive, despite being a little overweight. He thought she was too tall for absolute beauty, as he usually liked petite women. Her teeth were very good though, and her hair lovely, despite being of a colour he was not particularly fond of, as he much preferred blondes.

He thought her eyes were rather lovely, even though framed by thick, almost black eyebrows, but she was undeniably intelligent and highly accomplished. Several nights spent listening to her play his favourite pieces on the piano was proof of her talent, that and the fact she had lived in and survived India, when so many children hadn't, made her a far superior candidate for marriage than any other woman he'd met in England.

Despite her shortcomings, he saw her as a potential wife because he was sure she adored him, even though she did at times have an annoying habit of contradicting him on matters he felt she should know nothing about.

Being an orphan only added to her charms. There was no

doting parent to make demands on her time and take her away from her wifely duties and, despite the fact her parentage was a little cloudy, he'd been assured her father had been educated at Eton, was English through and through, and had left his daughter a small annuity for her personal use only, the comfortable sum of five thousand pounds, which would be his on the day of their marriage.

Though when faced with the real prospect of marriage, there was the sudden realisation he might not be able to please himself any more. He'd momentarily forgotten about the pleasures of his club, and the freedom bachelor life brought. It was pleasant to be always available to balance the table at dinner parties, and to be surrounded by admiring women hanging on his every word.

Then there was the thrill of big game hunting, the drinking till all hours with his male friends, whose company, he had to admit, he preferred more than any woman he'd ever met. And, of course, there were all the other delights India had to offer. A thrill ran up his back at the memory of past pleasures. There were indeed compensations for a life spent as a single man, and a wife would be sure to get in the way of all that.

He'd decided after all to return to India and resume the pleasant life he'd always lived. It was only when Sara had told him about her potential engagement to another man that he had felt a sudden pang of regret. Somehow, he'd always imagined her as his own to take or leave as the whim seized him, and now there was someone else in the picture he felt as though something had been stolen from him. The thought of the other man being in the way meant nothing to him. He felt sure she'd choose him over anyone else, regardless of the consequences.

When she agreed to marry him, though, it came as a shock. But, like a man, he accepted it and there was no turning back, despite at first an almost overwhelming urge to run in the other direction.

In the end, though, it was his desire for a son and heir that finally convinced him he'd made the right choice. And he liked her, really liked her. She'd be a splendid companion for him. Now, all she had to do was fulfil the role that was expected of her, and there was no reason why their marriage should not be a success.

For Sara, alone in her room at the end of the momentous day where she had at last fulfilled the destiny expected of her, she stood before the mirror and closely examined her reflection, running her fingers over her face as though to smooth away the lingering signs of doubt. The blinding realisation had come to her as quite a shock. She'd agreed to marry a man she didn't really know and would go to the other side of the world to live with him.

Only a few months before, the question might not have arisen, but now she asked herself ... What would the ladies from our Female Emancipation group say?

It was while she had been running errands for her aunt that Sara had been stopped by a young woman bearing a placard saying, "Women of the World Unite!"

She was almost mannish in her dress and clearly not wearing stays.

"Come on in," the girl said, laughing. "We don't bite, and you look like it might do you some good."

The church hall was almost empty; even so, the speaker talked with a truth and passion difficult to resist. She spoke of the unfairness of the marriage laws, and why women should have the vote; the terrible injustices inflicted on their sex, and of the foolish and restrictive nature of the female dress. For Sara, it was the beginning of an understanding she had always been dimly aware of, but, once enlightened, had changed her thinking from that day forth.

Now she saw tyranny everywhere, especially in her own home. It appalled her to see how her aunt had to pacify her husband in order to keep him content. Where once she'd grudgingly accepted the petty rituals of warming her uncle's slippers before the fire, or listening silently while he expressed his opinions, she now eyed him with a deep and bitter resentment, longing to say what she really thought, but having to bite her tongue for the sake of peace.

The young woman in the plain blouse and skirt, known to her later as Mary, had shouted out her warnings with a raised fist, and Sara was very aware of the truth of her words.

Though she was sure she was in love with Charles, deeply in love even, and she was equally sure she was marrying a man who loved her. Also, it was three days before her twenty-third birthday, considered far beyond the turning point of being either an eligible young lady or a hopelessly lost old maid.

But it wasn't just the fear of spinsterhood driving her to accept him.

There had been a terrible row, a row that had caused such a storm she felt it was impossible for her to stay in her aunt's home a moment longer.

She had been secretly meeting with the Ladies Emancipation group under the pretence of attending bible studies with other so-called respectable girls when she'd been discovered.

Someone had mentioned Sara had been missing from the bible meetings for some time. Then a pamphlet on women's rights had been found in her room and placed before her outraged uncle. For a moment she considered denying it was hers, then she admitted it and, what was more, admitted it proudly, and announced she would continue to go to the meetings no matter what.

For her uncle it was the final straw and he washed his hands of her, only making it clear he wanted her out of his sight as soon as possible.

Now, though, none of that mattered.

She could go back to India at last, India! Mother India! Her lost home that lately had haunted every thought and called her with an urgent and relentless cry, even as she slept.

They married on the day of their planned departure, in the church Sara had attended for nearly seventeen years, knowing a few hours later they'd be together for the rest of their lives.

She took a furtive look at him through her silk veil, hoping for a look of reassurance, as she was almost overwhelmed with sudden feelings of doubt. Though, when he felt her eyes upon him, instead of a returning smile, he seemed to visibly pull himself together, straightening his shoulders and swallowing hard.

Her heart sank. It seemed to her that Charles was steeling himself for something unpleasant, something he must endure, and see it through to the end at all cost.

A screeching note from the organ made her jump, and her stomach gave a sickening lurch. It came to her in a blinding flash. She may not love him after all! And perhaps he didn't love her! And was already regretting his choice even though he'd just spoken the words, "I will" in an almost inaudible shaky murmur.

When it came her turn to speak she hesitated, caught between a desire to make a run for the open door of the church and a yearning to cling to the man who offered her a lifeline to a new world.

She glanced around in a frantic effort to find an answer, but saw instead the face of her aunt, alarmingly pale, though smiling bravely, and her uncle, nodding furiously at her with a tight grimace on his lips, clearly willing her to get it over with.

She must have responded, as the final words, "I now pronounce you man and wife", were uttered at last, but Sara, at the threshold of what she felt every young woman must desire, instead of feeling the expected rush of joy, felt an overwhelming sense of doom.

Then, as she turned to walk down the aisle towards her new life, her aunt seemed to haul herself to her feet as she reached out to the new bride for a congratulatory kiss, swayed a little, then, grasping the folds of Sara's gown in her fingers, fell in a crumpled unconscious heap at the feet of the bride and groom, clutching a torn piece of silk from the wedding veil.

The illness was serious, and inevitably fatal. When her aunt begged her to stay to help nurse her it seemed unfeeling to do otherwise and, even though she expected Charles to protest, he was remarkably accepting about the prospect of travelling to India without his bride.

"In some ways it's a good thing," he said as he tried to reassure her.

"My house is a mere bachelor's hut and this small delay will give me a chance to find you something more suitable, and you can brush up on your Hindi. Tamil will be beyond you, I feel. But Hindi will come in very useful in dealing with the servants. Also—" he gave her a furtive glance "—my position demands my wife be well dressed. Lady Palmer entertains on a regular basis and you'll be expected, as my wife, to make a bit of a splash."

"Oh ..." Sara blushed as she looked down at what was meant to be her going away outfit, an ill-fitting mustard-coloured dress which did nothing for her complexion, adorned with oversized leg-of-mutton sleeves too tight under the armpits.

All her clothes had been made by her aunt's dressmaker, a lady who specialised in a style that had died out in Paris at least twenty years before, despite still flourishing amongst the vicars' wives and spinsters of Hampstead, and any suggestion that poor Miss Blunt might be exchanged for someone more modern was quickly suppressed.

Though her fears about the suitability of her clothes seemed trivial compared with the cruel reality that Charles would be leaving her any moment, her husband but not a husband, not till they spent a night together under the same roof.

In an agony of misery she threw her arms around his neck, unwilling to let him go. There was no question of his staying; he'd extended his leave already and was anxious to return to his duties.

He reached up to remove her arms from his neck, gave her a final brief kiss, then hurried away without looking back, while she flung herself down on the settee and cried as though her heart would break. To be so close to freedom, then to have it taken away, was almost more than she could bear.

Later, when her tears were exhausted and she felt nothing but an empty despair, she'd climbed wearily to her feet and made her way upstairs to the sick room.

Chapter 2

The shoreline moved closer still, and the mirage formed into a blinding reality. They would be there soon. Sara pulled a mirror out of her bag and examined the clear light topaz eyes squinting back at her. They appeared unimpressive in that harsh white glare, but she knew they would be lovely again once she was in a softer light. Her eyes were the only feature on her face she wouldn't change, and the rest of it she found more acceptable now, with the miraculous clearing of her skin and an equally miraculous dramatic weight loss.

The first small signs of improvement had come soon after the marriage ceremony. She had lost at least fifteen pounds in only two months, forcing her to buy a completely new wardrobe, and her doctor pronounced her excess weight and her skin condition as being based in nervous tension, hinting it was not unusual for single women to improve in looks with the marriage state.

She didn't tell him that, even though she was a wife, she was still technically a virgin, and perhaps the real reason for the improvement was she was no longer made to feel ashamed whenever the subject of marriage was mentioned.

After being at sea for eight weeks, including a further month spent in the Canary Isles due to having to mend a split mast, where she'd gorged herself on fresh fruit and vegetables, the almost constant faint rash around her nose had miraculously disappeared. Then the fine red bumps on her cheeks and forehead had faded completely, revealing a surface with the fresh even tone of rich cream.

Her true beauty however, lay in her bone structure, a beauty that would last long beyond the freshness of youth. Without the excess weight, her face became more refined, making her eyes appear much larger. Her posture had always been good, and her straight back and long neck gave her elegance, far from the clumsy girl of her youth.

Though it was the new shape of her once heavy eyebrows that gave her the most pleasure. Never could she have imagined such a small change could have produced so dramatic an improvement to her face. The mysterious ritual of threading, performed by an Arab woman in a tent in a Canary Isles market, had turned her shaggy brows into a blackbird's wings, giving her face a striking new beauty. Now she secretly plucked them to keep their shape, knowing her aunt would be horrified had she known, believing a lady must learn to live with her imperfections, and any thought of artifice was vulgar in the extreme.

Sara had no such feelings as she smiled at her reflection and smoothed her skin with a cautious finger. She hoped fervently the hated rash had been banished forever, though; it seemed the further she travelled from England, the healthier and lovelier she became.

Her much improved looks were a novelty still, and sometimes she found herself studying her face in the mirror for longer than necessary.

Though, as time wore on, she trained herself not to think too much about her new-found charms, but secretly enjoyed the long slow looks men gave her as she passed them on her walks around the deck of the ship.

She snapped the mirror shut and slipped it back into her bag. While she'd been dreaming, the shoreline had drifted closer still. The clear blue waters had changed to a dirty yellow, and the once vague outline of the distant bank had turned into buildings set amongst tall waving palms and enormous trees spreading their branches along the baking paths like engorged pythons.

Some of the structures were prosperous and ornate, more bizarre, romanticised reflections of their respectable English cousins, while others, mere piles of other people's cast-off rubbish and the fallen branches of coconut palms, were turned into little caves to huddle under for a moment's respite from the merciless sun and the endless mass of humanity.

Towering over even the grand buildings of the British were the temples, shimmering through the damp heat, many storeys high, barbaric and mysterious, intricately carved with unlikely gods and decorated with gaudy impossible colours and gold leaf. There were dozens of them, punctuating the tropical landscape every few hundred yards and soaring towards the heavens like the wild and fantastic imaginings of a dream, monumental and overwhelming.

Remembered snatches of whispered stories of ancient and primitive rituals carried out in the dark recesses of the temples crept back into her mind, making her shiver: stories too horrible to be spoken of out loud, used as a weapon by the servants when she was naughty, to frighten her into good behaviour.

Sara stared out towards the shore, her eyes squinting in the fierce sun. There, rising and falling with the motion of the waves, something floated on the surface of the water.

She peered over the side of the ship, then reeled back, shaken and drained of colour. Afloat in her funeral bier, a woven basket lined with a mass of faded flowers and wrapped in white gauze, slept a perfect child of a few weeks old.

A loving hand had placed the fragrant flowers around the halo of the child's head and over the little body, before releasing it into the sea. An unwanted girl, perhaps, who'd died conveniently, but had clearly been loved by someone in her short life.

The child floated past, an image of unbearable loneliness at the beginning of her journey. Sara's eyes followed the little voyager, smarting with painful tears till the yellow water turned deep blue again, and for a brief moment she was comforted by this.

Then her stomach lurched, and for a moment she thought she was going to be sick. She clutched the rail and squeezed her eyes till she saw stars, praying with a sudden fervent superstitious fear, to crush the image lingering in her mind.

She began to pace again, now with a more urgent step. It seemed they would never reach land and the shore was further away than ever.

Then, slowly, as she watched, the scene before her sprang to life. A tree swayed in the gentle breeze, and the thousands of coloured dots moving along the shore evolved into human beings.

Children began to play, running back and forth on childish missions. Thin wisps of grey smoke rose from the cooking fires where women sat, draped in vivid saris, their movements impossibly elegant for such humble everyday tasks.

Then the first sounds, laughter and shouting in Hindi, and Tamil, and music, a strange off-beat medley to western ears. There was a procession somewhere.

The handful of European passengers appeared on deck one by one. Already there was a distance between them, making it clear their relationships had been held together almost solely by the confines of the voyage.

Secretly, Sara intended to keep few of her promises of undying friendship if she could help it, though, much to her regret, with Cynthia Palmer there might be no choice.

Sara watched Cynthia with mixed emotions as she moved through the crowd on the deck, languid and unhurried, smiling her goodbyes, her white toy poodle, recently bought in an elegant pet shop on the Rue de la Paix, clutched in her small gloved hands, stopping now and then to speak to a friend, her voice hardly ever raised above a quiet murmur. Sara crushed a pang of rising irritation. If only she could believe in the value of such self-control it would have made her life so much easier.

A sweet young girl's voice, heavily laced with the rounded vowels of the well brought up, called out her name, and Sara looked up with a start from her daydreaming.

"Cynthia, how fresh you look. How do you do it, in this heat? I'm melting already." Her voice sounded false even to herself, and she wondered how Cynthia could not fail to notice it.

But then, Charles had made a point of how important it was for her to become friends with Lady Palmer and, even more so, her daughter Cynthia. She recalled his words in his letter: "I'm sure you'll become as fond of them as I am for, as we often say in our little community, it's impossible not to love Cynthia and her mamma."

Sara was fairly sure she didn't love either of them, and at times positively disliked Lady Palmer, though she was clearly outnumbered.

Cynthia was as pretty and fragile as a Dresden figurine, though it soon became clear her fragility was misleading, disguising an unbending core combined with a steely determination, at least when it came to having her own way. Though there was never any need to exert any pressure when it came to getting what she wanted; it seemed to happen naturally, as though it was always meant to be.

She had a habit of grasping the arm of the person she wished to beguile, holding them rigid, like a fox with her teeth on the neck of a rabbit, but, as a kind of compensation, she held them under the impression they were the only person in the world worth knowing. When she wished to move on, her small white hand would relax, releasing her captive, now limp with admiration, and left with a desire to be singled out by her again as soon as possible.

Though, when away from her mother and alone with Sara in her cabin, they could spend almost happy hours together as each girl talked of their hopes of the future with their respective husbands. Cynthia's intended would join her in Madras in a few months' time, where they'd be married before returning to Europe for their honeymoon and a new life in England. She'd met her fiancé William when he'd stayed with her parents in Madras and he'd fallen in love with her then. His health was precarious though, and more than a few months in India was dangerous for him. Cynthia's face would take on an almost childlike radiance as she spoke of her husband's country estate and her hopeful future away from the hell of India. It was at these times Sara could sympathise with the girl, knowing from personal experience how painful it was to be trapped and powerless, and at the mercy of another person's demands.

Her mother, Lady Palmer, was a big woman with coarse sallow skin, large features and a passion for extravagant clothing, who seemed constantly astonished to have given birth to such a fair and dainty child. Her main concerns, apart from her daughter, in whose life she took an almost unnatural interest, were the comings and goings of Madras society and all who moved within it. She set the standards of behaviour and it was up to everyone else to observe and follow, and woe betide anyone who didn't.

"I expected Charles would have married one of the girls at home ..."

Lady Palmer had scrutinized Sara shamelessly through her lorgnette. "Personally, I saw no need to look further than our little community, and there were many girls I thought more than suitable for him to marry." This was said with such an air of wounded outrage Sara had laughed aloud, then said, "Well, why didn't he then if they were so suitable?" causing Lady Palmer to glare in return.

"It's no laughing matter, my girl. Marriage is a serious business.

However," she conceded, "I'm sure dear Charles had his reasons. Indeed, I do believe at one time he might have asked Cynthia. Charles always seemed to pay her such particular attention, and we are so very fond of him." She frowned, as though recalling past times. "We'll miss him to balance the table at dinner. He was always so useful as a single man."

Sara could only laugh, knowing with a sure instinct nothing she could say would alter Lady Palmer's behaviour. Her role was supposed to be to endure and smile, but so far she had only questioned and scowled.

Their relationship was bordering on disastrous but, just in time, a small voice in Sara's head had cautioned her to be careful. All those years in an English boarding school had taught her it was vulgar to express what one really thought, and she would give Lady Palmer another chance, for Charles's sake.

Sara sat in the longboat, waiting to be taken ashore. She'd been there for some time, wilting in the stifling glare of an unbearable heat with the muddy waves slapping with an uncomfortable violence against the sides of the boat. She was jammed between a fat matron holding a bird cage containing a fast wilting canary and, on her other side, a fretful seasick child, all due to a dispute as to whether Cynthia's poodle should or should not be caged for the trip ashore. The purser was insistent it should be so, and Cynthia was equally insistent that it should not be. The other passengers were becoming increasingly irritable at the long delay, though Sara was almost thankful for the wasted time as it put off the inevitable a little longer.

She scanned the indistinct mass of faces on the distant shore, her stomach a tight knot of nausea, not knowing if her misery was due to anxiety or seasickness. Was Charles there amongst the crowd, staring out to sea, perhaps regretting his choice of bride or, worse, lying dead somewhere from an all-consuming tropical disease, as her uncle had often predicted? Was she abandoned before even beginning to be a wife? It was impossible to know. Charles was a poor correspondent and during the space of the fourteen months since she'd seen him last he'd written perhaps only half a dozen letters. In vain she'd scanned them for the passionate declarations of love she so longed for. But the contents of his notes were usually about the terrible state of the weather or graphic details of the outbreaks amongst the various castes. She wondered sometimes if he was trying to put her off coming at all, but at the bottom of the page there was his usual declaration, "Love Charles". That one word kept her hopes for future happiness alive.

At last, Cynthia made her way to the head of the ladder leading down to the longboat, her poodle in her arms and a self-satisfied smile on her face. She had won, as she knew she would.

A group of Indian workers, hired to help the passengers with their luggage, hovered around the launch, their fragile boats rising and falling with an uneasy violence at each surge of the waves, and it seemed must be thrown into the dense yellow water any moment. They watched the passengers with anxious eyes as they jostled for position. Charles had written the region was in the grip of famine and it was clear these men were hungry ... hungry with a desperation that made them careless.

Halfway down the ladder the dog began to struggle, being all at once aware of being poised above water. She made a frantic attempt to hide her head under her mistress's arm, thinking in her dog mind that if she couldn't see the danger then it wasn't there. Her struggles became more frantic, the dog's hard little legs working with a mindless terror, clawing for a more secure foothold against the shiny silk of Cynthia's gown.

Her mistress let out a piercing scream as the dog threw itself into the air with a yelp of fear.

The poodle fell like a stone. At first sinking from sight, then emerging from the muddy sea where a little wet head could be seen swimming in useless circles just out of reach of the boats. Some of the Indians laughed.

Their lives were too harsh to care about the fate of one small dog, though the shrewd amongst them saw it as an opportunity sent from the Gods.

Sara watched transfixed as one old man stood with shaky determination in the prow of his boat, letting go of his hold on the side. He was a tragic knight, his armour a useless rag serving as a kind of cloak knotted around his painfully thin body and his weapon a gnarled walking stick. Sara cried out in a whisper, "Don't! Please don't!"

He was too old to be out competing with the younger men. He should have been resting under the shade of a tamarind tree, smoking a cheroot and enjoying the last years of his life in peace and tranquillity. But, with desperation driving him, fate had decreed otherwise.

His smile was of an unusual sweetness as he reached out towards the dog, murmuring words of comfort and encouragement.

But there lay his mistake; by now, the others had realised the value in saving the dog and all rushed at once to get to the prize first. A sudden lurch of the boat and the old man fell like a shot bird over the side, his ragged cloak black against the sky, barely making a splash. He recovered quickly and swam towards the dog, his arms stiff awkward paddles. There was a hideous battle, an almost comic game of catch-me-if you-can, as the dog seemed to almost deliberately swim further out of his reach.

"Mother! Do something! Poor Fanny!" Cynthia covered her eyes and fell back in a faint.

Lady Palmer called out the price of the dog's life, and there was a sudden desperate jockeying to reach the dog first, and the old man was forgotten in the rush. An untimely swell from one of the larger boats drove him further away and he called out, a weak and almost apologetic cry. A couple of boats halted, looking first at the old man and then at the dog, but the prize made the decision an easy one.

The old man made a last feeble attempt to save himself, a hollow snatching at thin air, then there was a sudden jerk of his head as though something unseen was pulling at him from underneath the waves.

The thick water rose in a swell and he rolled with it. His face appeared for a moment, and Sara caught the full impact of the certainty of his own death.

Her scream seemed to recall him to life, and he struggled for breath with the last of his strength.

For a transient moment they made eye contact and in his look was a pleading that cut through to her soul. She leaned out towards him as far as she could, stretching out her fingers in a futile attempt to reach him, her eyes fixed on his.

"Try! You must try!" His eyes widened for a brief moment, then flickered and closed, as though resigned to his fate.

A cry, more like a sigh, rang out. "Prema!" Then, with a final thrashing on the surface, he sank under the yellow water.

There was a flurry of panic on deck as the captain ordered a lifebuoy to be thrown. It hit the water near where he'd disappeared, but the old man did not surface again.

The crowd rushed to the side of the ship, peering down into the old man's tomb, some of them trying not to show how they were enjoying the drama and congratulating themselves on their good fortune to be alive while the old man was with his Gods.

Surely, Sara thought, suddenly hopeful, it's a trick ... The old man's a *fakir* and any moment he'll rise up and the crowd will reward him with a few coins. But he didn't appear; his life was over in a terrible paltry moment.

The trip to the shore was made in an uneasy silence. The dog was back in her mistress's arms, unaware of the catastrophe it had caused. Cynthia, though, was a little shaken out of her usual self-control.

"The silly old man ..." Cynthia straightened the dog's wet pink ribbon "... I do feel sorry for him, but what could he have been thinking of? And now he's paid the price of his foolishness."

Her mother sat close, patting her daughter's arm with clumsy affection and murmuring, "My poor child, how dreadful it might have been."

"It's all right, Mother. Don't fuss! It turned out all right after all. Fanny is safe, aren't you, darling ..." she cooed as she wrapped the wet squirming dog more tightly in her pink cashmere shawl.

"It didn't turn out so well for the poor old man!" Sara spat the words with a bitterness she couldn't hide. She couldn't help it, even though she knew the words were the first nails in the coffin that sealed her social fate. Both women turned to her with unmistakable dislike—she had shown her true colours and they'd never forgive her.

She turned away, pressing her palms into her aching eyes, trying to drive the image of the old man's last moments out of her mind.

"What was he trying to say to me? Prema? What could it

mean?" Malika would have called it a bad omen and rushed to place an offering at the temple to ward off further bad luck, but she, as a civilised English woman, could only try to crush the horror of the event she knew would haunt her forever.

News of the disaster had reached the shore, though there were no obvious signs of grief from the crowd, only an air of quiet resignation. From some quarters there was almost an air of gaiety, as though the old man's death, not necessarily a misfortune for him if he had lived his life well, had spelt good fortune for someone else.

The sharp-eyed boatman who'd saved the dog kept a watchful eye on Lady Palmer, following close on her heels, accompanied by a group of his fellow boatmen who congratulated him on his good luck with open envy.

Lady Palmer kept her eyes averted, her hands clutching her purse with a tight grip despite the man's pleas for his reward.

"All in good time, all in good time," she murmured while the man followed behind, all the while grinning and nodding around at the crowd who'd gathered in increasing numbers, sensing a chance for the British ladies to appease the Gods by paying generous baksheesh. The people crushed closer, hands out, grasping and desperate, begging and pleading for coins, fighting each other in the scramble to be noticed.

"*Memsahib!* Dear and good *memsahib! Baksheesh! Baksheesh!*"

Sara bit her lip as she began to feel a rising panic.

"Perhaps, Lady Palmer, you could pay the man and the crowd would go away."

"Well, I would if I had any money," the woman snapped in return. "It's just that I don't have any on me at this particular moment. Indeed, I never carry it. Perhaps you could pay the fellow."

"Me? I don't have any money ... at least no Indian money, only English pounds and I don't think that would do."

"Well, give the fellow what you have," Lady Palmer replied, dismissing the matter and considering her part in the business now over.

Sara opened her purse and the man moved closer, his eyes fixed upon the contents. She held out a pound note and in an instant the man snatched it out of her hand and at first stared at it with disgust before throwing it down in the dust with a cry of anger. Then, in a flash, a gnarled brown hand darted out through the crowd of dusty bare feet, picked up the note, and someone more knowing quickly disappeared with it.

The boatman then turned all his attention to Sara. Lady Palmer had been forgotten. "Give me!"

Sara was angry now, and wondered how it came to be that she was bearing the brunt of Cynthia's selfishness and her mother's stupidity.

The crowd surrounding the besieged women stared with curious fixated eyes made wild with hunger. They crammed more tightly against each other in a tight rancid mass of unwashed bodies, allowing small ragged, almost naked children to scamper like mice over their heads, while the women stood clutching each other for protection in the ever-decreasing circle. The over-excited children, leaping in a grotesque dance on the heads and shoulders of the people, called out in halting English, "Give me money! I have no mother! I have no father!" thrusting their fingers in open empty mouths, while dodging angry snatches at their hard, thin legs from the furious onlookers.

Sara felt a furtive hand touch her thigh, then, as though being assured she was real after all, felt it again, this time with an added hard pinch.

She let out a faint scream of fear as she felt something hard hit the brim of her hat. Her first thought was that they were trying to kill her, then she looked up, astonished to see a glittering shower of coins fly high over her head, followed quickly by another, then another.

The children let out animal-like cries and flew after the path of the coins, followed by most of the crowd and leaving Sara standing alone in a cleared space. Though a number of the onlookers were so overwhelmed by the unfolding scene they froze on the spot, then fell to prostrate themselves at the feet of the man who stood before them, his legs sturdily apart and his commanding arms crossed over his chest.

Chapter 3

It was clear the blood of two races flowed through his veins, uniting to produce a man of such dramatic appearance Sara found herself staring at him in awe. He had the air of a person who was used to attention, so much so that he'd mastered the art of appearing to be unaware of the impression he was making.

He was taller than the average native Indian, and of a bulkier build, being broad-shouldered and thickset. His heavy masculinity was an odd contrast to his clothing, as he wore an almost transparent muslin *kurta*, through which could easily be seen the powerful contours of his chest straining against the fine fabric where it met his folded arms. A long white muslin *dhoti* hemmed with a wide band of gold thread hung around his waist and down to the ground in the manner of a Brahmin priest.

Standing out amongst the almost black servants, the unusual pale gold of his skin revealed at least one of his parents had European blood, though his hair was as blue-black as a leopard's pelt. He wore it combed straight back off his forehead, falling almost to his shoulders in the style of a Mogul prince.

His European ancestry showed too in the colour of his clear light grey eyes, making the irises appear more intensely dark and hypnotic. Though there was nothing dreamlike about his expression and, despite his prophet-like clothing, he glared out at the world with ferocity from under his black winged eyebrows, and an expression that seemed to say, *I defy you all!*

There was something there too in the corners of his full, sharply defined mouth that hinted at contempt, but at whom or what Sara couldn't tell.

Lady Palmer sniffed and turned away in an elaborate display of disapproval, even placing herself between him and her daughter as though his presence alone could be contaminating. Her behaviour did not escape the stranger's notice, though, instead of being shaken by her obvious dislike, he seemed to struggle to hide his laughter.

Sara gave a slight bow of her head in his direction, hoping to initiate an introduction, but Lady Palmer didn't attempt to even acknowledge the man.

He took a step closer and bowed. When he finally spoke, it was with a heavy accent as though English was his second language, though there was no sing-song note to his voice as with other Indian people. He spoke French with the accent of a Parisian.

"*Pardonnez moi, mesdames.* I apologise for the crudeness of my tactics, but, as you see, it is effective."

Lady Palmer turned her face away from him without a word, and Sara, feeling the shame that should've been Lady Palmer's, thanked him again with genuine gratitude.

A group of women in saris of gorgeous colours and wearing huge gold nose rings sat clumped together nearby, giggling behind their hands and pointing at Sara, their heads swaying like snakes as they came together to whisper their secrets. Little snatches of remembered Hindi came back to her. They were saying something about her hair and wondering if she used henna. The stranger heard them too and glanced in Sara's direction, his eyes focused on her hair. She flushed bright pink, without knowing why, and stared down at her feet, as was her habit as a child when she was in trouble. He sensed her discomfort and smiled to himself in an unpleasant way, as though wondering how he could exploit the situation.

He appeared to reject the thought at once, feeling it was beneath him, and he raised his eyes heavenwards, as though the whole episode was nothing more than an unpleasant interlude he must endure. Then he turned to face the crowd, his palms held outwards like a prophet. "What is the problem here?"

No one seemed willing to answer now they had the chance, and after an impatient few moments he chose a quiet old man with the face of a saint and commanded him to speak.

The stranger's face changed with the telling of the events, first showing only a raised eyebrow at the fate of the drowned man, then a sharp exhale from his rather strongly shaped Gallic nose. A slow scornful smile spread over his face as his eyes flickered towards the group of British women.

Lady Palmer held her face averted while Cynthia stood aloof, an image of picturesque innocence as she held Fanny in her arms. Only Sara seemed connected to the scene, with her purse ajar and her face flushed with guilt, showing she'd been responsible for the entire debacle. By now the crowd had turned resentful and some even shouted angry words in the direction of Cynthia, who held her dog closer to her chest.

The stranger clapped his hands and everyone stopped at once. He'd heard enough and his patience was at an end. He snapped his fingers and a servant hurried to his side. In a second the boatman was paid his due, and hurried away.

Sara felt she must say something, even if the others wouldn't. "I'm sure Lady Palmer would be happy to reimburse you the money if you would leave your name and address."

"She knows who I am ..." the man gave her a slow and almost unpleasant smile "... and where I live." He then bowed in an almost military fashion, before turning away from her with a final blank stare.

Something in his manner drove her to make him notice her. Perhaps it was a desire not to be included with Lady Palmer and Cynthia in his obvious dislike, so she summoned all her powers to confront him.

"Well, I do not, sir." She smiled, hoping to charm him a little. "May I have the pleasure of knowing who I am indebted to?"

He glared back at her, fixing her with his strange hypnotic eyes, and she wondered if perhaps he was a prince and she'd broken protocol by even speaking to him at all.

"My name is Sabran. Monsieur Ravi Sabran."

She breathed a sigh of relief. He wasn't a prince after all.

"And *mademoiselle* ... will you allow me to know your

name?" This time his voice was soft, almost a purr, but Sara had the distinct feeling he was being polite against his will.

"Not *mademoiselle* ... I am ..."

Before she could finish speaking, an old man rushed to his side and spoke excitedly in Tamil while pointing to the crowd.

"Excuse me, *mademoiselle* ..." He raised a hand to stop her, and she glared; he was clearly not listening to her at all.

"This matter is not yet at an end. There is another act to this tragedy."

As though on cue, a woman pushed her way through the remaining onlookers and stood before them, her chin raised in wild defiance, her hard eyes darting from left to right, appraising the scene before her. Her skin was almost black, with wild uncombed hair flaring around her sharp fox-like face. Though, unlike the other Indian women, she wore her faded and torn sari blouse with a flared embroidered skirt worn low enough on the hip to show a beautiful and sensuous midriff, causing a few of the men to stare at her with lustful looks, despite her fierce and forbidding appearance. Sara recalled the tales from her childhood with vague fear. The woman was a Tribal; like gypsies, they were rumoured to be child stealers. She balanced on her bare hip a tiny girl, no more than a year old and naked except for a cheap gilt bracelet around her wrist, showing someone had thought her worthy of adornment, even though the woman held the child carelessly and without love.

The child, though unaware of this last cruel blow of fate to her short life, seemed to know she was the cause of all the commotion, and sat, her body limp and hopeless, on the woman's hip, looking around at an unfriendly world, her huge kohl-rimmed eyes too frightened for tears.

The old man began to shout once more and pointed at the baby with his stick, while Sabran listened, his hand held high to prevent interruption from anyone else.

Then, after the speech had ended, he thanked the old man with more coins and after a brief, almost disrespectful bow, turned to Cynthia, who, outraged that he'd dared to speak to her at all, clung to her mother's arm for protection and stared back at him with her most haughty glare.

"This baby is the dead man's granddaughter and has no other family. This woman was minding the child. He promised her a few rupees when he returned ..." He added, with scorn he didn't bother to hide, "And as there is no doubt he will not return, she thinks you should pay her for her lost earnings."

Cynthia pouted, not looking at him but at the air above his head. "You must know what thieves these people are ... It's probably her own child and she's hoping to profit by it," Cynthia replied before turning away, the matter at an end.

Only a faint twitching around his nostrils betrayed Sabran's anger at the insult. At first it seemed as though he might say something in return, but then he smiled to himself, a smile slow and somewhat sinister, as though he was imagining what kind of revenge he might inflict later and at his leisure. Sara caught his look and shivered. She felt the danger in offending him, even if Cynthia didn't.

The woman was persistent. She came closer, holding the baby up for all to see, then made a sudden snatch at Cynthia's gown. "*Baksheesh!*"

It was as though a spider had crawled on her dress, and Cynthia leaped back a step, appalled at the woman's touch. "No! No *baksheesh* ... You don't deserve it, go away. Go away at once!"

Sabran spoke to one of his servants, who immediately threw a handful of coins at the woman's feet.

In a flash, the child was dumped without ceremony on the ground, the coins snatched up with a savage snarl at anyone who might steal them from her and, with one final disdainful look at Cynthia, she dissolved into the crowd as if by magic.

Sabran laughed, though it was clear he was not amused. "It seems it wasn't her child after all."

The baby sat alone in the dust, looking around at the sea of strangers, her eyes wide and helpless, though managing to convey a real or imagined accusation in her stare. Her look failed to hit the mark with Cynthia, though drenched Sara with an overwhelming sense of responsibility.

"There must be someone? Surely she can't be entirely alone." Sara's questioning looks were met by blank disinterest, though somehow it was implied that by speaking at all, the future of the child now rested with her.

In a curious way she felt it too, and at that moment she knew she couldn't walk away. The girl child she'd seen floating on the sea had been an omen—a message, for her eyes only! The feeling was something she'd only ever read about: a lightning strike of realisation!

She crouched down to stroke the child's velvet skin. "Poor little thing." She hardly mouthed the words. Even so, the child let out a terrified howl.

The child sat forlorn and alone in the dust, crying as though she already knew her fate lay in the kindness of strangers, and Sara couldn't bear it.

Then she remembered an Indian lullaby Malika must have sung to her as a child. Forgetting to be self-conscious, Sara began to sing, a lilting pretty tune in Hindi. "*Nini baba nini … mera baba soja …*"

The child stopped crying to stare at her, and for a few moments the chaos was stilled and everything was quiet. Even Ravi Sabran's manner had softened a little under the calming effect of the lullaby. Now he looked at her with a genuine curiosity.

When she finished, Sara rose to her feet, brushing the yellow dust off her skirt. "Well, I'm not leaving till I find out who will take care of this child."

At first no one came forward, then, after a few words spoken with ferocity and obvious impatience by Sabran, everyone, including Sara, jumped. A servant hurried forward and stood behind the child like a sentry, every now and then guiding her gingerly with his stick if she attempted to crawl away from the spot.

Lady Palmer had had enough. She called out, in her anger forgetting to be ladylike, "If only my husband were here … Why is no one here to meet us?"

There was an uncomfortable silence, then, as though answering Lady Palmer's prayers, separating itself from the noise of the crowd, came a male voice, deep, familiar and reassuring.

"Move along will you? Out of the way." His tone was calm at first, then as though through gritted teeth. "Move away at once, damn you!"

A shower of batons slashing wildly over the heads of the crowd preceded a sudden tide of hard-faced policemen in mustard serge uniforms, creating a path through which Charles emerged, his handsome face red with frustration.

In a moment he was standing before his wife.

"Sara?" There was a flash of shock in his eyes, as if he couldn't quite believe it was her.

"Charles ..." she called out, forgetting to be restrained in the joy of the moment. She fumbled with her hair, then was suddenly shy. She could say no more.

Lady Palmer pounced. "Charles ... At last ... Praise the Lord you're here. Take us away at once."

"Lady Palmer, welcome back." His words were directed at her, but his eyes were fixed on his wife.

Cynthia slipped her arm into his and hung on tight, gazing up at him with what Sara thought were adoring eyes. "Charles! Where have you been?" Her voice had changed to a babyish lisp. "We've had the most dreadful time."

"Yes, my poor girl, she's suffered so much ..." Lady Palmer clung to his other arm.

Charles hesitated, feeling besieged and unsure of which direction to take. Then he gently extricated himself from the arms of the clinging women with a stiff bow and took Sara's hand to raise it to his lips.

"My dear Sara, I'm so sorry to be late; there was a serious incident and it couldn't wait, not even for you."

He looked down at her, scanning her face till she squirmed. Then he leaned down to whisper in her ear, "How lovely you are. I must have forgotten." He was genuinely puzzled. He had retained the image of her when he had seen her last on the day of their marriage and couldn't imagine she would be any different. He remembered with a shudder the too tight mustard wool dress, the almost matronly hairstyle. That image was replaced by a face verging on beautiful, mostly due to her lovely eyes and clear pale skin. He had never noticed the shape and colour of her lips before. Surely in England they were unremarkable? Her teeth had always been good, better than most English girls he knew, but surely much whiter than before. Her fine muslin blouse showed a tantalising hint of small but perfectly shaped breasts above a slim waist, held in check by a wide black belt adorned with a bunch of fabric violets. Her dark green skirt was almost shockingly modern in the slimness of its cut, but the overall effect was of fresh elegance so far from the musty, plum velvet heaviness of the middle-class drawing room he'd left her in.

But it wasn't just a question of her slim figure and smart clothes. The expression on her face confounded him.

Then he saw it in a flash of rare understanding. He'd left behind a doting awkward girl and was reunited with a sophisticated woman who seemed, in the year or so since he'd seen her last, somehow to have acquired a style and assurance of her own.

"You have missed me then?"

He answered her by giving a look that caused a little shiver to run up her spine, then, putting his arm around her waist, he gave her a discreet kiss on the cheek.

A flash of pride shot through her body.

He was even more handsome than she remembered, though perhaps a little thinner. His skin, once a healthy light brown with patches of high colour on his cheeks, was now burnt to a dark tan, making his thick blond hair appear almost white, and his eyes a brilliant blue. He looked tired, and for a short moment she experienced a brief burst of concern, but then it died away almost at once. His back was ramrod-straight in his grey serge suit. She knew it would take more than mere soaring temperatures to defeat him.

He turned on the crowd, shouting irritably in Tamil. They drew back at once and it was clear his authority wouldn't be questioned.

Her arm slipped through his, bringing him back to face her once more.

"I hope the trip wasn't too dreadful ..." He could hardly look at her without his cheeks flushing a bright red.

She mumbled an answer, over-polite and on her best behaviour. "Not at all, we had good weather for most of it."

He looked away, obviously distracted and, it seemed, a little angry.

She searched his face, wondering what could be wrong, but his attention was taken by Cynthia, who stood smiling up at him from under her forget-me-not blue bonnet that suited her eyes very well.

Sara watched his beaming face with a rising tinge of jealousy. He really did look very pleased to see Cynthia. Too pleased, perhaps?

"Your trip went well?"

"Very well. William's family are charming, but of course it's what one would expect from people of such high standing." Cynthia's eyes held his for a long moment and it seemed he was enthralled.

"I can't tell you how devastated we all are at having you taken away from us."

"Of course I'll miss all my friends ..." she smiled "... especially you, Charles." Then she touched his arm with her tiny pink fan, leaving him helpless and trapped by her charm.

"Well, Charles, we've found ourselves in a tiny mess." Then she made a dab at her eyes with her lace handkerchief and moved closer to him.

"You always seem to know the right thing to do."

Sara almost laughed out loud at such obvious flattery, but Charles seemed not to notice how he was being manipulated.

"Now, my dear Cynthia, what's all this fuss about?" Charles had to lean down to hear her as, even standing on tiptoe, her neat little head only came to his shoulder, making her seem all the more vulnerable.

Cynthia whispered into his ear, sometimes taking quick looks at Sara as she did so. He listened intently, then gave the baby a brief glance; she now sat content with a piece of dripping mango in her chubby fingers, encircled by people making half-hearted efforts to amuse her, all of them now anxious to appear to have some part in her ownership, having seen there could be money in it.

"Most unfortunate," he murmured. "I'll deal with it." He clapped his hands and called out, "Shakur! Get here at once, you lazy devil!"

A manservant appeared before them, staring at Sara with a wide grin on his face, hardly taking his eyes off her except to look around at the crowd, hoping they would notice his importance.

"This is Shakur; he's my head man."

As a mark of the position he held, Shakur wore one of his master's cast-off shirts over his long *dhoti*. His thin neck stuck out of a frayed collar that was too big for him, but somehow he presented himself with a dignity impossible to ridicule.

He bowed again, pressing his palms together and touching his forehead in a blessing. Sara liked him at once. He grinned at her, showing large perfect white teeth.

"Is this lady the new madam, *sahib*?" He moved his head from side to side in time with his high sing-song voice.

"Yes, this lady is my wife, and mind you don't forget it."

Sara softened the moment with a smile.

"How do you do, Shakur?"

"I am well, madam." He seemed to study her face with obvious delight and blessed her fervently once more. He admired the fine bones of her hands and wrists, her white skin and her hair ... a very auspicious colour ... the colour of dark saffron threads.

Sara smiled again with genuine kindness, and he blessed her once more before stealing a hasty look at Lady Palmer and visibly shuddering.

Charles seemed irritated again and took charge. "Enough! Shakur, get the luggage and I'll see you back at the carriage."

"At once, *sahib*!" Shakur bustled around long enough to ensure that his importance had been acknowledged before hurrying off, saying as he left to anyone in his path, "Move along, move along, will you," in a peculiar imitation of his master's voice.

Charles had taken Sara's arm to lead her away, but was distracted by the sight of Sabran, who'd retreated to talk to someone in a waiting carriage standing apart from the chaos of the wharf.

Charles was clearly very put out and flexed his hands behind his back as though trying to control his fury. Sara followed his eyes to where an exquisite girl with a face from a fairy tale was looking out of the window of the carriage, but when she felt herself being observed the vision modestly drew back with such haste it was almost as though she hadn't existed at all.

Sabran let go of the girl's hand and threw Charles one of his enigmatic looks.

Sara looked up at Charles' face, trying to read his expression. His lips were white against his high colour, and his bright blue eyes seemed almost glassy as he stared back.

"Oh, do you know them, darling?" The endearment sounded odd to her ears, but it got his attention. "The gentleman was most helpful. I don't know what would have happened if he hadn't come along when he did. Charles, we must thank him."

"I think referring to Sabran as a gentleman is perhaps too

generous. However, you weren't to know, my dear. We must leave, now."

"But Charles, something dreadful has happened ..."

He wouldn't look at her, but kept his gaze fixed somewhere in the middle distance.

"Yes, I know ... Cynthia told me ..."

"Then you'll understand how we are responsible ..."

"Not responsible, surely ... but I'll arrange for one of my men to take the child to the nuns. We can't adopt her ourselves. It would cause trouble amongst the servants. You've forgotten how strict the caste rules are here. Anyway, as soon as the real mother realises there's no money to be had, she'll turn up. I've seen this sort of thing before."

He took her hand and held it firmly. There would be no more nonsense. Lady Palmer and Cynthia had made their way to the carriage, still surrounded by curious onlookers. They gave her furious impatient glares but, even so, Sara resisted, not being able to tear herself away from the child playing in the dust.

"Charles, we must do something ..."

He lowered his voice to a whisper. "Lady Palmer would never allow her in the carriage. We must leave at once."

"*Pardonnez moi.*"

Charles swung around to face Sabran, who stood before them with an air of barely controlled irritation. He'd been a witness to the scene between the couple and had been waiting for an opportunity to interrupt.

"Fitzroy." He said the name as though it cost him a great deal.

Charles gave a curt nod in return. "I believe my wife has reason to be grateful to you. I want to reimburse you for your trouble."

Sabran ignored the offer with a dismissive wave of his hand. "I do not want your money."

Sabran stared curiously at Sara, then back to Charles. His face showed a faint glimmer of surprise, then a half smile of what she felt sure was derision, accompanied by an exaggerated, almost sarcastic bow, waving a hand before her like a courtier, and dazzling her eyes with a huge rough-cut yellow diamond set in heavy gold he wore on his wedding finger.

Usually she couldn't bear jewellery on a man, thinking it effeminate and a sure sign of vanity, though on his hand the primitive cut of the stone seemed only to add to his air of mystery, as a sorcerer might use a wand to hypnotise his victims.

She'd caught his flicker of surprise, and even distaste also. She was shocked to see that the man didn't admire her and might even dislike her.

"I'm here to tell you, madam, I will take the child! That is the end of the matter!" he announced.

Then, bowing again briefly in Sara's direction, he snapped his fingers at his entourage. "Come!"

"Forgive me, *monsieur*, but I'm not so sure."

At first there was a faint gleam of pure white teeth, a polite but failed attempt to cover a snarl, then, while his dark enigmatic eyes swept over her with now unconcealed dislike, he snapped his fingers and his entourage sprang to attention again.

Charles took her hand to lead her away.

"I think the matter is decided at last, my dear."

"But the old man wanted me to take her!" She touched her heart with the tips of her fingers to emphasise the truth of her words. "I'm sure of it! And he died at peace because he believed, somehow, that I would take his granddaughter."

There was an uncomfortable silence at her public display of passion, including Charles, who felt compelled to step in and restore order.

"My dear girl, you're letting your imagination run away with you. Let Monsieur Sabran take her. At least, with him, she'll be at her own level."

Again, it took all of Sabran's self-control to ignore Charles and speak to Sara with a calm voice. "The English have taken everything else from us. You must at least leave us our children."

Sara stared. There was nothing more she could say, realising the truth of his words.

"But you must come to visit her often," he said in a softer tone. "You will always be welcome." His thickly accented voice poured over her like heavy silk. He glanced at Charles to see how he would take the invitation and was clearly pleased to see him bristle and clear his throat again.

"To make certain I'm not ill-treating her," Sabran added, laughing softly.

"Now!" He slapped his hands together, and everyone jumped again.

"I must go, and so must you. That's the end of the matter".

While still dazed by his sudden display of charm, Sara

watched as a waiting attendant picked up the child and held her dangling at arm's length.

"Don't be a fool! Give her to me!" Sabran almost snatched the child from the servant, gave Sara a final bow, then, with a dismissive look at Charles, marched away with the child, who was now crying loudly, tucked under his arm like a parcel, with his entourage hurrying along behind.

Sara had to hide her smile as she said goodbye in return. Then, as an afterthought, she called out, "Wait! What's her name? Does anyone know anything about her? Anything at all?" She looked around at the remaining people, who stared back at her with vacant eyes.

Sabran stopped in his tracks; the baby had wet herself and left a damp patch on his clean linen. He turned and glared at Sara, his patience obviously reaching an end.

Charles hissed at her, "For goodness' sake, my dear girl ... How obstinate you've become. Lady Palmer is furious; please try to understand my position."

"Just a minute, Charles, please ... forgive me. It's not a lost puppy we're talking about, she's a child!"

She held his gaze with her lovely eyes and, despite everything, he softened.

"You're right, of course. She must have a name, Monsieur Sabran ..."

"She must, I suppose." He muttered a string of words in French, spoken too quickly to make out, though Sara was sure they were not flattering to her.

"What do you think of Prema?" He held his face in a tight grimace. "It was my grandmother's name. Will that do?"

"Prema! It can't be! It can't be!" She swayed and for a moment she thought she might faint.

Sabran put out a hand to support her, but Charles moved quickly, at the same time giving a warning look. Sabran dropped his hand, though not without his mocking secret smile.

"The old man called out that name, just before he ..." Her voice faltered, husky now with suppressed tears. "He did! It was Prema! I'm sure of it now! It must be a sign, it must be ..."

"Prema ... is that your name?" She bent down to gaze into the child's eyes and the baby turned her head and gave a half smile as if to answer.

"It is!"

Sara stared at Sabran, her face shining, asking him to share in her astonishment and the absolute marvel of the thing. His eyes flashed with what she thought was a touch of alarm.

"So superstitious, madam, and you've only been on our shores an hour ... but then, so much that happens in India is unexplained. I will ask my guru about it."

His face was dark and frowning now, as though the whole incident had taken on a new meaning, though Sara's face showed only glowing relief.

"Well, then ... now I feel absolutely she'll be safe with you, because of your grandmother's name."

"My deepest thanks, madam." His mood changed again and it was clear he was laughing at her.

"Wait! What does the name mean in English? I've forgotten."

"It means love."

There was a faint snort of derision from Charles, but Sara was thoughtful, and sad. The memory of the old man's drowning came over her in a rush.

"Then someone must have loved her very much, to give her that name."

She watched Sabran's mouth compress, as though he was going to smile, but only his eyes gleamed as he waved his hypnotic ring before her eyes once more.

"I'll look forward to your visit, madam; it's not often we have such a charming addition to our barbaric shores."

"But where do you live? You must give me your address."

"Fitzroy knows where I am. Everyone knows my house, though some may pretend otherwise." He gave Charles another derisive look.

"It's 'Sans Souci', or, if you prefer the English, 'Without Care'."

Then he was gone, the faint sound of his laughter echoing in the distance.

Chapter 4

An exhausted and uncomfortable silence descended upon the occupants of the carriage as they turned from the hot dusty chaos and noise of the port. Lady Palmer sat with her lips firmly compressed in a disapproving grimace, every now and then looking at Sara and snorting loudly, while Cynthia lay back under her parasol with her eyes closed, waving at her hot face with her tiny fan. Charles kept his gaze fixed ahead, seemingly unaware of Sara sitting by his side. She stole a quick glance at his averted face then slipped her fingers through his.

He started and stared at her, his face showing shocked surprise.

It was almost as if he had forgotten she was there.

They moved into a wide street bordered by centuries-old tamarind trees, their dark sinuous branches meeting overhead and intertwining to form a refuge from the heat of the relentless sun.

Civilisation in the form of English rule had asserted itself in the prosperous, mostly new buildings. They passed the High Court with its peculiar lighthouse built on top.

"That is where I hope to hold ultimate influence one day."

Charles raised his chin high as they passed, and for a moment Sara thought he might even salute. She'd never really given his work as District Magistrate very much thought before, being so blinded by love she wouldn't have cared how he earned his living, but now she saw how very important his work was to him. He was ambitious and, she realised with a sudden small tweak of clarity, he expected her to be ambitious too.

Pepper pot minarets adorned several other buildings, flashing in the morning sun and giving the town a cheerful feeling of domesticity and a sense of safety from the great wild expanse of India. Though, despite the monumental solidity of the buildings and the well-dressed Europeans going about their errands with their attendant servants, there was the strange ever-present feeling the grip was fragile, and it could all disappear in a heartbeat, as though a genie had transplanted a foreign world into an incompatible landscape. Even the colours of nature had an otherworldly air of unreality. It seemed impossible that such hues could exist outside of heaven, despite the fine layer of yellow dust reducing the landscape to a watercolour wash.

"I feel as though I'm in a tale from the *Arabian Nights*." Sara squeezed his hand, forgetting to be shy in her happiness. "I didn't realise it would be so beautiful."

"Mount Road," said Charles as they passed a wide thoroughfare leading west of the city. "Of course there was nothing here till we British came." He waved his arms wide as though to embrace the whole street. It was as if he had built it himself.

"Yes, of course." She frowned, trying to summon up a memory. The name was there somewhere in her cloudy past, though the road itself had changed so dramatically from the once dusty path she vaguely recalled from her childhood.

Her eyes narrowed against the glare of the sun. There, in the far distance, shimmering through the dust, was a small hill. "St Thomas Mount," Charles said, reading her thoughts.

"Oh, yes." Sara remembered now. "Isn't that where it was believed the saint was murdered after he had been sent by the Lord to convert India to Christianity?"

"That's all a lot of nonsense, of course." Charles scoffed, "but the Indians believe it absolutely. They claim they have the remains of the Saint's finger in the church."

Sara smiled to herself as she remembered, with sudden clarity, her father taking her to the church built on the site of Saint Thomas' martyrdom, and being shown the very cross he was believed to have clutched to his chest at the moment of his death. The cross itself was reputed to sweat blood at various intervals, but, tired out from watching and waiting for the phenomenon to occur, she had fainted dead away, very much impressing the pilgrims who had gathered there, claiming she had experienced a vision.

Though now, as she looked around her, Sara felt none of the influence of Christianity, despite the Protestant churches built by the British. The heat itself seemed designed for a religion based more in nature than anything conjured by man. Even the twisted primitive shapes of the trees seemed to reflect the animism of the Hindu religion. They spread their thick tendril-like branches into the air and snaked along the ground, forming little arbours decorated with scraps of silk and flowers housing small figures of Ganesh the Elephant god, and Hanuman, King of the monkeys, or Shiva himself, Lord of the Dance, despite his human form, adorned with the horror of his myriad snakelike arms.

Beneath this shaded canopy, the people of this underworld had set up their homes and businesses, little makeshift boxes containing whole worlds of domesticity and industry. Glimpses of humble home life passed them by. A child, standing naked beside his home of rusty tin and grey rags, as his mother sat squatting in the dust before him, her bracelets jingling as she scrubbed him from head to foot with soapy water, inches away from a stream of running stinking waste. A faded turquoise sari nailed to a tree lifted in the faint breeze to reveal a sleeping place for a group of small children, watched over by their grandmother as she made chapatti on a cooking fire burning in the corner.

Sara welcomed it all, despite feeling a little detached as she sat next to Charles in the woven cane landau, a relic from the beginning of the nineteenth century, pulled by a pair of small sturdy horses, her parasol raised against the already blazing morning sun. She was still reeling, with not only the unusual sensation of finding her land legs again after weeks at sea, but also the conflicting emotions of her dramatic encounters of the past hour. Then the climax in the form of Ravi Sabran as he'd swept away with the child on his hip, his servants running along behind, trying to keep up with his impatient step. It seemed as though more had happened in one short hour on Indian soil than all the years she'd spent in England.

She thought of Sabran's parting words: "Sans Souci." An almost frivolous name for a house but alluring too; she would visit there as soon as possible.

Every now and then she stole a glance at Charles's averted face, not quite fully being able to believe she was actually with him at last.

Her mood darkened as she was all of a sudden overcome with a sharp twinge of anxiety. "Who is this man I have married? Do I still love him?"

A beam of sunlight broke through the intertwined overhead branches and illuminated the scene before her.

It was a festival day, and armloads of brilliantly coloured flowers were being made into garlands for temple offerings. A young girl of almost mythical beauty, draped in a cyclamen pink sari, sat squatting in the bright dust by the side of the road, weaving garlands of marigold and tuberoses. As she worked she sang, her voice lilting and mysterious, seeming to intertwine with the movement of her deft fingers as she twisted the flowers into fragrant ropes.

Charles glanced at Sara and was overcome with the need to do something gallant. He called to stop the carriage, then he threw the girl a few rupees. She caught them deftly, then, choosing a garland of intensely perfumed white jasmine, she draped it around Sara's neck. The girl raised her slender hands to her forehead in a joyous blessing. There was no sign in her eyes that she expected any other reward; the blessing was given freely, from the purity of her innocent heart. Charles felt it too and was moved to say, "She seems a decent little thing."

Sara smiled, touched by his gesture. He cared for her after all, and everything would be all right.

Then, from the distance came the beating of drums, discordant and sinister, and the people hurried off the road to stare.

A procession was moving towards them, the mass transforming into men dancing as though in a trance, kicking up the yellow dust of the road, convulsing their bodies in wild almost obscene movements, their eyes wide and crazed.

They carried a bier shaded by curtains and decorated with marigolds, but when the breeze shifted and the drapery briefly parted, a corpse could be seen, frozen by rigor mortis into an almost demure sitting position, though with one shrivelled and blackened foot sticking straight out into the open air of the living.

As the procession moved closer the grotesque shrunken head could be seen, bound in a white turban hung with cheap paste rubies, jerking in time to the beat of the music and the dancing feet of his bearers, the mouth set in a grim smile, as though enjoying its final macabre journey to the funeral pyre.

Cynthia's hand flew to her nose. Over her handkerchief her eyes showed an expression of deep horror, though Sara was struck by how quickly her own feelings of revulsion evaporated. There were no lingering feelings of sadness; the death was accepted as inevitable, and faced head-on as a natural part of life. She shuddered as she remembered the funeral of her aunt, the icy rain pouring into the muddy grave, and the despairing empty sound of the clods of earth as they fell onto the lid of the coffin.

At that moment Charles took her arm and held it close within his own. He smiled at her. "All right, are you? Not too horrible."

"No ... somehow it seems more preferable than a tightly sealed grave."

He looked at her oddly. "Of course, but I don't think it would be the thing for us English to follow the same course. A little undignified, don't you think?"

She gave a small laugh, thinking he was joking, though when she examined his expression she could see he was deadly serious.

The respectable stone buildings of the town were almost left behind now, and the ramshackle small buildings and rich temples of the Indian population clung closer together, a mixture of homes and businesses, the alleyways now mere burrows, leading to a seductive mix of shops selling spices heaped high in multicoloured cones, to brothels where young girls sat on embroidered cushions in open windows, their childish forms burdened with cheap gold jewellery and bright cotton saris, their haunted eyes painted with wide black streaks of kohl in an attempt to make them more alluring to the passing trade.

Cynthia suddenly let out a shriek of horror as a holy man, almost naked except for his long matted hair hanging almost down to his feet, and smeared from head to toe in a grey ash, threw himself before the carriage to beg for alms. It was impossible not to notice his long limp penis, covered like the rest of his body with grey dust and half hidden with the cotton rag hanging from the man's waist. It was the first man Sara had seen naked and she could barely drag her eyes away from the lower half of his body.

She gave Charles a hasty curious look, then turned away, uselessly rearranging the gloves on her lap to cover her fears. It seemed so strange that because of a ceremony performed in England over a year ago, she would now have to share this man's bed and do whatever intimate things married people did together. She wondered how on earth she would be able to go through with it and wondered if he would insist she sleep with him in his bed that very night.

"Move on, Shakur, you fool! What do you think you're playing at?"

It was obvious Charles was as embarrassed as she was and was hiding it with anger, though she couldn't help thinking it would be better to laugh instead.

Shakur flicked the reins but the horses refused to budge, prolonging the discomfort of everyone.

"Forgive me, sir; this fellow wants money, then he will go away."

Charles hurriedly threw the man a coin. "I'm sorry, ladies," he mumbled, blushing.

The Sadu followed behind, torturing them once more with his nakedness, blessing them all fervently and often, as Lady Palmer tried to shoo him away while holding her other hand over her daughter's eyes.

Sara now found it difficult not to laugh and was almost bent over, trying to suppress her giggles.

The shock from the sight of her first naked male body had receded almost indecently fast, and her interest was taken by fresh scenes of life as it swarmed around the barely moving carriage.

Small herds of cattle, their horns painted bright colours and interwoven with flowers, stood in caramel-coloured unhurried clumps in the middle of the road. The carriage was forced to stop as a newly born calf struggled into the world on the road before them.

The calf rose, still crumpled from the womb, the umbilical cord trailing in the dust as its mother gently nudged it to stand, a picture of placid maternal devotion in the commotion around them. Sara and Cynthia looked at each other in a rare moment of genuine connection. For both of them it was the first time they had witnessed birth.

They crawled slowly past the gates of a huge temple where crowds had gathered to wait their turn to seek an audience with the Brahmin priests, ready to pay a rupee or two for a *puja*, a blessing, to further their chances of success in love or luck.

These men, the highest of all the castes, were mostly plump and well-kept like the spoilt concubines of rich men. They idled on the steps of the temple, gossiping and laughing, their bodies wrapped in robes of pure white cloth, their fat shiny necks ringed by garlands of marigolds.

Lines of the crippled and deformed had taken up their positions in front of the entrance to capture the pity of the crowd as they passed. Sara reeled back with a sickening lurch to her stomach at the sight of a deformity that surely could never have been created by nature alone. A young man, his legs and arms bent in a grotesque shape, sat patiently on a wooden trolley he propelled with a stick, his beautiful saint-like head being the only feature of his body not defiled.

"For God's sake, give him some money," Sara gasped. Charles, too, was moved by this special horror to hastily feel in his pocket and throw the coins blindly in the direction of the boy. Sara looked back to see the other less deformed pick up the coins to place them in the boy's faded cotton sack he wore around his neck. Even amongst the desperate they recognised the dishonour of stealing from such an unfortunate being.

They followed the seafront now, and the high grey stone walls of Fort St George, topped with the English flag flying from the battlements loomed ahead, clinging to the water's edge and protected on the south side by a wide muddy river. They passed through the outskirts of a settlement of dense streets and warehouses, built up against the fort walls and giving the area the look of an Arabian Souk. There was something vaguely familiar about the place, and Sara broke out in a gentle smile. The memory must have been a happy one.

The population had become more diverse, and Muslim families had set up businesses alongside Chinese, Hindus, Tamils and Parsees. Veiled women and Europeans squeezed up against

72

each other in the narrow laneways and shopped and bartered loudly in foreign tongues.

Sara heard snatches of French and Spanish as they passed, and once, as two men stood aside to let the carriage pass, she heard softly but distinctly, "*Cochons Anglais*!" The words were uttered with such ferocity she blanched and looked back to see one of the men bow at her in an insulting, mocking way.

"That's Blacktown!" Lady Palmer gave a haughty toss of her head. "And most appropriately named. We try to pretend this place doesn't exist, though I suppose it's a necessary evil. Catholics and Muslims and God knows what else!"

Sara thought it wise not to respond by keeping her face averted, and only turned when Lady Palmer poked her on the arm with the end of her parasol and pointed to a group of pretty painted houses facing the river.

"That very vulgar house with the bright green shutters belongs to the McKenzies, an Anglo-Indian family. We don't socialise with them." She placed extra emphasis on 'them'.

Sara gave Lady Palmer an enquiring look, but the woman shuddered, raising her hand at once to dispel any further questions.

"When you see them, you'll understand. The mother and daughter are very black. Even though the father was a Scot, dead now, mercifully, the mother is Indian, and as ugly as a gnome. You may see them in the street, but it is best to ignore them if they attempt to speak to you. The girl in particular is most annoyingly present in English society, despite all efforts to discourage her."

Sara made a mental note to be sure not to snub them if

she did somehow meet the marooned family in question, while her dislike of Lady Palmer rose to new heights.

Sara scanned the scene before her with fresh interest. Each house they passed might perhaps have been the home she'd lived in as a child, though none of them provoked even a hint of recognition. The house she remembered had a wide veranda with tall white columns and stood in a lush garden. None of the houses she passed were large enough, and gardens were almost non-existent in such a crowded place. It seemed an impossible task.

They'd come at last to the high stone walls of Fort St George and stopped at the southern-most entrance. A sentry saluted and raised the boom gate to allow them to pass.

"You'll always be safe here, my dear." Charles acknowledged the sentry with a haughty nod. "White town is for English Christians only, and no Indians are allowed to enter except for the tradesmen and, of course, our servants."

Sara looked behind her at the busy streets and felt a strong pang of longing. It seemed they were leaving life itself behind, and entering a kind of well-preserved tomb, dedicated to a country thousands of miles away.

Inside the fort was a tidy world of chalk roads and white timber and stone houses of varying sizes, according to the social status of the people within, and bordered with prim English flowers and well-watered lawns. They passed a pretty white church surrounded by struggling rose bushes, and low wide windows open to the outside air, though hung with thick shutters capable of deflecting a typhoon. A middle-aged parson in a flat black straw hat, about to enter the church, stopped for a moment and waved.

Lady Palmer called to him, and Sara was amused to see how quick he was to respond to her summons. After the initial greetings, Sara was introduced.

"You'll have a new face in church this Sunday, Mr Hobson. Mrs Fitzroy, Charles's wife."

The little man squinted up at her through horn-rimmed spectacles.

"Welcome to our little parish, Mrs Fitzroy," he chirped. "I think you'll find our activities will keep you as amused as if you were back in England. We have tea with the other wives every Wednesday at three, you will be very useful in taking the bible readings with the converts Thursdays at ten, and there's the sewing group where we make articles to sell for charity, which I'm sure you'll be able to attend ..."

Sara nodded and smiled and, despite doing her best to listen to the man, she found herself unpleasantly reminded of the suffocating rituals that made up most of her life in England. It might not be so easy to escape the stuffy air of parsons after all.

Chapter 5

Despite longing to see her own home, lunch at Lady Palmer's at least put off the inevitable moment when she and Charles would be alone, for better or worse. She sensed he was feeling the same, as he didn't even attempt an excuse when Lady Palmer insisted they join her for lunch.

The Palmers' white stone palace was more like a public building than a home, standing with majestic grandeur in the centre of a neatly manicured wide green lawn, and towering over the surrounding houses of lesser public officials.

A pack of excited pugs ran down the front steps to greet them and, for the first time, Sara saw signs of genuine affection spreading over the proud features of Lady Palmer as she bent to kiss their wet, snuffling noses.

Lady Palmer presided like a queen over her staff of at least one hundred servants and, even while claiming she loathed being back in Madras, it was plain being able to command such power over so many was a huge comfort to her.

A group of servants hovering at her elbow looked at each other as though longing to escape.

Sara hid a smile. While Charles sipped his tea his mind was elsewhere, till he burst out, not being able to contain his thoughts any longer, "I thought Sabran was a bit thick with the compliments towards you, Sara, my dear." Charles mimicked Sabran's heavily accented tones, "'It's not often we have such a charming addition to our barbaric shores.'" I almost laughed out loud."

Sara squirmed in her chair. What a fool she was, so easily taken in by a bit of fake charm.

"It was a remarkable coincidence though, Charles, his grandmother having the same name as the baby. Surely you can see that?"

"He most certainly made that part up. He probably already knew the child's name, and I believe he was flirting with you. What a cad the man is."

Sara was silenced for a moment, then she spoke up, a little fever in her heart telling her he was being unfair.

"He's a Frenchman after all. Perhaps he thinks it's expected of him."

"Well, half a Frenchman anyway; the rest of him is pure Indian! And with all it implies." His voice was raised just a little, but enough to show how deeply he felt.

"He was being kind ... taking the baby ..."

Her words were wasted. Charles was listening to something Cynthia was saying about Paris, but he patted her on the arm as though it should be the end of the matter. Sara was glad they had changed the subject as she wasn't sure she could contain her temper, though there was no escape from the persistent thoughts buzzing around in her head like a trapped fly.

I should have taken the child ... I should have taken her ... The old man meant me to take her ...

Lady Palmer drew herself up and pursed her lips. "No one knows where Sabran gets his money, but he's most vulgar ... He bought a house that rightfully belongs only to those of English blood."

"I believe he bought it just to irritate us." Cynthia sniffed.

Sara roused herself at last to respond. "You've been to his house? Is it far from here?"

"I most certainly have not been to his house! And I wouldn't go even if he asked me ... but those who have been there say it's terribly common, and that he has all kinds of dreadful people staying there ... Indians and God knows who else."

Sara couldn't help herself. "Well, it is India after all."

Cynthia pursed her lips and looked for a moment remarkably like her mother.

"Even so, he has a bad reputation. They say he keeps a group of dancing girls ... to entertain him day and night."

The girl looked so excited by the lewd possibilities, Sara laughed out loud. "Surely you exaggerate. He must sleep some time. Poor man, he must be exhausted."

Lady Palmer rushed to defend her daughter. "My daughter does not exaggerate!"

Charles whispered an explanation for Lady Palmer's unusual attitude.

"It is Lady Palmer's particular concern. She believes the dancing girls are responsible for the moral breakdown amongst some of our young single men."

Lady Palmer's lips had shrunk into a thin line. "I most

certainly do. Waving themselves about, practically naked, in front of our boys. It's outrageous!"

Sara felt a warning nudge from Charles, but her spirit rose within her.

She laughed again, trying to make light of the situation. "Well, I suppose I'll find all this out when we go to visit the child."

A teacup hit a saucer with a loud crash.

Charles cleared his throat and was about to speak, when Lady Palmer uttered the words for him. "You can't be serious, my girl. You can never visit her ... ever, especially not alone."

"But Lady Palmer, times have changed. Why, in London now it's not so unusual for a young lady to make visits alone, or to work, and even to have her own rooms."

"Well, in that case she most certainly isn't a lady!" Lady Palmer was emphatic.

Sara turned to her husband for support. "Well, I'm sure Charles will accompany me, to protect me from Monsieur Sabran's rather florid compliments."

She smiled, with not much humour, hoping to encourage Lady Palmer in a returned smile, but the woman only snorted her disapproval.

Sara watched Charles's averted face, but there was no reaction.

"Charles?"

"Sabran isn't received anywhere," he said at last. "At least not in any decent home." He lowered his voice to a whisper.

"He keeps a woman, but, instead of being discreet about

it, he flaunts her, and she's already married ... She was with Sabran today ..."

Sara remembered the glimpse of the beautiful face, one not easily forgotten.

"Her husband's a very great Maharaja, and very useful to us in the collection of taxes from the farmers in his district. So you can see how I'm placed in a difficult position. He's insisted I help return her, even though she's the lowest of his wives."

"'The lowest of his wives!' How cruel, if she means so little to him, he should let her go.'"

"It's a matter of honour for him, and it's not my place to have an opinion on the matter."

"Perhaps he was unkind to her," Sara persisted.

"I want to tell you more about Paris, Charles ..." Cynthia had moved a little closer, hoping to turn the topic back to herself.

Charles mumbled an apology then returned to Sara. "It's none of our business. My business is to return her to her husband, and Sabran flatly refuses."

"He must love her very much."

"Love! What a hopeless romantic you are, darling. He could afford a hundred such women. He keeps her to annoy me! That's the sum of it. The man is arrogant beyond belief, and it's not clear where he gets his money ... We think he has some interests in opium ..."

"Opium!" Now it was Sara's turn to drop her cup too loudly on the saucer. "But if he's so bad, why would he bother with a stray child?"

"Well, it's not as though he'll ever see it ... One of his servants will take care of it, and he's as rich as Croesus, and he takes good care to see we British won't be getting any of it."

She felt the frustration rise once more. "Even so, I must see the child once more, just to be sure. Then I'll have discharged my responsibility."

He spoke slowly, as if to give more weight to his words. "Darling, you must never visit him. Things are different here, it's a small community and people talk. A woman's reputation is very important, even more so than in England, and remember you're the wife of the District Magistrate. We must set an example to the natives, otherwise they'll lose their respect for us. Anyway, he'll have forgotten about you by now. Your promises mean nothing to a man like Sabran."

"He doesn't seem to like you much either."

"He has no reason to like me. We've clashed often over various legal issues. He simply won't accept English justice ... fights tooth and nail to defend the indefensible. But I don't want to talk about him. I'd much rather talk about you." He bent to kiss her again, giving her at the same time a particularly tender glance. "But we can't avoid seeing him sometimes, even if I wish him gone to the devil. He's managed to get his polo team to the finals. There's the last match of the season in a few weeks and I intend to thrash the brute."

"He plays well then?"

"Too well. So far we haven't managed to beat him ... But this time ..." Charles banged his fist down on the table, making the teacups shake.

Sara was shocked by the anger in his voice. He seemed

almost obsessively determined. "Is it really so important you beat him? Really, Charles, does it matter that much?"

He answered her with a silent nod, then turned away, the conversation at an end.

Charles rose to join Cynthia on the other side of the room, and Sara's spirits sank within her. She unconsciously pulled at the neck of her blouse as she looked around Lady Palmer's over-furnished drawing room. The brilliant day had lost its beauty, and what she had so recently thought exciting and exotic appeared shoddy, ugly and dull.

She toyed with Charles's gift of jasmine she had tucked at her waist so to admire it better. Already it had turned brown and hung lifelessly from her belt, its once heady fragrance now sickly and rancid.

Chapter 6

Sara hated herself for her failure to like her new home, even though it was one of the largest and best built in the community, and, at her first sight of it, had to struggle to hide her dismay, though Charles spoke with unmistakable pride in his voice.

"What do you think of it? I like to see it as our own little patch of England."

The house was an exaggerated version of a Surrey country cottage, burdened with both mock Tudor features and a prim picket fence. There was something ridiculous about it, like an Englishman Sara had met on the ship, who wore heavy tweeds despite the heat and always carried an umbrella.

A dainty path bordered by half-dead roses snaked from the veranda across a faded yellow lawn to the front fence. It was clearly her husband's pride and joy and as he paused at the front gate he solemnly contemplated the grass, poking at the bare patches with his walking stick.

"My home," she murmured, but even to her own ears the words seemed wistful.

The servants appeared to welcome them, laughing and generously bestowing blessings on their new mistress. She was swept towards the house while fragrant flowers were thrown in her path. Only one servant hung back, unsmiling and watchful, her eyes fixed on Sara. Even the drab brown of her servant's sari couldn't disguise the fact that she was lovely in a way that set her apart from the rest of the servants.

Charles seemed not to notice her beauty. Her presence seemed only to inspire him to anger. "There you are! Quick! Come here at once and meet your mistress."

The girl crept forward and prostrated herself on the ground before them both, then slowly raised her kohl-rimmed eyes, her expression a mixture of fear and curiosity. She glanced in Charles's direction as though asking for permission to speak. Despite her heavy gold nose-ring disguising almost half her face, it was plain she was not from South India. Her pale skin and slightly curved nose showed something of Arabic roots.

Charles gave her permission to speak.

"I am Lakshmi, *memsahib*." Her huge almond-shaped eyes flashed, then were cast down once more.

"Lakshmi, what a pretty name—it means the goddess of good fortune, doesn't it, Charles? I hope we will be good friends, Lakshmi."

The girl gave Charles another furtive look before venturing to speak.

"Thank you, *memsahib*."

"That'll do. Wait over there." Charles was cross again and Sara couldn't understand why.

"Is something wrong?"

He answered her at last, speaking as though she were a small child who must be humoured. "Darling, you don't have to be friends with her, but from now on Lakshmi will do everything for you."

"Couldn't it have waited a little? I would've liked to choose my own maid. Perhaps we won't suit each other."

"My sweet girl, you know you can't turn up in your own home without a maid; the servants will despise you if you do. Anyway, it's not for her to decide if you suit her. She's here to do what you ask of her; that's all there is to it."

"I would like her to be happy, just the same."

"As I said, her happiness is not an issue. She's a hard worker, that's what's important, and trained by Lady Palmer herself. She's been given to you as a wedding gift and you're very lucky to have her."

"A wedding gift? I was under the impression that slavery was illegal."

"We do pay her, you know." He spoke with a tinge of impatience in his voice. "Very well, as it happens, and she's very grateful to have the position, I can assure you."

"Then I must thank Lady Palmer when I see her," she replied almost sweetly, though her eyes showed her resentment. "She's very pretty."

"Is she? I hadn't noticed. One can never think of the Indian women as pretty ... but of her type I suppose she's attractive enough."

Sara smiled up at him, wanting to break down the stiffness between them. "Has she a sweetheart?"

"Of course not ..." he spluttered, and shook his head almost

85

violently, as though the idea was unthinkable. "The men won't have her ... She has no family or dowry!"

"Poor girl ... Is that why she seems so unhappy?"

He frowned, his patience at an end now. "Sara, my dear, you really do have an over-fanciful imagination. How can you tell if she's happy or not without even knowing the girl?"

Sara was taken aback by the passion of his response, but at the sight of her shocked face, as soon as the servants were dismissed from the room, he hurried to console her.

"I'm sorry ... Forgive me. It's just that, after all this time, it's a strain for us both and," he added, taking her hand to kiss it, "I'm not used to being in the company of such a lovely and accomplished girl. I've forgotten how to behave."

The gentle tone of his voice softened her a little, and she didn't protest when he put his arms around her.

"I can't believe you're here at last."

"I would have come at once if you'd sent for me." Her tone was cool. She had to admit to having harboured a secret resentment towards him. It had been a niggling and often painful thought in the back of her mind that if he really cared for her there would've been no delay. In her heart she felt he should have swept her up in his arms and insisted on taking her on the ship with him, despite her aunt's sudden illness. Though, even though she thought it, she studied his face and saw the truth of it. Despite his romantic exterior, it wasn't his way to be impulsive.

"Well, you're here now, and we have the rest of our lives together. Anyway, I couldn't take the risk of you falling ill. You must trust me. We lost two of our community to the cholera this last time, one of them a young woman about your age ..."

"Then you do care for me?" she asked with a smile.

"Of course I do, perhaps even more than I did before."

He put out a hand to touch her hair. "I don't remember you being so lovely; it's come as quite a shock to me."

"Have I changed so much?" She raised her face to his, while his eyes lingered on the tempting shape of her upper lip. He wondered why he'd never noticed it before.

"As I said, it's almost as though you're a different person. I wasn't sure if you still loved me." His voice was almost harsh now. "I suppose I need you to be devoted to me. Like any new husband."

"Well, I am devoted to you." She laughed, surprised at his intensity. "And prepared to love you, even more than I do already, if you give me half a chance."

He studied her face as she gazed at him. It was impossible not to see how eager and sincere she was.

He nodded, satisfied at last. In truth he was a little disappointed to discover he'd married such a beautiful girl. It had never been his intention to marry for beauty. He felt a wife was expected to be a wife, not an ornament. It made him uneasy to think other men might now look at her with lustful ideas. It increased her power over him, and he hated to be at a disadvantage. He changed the subject at once, not wanting to linger on unpleasant thoughts.

"I've arranged for us to leave for Tanjore as soon as I can get away."

"Tanjore?"

"South of here. you'll like the place. It'll give us a chance to get to know each other, away from prying eyes. One is never really alone in Madras."

His eyes lingered on her body, taking time to appreciate her shapely form. She unconsciously crossed her arms over her breasts, at the same time experiencing a strange little flutter in her chest. It was real, after all. She really was married to this man standing before her and he had a right to look at her in that way.

"Our honeymoon ... Of course, I'd almost forgotten." She blushed and looked away.

"I don't see why you're so shocked." He laughed, for the first time showing a touch of humour. "That's what you're here for, you know, to love, honour and obey."

She bit her lip and stared down at her hands, wondering what to do next. Then, before she could stop herself, the words spilled out. "I will love and honour you, but I have no intention of obeying you, Charles, unless I want to, of course."

He stared at her for a long moment as though weighing up her words and struggling with his own thoughts, then he stepped forward in a determined way and drew her to him, kissing her hard on the lips.

It was the first time they had actually kissed with any kind of intensity, and she wasn't sure if it was pleasurable or not; his transformation from practicality to passion came as such a shock.

"I can't wait. I can't wait to have you to myself," he breathed. She was aware of his beating heart as she was pressed almost violently against his chest. Then she felt the warmth of his fingers as they stole up the back of her neck and grasped at the strands of her hair, pulling her head back to be kissed once more.

She gave a little gasp. It was almost as if he was another man. Then for a blinding instant she saw a little into his soul. He kept his feelings close, and only sometimes would he allow them to be seen. This was what marriage was about; she must try to understand him, and with that understanding would come a deeper love. It was such a relief, such a relief to know, deep down, she hadn't been wrong about him after all.

Chapter 7

It soon became clear that, apart from the climate, there was very little difference between the life Sara had left behind and the society she now found herself marooned in. The only difference being that the codes of behaviour were even more rigid for women than for men.

Even the regulations themselves were frozen in the earlier time of dusty Victorian rule, as antiquated as the horsehair sofa she sat upon most evenings in the drawing room of Lady Palmer's cloying over-furnished mansion.

At yet another gathering where it was deemed essential she attend, she looked around at the assembled guests, trying to discern signs of unease in the faces of the other women. Were they too struggling with the endless rules of behaviour imposed on them? But their faces betrayed only contentment, even pride, as they fanned themselves against the insufferable heat and watched their menfolk at play.

Many of the women she knew had come from the lower middle classes of England and had once been part of the "fishing fleet" of the past years. They'd found husbands amongst either the minor civil servant community or the military and were now in a society they could never have hoped for in England. Here in Madras, even those from the most humble of backgrounds had at least a dozen servants who enabled them to live with total freedom from domestic servitude.

They were proud of their new status and couldn't help but boast of it with, it seemed to Sara, sometimes an almost vulgar display of arrogance against the Indian natives. Her compatriots were more than happy with their position, and it was unlikely they would buck the system they had so recently found themselves a part of.

At the far end of the room a group of men were standing together, arms around each other's shoulders and singing a faintly disreputable ditty from one of London's faraway music halls. She tried to be indulgent as it was harmless enough, but she resented the fact that men could be silly and loud and drink too much and stumble the night away without any recriminations, while she was supposed to be restrained and corseted, as stiff and emotionless as a mummy in a tomb.

Her face was outwardly serene, but inside her head her thoughts were in turmoil as she ran through the endless list of rules an Englishwoman in India must abide by.

A lady must never be seen alone in the street without at least one servant. A lady must never appear too forward in the company of a gentleman or discuss politics with an air of knowing something about the subject. A lady must always defer to the opinion of the gentleman, even if she felt he was wrong. A lady must not interrupt a gentleman while he was speaking. And, above all, she must never be seen to be amused or interested in the company of an Indian man if she should ever meet one, no matter how high his status. She must always be aware any relations between the races must be kept strictly at arm's length.

So far, she had broken nearly all those rules, and on the first day of her arrival in India, and had been made to pay for her unconventional behaviour with sly looks of censure and haughty glares, especially from Lady Palmer.

Sara's head spun with it, and she experienced a familiar tightening in her throat whenever she was in Lady Palmer's drawing room.

Card tables, occasional tables, vases of dried flowers and tall brass buckets of peacock feathers, silver picture frames, large bronze statuettes and examples of the local bird life preserved under domed glass, their brilliant plumage ragged and dusty. They jammed up against each other and competed on the walls with damp and dreary landscapes of the Scottish Highlands, and scenes of quaint English villages brought from "home".

Sara's own house had been adorned in much the same way when she first arrived, and Charles had confessed the furnishings were due to Lady Palmer's influence. Within the first month, though, Sara had removed the dusty trinkets and condemned most of the heavy Victorian furniture to a storeroom. The walls were painted white and she hung curtains of a vivid turquoise blue and decorated the rooms with exquisite antiques and weavings she'd found in the marketplace for a pittance. The finished result was light and elegant and, most of all, unique, despite the objections of Charles, who declared the look a trifle bohemian. He was concerned about how Lady Palmer would react if she ever found out. But, being in the first throes of fascination with his lovely new wife, he soon adjusted to the changes, only keeping the stuffed head of a tiger in his study, and the largest of Lady Palmer's paintings, a gloomy still life of a collection of dead animals arranged on a tartan rug after a shoot, which took pride of place above his narrow bed in the dressing room, causing Sara to emit a little shudder of horror whenever she walked past.

A servant bearing a tray of wilting cucumber sandwiches roused her to her present world. She took a bite then put it down at once; it was warm, and tasted vaguely of rancid butter. A sudden roar of coarse laughter from the other side of the room made her flinch.

She longed to be alone, but she knew Charles would be disappointed if she asked to leave before he was ready. He liked nothing better than to be at the centre of a gathering where he knew he was respected and admired. He was at home with his people and, for a clouded moment, Sara had a fear that she'd never feel the same way. But she told herself it was nonsense to be so uneasy. It had only been a few weeks, and there were bound to be difficulties at first, and with time she'd carve her own niche in this new world.

Though she was beginning to wonder what she had committed herself to.

Where was the adventure she'd so longed for? There was

none in being transported across the world from one drawing room to another.

For a wild fleeting moment she wished it wasn't taboo to be alone with a man before they married, if only for a few hours, just to discover what happened in the bedroom before a bride was bound for life.

To prepare her for these unknown rites, her aunt had mumbled a few incoherent words, accompanied by torturous blushing and squirming so distressing to her, Sara had felt compelled to spare her any further agony and put a stop to it at once.

"There are things you might not want to do," her aunt had managed to splutter at last, "but it's quite normal."

These words, accompanied by a horrified shudder, were the extent of her knowledge of the facts of life. She closed her eyes, trying to squeeze the thoughts from her brain. She didn't want to think about what happened when she and Charles were in bed together.

The first night of her married life she'd spent curled up on the other side of the bed, watching him sleep and wondering how he could, after such a momentous event. Somehow, she'd imagined more tenderness and care.

She hadn't expected the almost savage attack as he'd held her pinned down, roughly spreading her legs with his knees and forcing himself into her while she winced in pain. His panting face had loomed over her with an expression she'd found difficult to read. It was almost as if he hated her.

When it was over at last he'd taken pity on her bewildered

face. "Poor little girl. Didn't anyone tell you what was expected of you? Don't worry, you'll soon get used to it."

She felt she was being watched and looked up to see a short, florid-faced man with pale, rather protruding eyes and a thick neck on the other side of the room, leaning against the piano. He raised his glass to her and gave her a lascivious smile.

George Perry always made her squirm, but he was Charles's closest friend and already, Sara suspected, more than a little attracted to her. He was courteous to the point of almost being a nuisance, but it was clear Charles admired him so she took his attentions with a mild grace.

At first she was quite willing to forgive his imperfections, till she discovered him drunk in the library one night beating his manservant over the head with his riding crop because he'd spilled brandy on his master's trousers. When she'd called out and insisted he stop, he'd tried to make a joke about it, but ever since she could see him in no other light than that of a tyrant to be avoided as much as possible.

All the men drank more than was good for them, and even her own husband, who had so much self-control, showed a hard light in his eye and a sharp tongue when he'd drunk too much brandy. Though it was accepted as inevitable the men would turn to alcohol. The climate encouraged it.

Even the women betrayed flushed faces and high-pitched giggles as they sipped their gin and quinine behind their fans. More than once a lady was seen leaving the room, her legs wobbling as she was supported on both sides, being ushered out to the reviving air of the terrace, or to be discreetly sick amongst the hibiscus. Though it was considered bad form to notice it, let alone speak of it.

This was a new experience for Sara, having never seen a woman drink even a thimbleful of alcohol before, except as a tonic when faint.

As she watched, after an evening of slow but continuous drinking, the mood become more menacing as the men, driven by boredom, turned to a type of schoolboy violence for amusement. She'd seen it all before and wanted to leave before the games began.

She looked up and caught Charles's glance from across the room and beckoned with her eyes for him to come to her. Cynthia was in the middle of whispering something in his ear, but he put out a hand to halt her in mid-sentence and, frowning a little, he made his way to where Sara sat on the sofa.

"Whatever's the matter, my sweet? You look quite cross." He staggered a little as he bent down to her and his words were slurred.

"I want to go. I'm rather tired ... It must be the heat." Up close, his cheeks showed a bright red flush and his pale blue eyes had a familiar hard glitter.

"Not yet, darling. It wouldn't look right to leave so soon. They expect me to stay."

"Then I'll have Shakur take me home."

Sara rose to her feet, but Charles leaned close to her face and spoke through clenched teeth, forcing her back onto the settee. "I said *not now*. Lady Palmer would be offended.

If you'd put yourself out a little you might find you enjoy it."

A voice rang out from the other side of the room, causing them both to start. "Choose your mounts! We'll have some practice before the match."

Charles laughed, his anger fading at once. His eyes were no longer stern and he patted her arm as though to appease her, before leaving. She watched him as he made his way towards his waiting friends. He'd forgotten her already.

A few moments later the male servants were called from the anterooms and assembled to be chosen for the teams.

Sara rose and left the room, hurrying towards the relative peace of the terrace. At least there she wouldn't have to be a witness to the humiliations that were bound to follow.

A favourite game of the men was to ride their servants around the room in a pretend game of polo, where, as they became more excited, the drunken riders beat their servants as they scrambled about the floor chasing the ball. Sara wondered why she didn't find it as funny as the other spectators obviously did, their heads flung back in uncontrollable hysterics, with even the women shouting from the sidelines and betting on the winners.

Cynthia followed her out onto the terrace, her usual controlled self, though her eyes showed an eager curiosity disguised as concern. "What are you doing out here by yourself, Sara? Are you unwell?"

Sara didn't turn around, unwilling to reveal the bright tears smarting in the corner of her eyes. "I just can't bear to watch. It's all so humiliating." She wasn't in the mood to speak and disliked being disturbed, especially when she felt she might betray her emotions to Cynthia's gossiping tongue.

Cynthia slapped Sara's arm with her fan, as was her habit. It was meant to be playful, but there was a real reproach in the slap as well.

"You sound just like my governess! They've little enough to amuse them, and the poor boys are so far away from the usual pursuits of gentlemen."

"Well, that's my point ..." Sara almost snapped, forgetting her strict training and unable now to hide her resentment. "It's beneath them to behave in such a way."

"Oh, for heaven's sake ... It's only a game, and the servants enjoy it too. You're too severe, come and join the others. Poor boys ... If they could have a little fox-hunting, perhaps ... It only seems fair, now that the tigers seem to have all but disappeared."

Sara thought about replying but felt nothing she could say in defence of tigers would have any effect except to annoy. She merely smiled, then collected her cashmere shawl from the seat beside her. "Tell Charles I'm going home."

She left at once, leaving Cynthia to wonder why Charles would've thought it necessary to marry someone so unsuitable, and who seemed to take pleasure in ruining everyone else's fun.

Chapter 8

The polo match was held in the coolest part of the afternoon, as the sun's rays cast long mauve shadows across the sparse, almost bare expanse of grass that had been hacked out of the always encroaching jungle.

A raised dais stood in the corner of the field, decorated almost too lavishly with garlands of brilliant flowers and bunting representing the colours of the British Empire. A line of cane armchairs had been set up on this dais for the chief dignitaries, first amongst them being Lady Palmer and her daughter. Sara too had a place of honour, raised high above the other guests, as the wife of the captain of the British team.

She would have preferred to be amongst the crowd below, who had set up their own picnics under the shade of trees or under festive little tents, but Charles was keen to show Sara his horsemanship, and also to display his beautiful new wife to as many people as possible.

All the women had dressed in their best, including Sara, who wore a dress of the finest embroidered white linen, matched with a rakish straw hat turned up at the front and trimmed with a wide green ribbon. The brim cast half her face in shadow, but the heavy gold-fringed earrings she wore gave her topaz eyes a glow, as though lit by candlelight. The earrings had once belonged to her aunt and, even though they had sometimes had a difficult relationship, she felt near to her when she wore them, and missed her despite everything. Especially now, when after only a short few weeks of marriage she was ridden by confusing thoughts. She shook her head as though trying to push away her nagging doubts, and the earrings danced. She told herself it was best not to think about it and turned her attention back to her surroundings.

In the distance just beyond the field, she could see the teams of polo ponies waiting with their individual handlers. The thoroughbred horses of the British were on one side and the Arabian horses belonging to the Indian team on the other. She could see a curious ceremony taking place in front of the Indian team. A Brahmin priest was giving a *puja* for luck, and the acrid sweet fragrance of incense wafted through the air towards her, lifting her spirits and making her heart race with the thrill of it all. The Englishmen stood to one side, hands on hips or pacing back and forth, waiting for the ritual to be over, and even from that distance she could feel their contempt for such primitive behaviour. After the strange events on the day she'd arrived in India she could feel no such contempt, only a faint sense of apprehension, and a fresh wonder at the mystery of India.

A man with long black hair, wearing a white shirt and cream jodhpurs, walked with long, almost languid steps to where the *puja* was being held.

He bent his head to be given a garland of bright marigolds and receive a blessing, then he straightened his back, combed his hair back from his face with his fingers and wrapped a white turban around his head and face.

She knew it must be Ravi Sabran. There could be no one else in Madras with that proud tilt to his chin and air of impending drama.

A strange current of something like pain shot through her body.

She wasn't sure what that feeling was—apprehension perhaps?—as she had planned to ask him when she could visit him, despite being told she could not. She knew, though, she must see the child and be sure of her happiness till she was old enough to find it herself. She felt with absolute certainty she owed it to the old man who had drowned, and nothing or nobody would stand in her way.

Servants bearing trays of fragrant food and long cool drinks milled about, paying particular attention to Lady Palmer, who was relishing her role as queen of the proceedings. A small gilt trophy waited on a stand at her side to present to the winner, and Charles had assured her that this time it would be presented to him.

Cynthia leaned back in her chair, waving her pink lace fan against the heat. She looked cross and bored, and every now and then cast a resentful eye in Sara's direction. She felt it was wrong any other girl should share the limelight with her, especially someone she saw as being of inferior rank, and even possibly more attractive than herself.

A military band played, first marching across the field then back again, giving the signal for the game to begin.

The British team rode out first, cantering across the field in their immaculately pressed khaki jodhpurs and jackets. They stopped before the dais and raised their mallets to pay their respects to Lady Palmer and in return receive her regal blessing. Cynthia roused herself for the first time that day, leaning forward and gripping the arms of the chair in her excitement.

"Make sure you beat them, Charles! You must! It's a matter of honour."

"I will!" he called back. "I'll make sure I do!"

Charles blew Sara a kiss, then took off his white helmet and bowed his head in her direction. She thought he had never looked so handsome, with his white-gold hair shining in the soft evening light.

"Good luck, darling!" she cried and threw him the tuberous she wore in her belt. He kissed it and placed it in his button-hole, before cantering onto the field with his men.

Ravi Sabran and his team rode out next. All the men except Sabran wore wide baggy pants and a type of gaily embroidered waistcoat over loose muslin shirts. Thick turbans were wound around their heads and chins to act as a helmet, giving them the look of wild marauding Arabs.

Their fierce black eyes darted everywhere, keen to start, and determined to win.

They performed a ferocious race around the field first, raising their mallets high in the air like bayonets, then, pausing in front of the rotunda, gave a hasty salute, before galloping away onto the field to a loud roar of approval from the Indian crowds.

Only Sabran had dismounted, swinging down from his fine Arab stallion with an easy unhurried grace. A servant rushed forward to hold the reins while he made his way to the dais.

Lady Palmer received him with a cursory impolite nod, but Sara rose from her chair and walked down the steps to meet him. From behind her back she heard the words, "Mrs Fitzroy, totally unnecessary!"

Up close she could see his white linen open-necked shirt and jodhpurs were spotless and perfectly tailored. She wondered where such things could be bought, as everything she had seen made in Madras so far had a shabby half-finished look. She experienced a faint feeling of disdain, thinking the man was most likely vain as well as arrogant.

She caught a hint of the musky scent of sandalwood rising from his clothes, bringing back vividly the sudden memory of her father, when, as a child, he had lifted her in his arms for a playful kiss. The memory was so powerful, for a moment she almost forgot where she was and had to rouse herself to face him.

It was difficult to see if Sabran smiled or not, but she felt he didn't. His eyes gave him away.

Like the rest of his men, he wore his white turban wound around his head and neck like a Bedouin. Only his eyes were visible, reminding her of the eyes of a falcon she had once seen on a visit to Scotland, being trained to kill sparrows on command. They were wary and at the same time alert, and perhaps even pitiless.

He unwound the scarf from his face. There again was that strong nose and firmly carved red mouth, and the same expression she remembered from their first meeting, giving the feeling she was standing before a great prince who had lowered himself to speak to one of his subjects.

"Madam Fitzroy. We meet again." He slowly raised one corner of his mouth in a kind of smile, but it was enough to encourage her to step closer to him.

"Monsieur Sabran, I had hoped to see you. How is Prema?"

He seemed a little insulted by her question, almost snapping his answer.

"The child is well, of course!"

Even so, he took her hand as she skipped lightly down the last step, then raised it to his lips in the French manner, while bestowing on her one of his enigmatic looks.

He took her in at a glance. He thought she was looking thinner, and not quite as blooming as when she'd first arrived in India. There were faint mauve shadows under her eyes, and a hint of something like depression concealed in their beauty.

Then, as though performing a role, his manner changed to that of the perfect French gentleman. "What a very charming hat you are wearing, madam, absurd but charming."

"Well, thank you, *monsieur*. I was under the impression it was fashionable. Forgive me." Then she laughed to show him she didn't care what he thought, and he laughed too, forgetting for a moment he didn't like her.

A loud disapproving cough caused them both to look

around to see Lady Palmer, her lips firmly pressed together, shaking her head and making it clear she was displeased.

Sara pulled a face only Sabran could see, making it plain she had no intention of obeying the woman, and that one simple act made him like her a little bit more.

"I want to visit Prema. When can I come?"

Her voice was low and soft, with a slight husky inflection. He decided he liked that too, as for him the sound of a woman's voice was more important than her beauty.

"I will be away for a week or two, but then you can come … Are you brave enough to visit the home of the notorious Sabran? I think you are not supposed to be speaking to me … Your behaviour will be all over Madras by nightfall."

"I will come nonetheless. I must."

Lady Palmer's voice rang out, impatient now. "You are holding up the game, Mr Sabran. Kindly finish what you have to say to Mrs Fitzroy and go."

Sabran wanted to ignore her, but even his dislike of her wasn't enough for him to disregard the privileges due to a lady.

"Allow me one moment, madam." He smiled at her, and Sara could see even Lady Palmer was momentarily dazed by his charm.

He called for his servant to come forward and bring the beautiful stallion. "I want you to meet Sultan. He is a prince amongst horses."

After touching the animal very lightly on the foreleg, he performed a delicate bow in Sara's direction. She was bewitched.

She couldn't help herself and, on an impulse, kissed the lovely creature's neck, laying her face against his silky flank, while relishing the powerful pulse of life under the warm skin.

She let her guard down for a moment and sighed aloud in her pleasure.

"Oh, he's lovely. I wish I could ride him. You make me jealous."

He was taken aback by the expression of pure joy lighting up her face and, he had to reluctantly admit, making her beautiful. He was momentarily transfixed by her long slim fingers and fine wrist, circled by a thin gold bangle, as it lay on the animal's neck.

"You are not afraid?"

He frowned as he studied her face, his interest in her piqued a little.

"No, of course not," she almost scoffed. "I love to ride. It was almost my only pleasure at my hideous boarding school, and the only time I could really escape, except in a book. Though I was always in trouble for being late bringing my mount back ... but ... oh, I want a horse just like this ... Perhaps you could advise me where I could buy one so I can ride every day ..."

"You will never find a horse like this one. He has Manipuri blood as well as Arab. The British mock the strain as being half caste; they much prefer the thoroughbreds, so perhaps your husband will think the breed an unsuitable choice for an English lady."

He was being sarcastic again; she could tell by the faint

malignant glow in his eyes. "I always play the last chukka with him; he never loses."

Sultan was led away to await his turn in the game. His step was as light as a dancer, and Sara watched his proud arched neck and high step with pure envy.

A bugle rang out, signalling the start of the game, and Sabran turned to leave, giving her his customary low bow.

She put out a hand to halt him, and Lady Palmer let out a loud protesting snort.

"Forgive me, *monsieur*, but I must know ... is it true? Was polo first played with the heads of captured enemies?"

He laughed. "Such an unladylike question, madam, but history says it was the women who played the game first. The men would toss a head to them after a battle to keep them amused."

"That's horrible. I don't believe you. A woman could not possibly be so barbaric."

"Well, madam ..." he looked directly into her eyes, unsettling her again, and causing her to step back a pace "... I disagree; in the game of love many a man has been left feeling headless and beaten at the amused whim of a beautiful woman ... such as yourself."

At first she felt a little thrill at the compliment, then she was angry at herself for allowing her thoughts to drift that way; he was being predictable and was now a disappointment to her. She remembered her husband's words, and how he had laughed at her for succumbing to Sabran's false charm. She would not be taken in again.

"I think you are playing a game with me, *monsieur*, and you insult my intelligence."

He raised his eyebrows at that; he wasn't used to a woman questioning a compliment. "And you, madam, insult my honour; I never say what I don't mean."

He was confused by her answer. He had meant what he said, and in return he expected her to flirt with him, as a Frenchwoman would, but instead she only raised her chin and gave him a haughty stare.

He was tired of the sport already. She was as he'd first thought, a strait-laced Englishwoman, not worthy of his faint interest.

Lady Palmer's voice rang out again. "Monsieur Sabran, please ... We are here to watch a match ..."

In response, he turned his head in a slow, insolent way to see the British team riding in impatient circles in the centre of the field. Charles had dismounted and stood with his arms folded over his chest. He was obviously trying to contain his fury, and Sabran knew it was because of his wife more than being held up for a minute or two.

This pleased him. There were the fading traces of a mocking smile on his lips as he turned back to speak to her. "I must go. It seems the gentlemen are anxious to be beaten."

"You are very sure of yourself, *monsieur*."

"Not so sure as you might think; the Brahmin said it was an inauspicious day for me ... He didn't want me to play, but perhaps if you wish me luck it will change the course of destiny?"

Again, there was the flirtatious touch in his words she so distrusted, and her voice was almost cold when she spoke. "I will wish you luck, of course, but I want my husband to win, naturally."

Her answer angered him, and he felt driven to win all the more.

Then he laughed at himself. Why should he want the approval of this woman? She was nothing to him. It amused him, though, to ... what was the English expression? ... to put the cat amongst the pigeons."

He wrapped the scarf of his turban around his face, sprang onto his horse without looking back at her, then galloped onto the field. There was a rumble of hooves followed by a sharp thwack, a cloud of dust, and the game was underway.

109

Chapter 9

Later, when she was home at last, Sara did what she rarely
did. She poured herself a large glass of brandy and drank
it almost at once. Men did it all the time to blot out an unpleasant
memory, and she thought perhaps it might work for her ...

The game was exhilarating, her heart was racing with the
thrill of it, rising to her feet and cheering as the teams thundered past, vying for the ball with a recklessness bordering
on insanity.

Sabran's men were especially fearless. They rode their tough
little ponies as though they were charging into a battle of life
and death, and more than once she could see fleeting signs
of alarm on the faces of the British team as their opponents
hurtled towards them.

Charles rode well, with an equal determination and skill,
as did his team, but she could sense he alone was driven by
a desire to win beyond what was normal. They had come to
the last chukka and the teams were equal, then Sabran had
the ball, and was racing towards the goal with only a minute
or two left.

The beautiful Sultan dashed past the dais, his mane flying.

Sabran's eyes were fixed on the ball, glowing with the knowledge of certain victory. He raised his mallet high to strike what was a sure goal.

Charles thundered alongside, the flanks of his horse dangerously close.

Too close. Then, as she watched, her heart skipped a beat, knowing with a terrible certainty something disastrous was about to happen.

She caught a glimpse of Charles's face as he flew past her, his mallet raised to attack, and his expression frightened her. He was smiling, but it was a cold smile and twisted with a furious intent.

Then it happened. Charles's mallet caught between Sultan's forelegs and the horse fell with a horrible shriek.

Sabran was down, lying in the centre of the field, his turban unwound and his face almost as white as his once immaculate shirt. She leapt to her feet, a trembling hand on her heart and, before she could stop it, committed the unforgivable act of screaming aloud.

All manner of thoughts had flown through her brain. Was this strange and powerful man, who seemed to be exempt from the fate of ordinary mortals, going to be struck down before she had the chance to know him?

In a few moments, though, he had staggered to his feet, his hands covering the anguish on his face, then a few minutes later, as the crowd fell silent, a group of men collected to screen the act that was to follow. A gunshot rang out, and the poor screaming creature was hushed at last.

Then, when the curtain around the scene lifted for a brief moment, it revealed the awful sight of Sabran, almost crazed in his pain, bent over the horse's body, his face hidden in his beloved's neck. From her position on the dais, she saw his body shake violently, and she knew he was trying to suppress his tears.

Then he leapt to his feet and threw himself at Charles, clearly wanting to kill him. It took four men to pull him away, while Charles stood before him, arms wide as if to declare his innocence, but with a look that was both taunting and threatening.

With an enormous effort to exert himself, Sabran insisted on finishing the last chukka, playing now with an even greater ferocity, his face white with rage, his black hair flying unbound, till his team won, and Charles had to bear the humiliation of watching Sabran take the cup from Lady Palmer without a word, then throw it contemptuously to the crowd, at the same time announcing he would never play with an Englishman again.

Even though the warmth of the brandy had numbed her senses a little, she paced the room, her hands over her ears, trying to block out that horrible sound and the expression on her husband's face as he'd raced towards the ball.

There had been a lot of dust, but it had cleared for just a brief moment as they'd thundered past her position on the dais, and she'd thought she'd seen Charles lean wide to deliberately trip the horse, even though he'd sworn he had slipped in his saddle and the accident was unavoidable. She began to think she must have imagined it, but still the horrible thought nagged at her.

No one questioned it except Sabran. Charles was known as a gentleman, and sadly horses died sometimes, but now she watched her husband with a caution she hadn't felt before, searching for signs that might betray his guilt, even though his behaviour didn't alter when the subject was mentioned. He remained impassive, at times almost chillingly blank; the only comment he made about the whole event was that of course he felt bad about the whole thing, but half-caste horses had no stamina, and Sultan had stumbled due to exhaustion.

Chapter 10

When Sara married Charles, she felt it was for life; the line, "to forsake all others", she took for granted, though after only a few weeks of married life there was an ever-widening breach between them she had not yet been able to heal. On her part there were the events on the day of the polo match to overcome, and the constant battle she had with those suspicions that clouded their relationship. The image of Sultan on the day of his death continued to haunt her. The powerful glossy flanks she had caressed so fondly were not those of a weakling bred purely for his beauty, and she knew beyond doubt that Sabran would never risk losing his favourite horse by pushing it beyond its limits. It was clear to her Charles was looking for excuses to somehow lessen his guilt in the matter, but most of all it was his comment about the horse being half-caste that troubled her the most, as she suspected it was a veiled sneer directed at Anglo-Indian people like the McKenzies.

She had written to Sabran offering her sympathy, and asking again when she might visit Prema, but had received no reply, and she assumed that, as the wife of Charles Fitzroy, he had no wish to ever lay eyes on her again.

Though something good had come out of the horror; she had bought a beautiful mare and had her stabled in a nearby field so she could ride in the cool of the day, giving her the exercise she craved. But most of all it gave Sara freedom, and the solitude she needed.

She had expected Charles to object, and suspected he'd only agreed because he sensed she still had doubts about the part he had played in Sultan's death. He only asked that she should stick within the confines of White Town, or to the main roads of Madras to avoid any trouble with the Indian men.

He felt it gave him added status to have a wife who rode well, and who looked so beautiful in her riding habit. There was something aristocratic about her when on horseback, raising her above the other women in his community. But this fact soon began to have repercussions, and jealousies began to form, first whispered in the drawing rooms then spoken aloud, especially by Lady Palmer, who saw the lovely Mrs Fitzroy as a threat to her well-ordered standards of behaviour.

Sara was aware of the gossip and, because of it, began to avoid the public places of the British, and ride further afield. She crept out of bed at dawn while Charles slept, knowing she had two hours of freedom before he awoke and she became a wife once more. Then she fled to the nearby beach for a wild gallop on the sands, or a wade through the deliciously cool waves, before any of the English community awoke and set tongues wagging again.

In the early morning mist, heavy with smoke from the thousands of dung fires, the sky was a magical turquoise washed with an innocent pink; however, she was often aware of a sense of unease, especially if she happened across the groups of holy men performing their strange rituals at the many temples lining the shores. They would look up at her as she rode slowly past, their kohl-rimmed eyes vacant and staring as they smoked long cones of ganga, their almost naked, emaciated bodies smeared with grey ash and heavy with holy beads and talismans. But, despite the ever-present faint sense of danger, she felt drawn to the place and couldn't stay away, and every day became more adventurous with her exploring.

At the far end of the beach lay giant sun-bleached boulders littering the shoreline like monstrous marooned whales. It was there the holy men usually collected, as ancient carvings were depicted there on the sandstone rocks, and they were usually kind, and were grateful for the coins she gave. She felt no fear from these holy men, but the atmosphere permeating the area was heavy with a strange, almost mesmerising spirituality that sometimes made her feel light-headed, as if she was under a spell. Even the rhythmic flow of the waves and the touch of the caressing wind against her face seemed to overwhelm her will. It was almost as though she was being lured there by something unknown and frightening.

Because of an important holy festival in Madras, one morning the place was almost empty except for a chapatti seller who had set up nearby to catch the early morning trade, so she dismounted to take a closer look at the carvings.

What she saw made her reel back with shock.

The naked bodies depicted on the giant stones were intertwined, their long, delicately carved eyes heavy with passionate abandonment, frozen by time and stone into decaying ghosts of what they'd been in life.

A lovely girl, her rounded body as luscious as a ripe peach still, though partly eroded by wind and sand, stood on tiptoe to kiss a handsome, crumbling god with a huge erect penis. He held another girl in his muscular arms and she lay back in his embrace, hips thrust forward as she exposed her naked self with careless unconcern. Another man, on his knees before her, his face a picture of sensuous delight, was intent in giving the girl pleasure in a way Sara could never have imagined.

Everywhere she looked were images of even greater eroticism, repeated over and over, tier after tier of figures, all of them depicted trapped in the moment of ecstasy that would last till they crumbled and turned to dust, as the original models for the work had, thousands of years before.

She felt a powerful surge of pleasure shoot through her body, making her legs tremble and her face flush. She looked about, feeling sure that as her reaction was so strong it would be written clearly for all to see.

She didn't know people did such things, but in moments of solitude she had to confess to thinking there must be more to what happened in bed between a man and a woman apart from what she and Charles did. She felt instinctively, though, that Charles would probably be repulsed by such behaviour.

He was fastidious in his love-making, usually hurrying out of bed immediately afterwards and washing himself with a great deal of splashing, leaving Sara to feel dirty and ashamed when she knew, instinctively, there should be no shame.

She looked around to see the chapatti seller staring at her with an odd, almost insolent smile, and she began to feel the danger of lingering there any longer. Her first thought was to get away before she was seen. The beach was beginning to fill with people, and in the distance a rider was fast coming towards her.

She decided to stay where she was till the rider passed, in case it was anyone she knew. Pulling her horse behind the highest boulder, she stood motionless and listened, her heart pounding. After a moment the sounds of galloping retreated into the distance, so she quickly mounted her horse, pulled her black net veil over her face and began to ride away, congratulating herself on not being seen.

But she had been seen. Ravi Sabran had turned on hearing the faint sound of her horse and saw the young Mrs Fitzroy, wife of his hated enemy, riding away from what he knew to be, at least to English ladies, a forbidden area. He knew the sculptures well, and what they depicted, and couldn't help but wonder what kind of effect they had had on her.

He dismounted with extra stealth, as silent as a hunter, and under cover of the giant boulders led his horse to the same spot she had so recently left. There was one of her footprints clearly marked in the sand and, on a strange impulse, he measured his own foot next to hers.

She had stopped a few metres away, allowing him time to fully appreciate the sight of her slim figure on horseback. He thought she looked very dashing in her green habit and black veiled hat with a green feather. He smiled to himself; she seemed to have a passion for absurdly pretty hats.

Her back was very straight, even though she was burdened by having to ride side-saddle. He thought it an unnecessary punishment to inflict on a woman; it was dangerous and selfish too. He couldn't understand why society would go to such lengths to deny a woman an accidental pleasure by her riding astride.

One of her legs was hooked over the pommel, and her neat booted foot and slim ankle were peeping out from below her skirt. The sight of her ankle stirred in him a powerful sensation he did not want, and he crushed it at once.

He began to feel like a Peeping Tom and thought about making himself known to her, but he knew she would be embarrassed to be discovered in such a place, and he could at least save her from that.

As he watched her, he could see she had somehow become aware of his unseen presence. She began to look nervously about, like a startled fawn sensing a predator on the air; her horse made little restless movements, which she calmed with gentle pats on her neck and soft words of reassurance.

Then, all of a sudden after taking a final quick look about her, she broke into a wild fearless gallop, her skirts billowing behind her, leaving him to struggle with all kinds of conflicting feelings, including disappointment at having let her go without speaking to her. He wanted to hate her; he must hate any woman who had chosen to marry such a man as Charles Fitzroy.

But now his hatred had been replaced with something else, but he wasn't sure what or how strong that feeling might be. He was familiar with lust, but this was different; he only knew she disturbed him in a way that might be dangerous.

He made a silent pact though to crush those feelings. He needed a clear head if he wanted to exact his revenge on Charles Fitzroy, and he would not allow any signs of tenderness to stand in his way.

Chapter 11

Almost a month had passed since the polo match, and the social events continued unabated, so even in her home the constant presence of the servants made intimacy between her and Charles difficult. The walls were thin, and it seemed ears were alert for any sound uttered from the mouths of their masters.

The meals were gruelling affairs, as they were watched closely by the retinue of servants waiting behind every chair and in every corner of the room. Their voices seemed loud and artificial in such an environment, and the clinking of cutlery and glass in the painfully silent room made conversation difficult and stilted. Though in a way Sara was grateful, for the constraints imposed on them hid what really lay beneath the surface: Sara's unspoken distrust of her husband.

Their honeymoon too had been postponed more than once because of bad weather down south, though it seemed Charles was in no hurry to leave Madras, despite Sara's desire for a break in their gruelling social engagements.

He relished the company of his friends and followed

steadfastly the pattern of his life before he was married; the only difference being, now he had the added advantage of a lovely wife by his side.

"I'm a lucky man," he murmured as they entered Lady Palmer's drawing room. "There's no one here to equal you."

She looked at him with wonder mingled with apprehension. Remarkably, there was no sign of dissipation on his face from the almost constant heavy drinking, only a faint grey shadow under his blue eyes, and a slight pink flush on his cheeks that seemed to even improve his looks.

She knew she was looking her best. She could always tell, by the silent nod of approval he gave her, combined with a proud squaring of his shoulders as he glanced around the room to see if others had noticed how well she looked. He had recovered from his disappointment at finding her so attractive, and instead took an interest in how her good looks and charming manner could promote his career.

She had left London with six oak chests, packed with twenty sets of the finest lawn underwear, two dozen embroidered silk nightgowns and fifty gowns still packed in their tissue paper, along with a dozen pairs of fine linen sheets, one hundred and twenty Scottish crystal glasses, and a Worcester dinner service for twenty places.

Her evening gowns and day dresses in various shades and fabrics were commissioned from an unknown French dressmaker who had set up a small boutique in Chelsea, an area much frowned upon by her aunt as being disreputable and totally forbidden.

Sara hadn't really cared about fashion before, having always been a bit of a tomboy, and had heartily disliked the complex ritual that went into turning a healthy female body into a trussed-up confection of frills and whalebone that prevented her from doing all the things she liked to do, such as riding or playing tennis.

But these gowns were different; they suited her newly slim body and brought out in her an innate femininity, and a desire to be well dressed for the first time in her life.

Her dresses were modern, in the style and colours of the fashion the women of the Chelsea artist community chose to adopt and didn't conflict too strongly with the beliefs of the new Rational Dress movement who believed in freedom from constraint for the female body.

The end result meant her wardrobe was striking in its simplicity. Where other girls appeared at a dinner or ball dressed in heavy silk gowns with leg-of-mutton sleeves adorned with abundant lace and absurd bustles, Sara would wear a gown of simple cut, with tiny puffed sleeves and a low curve to the neck and shoulders. She favoured almost straight skirts, showing the natural shape of her hips, shocking Madras society with her non-existent bustle. Her corsets were of the new French style and made of silk, and so light she was barely aware she was wearing a corset at all, making it possible to dance longer than anyone else without feeling faint. She wore little jewellery, usually the heavy fringed earrings or a simple gold chain necklace and engraved locket containing the miniature of her father as a young man. Her dark auburn hair was brushed to a deep glossy shine and held with a pair of gold filigree combs of Spanish design once owned by her mother. She held her chin high, showing the curve of her beautiful neck, and walked with an unusual elegance, moving from the hip with long slow strides. There was something in her walk that made men look, even though there were other, perhaps prettier, faces in the room.

Charles found himself bewitched by her beauty, even though he often declared her taste a little unconventional. It was while he'd watched her dress for dinner that he'd commented on the fact she rarely wore any colours other than white, green, mauve and black.

It had taken her some time to answer him, as she knew the real answer would not please him. They were the colours of the Suffragette movement and a symbol of her secret growing support. The white was for purity, the green for hope and the mauve for dignity. She knew he would not be sympathetic, but she had hopes he would change his mind when he knew more about the movement.

So she made up a lie about wearing her mother's favourite colours as a tribute to her memory. Black she wore for elegance, and also as a sign of eternal mourning, for the parents she would never see again.

But now, as she thought about the evening ahead in Lady Palmer's drawing room, she began to feel she'd fallen into a kind of trap, and the pressure from Charles to be perfect at all times was beginning to be a burden. She was bored with it all, and at the same time overwhelmed with the realisation that the life spread out before her would not be enough.

A hand on her arm shook her back to reality.

"Sara, you really are the deepest daydreamer."

"Charles! I'm sorry, it must be the heat."

"Well, buck up, my dear. There are some ladies I want you to meet."

She almost groaned aloud but managed to disguise it with a cough. She had already overheard some of the ladies in the bedroom next to her own, where they had retired to cool down after their journey. Over the general chatter and giggles, one voice in particular had a way of carrying through walls.

"It's safe ..." Cynthia giggled "... I saw her go downstairs a while ago."

"And just who is she? I've heard she's not like us at all."

Then Cynthia's careful response. "Well, at least she's a lady, though not exactly what I would've wanted for dear Charles, but I suppose once he was trapped into it, he couldn't withdraw. He did mention to me she's changed so much she wasn't the girl he'd married, but you know what he is, so very honourable ..."

Sara, listening from the next room, couldn't help but be disappointed, because there had been times when she had really liked Cynthia. It was impossible though they could ever really be friends. Sara knew she was not as girlish and carefree as other young women, and sometimes lamented that her harsh early life had blunted that side of her. Lately, though, she'd begun to take a certain pride in being a little apart from the crowd and, despite the safety of acceptance, she didn't care to become part of it, especially if it meant she must lose her individuality.

"Here she is ... my wife, the loveliest girl in Madras ..." Sara cringed as Charles introduced her to the women who had earlier maligned her. She hated it when he spoke of her that way; it made her feel like one of his possessions.

"I'll leave you ladies to your nonsense," he said before leaving her, and those words too made her flinch.

The expressions of the girls were not hopeful as their eyes made swift calculated darts over her face and figure, and one of them, a plump girl with round vacant eyes, opened the conversation with the mention of a name Sara would prefer not to think about.

"We all saw you at the polo match, Mrs Fitzroy, talking with that Sabran fellow. You must be careful of him, no matter how pleasant he pretends to be."

Before she could reply, another girl, introduced as Milly, and of equally bland appearance interrupted her. "All the Indian men want a white woman. It's common knowledge. So you must never make eye contact with any of them, in case they lose control, and you know ..." Here she rolled her eyes and giggled, before lowering her voice to a whisper. "And our wicked Monsieur Sabran is the worst of all ... The things one hears about him, enough to make one's hair curl ... You can't imagine ..."

Sara looked around for an escape route. She had never been

interested in gossip, especially now, when she knew most of it in her present circle was centred around herself.

"No ... I can't imagine ... He seemed perfectly charming to me."

"Well, the rumour is he keeps at least three women, and not all of them Indian ... They say he has a French actress in Pondicherry ..."

Charles appeared again to rescue Sara from any more unlooked for sensational intimacies, although she had to grudgingly admit she was just a little curious about what the girl was about to say about Ravi Sabran's romantic affairs.

Charles took her arm in his, claiming ownership with the same determination with which he dealt with every other matter he felt was under his control and drew her away, whispering something about the garden, and his desire to kiss her, when a small white hand grasped his coat sleeve.

He swung around to attention with just a faint tinge of irritation in his voice. "Sara and I were just about to take a walk in the garden ..."

"Oh, no, you don't, I haven't finished with you yet ... I need you to explain something ..." Cynthia gave Sara her most charming smile and took a firm hold on his arm.

"You must excuse me stealing Charles so much; it's just that he's always been such a help to me in the past, and you know how I've come to rely on him for all manner of little things ..."

She had a habit of dropping her lashes over her blue eyes, then holding his gaze with a coy half smile. Her look seemed to have the desired effect and he was transfixed, and Sara wondered what might have been the outcome if Cynthia's fiancé was not a rich man, and the eldest son of a Baronet.

Sara laughed. "No, please, take him. I was brought up to share."

Cynthia was put out; it wasn't the reaction she was hoping for, and she gave Sara one of her hasty up and down looks, then turned away.

In doing so she bumped into a servant who had appeared before her holding a letter and Cynthia took the opportunity of venting her anger on the man, showing the usually hidden side of her character. He'd stood on the hem of her gown, and she tore it away from his touch with a look of utter distaste. "Now I'll have to change."

There was a cold warning in her tone that spoke of future punishment, and the man picked up on it at once. He almost prostrated himself before her. "Forgive me, *memsahib* ... but this letter is very important. The messenger said it must be delivered at once."

Cynthia waved him away and he hurried out of the room, pleased to escape.

She opened the letter, read it, and for a brief flickering moment her face showed interest, then almost at once fell back into her usual haughty expression. "It seems the Maharaja of Chittipore is hosting a garden party on Wednesday. Listen to this: "'It would please me if you can extend this invitation to the wife of our most respected Mr Fitzroy ...'" How on earth did the old fool know she was here?"

Charles placed a possessive arm around Sara's waist and smiled upon her. He was clearly very pleased. "Oh, nothing is a secret in Madras ... By now everyone knows there's a new face in town ..."

"But why would he be so particular about inviting Sara when other girls who've lived here for years have never been asked? Why poor Millicent would give anything to go. It doesn't seem fair." Cynthia pouted, and gave Sara an almost resentful look.

Sara wasn't unaware of the cattiness of the remark, but again, most of Cynthia's comments washed over her, feeling it beneath her to notice such childish behaviour. But she was a little intrigued by the unexpected invitation after all. "Forgive me, but why must I feel so honoured?"

Charles rubbed his hands together and spoke with a kind of glee. "Well, the invitation is a compliment to me, of course, and the Maharaja would be interested in my choice of bride, it's only natural. The natives show an insatiable curiosity about our lives. Rather pathetic really.

The fellow's from a little province north of here, but he always comes to Madras for the season. He's a shrewd old thing, and well known as an eccentric ... but his jewels are the best I've ever seen ... and his palace is said to be worth a visit."

Cynthia's mouth was hanging open a little, just enough to show her wet mouth and teeth. "Just one of his better diamonds would be enough to buy a small country house in England, but it pains me to see how he apes our customs. A garden party indeed! It's enough to make one squirm. But I suppose we should go, even if it's only to admire the old fool's diamonds." Cynthia had a rather raucous laugh for a well brought up young lady, and it seemed to Sara there was very little humour in it.

Charles joined in with her laughter. They seemed to find the whole matter irresistibly funny.

"I'm pleased you find the whole thing so amusing. I only wish you would let me in on the joke."

Charles became serious for a moment and, speaking slowly so Sara would get the full impact of his words, raised her chin to face him. "Because, my lovely wife, he's extremely proud of them and it's most important you admire them. It's protocol. So you must admire them; he'll consider it a personal insult if you don't."

She pushed his hand away. She didn't like it when he spoke to her in such a way. It made her feel like a naughty child who must be taught a lesson.

"It seems like an odd thing to expect, but if it will make him happy I suppose I must."

"It will make me very happy also, my dear, so mind you don't forget.

He's singled you out for special regard so it's a huge compliment.

I'm looking forward to it," he said, unaware that Sara was not looking forward to it at all.

Chapter 12

The Maharaja had taken up rooms in the best hotel in Madras, a confection of gilded domed turrets and lace-work balconies, once built by a successful English trader who'd made a vast fortune in the tea trade. It was looking a little shabby after many years in the merciless Indian sun but, even so, managed to impart an air of refined grandeur in the dusty landscape.

Outside the entrance, elegantly dressed guests filed towards the open double doors leading to the cool marble corridors, which in turn opened onto the wide grassed inner courtyard filled with the Maharaja's entourage, though his female house-hold were hidden from view, and could only peep through veiled eyes from shuttered windows onto the splendour of the scene below.

Tables covered with crisp white linen, laid for a lavish tea, dotted the setting, while large arrangements of brilliant flowers in extravagant vases competed in beauty with their earth-bound cousins in the gardens. Where there were no trees, huge umbrellas of richly coloured silk blocked out the sun, forming patches of shade on the armchairs placed for the comfort of the guests. The finished result was a room without walls, but so beautiful it was almost unearthly.

"I'm glad I came after all, how lovely!" As always when she was in the presence of beauty, Sara's eyes filled with tears.

Charles snorted his contempt. "It must have taken an age to get all this stuff together. Why not simply hold the party indoors with the windows open? The man is simply showing off."

Sara chose not to reply and turned her face away. It was clear Charles was in a difficult mood and her own mood darkened despite the beauty of the day, though she recovered her spirits almost at once as fresh distractions were placed before her.

The Englishwomen, uniform in their white silks and muslins, hiding delicate complexions under hats heavy with ribbons and flowers, moved through their exotic backdrop, trying to keep at bay the creeping evils of perspiration stains and the danger of fainting from too tight stays. The men, inconspicuous in black or grey, were a sober contrast to their surroundings, though every now and then a member of the more flamboyant militia punctuated the crowd with a flash of scarlet and gold. In the background a group of Indian musicians played an off-key, self-conscious medley of English classical favourites. Sara smiled at the charm of it and looked at Charles, hoping to share the moment, though he kept his chin up and eyes averted, determined not to notice.

Sitting alone on a raised dais in the middle of an emerald-green sofa shaded by a pink umbrella sat the Maharaja, surrounded by a small army of servants and officials who stood behind him, getting in everyone's way, while ready to jump to attention at his slightest whim.

He sat heavily in the drenching heat, his limbs splayed, giving the impression that it had taken some effort to get into his present position and there he must stay till he could be moved. His plump legs, tightly bound in silk cream puttees further added to his discomfort and made him look like the cocoon of a giant caterpillar about to burst out of his skin. Despite his physical unease, he seemed to be blessed with a benevolent nature and he smiled serenely on all, tapping his little finger in time to the music, though his eyes gleamed as shrewd as a fox, missing nothing, as he took in all about him.

His jewels were as spectacular as promised. Along with his jewels of state, sitting almost lopsided in his turban was a sapphire as large as a bird's egg, and on the huge mound of his chest and belly lay rough-cut diamonds, emeralds and rubies, plus a generous sprinkling of gemstones from the lower orders, amethysts, zircons and topaz, all of them set in a brassy overly ornate gold filigree.

He received his guests one by one at the faint signal of his own delicately raised forefinger, at which, his chief official rushed out into the crowd, captured a guest and brought them back to stand before him hypnotised, like a titbit to be savoured for his pleasure.

Sara was too far away to hear what was said, but every now and then a faint, well-controlled wave of polite laughter burst forth from the crowd hovering about him. Then, when the visitor had exhausted themselves and their wit, they made a discreet backward retreat into the assembled company, where, after a proper interval, a fresh sacrifice was called for to come forth to entertain.

"I must make it known that we've arrived." Charles rushed from her side, suddenly businesslike, leaving Sara with Cynthia. Sara had never seen Cynthia so on edge and attributed her manner to the ordeal before her.

She stood at the ready like a terrier on the scent of a rabbit, and the signal to spring came in the form of one of the Maharaja's officials who seemed to appear out of nowhere.

"My felicitations, my dear, most beautiful madam." The man bowed so low his turban almost touched the ground. "His Majesty requests that you will spend a few moments of your most precious time with him." He bowed again, this time at Sara's feet.

"It would be a pleasure." She nodded her head in return, and was about to move off when Cynthia sprang forward.

"Delighted," she said, and was gone in a flash towards where the Maharaja sat.

"Oh!" was all Sara could say, and she blushed not for herself, but for Cynthia.

The official was put out, but he contented himself with a sly knowing smile and a slight shrug of his shoulders.

"It seems you have been outrun." A cynical laugh accompanied the voice at her side.

When she turned, she saw it was Ravi Sabran. Sara was taken by surprise and stepped back a pace. He was wearing western dress but, instead of the more conventional morning suit, he wore a loosely cut suit of cream linen, matched with a wide black-ribboned panama hat in the style of a Frenchman on holiday in the south of France. It was as though he was a different man.

For a moment the dark shadow of his hat covering the top half of his face created the illusion his eyes were rimmed with black kohl such as the Indian women wore, giving them an impenetrable density as he looked back at her. Sara was transfixed for a moment, and so caught by his gaze she was silent at first. But the illusion evaporated the moment he took off his hat with a flourish and bowed low before her. His eyes were as sharp as ever.

"Monsieur Sabran ..." She wavered a little before his still poise. Her voice was calm despite her inner turmoil.

Her voice dropped to almost a whisper, but she couldn't meet his eyes. "I wrote to you to express how sorry I was about your beautiful Sultan, but I received no reply."

She looked up and saw the momentary flash of pain in his eyes, but it seemed he was determined not to succumb to any sign of weakness in front of her.

"I received no letter, madam."

His voice was very cold, and it unnerved her a little.

"How strange. I wrote weeks ago. My letter must have been lost."

"Well, things don't always run smoothly in Madras. Indians are not as efficient as you British would like them to be."

"I'm not very efficient myself ..." she smiled "... I can hardly expect anybody else to be."

He didn't reply but continued to look at her in his enigmatic way. She was almost impatient with him now.

"And the child is well?"

"Very well. I saw her myself this morning, and I gave strict orders to indulge her as much as possible."

She could see his mouth twist slightly at the corners, as though he was trying to control a smirk.

"I was hoping I could visit her ... We had planned ... before that awful tragedy ..."

His face blanched once more and it was clear he didn't want to be reminded of that day. "It will not be possible ... I may be away for some time ..."

"Oh ..." She was very disappointed, and a little hurt, and he saw it in her eyes, but since he'd seen her on the beach he'd thought about her more often than he liked, and he'd sworn he would crush any feeling before it took hold.

"I have a horse now myself, a beautiful little creature I've named Pansy ... I ride often ..."

"I know," he said without thinking.

"How did you know?"

She thought she saw him flinch, but he regained control almost at once.

"Oh, nothing remains a secret in Madras for long. You must know that by now. I've heard the gossip, how the young Mrs Fitzroy exposes herself to all kinds of dangers by riding alone ... in places considered not suitable ..." he added with a touch of devilment.

He saw her blush, first with a secret discomfort, then with mutiny in her eyes.

"And do you think I'm being foolish to want to have some

freedom? Some time alone from ...?" She almost said, 'my husband', but stopped herself in time.

"No, of course not. From what I know of women, they are much more capable than they are allowed to be. Their lives are blighted by ridiculous rules ..."

She was intrigued by his comment and wanted to discuss it further, but they were interrupted by a voice at his side, and secretly both of them were a little relieved.

"Ravi, my dear, you must introduce me to this lovely creature. I've been admiring her from afar."

For Sara, it seemed to call Ravi Sabran 'my dear' was strange in itself, even brave, knowing how proud he appeared, though the lady's eccentric appearance was even stranger. Her eyes were very bright and heavily made up and applied in a hurry, judging by the smudges of kohl on her face. Her ears and neck were adorned with garlands of amber and turquoise beads, falling down to her waist over a dress long out of fashion, and in a colour not flattering to her sallow skin. Though Sara could see at once the woman's charm lay in being totally unaware of the effect she created, as she beamed in a friendly way from under an almost battered black hat.

Sabran took the woman's hand and kissed it warmly. "Lucy, my dear, I thought you were out of town." His voice was almost boyish as he greeted her. Then he became more formal as he gestured in Sara's direction. "'This lovely creature'", as you call her, and I would be a cad to disagree, is the wife of Monsieur Charles Fitzroy. This is Madam Fitzroy. Madam Fitzroy, this is Madam Lucy McKenzie."

It was too late to hide the expression of surprise on the woman's face, and the subtle looks that passed between her and Sabran, but she recovered her composure, at least outwardly.

"A newlywed, ah, that explains the radiance. Please accept my congratulations." She seemed to cool almost at once, and her previously friendly manner became more remote. "You are English? I must say I am surprised. I thought you were French at least. You look so different from the usual crowd one meets around here."

"You could not have given me a higher compliment. No one wishes to look like everyone else, especially me. I have a truly perverse nature. Is that very wrong?" Sara's smile was so open, and totally without guile, Lucy was charmed.

"Then if you truly want to set yourself apart," Lucy said with a look of merriment in her eyes, "I invite you to visit me and my daughter. You can show her what a truly elegant young lady is like. We are at home every Wednesday afternoon. Sometimes even Monsieur Ravi condescends to join us, but he is so wicked and so popular with the ladies, I discourage him as much as possible."

"You are trying to shock Madam Fitzroy. You will scare her away."

There was a challenge in his voice that was unmistakable and he watched Sara with veiled eyes.

He was unnerving Sara again, and her voice was a little unsteady when she spoke. "It will take more than Monsieur Sabran to keep me away. I look forward to our engagement very much."

Lucy gave her address and paused for a moment, as though waiting for Sara's reaction. "It's not a popular address. In fact, Blacktown is considered almost disreputable, but for me that is its charm."

"I admit to being a little bored with the attractions of so called White Town. It's a horrible name, don't you think? I want to see something of the real Madras ... So far I might as well have stayed in England."

"Then I will try to make it interesting for you. I'll see you on Wednesday around two then. I must go and eat something ... I'm starved ..."

And with that Lucy floated away through the crowd, her funny black hat bobbing up and down as she made her way towards the food table.

"Will you accept Lucy's invitation?"

Sabran was watching her intently again, and Sara felt a shiver run down her back as he leaned forward to whisper in her ear. "She is regarded as dangerously bohemian in certain circles."

Sara's memory was pricked. 'McKenzie ...' The very same family Lady Palmer had warned her against.

She was on her guard at once and raised her chin to glare at him before snapping open her parasol. "I do have a mind of my own, you know, and I'm not so gullible that other people will influence me when I don't want them to."

He opened his eyes wide, holding one hand over his heart. "Forgive me, madam."

She watched him closely through narrowed eyes, hoping he might let slip something of his true personality. "What do you mean when you say I allowed Miss Palmer to outrun me?"

He frowned with his head on one side, appraising her. "You really don't know?"

"Why would I pretend otherwise?"

"Well, you know that she hoped, by getting to the Maharaja first, she'll have the first pick of his jewels?"

"I don't understand."

He half closed his heavily lidded eyes and examined his nails. "Well, if she admires a jewel, he'll have to give it to her; it would disgrace him otherwise."

"So that's why ..." Sara blushed again with deep shame. How humiliating it would've been if she'd done as Charles had insisted and admired the Maharaja's jewels. She felt she'd be no better than a common prostitute.

"All the English ladies do it. That is, all the ladies who have the chance to do it ... It seems they are hypnotised by precious stones and lose all self-control when confronted with them."

She glanced at his own jewelled hand. "It seems you're a victim of pretty stones yourself."

"Ah! This ..." His voice softened as he held the jewel up to the light. "This is a token of undying love, and for this reason I can never take it off." For a moment he was lost in thought as he contemplated the ring, and it seemed he had almost forgotten she was there. She was affronted and wanted to jolt him back to life.

"And what makes you think I would sell my principles for a mere bauble?"

He swung around to face her. She'd succeeded in getting

his attention at last, and for the first time he saw how much lovelier her eyes were when lit with an inner fire.

His voice took on a mocking parody of the English upper classes. "A young lady should never accept a gift from a gentleman unless he's her betrothed." Then, with more than a tinge of sarcasm, "You have been very well brought up, though I think when you're confronted with a '"mere bauble"', as you put it, worth five years of your husband's wages, you won't find it so difficult."

She glared at him, her eyes narrowing. She had been right about him the first time. She could never like such a man. "So, you think that anyone can be bought as long as the price is high enough?"

"Well, I'll soon have the opportunity to find out. Here comes Miss Palmer and she looks very pleased, and, of course, closely attended by your husband."

His words made her start and she turned sharply to look at him. What was he implying? But his face was impassive again and his manner almost too courteous.

"If you will allow me a few moments of your time afterwards, I would be most grateful." He gave her a hasty nod and retreated.

"Of course, if you wish it."

He took a brief look at Charles before leaving, and she couldn't help but see the faint twitching of the muscles in Sabran's chest matched the spark of pure hatred in his eyes. She felt a curious sensation in her body, like the fear of being in the presence of a wild animal on the end of a taut chain that might suddenly snap.

Charles stood beside her as he watched Sabran stroll over to join some friends, followed by the sound of his rather caustic laughter from over the chatter of the crowd.

His mirth seemed to aggravate Charles to an irrational anger. He spoke through clenched teeth. "What did that man want?"

"Nothing."

Charles scanned her face, his eyes suspicious, making it difficult for her to regain her composure, until he was distracted by Cynthia, who hurried towards them as excited as a child.

"It was too easy. All I had to say was the sapphire was my favourite shade of blue, and he said I must have it to match ..." she hesitated for a moment, too breathless to go on "... to match my lovely eyes, he said. It's magnificent, perhaps five carats; he's sending it to me tomorrow."

She stopped for a moment then broke out, "But how silly I am ... I should have admired the diamond on his finger; he kept waving it in front of my eyes, almost as if he wanted me to have it. Oh, if only it wasn't considered greedy to want more than one jewel. Oh, well, next time. There's Mother; I must tell her about the sapphire."

Sara watched the girl's eyes. So Cynthia had a weakness after all. She had a passion for sparkling stones, and her pride was nothing when it came to satisfying that desire. Sabran had been right.

Charles tightened his grip around her waist, quietly angry. She saw he was watching Sabran again, who was now lounging in an armchair under the shade of a tamarind tree, sipping a glass of champagne. She realised Charles was jealous but, instead of feeling flattered, it made her feel like one of his possessions. She tried to move out of his grasp, but he held her more firmly and muttered, "Stay where you are, my dear, please."

When Sabran saw he was being watched he smiled a rather mocking smile and raised his glass at Charles, at the same time managing to make it appear an insult.

Sara felt her husband's arm stiffen, but he showed no other outward sign of anger. When he spoke his voice was calm. "The Maharaja has asked me to introduce you. Are you ready?"

"Must I?" Her voice shook a little.

"Of course you must. Who knows what may come of it?"

There was no getting out of it. It was clear Charles expected her to take a gift if it was offered.

But all she could see was Sabran's sure smile, so sure he would be proven right. She berated herself for a fool, but she couldn't help it; she couldn't bear to owe an obligation to anyone, even a Maharaja.

In a moment she was before him and she gave him a sweeping bow.

"No, no, my dear madam—" he seemed genuinely disturbed "—it is I who must bow before you. Thank you for coming to my little soiree."

"The pleasure is mine, sir."

"Charming." He smiled and indicated the chair opposite him. Despite his grandeur, Sara soon felt at ease, for she could see his eyes were intelligent and perhaps even kind, though he made no secret of his interest in her.

He allowed himself a long luxurious examination of her face and figure. He admired her white skin and dark red hair in half shadow under her wide-brimmed hat, he admired her straight back as she sat delicately upright on the edge of the chair, wearing a slim-fitting cream silk gown decorated with a dark green silk bow at her throat and wrists. He particularly liked the grace of her slim arm as it rested on the handle of her matching parasol. He nodded his approval and his entourage relaxed, as did Sara. She'd passed the first test at least.

The Maharaja's eyes twinkled as he leaned closer to her. "I have a weakness for garden parties. It is a passion I learnt from the British, along with a love of your Shakespeare."

"Oh, and do you have a favourite play?"

"It is the great *King Lear*, without question. It is tragic and violent enough to be a tale from an Indian classicist. You see I am not a total savage after all. I pride myself on being a modern man. I am not like my father, who was a complete despot. That is the word, is it not?"

"Yes. Though perhaps you are too harsh on your father." She began to relax a little and to lean back on the chair.

"Perhaps, but I don't think so. Amongst his more unsavoury practices, he had a fondness for using widows as tiger bait. He used to say there were more of them than goats and therefore they were more dispensable."

Sara was so incredulous she thought at first he must be teasing her, though his impassive expression showed that he was not. "He was indeed a despot, and even perhaps far worse," she remarked, trying to contain her outrage.

"Oh! Do not alarm yourself, my dear." His glinting black eyes saw her cheeks flush a bright pink. "He always shot the tiger before it ate the bait."

"I'm very relieved to hear it." She stared down at her hands, biting her lip and trying not to smile. Surely he was teasing her, but she dared not ask.

Instead she swung the conversation around to the safer ground of English literature once more, even managing to extract a laugh or two from him with her observations, causing his attendants to nod and laugh in agreement even though they had no idea what they were laughing at. Sara began to feel very much like Alice in the court of the Red Queen and she was very much inclined to break out in giggles. She groped around in her mind for more topics of conversation till she fell into an uncomfortable silence once more.

He was clearly waiting for her to speak but, seeing she said nothing, he prompted her. "Do you like jewellery, my dear?"

"Well, yes, sometimes, as long as it is of a simple design." She moved her parasol against the glare of the sun.

"What do you think of this ring; do you not think it is very beautiful?" He held his plump hand in front of her face. On his forefinger a gigantic crudely cut diamond set in old gold flashed in the sun. For a moment she was hypnotised by an alluring seductive power and her eyes followed his hand unwillingly as he waved it before her. She had to pull herself away from the stone's magical force before regaining her composure.

Her voice showed only a polite interest though it shook a little. "Is it a family piece? It seems very ancient."

He flinched, clearly taken aback. "There is nothing of mine you admire? Come now, here is simplicity itself, an emerald to match your ... if I may say ... your beautiful eyes ..." He tapped a large and roughly cut emerald on his belly with his fingertips. "Come, come ... Something to remember this occasion by."

So the compliment was a standard one. It was disappointing but it made it easier now to refrain from weakening. She kept her eyes averted. She could never say, 'Perhaps the emerald', not now. She pretended she hadn't heard him and stared into the distance.

"This is such a beautiful afternoon. I do believe the memory will stay with me forever." She moved a little on the chair as if to indicate that she was ready to leave.

He tried to read her face, frowning as though trying to squeeze a memory from his brain. "You remind me of someone. I've seen your face before." Then, regaining some of his regal charm, he exclaimed, "I must have seen you in a dream, that's it!"

She laughed at so outrageous a remark; there was nothing she could do except wish to be gone in case she should succumb to the lure of his jewels. This time when she changed position in her chair, he took the hint.

He struggled for a moment with his ungainly weight then called for his retainers, who rushed to his side. After a comic struggle where Sara had to look down to hide her smile, they managed to haul him to his feet.

"You must come to the palace for a long visit; you'll want for nothing."

She curtsied as she had when presented to an ageing Queen Victoria at the debutantes' ball on the night of her coming out. He was charmed.

"Your Majesty is most kind, most generous. Thank you for the great honour you have bestowed upon me."

"The honour is mine." He stood and held out his hand to her and there was a faint gasp from the crowd. Sara retreated with as much grace as she could, hoping that she wouldn't trip up on her skirt.

When she reached Charles's side he could barely contain himself. "The old boy never stands for anybody; you must have impressed him pretty much, I think."

"He did invite me to stay at his palace."

"I don't know if that's much good to you ... And a gift ... Did he offer you a gift?"

"No. He did not."

"You did admire his jewels as I asked you to?"

"We spoke of his jewels. Of course it was impossible not to."

She looked away so he wouldn't see her eyes.

"That's very odd. Perhaps it will come tomorrow ... That's it, it will come tomorrow ... He wouldn't dare to insult me." He broke off, his thoughts diverted again. "Look at that upstart, Sabran ... lolling about with the Maharaja. Look at them, as thick as thieves, and they probably are."

Sara watched the two men, their heads lowered. Someone had placed an armchair for Sabran by the side of the

Maharaja, an almost unheard of honour for someone not of royal birth.

Sara blushed to the roots of her hair and was grateful her large hat hid her face from theirs. So Sabran knew the Maharaja well … too well. She was glad now she'd stood her ground.

They both stared in her direction then fell back into deep conversation. They were talking about her. It was quite plain. She felt her cheeks burning again.

Charles noticed it too and it drove him to an unreasonable anger.

"Really, Sara—" his neck flushed a deep red "—I tried to warn you. Now Sabran thinks he can speak to you any time he feels like it. Absolute impudence of the fellow! You really must try to be less friendly to people who aren't worth your time. You know he isn't received, and if you're observed talking to him at functions like this you'll find yourself out in the cold. And I saw you speaking with that disreputable McKenzie woman. She's most definitely not the sort of person I want my wife to associate with, and I saw you curtsy to her—curtsying to a damned Indian, for God's sake!"

Her head snapped around to face him. She hadn't forgiven him yet for attempting to make a fool of her.

"If people are so petty and snobbish, then I don't think I care to be a part of the English community."

"You don't mean that!"

"Of course I do. I wouldn't have said it otherwise."

Charles spoke his next words with deliberate care so she

would get the full impact of his meaning. "I don't think you quite understand, my dear. When you married me you married my life. These people are my life, as well as all the rules that bind us together, and I expect you to observe those rules to the letter."

She stared at him incredulously, almost choking with regret, and before she could stop herself the words came tumbling out. "I can't believe how pompous you are. Surely you're joking."

"I wouldn't dream of joking about something so important to me."

In a white flash of self-realisation Sara realised what a fool she'd been. She'd married a man she hardly knew, and probably never even loved. She could see clearly now that it had been her desire to return to her beloved India that had deliberately blinded her to his faults, and now she was paying for it. Her hand flew to her throat and for a brief wild moment she had a vision of her future. She felt if she acted at once perhaps it wouldn't be too late to save herself from what she felt was a dreadful mistake.

The bitter words came out with a rush. "Well, then, perhaps this marriage was not meant to be after all, and we should reconsider our commitment to one another."

Except for a touch of white around his mouth, he showed no emotion. His face was as impassive as ever, though he scanned the crowd nearby, hoping no one had noticed their lapse in etiquette.

"You're tired. I'll forget you said that."

"I'm not a bit tired. And I don't want you to forget it." She left him while he stood rooted to the spot, afraid someone might have witnessed their public spat.

"How dare he? How dare he!" She was almost crying with frustration and fled to a quiet corner of the garden and flung herself down in the shade of a large parasol, glad to be alone at last. When she was offered a glass of champagne she took it, despite a look of disapproval from Lady Palmer, who'd been watching her hurried exit from Charles's side from afar, and swallowed it almost in a gulp.

At once she felt dizzy. The cloying heat combined with her wildly beating heart sent the champagne straight to her head. She closed her eyes to shut out the image of Charles's shocked face. It was all too much to think about; she needed time to plan what she'd do next. It was impossible to go back to England, to be pitied and scorned as a failure, and there was no home to go back to now. Her uncle had already slipped into a comfortable life as a widower, and in his last letter he had hinted that he was already contemplating marriage with someone else.

She wondered if it was not too late to have her dowry returned, though she'd seen no sign of it since her marriage. Charles seemed to consider her money his and would dole out her allowance almost resentfully.

Her mind was busy calculating how much ready money she had left in her bank account, and how long she could hope to exist on it, when a shadow fell across her face and the air around her was infused with the fresh scent of sandalwood soap. Even without opening her eyes she knew it was

Ravi Sabran who stood at her side. The Englishmen she knew all smelt slightly stale and unwashed, or heavily tinged with the odour of tobacco, all except for Charles, who always used bay rum cologne especially imported from Barbados on his hair and body. He was almost obsessive about it and had dozens of bottles of it sent at one time in case he should run out.

"*Pardonnez moi.* May I?"

She snapped open her eyes and moved over to make a space beside her on the settee. Sabran leaned back to light himself a cigarette, then let one of his arms rest with casual ease over the back of the seat, his golden-brown hand almost touching the skin on her bare neck. A shiver of electricity seemed to shoot from his hand and down her spine and to hide her discomfort she kept her eyes down till she could control her emotions. She stole a glance at his crossed legs, where the muscles of his thighs showed prominently through the thin fabric of his cream linen suit. It was obvious the polo kept him fit, despite his conscious efforts to appear indolent and inactive. He blew a cloud of fragrant smoke into the air and she watched, fascinated, as he savoured the tobacco with an unhurried sensuous pleasure. He looked at her through half-closed heavy-lidded eyes as he picked a tiny fleck of tobacco off the tip of his tongue.

"It appears I must offer you an apology; you have won our bet."

"I'm sure you think me a greater fool than ever," she snapped, forgetting to be distant in the heat of the moment.

"What woman isn't who turns down a fortune because of false pride? I'm sure I'll be made to regret it. Now, more than ever," she added under her breath.

A waiter appeared with more champagne. She took another glass and gulped it down. He watched her, trying to fathom her mood. It was obvious something had upset her.

"If it's any comfort to you, the Maharaja never wears his top-class stuff to these functions; they are rubbish really. The sapphire the very cunning Miss Palmer managed to pilfer is flawed. If it is cut, it will probably shatter. He's very shrewd, you know. He knows what's going on."

"Well, if he's so clever, why does he let them get away with it?" she said tartly.

He laughed, throwing back his head with a cold and cynical delight.

"Well, he must make a public show of his wealth; otherwise he would be shamed in the eyes of the world. However, it amuses him ... It amuses him to see them scramble for his jewels. It is the only comfort of a man whose pride is wounded by having to submit to foreign rule. Acceptance of the gift leaves them at a disadvantage, and he has the upper hand."

"Then I'm glad at least I wasn't a subject of his entertainment. My pride is worth much more than I lost!"

She spoke with such passion he was taken aback. Then he saw the signs of tears in her eyes.

He could feel other eyes upon him, and he looked up to see Charles Fitzroy watching them both from the other side of the garden. It became clear in a flash. There had been a quarrel. He looked at her averted profile and saw her clearly for the first time.

He admitted to a very faint attraction because of her unusual style of beauty, having never seen a woman with that shade of hair before, especially paired with the dark eyebrows and white skin. But the attentions he paid her were due mainly to a desire to irritate Charles Fitzroy as much as possible.

The child, too, he had used as a tool to humiliate Fitzroy. Another waif meant nothing; his household already was full of them. But now he was forced to change his opinion of her. She'd proven herself a woman of principle and character, and he softened. She sat trembling with restrained passion, twisting her hands together and biting her lips in an effort to stop her tears. Before he could stop himself, he found himself speaking, quietly but precisely.

"Try to remember, none of it is your fault. A man like that can never be a husband to a woman like you."

Her head snapped around but, before she had time to reply, Charles had crossed the lawn almost at a run and stood before them.

"We would like to be alone." His eyes flashed a warning. He'd been drinking and was on the edge of making a scene. Perhaps even a violent scene. Sabran decided for her sake, and for the other guests', he would retreat.

Even so, he took his time, rising from the seat in an almost provocative way, his movements as languid and threatening as a leopard before a kill, and as though at any moment he might decide to turn and unleash some of the restrained hostility he wasn't bothering to hide. Sara, seated between them both, felt the tense electric charge of their mutual hatred. It was an awkward moment but, with a derisive smile at Charles, Sabran bowed in Sara's direction and left.

Chapter 13

The next afternoon Sara attended church as usual with the rest of the British community. The droning of the sermon was smothered by the soft sigh of a giant fan pulled by bored *punkah wallahs* perched like gargoyles high up on the beams above, their almost naked brown bodies glistening with sweat. Back and forth they hauled the ropes, almost as listless as the more privileged people below, in a losing battle to keep out the stifling heat.

Sara caught sight of Cynthia's fiancé William, who had arrived from London at last and, though pale and weak, had left his sick bed to attend the sermon. She smiled at him and he rose to his feet, supporting himself with one hand on the back of the pew before slumping back again. She thought him a pleasant young man, though as weak in character as he was in health.

Lady Palmer stood by his side; she nodded rather stiffly as she took her seat. So far that morning they'd only exchanged a few words, but enough for Sara to know the woman was angry with her for what she saw as her breach of etiquette at the garden party. She was determined, though, to ignore the woman's scowling face, and she smiled pleasantly in her direction.

But Sara's smile evaporated almost as soon as it began, and panic took its place. She was all at once overcome with the feeling that she'd been in that particular church before. A black shadow moved over her senses and she was a child again, staring down at a coffin covered in a profusion of tropical flowers.

She remembered the rising nausea as she stood in a stifling crowd, her little legs shaking with weakness, the sickly-sweet perfumes of the blooms competing with each other to disguise the smell of the corpse creeping through the lid of the casket. Even from the distance of time, she recalled clearly the dismal sound of unrestrained wailing from what must have been Indians, as no English people she'd ever met grieved in such an abandoned way. Then the firm, no-nonsense grip of an adult's hand as she was led away.

The clatter of the congregation standing to sing the final hymn brought Sara back to the present, and she shivered despite the suffocating heat. Surely her vision must have been an omen, perhaps even an omen for her future. She laughed at herself; since living in India she was becoming more and more superstitious. Even so, she had to crush a sudden desire to flee from the church and never look back.

She reached out for Charles's arm to steady herself, as though anchoring herself to him for fear of carrying out her secret desire.

There he stood beside her, head bowed, his hands folded in front of him, his gold hair shining, an image of gentle piety.

Only a bright red blush on the back of his neck and a twitch from his shoulder blades betrayed his true feelings.

He flinched at the touch of her hand, angry with himself for having to beg her to stay with him. It was humiliating, but the alternative was unthinkable.

He could almost hear the laughter and scorn of his friends, especially the men. To have his wife leave after only a few weeks would be unbearable. It had been pleasant arousing their jealousy and obvious desire. He glanced at her profile as she stood next to him and, despite everything, he felt a surge of pride. In the dim light of the church he thought she resembled a portrait by Raphael he had seen once in a London gallery. He admired the deep auburn tones of her hair, haloed by the sunlight streaming through the stained-glass window, and the sharp line of her black eyebrows and eyelashes against her white skin. She seemed to grow more beautiful every day, like an orchid transplanted from the binding dry dirt of a hot house into the birthright of rich black soil.

He clenched his teeth. It crossed his mind that it would be within his rights to subdue her with a slap every now and then, but then that would be caddish, and it wasn't considered good form to strike a woman. He knew how to manipulate her. He would withdraw his affection when it suited him. He would control her passionate nature with a blast of cold scorn that would wither her where she stood. That was easily done, and would leave no bruises, at least none that could be seen.

Cynthia glanced at Sara from her position in the front row, though her eyes glinted with resentment through the veil of her hat. Sara knew it was because of the pearls. Cynthia's heart had almost broken at the sight of the necklace Sara wore at her throat. They had arrived from the Maharaja at the same time as Cynthia's sapphire, and by comparison the sapphire had seemed vulgar and crude. The stone itself seemed to condemn Cynthia's greed by its grotesque size, and Sara could almost hear the laughter of the Maharaja emanating from the glittering depths of the jewel.

The pearls, though, large and creamy, tied twice around Sara's throat and yet still falling to her waist, were a magnificent piece, shown to perfection on the background of her pale green silk gown. Cynthia had almost cried with rage.

Sara, too, was thinking of the pearls, and her fingers touched them with care, still not able to believe they were really hers. She'd protested the gift was far too grand, but the note that had accompanied them made it impossible for her to return them and, even though she didn't like to admit it, even to herself, she was very glad.

"I know you are not the type of lady to accept gifts, but for you to take this small token would give me great pleasure. It is an English custom, I believe, to allow the acceptance of a wedding gift, and for that reason you cannot refuse me."

Charles had been overjoyed at the sight of them, believing them to be a compliment to him rather than to Sara. But, despite their high value, she was very moved by the Maharaja's kindness towards her. Now she felt the weight of the pearls around her throat, not so much as a valuable piece of jewellery but more as a talisman, a protector against misfortune.

A messenger from the Maharaja's court had appeared on her veranda just before nightfall and, bowing low before her, he held up an exquisitely carved ivory box, almost as beautiful as the pearls themselves, then retreated, slipping into the shadows as silently as he had appeared.

As she'd drawn them out to admire their sheen in the setting sun, Charles had taken them from her and draped them around her throat. "I'm sorry," he said, before kissing her with extra tenderness on the nape of her neck. "Give me another chance, and I'll change. I love you so much."

His remorse seemed sincere and, despite her persistent doubts, she felt she had no choice but to try to make their marriage work. Divorce was unheard of except in extreme circumstances, and it was unlikely Charles would ever agree in any case.

She remembered Sabran's face as he'd said those words. "A man like that can never be a husband to a woman like you," and for a moment she felt a flash of dislike towards him for making her listen to his bitter remarks. It was all too unsettling, and she couldn't afford to let more doubt creep in when already she struggled to keep her thoughts under control.

'A woman like you ...' It was plain he thought her special in some way; otherwise he wouldn't bother to seek her out. If she allowed herself she might even feel a little flattered, though, always in the back of her mind, was her deep mistrust of Sabran. There was something hard and calculating in his eyes when he looked at her that made her shiver when she lay awake at night, alone with her thoughts, and Sabran entered her thoughts more often than she liked. And what did he mean when he referred to Charles as 'a man like that'? It was plain he hated Charles, but was there something else? Something Sabran knew about her husband she didn't: something that might make living with Charles impossible?

But she swore she would be careful in future dealings with Sabran not to take him too seriously. He was clearly mischievous and vindictive towards Charles, even more so now because of what had happened at that fateful polo match, and she knew her husband, no matter what might happen between the two men in the future, would never be forgiven.

Chapter 14

Sara learned very quickly that marriage alone wasn't enough for her, knowing instinctively she must find another form of fulfilment if she was ever to be truly happy. At first she was unsure how she was going to go about it, till a small twist of fate opened her to a new pleasure.

She'd been writing to her friend Mary from the suffragette movement about her life in India. It had started very simply, with a description of the merchants who came to her home almost daily to sell their goods.

"The man who sells semi-precious stones arrives around five o'clock every Friday. He is a most strange man, and you will find it difficult to believe but he brings with him a mesmerising aura of something otherworldly, despite the practical nature of his profession.

His hair is long and matted, and dyed a bright orange henna, which is known to be an auspicious colour and therefore may win him favour with the gods. His eyes are blackened with kohl, making him as frightening as one of the demons from Indian mythology, even though he is always kind and gentle. His fingernails are long, yellow and curved, and on these hideous claws he displays his goods, which are usually rings adorned with various jewels.

He sits himself down cross-legged on the veranda like a yogi, leaning his back against the post as, one by one, he opens the lacquered boxes that contain his treasures. It is useless to say one doesn't need anything, and it is rare that he will leave without selling some small thing. I bought one of his rings, made of a rich deep coral; he rubbed it with great vigour on his, I must say, rather greasy hair, to pass on a sacred blessing; he believes in his power so fervently that it is almost impossible not to believe him. Now I am afraid to take the ring off, in case I bring bad luck on myself ...

Then, there is the tailor who comes to make sari blouses for the female servants ... He manages to take their measurements without touching their breasts or waists; he stands at least six inches away from them and blushes profusely, but so far all the blouses fit perfectly ... He has the face of a saint, but also an odd deformity ... a tiny extra finger on each hand, though he uses his misfortune to his advantage to pull the tape measure through ... and leave his hands free to hold the cloth ... He is the sweetest man I have ever met ..."

She wrote too of the plight of the untouchables, who were considered so low in caste that even to have walked in their shadow was to cause that person to be unclean, and of the remarkable Jains, a people who were so afraid of killing even an insect by mistake, they screened their mouths and lamps with muslin, and went to their homes at sundown and stayed there till dawn, for fear of stepping on even an ant.

Her friend Mary was delighted with the letters, and suggested they be sold as a series of stories, or as a book, and would look for a publisher for her. They were to be called *The Diary of an English Lady in Madras*.

So far she hadn't told Charles, but instinctively she felt it was best to keep her plans secret, for in the letter she'd finished that morning she wrote a damming criticism of the English community and their attitudes towards the Indian population. The country had been in the grip of a terrible famine that had wiped out thousands of people, yet taxes were still being demanded from the barely recovering farmers to swell the coffers of the British government.

Only the night before there had been an argument with Lady Palmer herself, who had very little sympathy for the victims of the famine, saying if the people were so hungry, why didn't they slaughter the sacred cows and eat them?

But Sara had stood up to her, outraging Charles and some of the others at the gathering by suggesting it made much more sense to keep the cows alive.

She remembered her father telling her the cows were sacred for a very practical reason. They wandered freely amongst different families for many years, providing milk for children who would otherwise have nothing. Their milk could be turned into cheese to add protein to vegetables, and their dried dung was used for housing and fuel for cooking.

She finished by suggesting that, instead of criticising the Indian people, Lady Palmer, because of the grand position she held in society, might consider doing something practical to help. Her comment had caused gasps of outrage from some of the guests and furtive mumbles of support from others.

But she had made herself obvious, and had left under a cloud, and Charles had been cool towards her ever since.

Chapter 15

Lucy McKenzie opened the front door herself, an act unheard-of in a household of servants, but the warmth of her welcome made Sara glad she'd come, despite Charles insisting she do otherwise. Though, since the night when she had outraged Lady Palmer with her contrary opinions and felt so ostracised by most of the English community, including her own husband, she'd felt driven more than ever by a desire to seek out new worlds to help fill the widening void in her life.

She had to admit to feeling a little hurt and confused as to why her telling of the facts should be so roundly opposed, but at the same time she felt an odd perverse pride in her banishment because of her firm belief she was on the side of right. In regard to her own husband, though, there were more profound feelings to contend with. There was a deep sense of indignation that Charles felt it was more important to agree with Lady Palmer over his wife, even though he must know the woman was wrong. It made him appear weak in her eyes now, and the thought was so troubling it seemed almost insurmountable.

Now, as she stood on the forbidden doorstep, smiling back into the warm embrace of Lucy McKenzie's welcome, she felt an instant connection, and the promise of something she had been seeking.

"I saw you from the window, and you could have knocked me down with a feather. I was sure you wouldn't come. As you see ..." Lucy brushed her hands on her admittedly rather shabby sari "... I haven't changed yet. Forgive me."

"What a charming house." Sara had been admiring the gay wide blue shutters thrown open to catch the afternoon breeze. "I've been looking forward to seeing you all week."

The older woman enfolded Sara's arm in hers and led her into a studio at the back of the house, overlooking an enclosed courtyard thick with a lush overgrown garden.

In one corner of the room an easel was set up to catch the light, where an almost finished portrait of an Indian prince in full regalia and jewels of state stood next to a table of tubes of oil paints.

"I forgot the time. I always do when I'm working." She pulled a few stray hairs and pinned them into a knot. "What a fright I am." She laughed gaily, and Sara laughed with her.

"I didn't know you were an artist." Sara moved closer to admire the work. "It's very good. You are clever."

"It's very fashionable now for the royals to have their portraits done, but not so fashionable to pay me on time." She laughed again, as though not being paid was a fresh source of amusement, and reached for a cigarette while settling back in an armchair by the window. "Please sit." Sara took a seat opposite her.

"You don't mind if I smoke?"

"Not at all, I rather like it. It seems to suit you somehow."

"How very wicked of you to say so, Mrs Fitzroy. I can see I'm already a bad influence on you."

Tea and refreshments were put down before them by a girl in a bright blue sari, who flashed a joyful smile at Sara before departing.

"I deplore the habit of dressing servants in that dreary brown cotton. I must be surrounded by colour. Otherwise, it is so depressing. Don't you agree?"

"Yes, of course."

Charles insisted his own servants be dressed in the cheapest brown cheesecloth. Now it seemed small and mean, and she made a pact with herself to change the practice as soon as possible.

"Excuse me for asking, my dear Mrs Fitzroy, but are you quite well? You seem a little pale ... The heat is not too much for you, I hope?"

"Not quite as well as I would like. Not very ill, just a little nausea every now and then, that's all."

"Oh, I hope you will not be a jasmine wife, like some of the other English ladies who come here."

"What do you mean? What is a jasmine wife?"

"Well, they fade fast, or become ill and wilt like jasmine does almost as soon as it's picked, or their marriages fade just as quickly because of the strain. India is such a harsh place."

Sara looked into Lucy's eyes. Did she know something? They were shrewd, but sympathetic too. She longed to tell her what was bothering her, but she knew she would not. She was far too proud.

As though reading Sara's mind, Lucy gave her a sudden beaming smile.

"But, my dear Mrs Fitzroy, that term can never be applied to you. You are no wilting flower. There is something regal about you and, may I say, even defiant. You will never be crushed, though you may at times be trampled. You will bloom as long as you have a little nourishment, but it must be love of an exceptional kind, not a half-hearted lukewarm love, and you must return that love with the same passion, otherwise ..."

Lucy's large glistening eyes held a warning, almost a prophesy, and Sara felt a little chill run down her back. She wondered at the woman's insight. It was as though she had spelled out her own secret thoughts, and she couldn't hold Lucy's gaze for fear of exposing herself too much.

Then she felt an urge to unburden herself just a little, but they were interrupted by the door opening, and in trooped a gay little group of people, who took over the drawing room with a lot of loud chatter and mutual greetings. Amongst them there was an Indian poet who was translating Indian love poems into English, a French nun who was working with the poor in the slums, and a Scots naturalist and activist who was documenting the decline of the Indian tiger.

They were warm and welcoming in a way Sara had not so far met with in Madras. They laughed loudly, ate hugely of the food put before them and smoked Turkish cigarettes or little *bidis*, the Indian cigarettes made out of temburni leaves wrapped in tobacco, filling the room with a rich and spicy fragrance.

Someone had brought bottles of French wine, which enlivened the conversation further, becoming chaotic and sometimes fiery, with a lot of interrupting and much shouting. Every now and then someone would mention Ravi Sabran and ask when he was expected, and sometimes reveal little anecdotes about his behaviour, like the time he'd sent the nuns at the convent six dozen bottles of French champagne for Christmas, and enough money to feed the children of the convent for a year.

She learned he'd been educated at the Sorbonne and had spent at least ten years in Paris, living on the Left Bank, which explained his accent and his urbane charm.

All of the little snippets of gossip were in a way admiring and amused, and Sara could tell that even these more sophisticated and cultured members of Madras society were intrigued by him and his exotic charm.

To hear these indulgent comments about Sabran were in some ways pleasing, though in other ways again disturbing. It was a relief to know he was respected for his kindness and generosity and appeared to be not as evil as he had been painted by the British community, though she was not ready yet to fall under his spell as these people had. He had not replied to her letter, and she was beginning to feel slighted and ignored. It was frustrating too that she cared what he thought of her when he should have no power over her at all. Even so, she waited almost anxiously for him to appear and to see how he behaved when amongst his friends.

Lucy never bothered to change out of her old sari, and no one seemed to notice; she milled about, forcing food, drink and conversation on everyone. When it came time to leave, everyone swept out in a rush of laughter and clatter with promises to see each other the following week.

Sara had never been so amused in her life, and it was while she lingered after the others had gone for a more intimate moment with her new friend the sound of a door slamming broke into their chat, and a young girl rushed into the room while tearing at the ribbons of her bonnet. She was out of breath from laughing, and at first didn't see Sara on the sofa.

"Oh! Excuse me! Mother, you didn't say you had company."

She stood before them and dropped a little curtsy, giving Sara a chance to take in the girl's features. She was extremely pretty in her fresh white muslin gown, her dark eyes glowing with an inner joy, and Sara was charmed. Sara remembered Lady Palmer's remark about her being extremely black, yet her skin was hardly darker than her own.

"Allow me to introduce my daughter, Belle. This is Mrs Fitzroy, my dear. What have you been doing to make yourself so hot?"

"How do you do, madam?" She gave her mother a quick kiss, then threw herself down on the sofa next to Sara.

"I've been playing tennis with Harry Scott. He's coming for tea in a moment; do you mind, Mother?"

"Not at all. Now, please sit down and behave yourself."

"I know Harry, and his parents; he's a sweet boy." Sara had met both him and his parents at one of Lady Palmer's interminable soirees. Though she'd liked the boy at once, she'd felt an instant chill from his parents. They were both narrow-minded and suspicious, and very superior in their attitude towards anyone they considered of a lower station than themselves, and she couldn't imagine they would approve of their son's connection with the McKenzies.

Belle flushed pink when Harry was shown into the room; she was clearly infatuated with him, and it troubled Sara to know the girl would surely be hurt.

"Belle! You didn't wait for me!" Then he stopped and stared, his smile fading at once. "Mrs Fitzroy! I didn't expect ..."

He seemed agitated to find her there but sat opposite her and tried to make a show of good manners, even though the atmosphere in the room had changed. The boy fidgeted and squirmed, unable to stay still in his seat for the short time he stayed, and soon found an excuse to leave.

"I just remembered I have to go. I'm sorry, Belle. Excuse me, Mrs Fitzroy."

"But you said you wanted tea ..."

"I'm sorry, Belle ... I'll come back later ..."

"I'll see you out, Harry."

The girl followed him, her face showing her confusion, leaving Sara to feel responsible for having ruined their afternoon.

"I think he's afraid I might tell his mother I've seen him here. I won't, of course."

Lucy's expression looked for a moment unusually bleak. "In a way I wish you would, and put an end to Belle's hopes once and for all. She's totally deaf to everything I say. Their engagement is a secret, and against my own wishes, knowing how it is bound to end. Harry's family objects strongly to Belle because of her colour, even though Belle assures me Harry doesn't care about such things. I know, though, his parents would be terrified their grandchildren may be born black. '"A touch of the tar brush"' I believe is the vulgar expression." For the first time, bitterness crept into Lucy's voice and Sara was moved to a deep sympathy.

"It's all so ugly, and I'm sorry for it, but the world in which we live is a cruel and narrow place. Especially the small and petty world I inhabit, presided over by Lady Palmer and people like her."

Lucy looked at her now with a new interest, and realised too, by the tone of her voice, the lovely Mrs Fitzroy might well be suffering oppression of a different sort, though almost equally suffocating.

They were interrupted when a maid entered the room with a note. There was silence while Lucy read the message.

"Oh ... I am disappointed. Monsieur Sabran apologises for not coming today. How strange, he never misses our day together if he can help it. He sends his regards to you in particular, Mrs Fitzroy ... He says business prevents him from coming, as he will be leaving town for at least a month ... Even so ... so unlike him."

He was avoiding her. Sara knew it instinctively, and for the rest of the visit she couldn't crush the feeling that he had somehow insulted her, and she was more affected by that insult than she should have been.

Chapter 16

Sara woke to find Lakshmi standing over the bed. She couldn't be sure, but she had the feeling the girl had been there for some time, and the uncertainty made her feel uneasy. She always felt a little uncomfortable around Lakshmi, having the feeling that somehow the girl didn't like her. Not that she ever showed her dislike. That would be unthinkable.

She moved about the house on her tiny, silent feet, performing her tasks with an uncommon grace of movement, rarely smiling or laughing as the other members of the household did.

Shakur said it was because she was from Kashmir, where as a small child she had been found alone in the streets by a soldier and taken as booty back to Madras to be sold as a servant. It wasn't surprising she had no taste for humour. No one knew her real name, or if she had family, alive or dead.

That morning she had taken a bunch of tuberose and woven them into her thick black plait that fell almost to her knees. She was seldom seen without her hair tightly plaited in this demure fashion. Though once Sara had come across her in the garden as she was combing her black waves as she sang to herself, a strange high-pitched melody as beguiling as a swaying cobra. Her heavy-lidded eyes lay half closed as she anointed the waist-length coils with the deep musky fragrance of patchouli oil. There was something so sensuous about her movements, so voluptuous, it seemed impossible she had never known the touch of a man's hands on her body. Though Sara had seen her when the men in the house made any kind of suggestion to her. She sprang to her own defence like a wild animal, making sure that they never dared to do it again. They could only watch and desire her from afar.

She came close to the bed with the breakfast tray. "Good morning, madam," she said in her sweet, sing-song voice as she pressed her palms together in her usual greeting.

"The *sahib* has left for the day ... He said not to wake you."

"Thank you, Lakshmi. You look very pretty today; are those new earrings?"

"Yes, madam." Her hands flew to the fine gold drops hanging in her perfect ears, and a soft smile crossed her lips.

Sara knew Indian women loved gold, but still, she wondered how the girl could afford such fine things, but then, she had nothing else to spend her money on, having no family to support.

"Did he say what time he'd return?"

"He will not be home for lunch. He said he will visit Miss Palmer as she is not feeling well."

"Oh."

Sara's head fell heavily back onto the pillow and she sighed from deep within her chest. A sly, enigmatic smile crossed

Lakshmi's lips, and Sara was driven to an unreasonable anger, though she managed to hide it with a forced half smile. It was unfair on the girl to be so peevish.

"When will the weather improve, Lakshmi? It's so hot!"

"Soon the monsoon will come, madam, and everything will be green again."

Another long despairing sigh escaped her. She was unhappy for many reasons; the honeymoon she had so long waited for had been cancelled. An invitation had arrived the day before their planned departure, announcing Cynthia and William's wedding within the week. It appeared William had rallied enough to fulfil Cynthia's wish to be married before the monsoons might delay their trip back to England.

"Must we go?" Sara had asked, though all the while knowing what Charles's answer would be. "Is it so very important we attend? Surely, as it's the only time we have for our trip, we could be excused."

He pulled away from her, puzzled she should ask such an impossible favour. "How can you say so? Of course we must attend; Cynthia would never forgive me."

"She knew we were planning on leaving for our honeymoon; she might have waited just another two weeks till we returned. Sometimes I think Cynthia just wants you to dance attendance on her."

He didn't hear her, as he was already thinking of something else. "I believe she's making a great mistake in marrying William. She needs a man to take care of her, not a milksop. The boy's a weakling; mark my words, Cynthia will be a widow before long."

As it turned out, Charles was proved right in one respect, as within a week William was dead.

It seemed that because of his efforts not to disappoint Cynthia, after dragging himself out of bed while still in the throes of a raging fever, he collapsed and died a day before the wedding, only just cheating Cynthia out of widowhood, and the much longed-for title, by twenty-four hours.

Lakshmi's sweet sing-song voice roused Sara from her thoughts again. She daydreamed often now and slept as though in a coma in the afternoons, something she'd never done before, then woke irritable and restless. It seemed she was almost constantly suffering from a mild headache and nausea that left her feeling tense and out of sorts.

"What will madam wear today?"

The girl's footsteps were so soft they were never heard until she was by Sara's side. Her heavy-lidded eyes were cast down as usual, playing her role as the dutiful servant, though behind the eyes there was something else, something unreachable.

"Just a plain muslin, thank you, Lakshmi ... I don't think I'll go out. It's far too hot."

Sara watched her as she walked towards the wardrobe, her every movement charged with a seductive slow grace. The curve of the back above the gently swaying hips, the slim brown arms covered in bangles, the tiny waist and the hint of roundness in her belly.

As her eyes followed the girl around the room, Sara was overcome with a familiar lethargy and a vague unhappiness, though she tried hard to convince herself it was only the weather making her feel that way.

When Lakshmi left the room after placing the gown on her bed she felt more comfortable, and wondered at the girl's power to unsettle her.

After a moment, she roused herself to leave her bed and lock her bedroom door, then she crossed the room to stand before the cheval mirror.

Was she as appealing to men as Lakshmi was?

She raised her arms above her head and took off her lace nightgown.

Was she desirable? She wasn't sure. Her breasts were high and firm, though, she had to admit, not large, and her nipples were a rosy pink against the pale skin. Despite her occasional days of illness, her complexion was still clear and luminous, and people often remarked on her apparent good health, making sly insinuations about the benefits of married life. Again, she was overcome with painful thoughts. If only there was someone to ask. If only the subject could be mentioned.

She flushed as she remembered the events of the night before. She had been thinking of the sculptures she had seen on the beach, and how much pleasure the women seemed to be having, and while Charles was making love to her she had begun to move her body and, as she moved, she had felt pleasure for the first time, losing herself in a delirious ecstasy till Charles had snapped at her, "Don't! Don't do that! It's disgusting!"

"What's wrong?" she could barely whisper.

"Only dirty women do that ... Surely you know this." He pulled away from her as though reviled by her touch. She watched as he lit a cigarette, blowing out the smoke in furious short puffs.

Then, after a while, he turned to her, his manner softening. "I suppose you can't be expected to know. If your mother were alive, she might have told you ... Good women can't know any pleasure from this ... That's for men. For you it's only for creating children."

Then he had kissed her on the cheek and murmured that he forgave her.

She had lain there for hours after he had gone to sleep, frozen with shame and anger, and again feeling there should be no shame.

In her heart Sara felt that the enjoyment of sex must be normal, or was it only regarded as normal for members of the Indian population? The idea was ridiculous, of course, but even amongst her women friends from her female emancipation group, the act of sex in itself was never discussed, only the importance of having fewer children. No one had ever mentioned that secret part of a man's anatomy, even when she had attended a banned meeting on birth control, and it was suggested that half a lemon inserted high into the vagina was an effective way to prevent pregnancy. This proposal had been met mostly with horror or wild giggling, and at the same time created great difficulty in imagining there might be any pleasure involved after such a procedure.

Her aunt's comments about sex came back to her. "There are things you might not want to do, but it is perfectly normal for them." It was plain she meant good women were not meant to enjoy sex, and it crossed Sara's mind she would be thought a bad woman because she wanted to enjoy it.

Bad women were heard of and sometimes seen, wandering around the streets of London and the alleyways of Madras, poor, painted and sad, so it was clear, sex was not a happy choice for them.

She thought then about Ravi Sabran and his illicit relationship with the wife of another man. He was shameless, apparently, even proud of his love. He flaunted it, and also made no secret of his admiration of women in general. The images of the sculptures on the beach came back to her again, inflaming her body and causing a shiver to run down her back. Did Ravi Sabran do those supposedly wicked things? His own heavy-lidded eyes and slow sensuous smile were depicted there on the sculptures so plainly he might have posed as a model for them. Did he use his lips and tongue in the same way as those men? She thought of his firm red mouth and sudden flash of white teeth, and the way he had picked the tiny shred of tobacco off his tongue as he had watched her at the garden party, so slowly, so languidly, through half closed eyes ...

Then she roused herself, a little shocked at how her mind had followed such a wanton path. It was all so pointless really, and she was even more unhappy to think she might never know what it would be like to experience passionate mutual bliss, or even if it existed at all.

She slipped back into her nightgown and dropped down into the cane chair by the window to stare bleakly out at the borders of limp flowers, fast being bleached of colour as the morning haze became a harsh white glare.

In the background, amongst the clattering of pots and pans, she could hear the servants chatting in the kitchen, their voices rising and falling; every now and then an explosion of laughter would suspend their chatter. In a brief attack of paranoia, she wondered if they were laughing at her.

Soon Mutu would want to see her about the menu for the day, and she found herself sighing again. His cooking was atrocious; that was, his cooking of English food was atrocious, but Charles didn't seem to mind it. He had often said that they were lucky to have a cook at all, as most Indians were vegetarians and were revolted at the thought of touching red meat.

Charles insisted on plain food, as he said his stomach couldn't bear anything else.

Sara wondered at his apparent enjoyment of his meals. He rarely looked up from his plate as he chewed, but sometimes stared into the middle distance with a vacant, half smile of pleasure on his lips. She toyed with her food, pushing it around the plate and piling it into the edges to create the illusion that she had eaten more than she actually had. She often left the table hungry, though without any desire to eat. She'd become even thinner, while he'd become heavy, especially around his once trim waist.

She recalled the disaster of the day before, when Mutu, as usual, had waited on her for his daily orders.

When he'd seen her anxious face as she sat planning a menu that would be suitable for her husband, he'd leapt in to help her.

"I will have some fresh meat, madam ... I have asked for a young goat to be slaughtered this morning." Mutu said the words as though he thought the event a happy one, though Sara knew he was a strict vegetarian.

"Sir will be very pleased, I think." He beamed. "I can make an Irish stew."

Sara experienced a surge of nausea. A baby goat must die that day so she could eat it that night. The idea was unthinkable.

At that moment a delicious smell wafted towards her from the kitchen.

"What are you having for lunch, Mutu? It smells so delightful."

"You would not like it, madam ... It is only our simple Indian food, vegetable kofta, *dhal* and rice."

"Kofta? I'd almost forgotten. It was my favourite dish as a child ..." She smiled as she remembered how she was forever begging spoonfuls from Malika's plate after she had eaten her own.

"Can you prepare it for this evening? I can't think why you haven't given it to us before."

Mutu wrung his hands. "But it is not English food, madam ..." His face had taken on a look of extreme anxiety. "Sir will not like it, I think ..."

"I think I will like it, and I'm certain Mr Charles will as well."

"Yes, madam," he said, delighted, convinced at last. "I will make you something special, very special."

"Before you go, Mutu ..."

"Yes, madam?"

"Tell them not to slaughter the little goat ... It's such a lovely day ... Nothing should die on such a day. In fact, from now on, we will eat much less meat. I find it doesn't suit me any more."

Mutu beamed now. "You will win favour with the gods, madam." Then he bent low and kissed the hem of her dress.

Charles had said nothing when the food was placed before him but toyed with the dish of vegetables and cashew nuts. Sara watched him with an expectant smile on her lips, waiting for the nod of approval which would surely follow.

Mutu and Shakur were watching too from the dining room door, nudging each other and grinning. Mutu had worked all day to produce the most exquisite of flavours.

Charles took a bite, rolled it around in his mouth with a look of deep disgust, then took his napkin off his lap and placed it before him, before settling back in his chair.

"What do you think, Charles? It's not too hot, I think." Her smile was more a grimace now, her stomach slowly beginning to knot.

"We can't have their food," he said with absolute conviction. "We can't have them thinking that they have anything we may like."

"But surely that's absurd." Before she could stop herself, she raised her voice in front of the servants. "You know it's delicious. Anyone can see that!"

He stared at her with cold eyes and pushed his plate away. "It doesn't matter, even if it does taste good. They'll think

183

their food is better than our good English food, and then that's the thin edge of the wedge. They lose their respect for us ... Believe me, my dear, as I said many times before, you won't be able to do anything with them."

She stared at her plate, not seeing it, her fork frozen foolishly in the air, the food cold in her mouth. "Well, I'm eating it. It's delicious. You may do as you like."

"Please don't think I'm unreasonable, darling—" he managed a smile along with the endearment "—but, believe me, I know what I'm talking about. Do not forget the rebellion of fifty-seven. We'd gone soft on the devils then, and they repaid us by murdering women and children in their beds! It could happen again!"

"Shakur," he shouted, "take this back to the kitchen, all of it! Madam has made a mistake. Find us something else."

She had clung to her plate, refusing to give it up, and for a moment there was an embarrassing tug of war between her and Charles. In the end, because the servants were watching, he let go, and she ate the food before him, making a proud show of her enjoyment, even though it seemed to stick in her throat.

From that time on, though, she refused the Irish stews and various messes that passed for English food, and ate nothing but fruit and vegetables, adding yet another barrier between herself and her husband.

Sara roused herself from the chair and, instead of calling for Lakshmi to help her with her bath, she put off the dreaded moment for a little longer to write another chapter of *The Diary of an English Lady in Madras*.

But her thoughts overcame her, tangling with her words as she wrote, till at last she threw down her pen to pace her room once more.

She'd been living with her husband for four months and, despite all her efforts, she still felt nothing was as she'd expected. For a few horrible moments she bitterly regretted her marriage and longed to be a single girl again. The blinding white glare stealing through the shutters oppressed her and already her eyes hurt and her head ached. It would be a long lonely day, as even Lucy, her lifeline to sanity, had left Madras for at least a month.

Somehow the news of Belle's engagement had been leaked to Lady Palmer and, even though Harry had protested his undying love for the girl, he'd soon collapsed under the weight of general disapproval. He'd been packed off to Egypt with the threat of being disinherited till he came to his senses, and Belle was taken for a change of scene to Delhi to stay with relations, in an attempt to heal her broken heart.

Already Lady Palmer had made it plain to Sara she felt she had encouraged the engagement just by being a friend of Lucy's and, as punishment, she and Charles had been left out of an important dinner engagement. Charles had been furious and hadn't let her forget the snub.

Since then he'd been called back into the fold, but when sometimes Sara refused to accompany him in the evenings he didn't insist on her attendance, and she was almost officially seen as an outsider.

The clock in the dining room chimed ten o'clock.

Soon she'd have to call Lakshmi to help her bathe and get

dressed and she was already dreading her inquisitive stares. At first she'd insisted on bathing alone, but her plea for privacy had created a sensation in the household, with the other servants accusing Lakshmi of not doing her job. Charles had been met with Shakur's disapproving face the minute he'd arrived home from work.

"There is trouble in the house, *sahib* ..." He stared down at his bare feet as he spoke.

"Talk to madam about it."

"It is about madam, *sahib*."

Charles threw off his jacket and took the offered drink.

"Well, spit it out."

"Madam will not let Lakshmi bathe her, and Lakshmi thinks she will be dismissed ... She has been crying all day."

Charles marched into Sara's little sitting room and threw his arms up in a gesture of despair. He was angrier than he should have been. "Darling, what's this nonsense about not having Lakshmi bathe you? It's her job to do everything for you."

"I can't bear the way she looks at me when I'm undressed. I feel uncomfortable."

"What does it matter if she looks at you or not? She's only the servant ..."

"It matters to me," she said, determined to be firm. "Perhaps it would be best if we found her employment in another house or let her return to Lady Palmer."

"She's a gift!" he said, losing his patience. "And one does not return a gift, no matter how unsatisfactory in your eyes."

"She isn't unsatisfactory at all; in fact, quite the reverse. She does her job almost too well."

"Well, then, she should stay. Lady Palmer asks after her often, so I can't say we got rid of the girl. It wouldn't be a problem at all if you would only learn to treat the servants as though they're not here!"

"I can't treat another person as though they're invisible! But I'm not surprised you can." She turned her face away as she spoke. The cracks in her marriage were turning into chasms, and her heart was breaking.

Chapter 17

For over a month she'd heard nothing from Ravi Sabran, even though she'd written once more, asking if she could visit Prema. He had consistently failed to appear at the Wednesday afternoon soirees and, according to Lucy, it was most unusual. Now, Sara had to crush her anger at feeling insulted and ignored. At first, she put it down to the irregularity of the mail system, but now, as other letters had arrived without trouble, the excuse of lost mail seemed unlikely.

She wondered if it would be considered improper to appear on his doorstep without warning, but she had waited long enough and would risk being an unwelcome visitor.

It was no one's business but her own if she wished to visit Prema but, even so, her voice seemed unnaturally casual when she spoke to Shakur, who was polishing the silver, looking as bored as she felt.

"I think I'll go out today ... Will you drive me into town?"

He stopped polishing at once, as eager as she for a change from routine. "I will tell Lakshmi you wish her to accompany you."

"No, I would like to go alone." She didn't want Lakshmi and her secret smile.

Shakur stopped, his face puckering with concern. "The other *memsahibs* never go alone."

She flinched. He was mimicking Charles, and it was as though he himself stood before her.

"That will do, Shakur ... I'm going alone."

"Yes, madam." She watched his back as he walked away; she could read his disapproval there.

Then he turned and confronted her. "You cannot go alone ... None of the other ladies would go out unattended; you must have a woman with you. People will talk."

"Then I'll take the girl who cleans the shoes ... What's her name? Surinda ... I'll take Surinda with me."

"You cannot take her; she is an untouchable ... You cannot take an untouchable with you, and I will not drive her."

She wanted to scream, 'Is there anything I can do?' but she controlled her frustration.

"Then I'll go alone and that's that."

Shakur simply shook his head as he hurried out of the room.

Ravi Sabran's home stood at the end of a long line of grand English homes, situated a few miles from central Madras but separated by a canal and a wide stretch of jungle that had somehow escaped felling in the attempt at civilising the town.

The carriage moved along a winding road bordered on both sides with masses of scarlet bougainvillea, tumbling down and growing in amongst the avenue of ancient tamarind trees. There was scarcely a beam of light allowed through the mass of greenery, and even sound was muffled under the thick canopy.

It was a pleasure to be cool for a change, and Sara was lost in the joy of the moment when, all of a sudden, she was struck by a strange sense of familiarity. The feeling of déjà vu was so strong it made her stomach tighten with a vague nausea, though, as far as she knew, she'd never been on this particular road before.

The road turned into a path and turned a corner, coming to an abrupt halt at a set of wrought iron gates set into a stone wall, covered with a thick flowering vine that had insinuated itself into the very stones themselves. She almost leaped out of the carriage and stood before the gates, before parting the choking vine with her gloved hand to reveal a worn brass plate with the inscription, 'Tamarind House', and the date it was built, '1802'.

"Tamarind House?" She mouthed the words over and over again. She closed her eyes and tried to think. Surely she'd heard that name before somewhere?

"Are you sure this is Monsieur Sabran's house?"

"Yes Madame."

"But Monsieur Sabran's house is named Sans Souci."

"Yes, madam ... but this is still his house."

Shakur jumped up, preparing to open the gates. "I will tell them you are here."

She raised her hand. "No. You can come back for me in an hour or two."

"No, madam ..." Shakur was seriously alarmed. "This house is a bad house. You cannot enter alone."

Despite his protests, Sara could tell he was aching to see inside, but she didn't want him carrying tales back to the other servants.

"Come back for me before dark. Take the carriage and visit your mother; she will be glad to see you." She smiled at him, hoping to soften his air of disapproval.

Shakur shook his head sadly and drove off, looking over his shoulder with a sigh of reproach. Sara waited till he was out of sight, then pushed against the gate.

She paused for a moment, expecting the servants to descend on her, chattering and welcoming, as they did everywhere she visited in Madras, but she heard nothing to break the silence except the sound of birds and a faint sighing of wind in the trees.

She moved cautiously down the path, rounded a small bend and there, emerging from the disordered chaos of the garden, stood a lovely house with the pure uncluttered lines of the previous century.

Tall pillars supported a wide flagstone veranda running the length and the sides of the house. Wide wooden shutters, faded to a pale turquoise, were closed tight against the intruding light. The remains of a dried grass *tatti* hung from an outside window. Once it would have been green and sweet-smelling, freshly woven by the servants and kept cool and damp to protect the house from the searing summer heat. A shiver ran down her back; it had the look of the matted hair of a *sadhu*.

A creeper covered in sticky pink flowers ran across the worn stones of the veranda and up the walls, sealing the house and its secrets from the outside world. At her approaching footsteps, a mongoose with a dead rat hanging limp and bloody from its mouth raced across the veranda and into the bushes.

A nameless fear overtook her and she almost regretted sending Shakur away, then she broke out in a wave of dizziness, not knowing if it was from fright or the heat.

Afraid she might faint, she held tightly onto the curved stone banister as she climbed the steps, then she halted, transfixed by the faded front door where, in the centre, hung a heavy brass knocker in the shape of a gloved human hand. Again, a fresh wave of dizziness threatened to unbalance her. She had seen that very same knocker before. She shook her head and frowned as she struggled to remember.

Then she recalled the sensation of standing on tiptoe and reaching up, her own childish fingers just touching the cold metal.

"Surely ... this isn't ...?" She swayed a little and almost fell. She had to think, she had to remember.

Then, guided by some long dead instinct, she walked as though hypnotised around the side of the veranda. If she was right, there would be a little gazebo with carved wooden windows half hidden under an ancient tamarind tree.

She held her breath and leaned on one of the stone pillars for support. Yes ... there it was, the white paint faded now, but quite solid. There she had played as a child. It had been her mother's favourite spot in the cool of the morning and, amazingly, her wicker chair was still there, as though waiting for her.

Her feet moved forward mechanically as though under a spell, then she came to a stop at the open doorway.

In the corner of the room a small shrine dedicated to Ganesh showed the remains of a still burning stick of incense—someone came there to pray. She sat down in what had once been her mother's chair and gave herself up to an overwhelming grief, sobbing without a care for whoever or whatever might hear her. She rocked back and forth on the chair, the phantoms of the past surrounding her. Then she began to shiver with fright. The sounds of a lullaby, a haunting quivering sound, enveloped her. It was a song she well remembered.

The sound of the voice came closer then was stilled. A black shadow fell across the doorway as a figure stepped into the room then halted. An unearthly wail broke the silence and the figure dropped to the ground, lying crouched against the wall of the summer house, hiding her head under her sari.

Sara found her voice, speaking in Hindi. "I'm sorry ... Did I frighten you?" She put out her hand to reassure her, but at her touch the woman sprang like an animal into the corner of the room and peeped cautiously out from under her sari. Then she found the courage to speak. "You are real?"

"Yes ... Of course."

The woman rose and came forward, then, reaching out to touch Sara's head, she picked up one of the dark red strands and felt it. Then her eyes widened. "Sarianna!"

Sarianna! It had been years since she'd been called that name, and only one other person could know it.

"Malika!"

"Yes ... it is I ... Can it be?"

"Yes!"

The thin brown hands caressed Sara's face and smoothed her hair. Wild tears held back for so long were released at last.

"You have come home ... You have come home ..."

"Yes, Malika ..." Sara cried, her face contorted by sobbing "... I have come home."

The three graves behind the house were free of weeds, though the carving on the headstones had faded under the harsh sun and torrential rains. Sara traced her finger around the inscription.

'Lillian Catherine Radcliffe ... dearly beloved wife of William'.

"Radcliffe! Of course, my name was Sarianna Radcliffe!" She cried again, deep painful sobs that left her body exhausted but her heart lighter.

The name belonged to a happier time, and it was as though her soul had been returned to her.

She ran her hands over the third headstone. 'Daisy Rose'.

She mourned for a sister she had never known, who'd died when she was just two years old. At the base of each headstone Malika had placed a small stone figurine of Shiva, as though an added deity would carry more credit for those in heaven. Sara watched as she wiped the headstones with the hem of her sari.

"Why have you stayed so long ...?" She held Malika's hand as she studied the much-loved face, much older now, the once glossy black hair completely grey and worn in a matronly bun at the base of her neck. The large dark brown eyes, though, were the same, full of kindness and love.

"I have no family ... You are my family ..." and once more she raised her hand to Sara's hair and stroked it lovingly, not quite believing her eyes. "You are like your father. He had hair of this colour."

"Tell me what happened. I want to know how they died."

"She died first, it was very quick and she knew nothing, but the gods were merciful and took him soon after." She ran her fingers over the name on the headstone, as she had done many times before. "He could not have lived without her." Her eyes darkened for a moment, remembering past sadness. "Then you became sick. I took you from the house and cared for you myself."

"I remember ..."

"Then the English lady came and took you away from me ..." Her face crumpled suddenly as she relived the nightmare. "You were my child ... my child! I had no one else. When I was nine years old, my parents sold me to a man old enough to be my grandfather ... When he died, his relations said I must burn on the pyre with him ..."

The woman's eyes opened wide with remembered terror, and Sara felt a sudden surge of pity for the terrified child Malika had once been. "Your mother found me hiding in her garden. She paid my relations to forget about me. For many months she kept me by her side, in case they came back." She shuddered and bent down to clear the tomb of dead flowers and draped a fresh garland of marigolds over the stone. "I can never leave her, even when she is with her God."

"You've been here all this time ... If only I'd known."

"I said I would work for food only, as long as I could stay."

Then her face suddenly brightened. "The other people went back to England and Monsieur Sabran brought this house. He knows I can never leave ... Who would take care of the graves?"

"But you can't stay here forever ... I can't bear to think of you always being here alone ..."

"I am not alone ... There is a man who does the garden but, as you can see—" she waved her thin arm at the over-grown shrubbery "—he is very lazy. When Monsieur Sabran is here the house is full of people. But he hasn't been here for three months now, and he has written to say he'll probably not return for a long time; he says he might sell this house ... and I'll have to work for new people ..."

Sara stared down at the graves, overcome with fear. The new people might not like them being there and get rid of them somehow. There was only one solution. She brightened at once. She would buy the house herself.

"Where is Monsieur Sabran now?" she asked, unable to keep the excitement out of her voice.

"I do not know. He might be in his house in Pondicherry, or he might be in the Hills; he has a house there too, but I do not know where."

"Did Monsieur Sabran have a little girl with him when he went away?"

"Yes, an orphan baby. Sometimes he would look at her and say, "Make sure you feed her well, otherwise the English lady will say we are ill treating her." Then he would laugh, but he did not seem very happy when he said it."

"I think I must have offended him more than I thought."

"What do you mean, Sarianna? What do you know of this baby?"

"Nothing ... We won't talk about it now ... I want to see the house; can we get in?"

Malika led the way through the kitchen. A small pile of belongings folded neatly on the floor near the stove showed Malika's sleeping place.

"I can't bear to think of you lying there; why don't you take one of the bedrooms? There's no one here to see you."

"I could not, Sarianna; it is not my place to do so."

"Please, for my sake ..."

Malika shook her head. "Your mother would see me. She is still here."

Sara shivered a little. She could indeed feel an unexplained presence, but she was too sensible to believe in ghosts, no matter how much she would have liked to commune with the past. The heavy atmosphere was merely painful memories, and secrets as yet uncovered.

She followed Malika down the unlit passage into a spacious drawing room while she unlocked the doors leading onto the veranda, bringing in the dusty spiced air on a beam of morning light, and revealing the elegant proportions of the room.

Everything was so familiar, and surely the worn leather sofa by the window was the same she'd sat on as a child to learn her English alphabet. Her mother was still there, a ghostly form, holding the book, her embroidery basket by her side, as she listened while Sara lisped out the letters. Surely the scent of Attar of Roses was still in the room. Malika was right after all.

She groped her way up the staircase, almost overcome now with the pressure of more unshed tears and the rush of sensations coming to life. She clung to the banisters, dragging her feet up the stairs. She felt a gust of air pass close by, or did she imagine it? As a child she had run down those very stairs, eager to get outside to play with her dolls in the garden. She'd seemed to be always happy then, and the house had been full of people coming and going and life drifting on, unaware and unafraid.

The nursery lay at the end of the hall.

Inside the room, it was as though the children had left to play outside and would return at any moment. A child's cot, the white paint peeling and showing the rust beneath, stood in the corner with its cage of iron netting designed to keep out snakes and insects, though nothing could keep out the disease that crept unseen through the mesh, and killed so silently.

Malika opened a cupboard in the corner and dragged out a trunk, opening it with a key she wore around her waist. She reached in and pulled out a battered teddy and a doll dressed as a shepherdess.

Sara remembered how she hadn't been allowed to take any of her toys or books with her to England in case she would take disease with her too, and she relived the feeling of loss at leaving her favourites behind.

"Why did these rooms stay the same? Surely Monsieur Sabran would find them not to his taste."

"He liked them; he thought that he would have children some day so he kept the rooms ... But he will not have children with Maya ... I know ... I can see no children around her."

"Maya is Monsieur Sabran's ..." she hesitated, not knowing how to refer to the girl "... Monsieur Sabran's wife?"

"Maya is a bad woman. She is beautiful and good, but she is still a bad woman." Malika had the old-fashioned intolerance of a good Hindu woman. "I do not think they will ever be husband and wife. She says she will marry Monsieur Sabran when her husband dies but ... I do not know what it is ... something wrong ... The gods will punish them for not obeying our laws ..."

They moved silently down the hall, almost tiptoeing in fear of awakening the dead, and, without needing to be told, Sara recognised the door to her mother's bedroom.

"You remember, Sarianna? Now it is Monsieur Sabran's room."

Sara was torn between feeling that it was indiscreet to be in a strange man's room, and a desire to know more about the owner of the house. A bedroom told so much about the occupant, and this one was no exception. The room was furnished with good heavy mahogany and, to her surprise, she saw it was full of books in both English and French. They were everywhere, lying stacked up on the bedside table and on the window ledges.

The paintings above the bed and decorating the walls were modern, unlike anything she'd ever seen. They glowed with colour as bright as a hot summer's day, almost blinding in their brilliance. She stood before them mesmerised, soaking in the warmth radiating from the canvas.

In England, the walls of her home were decorated with dark portraits of past relations, dressed in sombre black and wearing forbidding expressions, layered with the dusty patina of age. She'd only recently read about Manet and the other Impressionist painters and how their new painting style had so horrified the French and English academies. She smiled to herself; it seemed that Ravi Sabran was not afraid of the modern but embraced it with enthusiasm. There before her were the luminous reminders of his French heritage: lovely scenes of French country life and the gay streets of Paris. The colours were vivid and restful at the same time, and oddly appropriate to their surroundings.

She tore herself away to admire the view from the window and imagined how pleasant it must be to gaze out upon the tangle of coconut palms and frangipani and, further away still, a distant view of the sea. Her hand rested upon a large armchair placed comfortably by the window and, as in the rest of the room, the table beside it was piled high with literature.

She picked up one of the books, left open as he must have left it, and saw it was written by one of the scandalous French novelists. She dropped it as though it burned her fingers, remembering how she had been caught with one of the same writer's books in boarding school. Her French teacher had left it lying around and, after reading a few pages, she'd been so tempted to learn more she had hidden it under her pillow to read after lights out, but, unfortunately, she had been caught, and the outrage that followed haunted her still.

Even so, she was pleased. Here was the other side of the exotic, flamboyant and arrogant man she'd met only a few times. Now she suspected him of being an intellectual.

Her brain was working fast, telling her she must live again in her old home. She ran a possessive hand over the coverlet on the bed and knew that she must have this room for herself, and sleep in the same bed her own mother had slept in. She felt only in that house could she ever regain her old happiness. Her mood lightened to a new feverish level, and she was all at once consumed with energy.

"I'll go to see him, I'll go to see Monsieur Sabran and make him sell the house to me."

Malika stared at Sara, her brow forming into a frown, before she reverted to her old status of nurse and shook her finger at Sara as she had done when she was a small child. "It isn't good for you to talk to such a man; he lives with a bad woman."

Sara laughed. Even if Ravi Sabran lived with fifty women, it wouldn't be enough to stop her from doing her best to find him again and make him sell her his house. She must have it, and she would do anything to get it.

Chapter 18

It was almost dark when Sara returned to Charles. She had parted from Malika with an almost agonising reluctance, being overwhelmed with the fear that once she was out of sight she'd evaporate into thin air and all her new-found happiness with her.

The house too had a stranglehold on her emotions. And, as she drove away, it seemed the vines surrounding the house had attached themselves to her, pulling tighter the further away she became, till finally snapping as she came to a standstill outside the little villa she only just existed in with Charles.

Before entering the house she stood for a while on the path outside the front gate as she contemplated the strange mock Tudor structure and what waited for her within those walls. Once inside the sphere of her husband's rule she knew she would fade as surely as the garden that surrounded the house. It was as though she left her true self at the doorstep and, after crossing the threshold, assumed a role that stripped her of her true character. She became as wooden as a puppet, speaking lines that did not belong to her, and smiling when she did not feel like smiling.

This, surely, could not be her home.

It took Sara some time to tell Charles about Malika and the house. At first it was excitement making it difficult for her to speak, but then she realised it was her unwillingness to share her treasure, knowing instinctively he would want to crush her dream of ever owning the house.

She wasn't afraid of him yet, even though at times she caught sight of what he might become if she did ever seriously displease him.

When at last she did speak up, her voice didn't sound as though it belonged to her. It was light and cheerful, as though the subject had to be broken to him gently. She was reminded of the voice her aunt had used when asking her husband for an increase in her dress allowance.

"Charles ... I have something important to tell you."

He didn't look up from reading his mail; he spoke in an offhand way. "What is it, my dear?"

"I found Malika ... You remember ... my old nurse ... I told you about her ... Malika! I found her! It's truly amazing!" Her voice rose to an excited pitch, then fell to almost a whisper when she saw his mouth twist.

"Your old nurse, are you sure? You know what tricksters these people are, and they do look somewhat alike."

A flash of anger surged through her body. "That's ridiculous, Charles, and you know it! Of course I'm sure. I'd know Malika anywhere. She was like a mother to me."

He put the mail to one side and stared up at her. "I wouldn't say that too loud if I were you. It doesn't sit right."

She confronted him now, but he backed away. "Why ever not? What do you mean?"

He picked up a newspaper and went back to his reading, not really listening. She watched the top of his head for a while, even though it said he did not wish to be disturbed.

"Charles, please ... I've so much to tell you ..."

He looked up then, but still held onto his newspaper.

"She's still living at my parents' house ... My parents' house! I found my parents' house! Isn't that an incredible coincidence? Isn't it wonderful, Charles? I found out the name my father used when he first came to India; he called himself William Radcliffe!"

Charles looked up, suddenly alarmed. "He changed his name?" Why would he do that?"

"I told you he'd quarrelled with his family, for whatever reason I don't know." She gave up all pretence now and rose to her father's defence.

"A lot of people change their names; it doesn't mean anything."

"I hope you're right. It wouldn't do if the fellow was hiding something unsavoury. But, as you say, it's unlikely. He was an Eton man, after all."

She almost laughed, thinking he was joking, but she soon realised he was deadly serious.

"But the thing is," she pushed on, even though his expression had changed to one of suspicion, "the house might be empty soon; we might be able to rent it, perhaps even buy it. Oh, Charles, it's such a beautiful house and ..."

"Sara, please calm yourself ... How can I understand you when you rattle on like that? Now, sit down and tell me your news quietly. How did you find the house, and what are you doing traipsing around the town by yourself? Shakur told me you refused to take Lakshmi with you."

"Well, I thought I should go to see Prema, so ..."

"Prema? You mean the Indian child; you went to see her?"

"Yes, I was, but she wasn't there; no one was there. That's when I found Malika, you see; it seems she works for Monsieur Sabran."

"I thought we agreed that you could never visit that man's home." As he stood his paper dropped to the floor unnoticed. "I know Sabran's house well. One of the best in the old style, I'll admit, but even if the house is available to rent, we can never have an Indian landlord, and especially a man who attacked me, and in front of everyone. I could have had him arrested. It's unthinkable."

"Don't be ridiculous, Charles! He didn't hurt you, and it's understandable as he was so upset. And does it matter if he's Indian? Perhaps he'll sell us the house and then he'll leave Madras. You should be pleased about that if he bothers you so much."

Charles flexed the muscles in one his hands and paused while examining his nails. She was meant to wait before him, like a child about to be punished, and she felt her anger rise once more.

He sighed loudly, as though his patience with her was exhausted, though determined to be patient still.

"And what will we do for money? Have you thought of that? I think you imagine we have more money than we have."

"I have my pearls. You said yourself they would fetch a good price."

"I don't think it's very ladylike of you to mention your pearls. You wouldn't have them at all if it wasn't for the respect I command here. I refuse to discuss it any longer. God knows what condition the place is in after Indians have lived in it."

"The house has been well taken care of." Sara struggled to keep control of her anger now. "If you only knew what the house means to me, how happy it would make me ..." She faltered this time, tears of outrage almost spilling over. "My parents are buried at that house ... Surely you can see ..."

"Yes, yes, of course I understand." He softened at once. "I could talk to the rector about having the graves moved into the churchyard, where you could visit them. It does seem barbaric they were buried in the grounds of the house at all, but then the rules were so very lax in those days."

"I want them to stay where they are, at peace. It seems wrong to move them."

He was impatient with her now, she could tell, and she knew also that he didn't really understand at all. The realisation made her feel cold inside and very alone.

"Charles?" Her voice couldn't hide her iciness now.

He sighed in response. "Yes, my dear?"

"Is the mail service very poor, here in Madras, I mean?"

"No, it's a very good service; that's something we've managed to teach the devils to do well."

"Then I can't understand why I've heard nothing from Monsieur Sabran. I've written a number of times and I've never received an answer; that's why I decided to visit the house without an invitation."

"Well, I did tell you not to expect too much from them; they aren't like us."

"Not so different, surely ... and Monsieur Sabran is an educated man ..."

He stopped her at once. "Perhaps, but nonetheless he has Indian blood and it makes all the difference."

"You sound like the perfect *sahib*, and a dreadful snob."

"Let me tell you something, Sara, that might help you to understand."

A moment of pure rage threatened to overtake her. To be patronized in such a way was unendurable. It took all her strength not to leave the house at once, but she managed to calm herself enough to speak, even though her voice trembled.

"I don't need help in understanding anything, Charles. In fact I think you should apologise to me at once."

He was quite taken aback, but he could see too how seriously he had upset her. "Please, my dear, forgive me; it's just that I don't want you to think too badly of me. I'm sorry, I really am, but now can I speak?"

She nodded, but without any interest. His words were meaningless to her now.

"Once I took an interest in an Indian fellow and accepted an invitation to tea at his home. When the hour came for the visit, he wasn't there. I walked around the back and found him hiding in the garden. It seems he didn't know what to buy for refreshments, so he pretended not to be home."

"Oh, the poor man. It must have been so horrible for him. I'm surprised you don't show more compassion."

"That is not the point. They're different, and we can never hope to bridge the gap."

"You must be right then." Now she didn't bother to hide her sarcasm, though he didn't seem to notice.

"I know I am." He smiled at her and patted her hand.

She flinched at his touch and drew back. This is the game I am expected to play, she thought to herself with a surge of bitterness. I smile and agree and in return he may grant me a favour.

"I must continue to visit Malika; she's getting old now and she's alone."

"Malika?" He flicked his newspaper again. "Oh, your old nurse ..."

"She's the only link with my past and with my family. I must see her."

Something in her voice caused him to look up.

"You cannot visit her there, but if it makes you happy you can have her live here with us. We can find room for her somewhere, I dare say."

"She won't leave my parents, not for long anyway. But she agreed she would come and stay with me for a day or two when I need her. That is, of course, if you don't mind."

He bent over and kissed her dryly on the cheek in a dismissive way.

"Well, I'll leave that up to you. I can do no more, and I have work to do, so if you will excuse me."

She was too angry to reply at first. She had tried honesty; now she would act in her own way. Charles had taught her to be cunning, and to play a game she must play if she was to get what she wanted.

"Charles, I'm going away for a few days. I'd like to see some of the country, perhaps Pondicherry ... It sounds so interesting ..."

His head swung around to face her. "Go away? What for? And to Pondi, of all places. It's full of French people. Aren't you happy here?"

"That's beside the point. I simply want to go away for a few days."

"But you have your duties here, in the house."

"I'm going, Charles, if you like it or not, but I would rather you be pleased about it."

"I don't like it, and I'd rather you stayed here."

"I plan to leave the day after tomorrow; there's a train ..."

He wouldn't allow her to finish. "You can't go alone, but if you insist on this foolish plan I'll ask Cynthia to go with you ... Poor girl; it might take her mind off her suffering."

It was on the tip of Sara's tongue to say that if Cynthia was suffering she hadn't seen any sign of it. Indeed, Cynthia seemed more angry than sad at her fiancé's death, and behaved as though the boy had purposely let her down by dying and depriving her of a title.

"Perhaps she won't want to come," she said hopefully. "I don't mind going alone ... I can take Malika with me."

"Cynthia will want to go; she mentioned she needed a change. I'll ask her."

"If you must." She scowled, but he didn't hear her. His mind was already on other things.

Later, before she retired for the night, he held her face up to the lamplight, then, as though she had let him down in some way, he dropped his hand and sighed before turning away from her.

Later, Sara drifted into her bedroom and sat down before the mirror, staring hard at her reflection in the hope of finding an answer to her misery there. Had she altered so much? She looked closer. There were changes after all. She was pale, it was true, and lately she seemed to suffer almost constant bouts of mild nausea, but there were also signs of disappointment around her mouth, and a new sadness in her eyes.

She picked up her hairbrush and began to brush her hair, slowly at first, then, overwhelmed with her own suffering, she pulled at her hair so hard it hurt. Then, in an agony of despair, she flung the hairbrush as hard as she could across the room, where it smashed against the window shutter. There was a flurry of voices outside the window before they subsided and all was silent again.

After a while she roused herself and moved to the window to retrieve the hairbrush. Looking through the timber slats, she could see Charles's lamp burning away in the summer house at the bottom of the garden where he often retired to work; his shadow was bent over the desk, innocently unaware of her unhappiness.

She opened the shutters and stepped out into the warm

night. The scent of incense drifted through the air and the stars were brilliant in the royal blue moonlight. The place was bewitching.

She decided that she would go to him and perhaps somehow try to recapture what they had lost, or perhaps had never even had. She stepped out onto the balcony and almost fell over the sleeping figure of Mutu, who was curled up on a mat. He jumped up, alarmed at first, then, seeing it was her, salaamed, his voice husky with sleep. "Can I get something for you, madam?"

"No! Nothing." The moment of enchantment had fled, and she hurried back into the room. In the background she could hear soft laughter. She peeped out through the shutters to see Lakshmi, sitting by the pond in the garden, combing out her long hair and singing to herself.

Chapter 19

In Pondicherry Sara found, recreated in the lush tropical landscape, a charming French provincial city, clean, prosperous and ordered.

It seemed the deception was complete, but there was an uneasiness in the air, and it struck her all of a sudden that here was a city under siege from India itself. It was as though the city was surrounded by invisible walls and those living within the walls were determined at all cost to keep the illusion alive. Smartly dressed Europeans strolled the elegant streets or gathered in groups in front of small cafés serving fresh cakes, so unlike the Indian variety, which seemed sickly and over sticky to western tastes, and where the fragrance of baguettes and freshly ground coffee scented the air.

But again, covering everything was the fine yellow dust settling on the pretty stone buildings, turning them a pale muddy gold. The dust combined with the humidity and mildew ate away at the stones and soon cracks appeared, through which strangling vines reasserted themselves, making it clear that crude indomitable nature was never far away. The

Indian inhabitants too seemed held at bay, living their lives on the outskirts of the city, or gathered together in faded and dusty coloured clumps in the corners and laneways of the polite streets. It was as though they crept through the landscape trying to pretend they weren't really there, almost apologising for the fact they didn't fit into this contrived setting.

Cynthia sat in the corner of the carriage, waving her fan over her hot face and pouting under her hat. She always kept her eyes averted when travelling through the streets, as she said the sight of so many dirty people depressed her. Though even when she was persuaded to look at an unusual sight or a scene of rare beauty it scarcely had an effect on her emotions, and Sara soon realised Cynthia's own world was more than enough for her, and anything outside of it she considered an unnecessary distraction.

Lady Palmer sat by her daughter's side and patted her while peering into her face looking for signs of heartbreak. Every now and then Cynthia's peevish voice could be heard. "Stop fussing, Mother!"

Sara could only agree with Cynthia, as she watched Lady Palmer with quiet loathing. At the last moment she'd insisted on accompanying the girls, using the excuse that it was impossible they should move amongst a foreign society unchaperoned.

They drove through the wide gates of the Pondicherry Hotel and came to rest at the front doors of a much smaller and daintier version of the Paris Opera. On closer inspection, though, Sara was amused to see the unmistakable signs of Indian workmanship showing itself in the tiny sculptures of the elephant God, Ganesh. There he was, hidden in the corners of the building in the hope he would go unnoticed, his trunk intertwined with the winged cupids of European imagination. It was unthinkable he could not be represented if there was any hope he might bring good luck on the building itself and those who stayed within it.

The French flag flaunted itself from every turret, and the sound of music played by an unseen distant orchestra came floating from the recesses of the building.

Sara pulled off her travelling bonnet and ran her fingers through her damp hair. The air was cooler in Pondicherry than Madras, cool enough to bring a faint streak of colour to her pale cheeks. A strong sea breeze brought a fresh wave of salt air, stirring the bronze wind chimes hanging from the hotel balcony. Her stiff muscles relaxed at last, and small tears of relief stung the corners of her eyes. She was shocked to discover how tense she'd been, accepting the pain between her shoulder blades as normal, and something she'd become accustomed to.

The air of gaiety was infectious, and even Lady Palmer was moved to exclaim, "How very jolly!" as she bustled about giving orders.

For Sara, there was an almost physical sense of a weight being lifted off her shoulders. She wanted to open her arms to the sky and laugh out loud, at the same time crushing the guilty thought that her joy was due entirely to being away from Charles.

Later that evening, Sara stood at the door of the dining room in a feverish daze of excitement. She allowed a calm moment of observation before exposing herself to the society of Pondicherry, who'd gathered in elegant groups around the supper tables. Even in those brief few minutes she could see they were different to the English set she was accustomed to. Here was a slight air of recklessness, a touch of disregard for what was proper. The women's gowns exposed more flesh and the men seemed less stuffy than their English counterparts. She noticed a few of them taking furtive looks in her direction, making her unconsciously cover the swell of her breasts above her low-cut gown by pretending to play with her locket.

Standing slightly apart from the crowd and leaning against the open balcony door stood Ravi Sabran, smoking a slim Turkish cigarette and watching her as she entered the room. He seemed absorbed in listening to the orchestra and was slowly tapping his fingers against his leg in time to the music, though his expression was anything but relaxed.

Sara felt something had seriously displeased him, though he was trying to keep his expression as impassive as ever. Each time she'd met him, it seemed she was shown a different aspect of the man. That evening he was dressed in the role of a cultured European gentleman, and even his skin appeared a paler shade against the severe black of his dinner suit.

He wore his hair slicked straight back from his forehead, showing his thick black eyebrows in greater relief against his skin. To the outward world he was as elegant and cultured as any other man in the room, but to a discerning eye there was no comparison. He appeared to have been tamed for the evening, whipping back his more exotic guise to walk amongst the common herd.

She felt no real surprise to see him standing there. It was almost as if she had willed it to be so. She'd had no real idea about how to go about finding him in a town unknown to her, but somehow in her heart she'd known he would find his way to her.

She was about to cross the floor to speak to him when, feeling a sharp tug from Cynthia's hand on her arm, she pulled herself up in confusion. For a moment she'd forgotten. Charles would be certain to find out, and Lady Palmer would inevitably make sure he did.

"If you go over and speak to that man, I'll never forgive you," hissed Cynthia, steering her to where Lady Palmer sat watching both girls with her ever vigilant eye.

Halfway across the room Sara stopped, asking herself why she should be rude to a man who'd only ever been of service to her, despite his scathing manner. His only real lapse had been on the day of the garden party, and even then his words had proved in some ways to be prophetic.

Every day of her life she was forced to be polite to people she didn't like at all, so why couldn't she extend the courtesy to someone, she had to admit, she had a sneaking admiration for? Besides, she needed him as a friend and, above all, she wanted his house and his servant for herself. She pulled her hand from Cynthia's grasp.

"Don't be such a snob, Cynthia. He would think me impolite if I don't."

Her path across the room seemed endless. Behind her were the audible gasps of Lady Palmer and Cynthia, and ahead was Sabran's insolent smile. She knew she had never looked so elegant, and at least in that regard she need not feel any shame, though she couldn't help but feel self-conscious with so many eyes upon her.

People stood aside as she made her way across the floor, her heels making the little click-clacking noises on the parquetry more obvious than they should be, as the orchestra chose that moment for a lull in the programme.

From Sabran's point of view, he saw a tall slim girl with high cheekbones and dark reddish hair and, even though she seemed much paler and thinner than he'd last seen her, her delicate appearance made her, in a way, lovelier still. She moved with a slow deliberate grace, her head erect as she held her skirt in her right hand in case she should trip. Her mauve chiffon gown draped over the hips and bunched behind, making her waist seem impossibly tiny. For him, though, the line of her long neck where it met her bare shoulders was the most beautiful feature of her body. For a brief moment he visualised what it would be like to make love to her, then he stopped himself from going any further. He thought he must have drunk too much wine and, anyway, he didn't trust her. He'd been fooled into believing her interest in the child was genuine but she was, after all, no different to every other Englishwoman he'd met.

She had proved herself unworthy by not fulfilling his original faith in her, despite her being married to a man he despised. Against all his feelings of dislike, he admitted to having a secret grudging admiration of her, but she had ignored his letter in a most arrogant way and was now not entitled to any particular consideration.

He straightened up when she stood before him and bowed with the grace of a courtier. It was clear the ballroom had brought out the most elegant of his manners.

"Madam Fitzroy." He spoke her name with a faint tinge of scorn that made her instantly on her guard. "This is an unexpected pleasure."

She was disappointed in him. It clearly wasn't a pleasure at all. He was barely polite, his strange grey eyes darting from left to right, avoiding looking at her, as though wanting to get the civilities out of the way as soon as possible.

"Your husband is not with you?"

"His work keeps him in Madras."

"You must find it very difficult to be apart." He seemed sincere, but his eyes were mocking.

She chose to ignore what she knew to be a provocative comment.

Then his voice took on a new level of iciness. "When I last saw you at the Maharaja's garden party, I made an unfortunate remark. I must apologise; it was none of my business. Now I can see you and your husband are very well suited."

She was hurt by his tone, but she wouldn't allow him to see it. "I must see Prema, if you will allow me. Is she well?"

"She is very well and here in Pondi. My Guru has recommended I keep the child with me. He considers her an omen of some sort."

"How very strange, and so superstitious; it doesn't seem the action of a modern man at all."

"Not so strange if you understand India, madam."

He was looking over her shoulder. Something had taken his attention.

"You left town with no forwarding address," she replied, furious at his lack of interest.

He returned to looking at her, and she almost lost courage under his cold glare.

"My dear Mrs Fitzroy ... I think you are playing games with me ... I wrote you my address and again I received no reply."

There must be some mistake. I have received nothing from you, and my servant swears it also." She bit her lip, puzzled. It occurred to her that perhaps Sabran himself was lying, though she could see no reason why he should, even though Charles had almost convinced her Sabran was avoiding her for vindictive reasons of his own.

He lit another cigarette while his eyes flickered over her body with, it seemed to her, an insult in every glance.

"But then, I have met English ladies like you before. You arrive in India full of pity for all you see around you, then become hardened within a week. I knew at once how it would be with you."

She was almost too angry to say more but, reminding herself she must tell him of the house and how much she longed to buy it from him, she composed herself to speak.

"It's not that way with me at all. I long to see the child, and all I need is an invitation."

"I await your pleasure." He was behaving like the perfect gentleman but his expression showed he was not convinced, and she must try harder.

She took a deep breath and began again. "I'm very glad to have met you here, *monsieur*. You see, I have a great favour to ask of you."

She held her head on one side and bestowed upon him her most winning smile. He thought her teeth were very good for a European lady and, unlike so many of them he'd met who bared their teeth like neighing horses, her full top lip curved charmingly upwards, revealing flashes of white as she smiled.

He bowed low. "I can never refuse a lady any favour. Name it."

"I wish to buy your house in Madras, *monsieur*, you call it Sans Souci, but I know it as Tamarind House. You see, it was ..."

He was on the alert at once. "I left the old name plate, it seemed a shame to remove it ... but before you say anything else ... will your husband live in the house with you?"

"Of course ..."

"Then my answer is no. I will not sell the house to you, not under any circumstances. And it will always be so!" He was already moving away from her.

She put a hand on his arm to stop him, and he gave her a hard look that made her take her hand away and step back a pace.

"But I heard the house may be for sale."

"It may be; I haven't decided yet. But I will never allow Charles Fitzroy to live in it."

"It's because of what happened to Sultan, isn't it? But he assures me it was an accident ..."

"I don't happen to believe him ... But there are so many other reasons, mostly for what he is doing to the Indian people. The cruel laws he seems to enjoy enforcing, his insistence on returning my beloved Maya to her husband when he knows she will most likely be murdered ..."

There he stopped for a moment, too angry to continue.

"Do you think I am a fool? I'll never let that man live in a house I love!"

His colour was heightened by an anger he didn't now bother to hide, and only his very formal manners prevented him from raising his voice. As an afterthought he added, "And madam ... I did not receive a single letter from you!"

Then he turned his face away from her. The audience was at an end.

He remained silent while she stood abandoned before him.

She watched the proud, determined tilt of his head for a moment. Then, as she struggled with her own thoughts and the truth of his words, she turned and walked away without a word.

The walk towards Lady Palmer and Cynthia seemed to take an age, aware as she was of his eyes fixed on her retreating back. In answer to the fury on their faces, she said, "I've done my duty. I need not speak to him ever again."

She sat beating the air with her fan, so distracted by their parting words she hardly acknowledged the, "I told you so," from Cynthia.

The orchestra began to play again, this time a waltz.

Sara mentally cursed Sabran. She had so much wanted to enjoy the evening, but now his insolent face and bitter words danced before her, blotting out her pleasure by increasing her distrust of her husband, and all hope of ever owning Tamarind House.

Every now and then she was made aware of his presence on the other side of the room. He seemed impossible to ignore; like a big cat, he paced the floor greeting various people with extravagant charm. She wondered why he felt it necessary to be so cruel to her when it was clear he could be pleasant when he wanted to.

Once, he engaged a very pretty Frenchwoman in conversation for at least twenty minutes, first kissing her hand in a lingering way, and, judging by her blushing face, also complimenting her on her considerable beauty. Even so, his mind seemed elsewhere. He cast Sara a furtive look and then looked away at once, before returning all his attention to the girl, giving Sara the distinct feeling he was acting out a performance for her benefit only.

Then she watched him while he at first ran an impatient hand through his black hair, flicked his cigarette into a bowl, narrowed his eyes with intent, then marched across the room towards her.

Halfway across the floor he seemed to pause and, for a moment, Sara thought he would retreat.

Then, with a quick step, he was there before her, bowing low in an exaggerated way with his hand extended. "May I have the pleasure of this dance?"

She was about to refuse with a haughty turn of her head when he took her hand and pulled her to her feet.

His grip was so tight, and the look in his eyes so determined, to argue would have resulted in an embarrassing tug-of-war with him right there on the ballroom floor. It seemed less trouble to dance with him, despite Lady Palmer's outraged squeaks of protest.

To make doubly sure she couldn't refuse, he tightened his arm around her waist as he led her to the floor and whispered in her ear, his warm breath coming in short sharp gusts, making her ear tingle in a disturbing way. "I'm sorry. I'm deeply ashamed, really. I was very rude. The sight of Lady Palmer's face always makes me behave in strange ways. It's as though the Gorgon herself has cast a spell on me."

She wanted to laugh but she hadn't forgiven him yet. "Is this the way you usually get ladies to dance with you?"

"Not usually, but I knew you would refuse me as I deserved. Please forgive me; I am very contrite."

She watched him, wary and unsure.

"I did write to you, more than once. I don't understand. My servant swears he sent them. The mail system must be very bad."

He looked into her eyes and saw her innocence. He wondered if he should enlighten her, then decided against it. He told himself she wouldn't believe him anyway, being so devoted to that fool husband of hers.

Soon the steady rhythm of the music combined with the movement of her body acted as a drug on her senses. She forgot she was angry with him and why. She even forgot she had a husband. After a moment the room took on a dream-like quality, as it always did when she danced. Nothing else existed except the hot tropical night, the candlelit room and the swirl of the women's gowns against the tempo of the music. It was as though her body was released from its weight and floated just above the ground, only his firm grip around her waist anchoring her to earth.

The change in her face was profound. He realised with a shock he had never seen her happy before. Of course, he had seen her smile and say charming things, but he had never seen her almost luminous before that evening. She turned away from him, made uncomfortable by his close scrutiny. Could she read in his eyes what he was thinking? He smiled to himself. Was it possible she was capable of such strong passions she was dangerous even to herself?

The pace of the waltz had heightened her colour, making her breath come in short gasps as he swirled her around. She almost slipped but saved herself by falling forward against his chest and clutching at his suit coat. The hard muscle beneath the jacket tensed and she coloured again before turning her head away, keeping her eyes fixed on his shirtfront. She mumbled a silly meaningless remark, then squirmed at her lack of sophistication. She began to resent him a little. It was his fault after all.

There was something about the way he looked at her that

caused her to lose her balance, in both a physical and mental sense. He tightened his grip on her waist and in that moment he felt a powerful frisson of desire. He could feel the warmth of her body through the thin fabric of her dress, and for a wild uncontrolled moment he imagined the pleasure of leisurely unlacing her corset to kiss the flesh underneath. The tingle of anticipation in his chest was almost painful. She looked up at him, her mouth parted and breathless, and in return his mouth contorted with the effort of maintaining a controlled exterior. He straightened up and flexed his burning hand behind her back as if to drive the sensation away.

She saw him flush and bite his lip.

"Is something the matter?"

He covered his feelings with a faint smile. "Forgive me, a cramp."

At that moment the music stopped and they unlocked hands to stand side by side, both relieved not to be touching each other. She put a hand out to steady herself against a chair, her legs weak and trembling.

A commotion at the door of the ballroom took her attention away from him for a moment, as a group of Indian musicians and women dancers, barefoot, but dressed in brilliant costumes, moved into the room and collected together.

The women removed their gauze veils to expose their midriffs and the swell of full breasts above low-cut sari blouses. Their breasts seemed impossibly round and luxuriant compared to the slight waists and full hips. Sara had always thought the classical carvings of the Indian female form were exaggerated, but now, standing before her, was the proof of the artists' sure knowledge.

She turned to Sabran, her eyes glowing. "I've been longing to see some classical dance."

He laughed out loud.

"Why are you laughing?"

"Not if Lady Palmer has her way. Look!"

The woman had hurried to her feet and rushed to where the manager of the hotel stood talking to the leader of the dancers. Her strident voice carried across the room. "Tell them to leave at once! At once, do you hear! I'll not have my daughter exposed to such indecency."

Sara couldn't keep the irritation out of her voice. "What on earth is the woman talking about? She's sending them away!"

It was true. To keep the peace, the manager was shooing the bewildered dancers from the room.

"This, I will not stand. Excuse me ..."

She watched him as he made his way to the door, the crowd parting before him.

After a few brief words and a generous handful of notes to both the manager and the dancers, they returned, while keeping a watchful eye on Lady Palmer.

The whole room stood silent while Sabran presented himself before Lady Palmer.

"You will forgive me, madam, I'm sure, when I remind you, you are on French soil now and therefore have no right to tell French citizens what they may do or not do." Then he walked away, snapping his fingers in the air as a signal for the dancers to start.

Lady Palmer's fury stalled him. Her voice rose above the noise of the crowd. "How dare you speak that way to me? I'll be informing my husband, Lord Palmer, of your behaviour as soon as I return to Madras!"

All of his charm evaporated at once. He turned and gave her a look that caused the crowd to hush. Lady Palmer blanched and stepped back a pace.

There was nothing left now of the European gentleman. He took some time to control himself, his eyes almost opaque with fury, his pale lips trembling. "If the dancing offends you, madam, kindly leave the room so others may enjoy it."

This time she was unable to speak, but stood, her mouth open, as he turned his back on her.

The musicians began to play, sometimes glancing in Lady Palmer's direction as though at any moment they might be called upon to stop, but till then were going to give their best while they still could.

After an uncertain start the dancers began to weave their magic. From her position by the open window, Sara watched, entranced by the beauty of their movements and secretly thrilled by Sabran's stand against Lady Palmer. The woman watched him with a fury bordering on hysteria, but there was nothing she could do. Pondicherry was indeed a French protectorate. She had no power outside of Madras and all she could do was fume.

Sara felt rather than saw Sabran join her as she stood by the window. She was on her guard at once, her skin tingling in anticipation, her body attuned to his movements as he stood next to her, so affected by his presence she found it difficult to speak for fear her voice would shake.

There was a profound silence while the dancers performed, then a rush of applause. It seemed the crowd were really congratulating the actions of Sabran more than the dancers and, as though realising this, he turned to the room and bowed. There was a murmur of well-bred laughter. To many of the French in the room, the English were still the enemy of battles fought not so long ago. This was a small victory to be savoured in the Pondicherry drawing rooms for some time to come.

She felt his warm breath on her cheek as he leaned towards her. "And, my dear Mrs Fitzroy, did you feel corrupted by such a sight before you?"

She stared straight ahead, not wanting to see the expression in his eyes, knowing he would make her colour rise in her face.

"Of course not. The woman's a fool, as you well know."

"She believes the dance indecent," he whispered, placing emphasis on "indecent". "She thinks their dancing inflames passion and lures the poor Englishmen into sin."

She wouldn't answer him but kept her face averted.

"But then," he continued, "the Hindus believe the European form of dancing is far worse. The idea of a man and woman who are comparative strangers locked in an intimate embrace, however temporary, is disgraceful to them. The waltz you and I so much enjoyed would be seen as provocative in the extreme."

Her head swung around to face him, her face aflame. His eyes caught hers for a moment, then she looked away, suffering almost intolerable discomfort.

Was there a hint of devilment there?

He had a habit of turning her safe world upside down with one simple sentence. She glanced around the room at the other dancing couples. They certainly didn't look guilty; why should she feel as if she was?

She took refuge in changing the subject. "I think I should go. I'm being observed, and I'm bound to pay for your courage in standing up to Lady Palmer, Monsieur Sabran."

He followed her gaze to Cynthia and her mother, who were pretending to eat their meal while casting furtive looks in Sara's direction, then he bent to whisper in her ear again, provoking a flutter of disapproval that could be felt from the other side of the room.

"On no account must you speak to the wicked Sabran; your honour is not safe with him." He straightened up with a shrug of contempt. "It's as though you are in *purdah*."

She turned on him. "You can't possibly compare my life to *purdah*. I'm perfectly free to do as I want." Though, even as she spoke, she was aware of her own hypocrisy.

"Then you will come to visit Prema while you are in town?" His dark eyes swept over her and she thought she detected a faint trace of eagerness there, despite his cool manner.

She glanced to where Cynthia and Lady Palmer sat watching her with apparent unconcern, though she knew they were scrutinizing her every move.

Her voice dropped to a whisper. "I'll come tomorrow if

I can, and I want to tell you something about the house."

He too lowered his voice in response, as though they were a couple of conspirators. "A secret? I love secrets. But why can't you tell me now?" He was teasing her, and for a moment he looked almost boyish. "I can't bear to wait when a secret is before me."

"No, not here. I wish to tell you in private. It's very important and I don't want to be interrupted."

"I will send someone to bring you to me."

"No, no, please, no one must know. I'll come to you."

This time he laughed out loud. "So you are free to do as you want, as long as it remains a secret."

He wanted to tease her again but stopped when he saw how shaken she was by his words. She stared down at her hands, not wanting to meet his eyes. He had hit upon a raw nerve.

"The carriage men outside the hotel know where I am. Just ask for my house. You will find it at the end of Rue des Fleurs. Everyone knows where I live."

"Of course, everyone knows where you live, *monsieur*." She laughed. "I expect nothing less."

A secret and inscrutable look came into his eyes as she gazed up at him, her face lovely in the candlelight, and made prettier still by the laughter in her eyes.

"I think I shall leave now. I have lingered too long. *Au demain*."

This time he couldn't meet her eyes. In fact, he seemed angry with her again.

Sara, watching him leave, saw he didn't bother to say good-night to anyone else in the room. He swept past the pretty Frenchwoman he had devoted so much time to earlier in the evening, while she looked after him with obvious disappointment.

And, as always after every meeting with Ravi Sabran, Sara felt the usual conflicting emotions of attraction and aversion. He was indeed a strange man.

Chapter 20

It was not possible to visit Prema the next day after all. Shops had to be visited and calls had to be made where Sara could not be excused, and it was not till late in the day she could send Sabran a note of explanation. She received a note in return, saying that he would be leaving town on business for a few weeks, and doubted he would see her for some time; even so, he had left orders with the household to expect her.

She breathed a sigh of relief. It would be so much easier if she didn't have to see him. It was useless to pretend he wasn't an unsettling presence and clearly a dangerous man to know, though she regarded him as such an exotic creature and so unlikely ever to be a part of her everyday life it was almost as if he wasn't real.

Her encounters with him had the magic she felt when she opened a copy of the *Arabian Nights* and spent a few guilty moments with a hero of fiction. Though in one respect he was more real to her than her own husband.

His words had hit their mark again and made her aware of her own weaknesses, more than any of her husband's incessant criticisms. He had shown her how she had failed herself, and how at times she had been timid and unsure when she should have gained strength from her marriage. She swore that from that time on she would not allow her husband's petty tyrannies to pull her down. Never again would her heart sink when he walked into the room, never again would she allow him to hurt her with his words. From that time on she would fight for what she wanted.

Two days passed before she had the chance at last to steal away from the claustrophobic company of Cynthia and her mother. It was almost as if Lady Palmer suspected something. It seemed she was everywhere, watching Sara with suspicious eyes whenever she left the room.

It was only when some ladies invited them all on a shopping expedition to a favourite milliner could she find an excuse to remain behind, pleading she was unwell. Lady Palmer's sharp eyes scanned her face, ready to contradict, but then unexpectedly relented. She could be excused just this once, as there was very little space in the carriage for both ladies and their purchases.

Almost as soon as they were out of sight, Sara left the hotel and asked to be taken to the Rue des Fleurs.

"Monsieur Sabran's house ... Do you know where it is?"

"Monsieur Sabran, yes, yes ..." The man grinned, pleased to have such an important fare, before heading off down the main street of Pondicherry, looking about and waving at the passing shopkeepers while nodding towards his passenger in the back seat, while she tried to hide under her parasol. It seemed he was determined to make her as conspicuous as possible.

"Is there no other way?" Sara called out. "Can we go a quiet way?"

He turned to look at her, at the same time pulling up his tiny horse just as Lady Palmer and Cynthia were coming out of a hat shop on the other side of the street. She ducked out of sight, all the while feeling very silly, but it was already too late. She peeped from behind her parasol and saw Lady Palmer staring in her direction with her mouth wide open as though in the middle of a shout, with her hand raised high in the air.

It would have been easier for Sara to pretend she'd changed her mind and was hurrying after them, but a spark of rebellion urged her to call out to her driver, "Quick! Quick! Move on!" The driver gave the horse a light touch with his whip and soon Lady Palmer's large, outraged figure shrank into the distance.

The man drove on while she sweltered in the heat for what seemed like hours, though it was only minutes. Then, when she was about to give up and ask to go back to the hotel, he raced down a dusty thoroughfare, stopping at last before a pair of tall wooden doors set into a whitewashed wall almost covered in a crimson flowering vine and bearing a brass plate announcing the residence of Ravi Sabran.

Despite the restrained domestic nature of the clean white wall and the elegant sign, there was an air of menace permeating the atmosphere.

A group of gaunt black-bearded men in faded weather-beaten turbans lounged about in front of the house smoking thin, strong-smelling cigarettes, or sat squatting in the dust of the street, staring with malevolent, narrowed eyes at anyone passing by. The men were from the far north near the Himalayas and had the reputation of being the fiercest fighters in India. It was well known they would die without question in the defence of the most trivial breach of honour and were to be scrupulously avoided should one ever be unlucky enough to be caught on the wrong side of them. They carried rifles heavy with silver and intricate carving and wore dusty grey cotton pantaloons and wide leather belts in the manner of eighteenth-century pirates, though these men travelled on tough little horses instead of ships. It was easy to picture them, galloping across the wide Steppes and waving their rifles in the air.

A few of them leapt to their feet when the rickshaw pulled up and surrounded Sara and the driver, peering at her with hard curious eyes, jabbering in a dialect she couldn't understand. Even in the bright morning sun she felt a shiver pass over her. There was something cruel and pitiless about them, even though they laughed with the appearance of good-natured banter amongst themselves, at what seemed to Sara personal remarks made about her.

She had made the mistake of being a woman alone without her maid and, even as a European lady, it made her a target for scorn.

There was nothing she could do, as all attempts to make herself understood were ignored. The driver seemed to sense their good humour couldn't be relied upon to last and might turn at any time. His voice shook as he managed to blurt out the words while pointing in Sara's direction. "Monsieur Sabran!"

They stood back at once and, after paying the driver, who snatched at the money and hurried off, all the while looking behind him in case they should change their minds, Sara made her way to the wooden doors and rang the brass bell suspended there, while the guards laughed after her.

A handsome servant, dressed in fresh white linen and embellished with the scarlet turban and sash of the household, opened the door just a crack, giving a tempting glimpse of a lush garden beyond. Then, seeing an English lady standing before him, her face flushed and her hat awry, he fell to his feet at once, bowing and bestowing blessings upon her. After letting out a string of abuse at the group of wild men before him for making her wait, he stood aside to let her pass, before locking the doors on the dusty chaos of the outside world.

The servant hurried ahead of her, every now and then glancing behind to give her a broad smile, as though unable to believe she was real. She followed him through a garden, thick with coconut palms and a wild profusion of tropical flowers. The beauty of the place was intoxicating and she found herself trailing behind, drugged with the heavy perfumes from the garden, spellbound, as though she had wandered suddenly into a sultry fairyland.

She was tempted to linger there and drink in the beauty of the place but when she saw the house she was drawn towards it like a sleepwalker. It was almost a miniature Taj

Mahal, complete with turrets and windows of carved marble filigree. The effect was so light and airy it seemed as though the house had floated there. She couldn't help but smile. It was so much a reflection of the owner. Here was the barbaric beauty of the Mogul princes combined with French elegance, an exquisite house from the *Arabian Nights*.

Her arrival had created a sensation. A young boy, who'd been cutting the heads off huge orange hibiscus, stopped to first stare then ran up the marble steps before disappearing into the house, leaving a trail of blooms as he ran. "A lady has come ... An English lady has come ..."

There was a series of shouts, then an echoed response coming from the depths of the house. Soon other servants appeared, staring with unabashed curiosity but bestowing blessings with warm smiles, saying as they kneeled before her," *Bonjour, madame, bonjour.* Come, madam, come in, please come ..."

From somewhere within the house, smoothing her hair and adjusting her sari, appeared an elegant Indian woman in her mid-thirties. Her greeting was full of unrestrained joy as she took both Sara's hands in hers and raised them to her forehead.

"You are here at last ... Monsieur Ravi said you would come."

"Forgive me for bursting in like this ..." Her voice trailed off. "I should have sent a note first."

The woman waved away any protests. "It is an honour to have you here at last. My name is Haria. I know you are Mrs Fitzroy."

237

She turned to a servant and, speaking with great urgency, sent him hurrying away down a long marble corridor leading into the further recesses of the house.

They moved into a type of drawing room, though the room was far from stuffy or formal like its English counterpart. There was no sense of being closed in, or of having any walls at all, and it was open to a wide terrace hung with a thick crimson bougainvillea. The floor and walls were of white marble stamped with a fine pattern of flowers worked in mother-of-pearl. Sara was never more conscious of her English background, having dressed in a cool white muslin gown, matched with a wide-brimmed straw hat. In her mirror at the hotel her clothes had seemed appropriate, but here in such a house she was as out of place as a snowdrop in a vase of tiger lilies.

She was aware of many pairs of eyes upon her, though when she looked around there was only a flash of colour retreating behind a door, a glimpse of dark shy eyes and a soft burst of laughter.

Haria clapped her hands briskly and all became quiet. "Please, sit. I have sent for Prema and Monsieur Sabran will be with you in a moment."

"Monsieur Sabran is here? But I thought he was to be away on business."

"He did not leave after all. A problem prevented him from leaving."

"Oh! Please," she cried, "don't disturb him. I've come to see Prema only."

She'd planned to leave him a letter, asking about Malika

and the house. She held it in her hand at that moment, though now there would be no avoiding meeting with him.

"No. Monsieur Sabran will be very angry with me if I let you leave without seeing him."

"You have known Monsieur Sabran for a long time?"

"Yes, since he was a child. I am his cousin."

"Oh!"

"He took me in when I was cast out by my husband's family."

"Oh, I'm so sorry."

"When Monsieur Ravi heard of my misfortune, he sent his men to find me and bring me here." She watched Sara's face, her eyebrows raised, as though expecting a response.

"He must be a very kind man."

"I would die for him." She said the words with such conviction, Sara had no doubt the woman meant it.

Her face clouded as she scanned Sara's face once more. "Then you think he is a fit person to look after a child such as Prema?"

Sara laughed. "Oh, I see; you're telling me these things so I'll think well of him."

"Yes, I am." She smiled. "But everything I have told you is true."

They laughed together, united by their secret.

Then there was a flurry of activity in the corridor, the sound of hurried steps and whispered furtive voices, then he was before her, running his fingers through his still damp long black hair. It was clear she had interrupted him in his bath.

Even so, he took her hand in his, kissing her fingertips, as gallant as ever. "Welcome to my home."

"Forgive me for not sending a note first; I had no time."

He swept her words aside, then he turned to Haria, speaking in Tamil, too fast for Sara to follow. The woman modestly withdrew, leaving them alone.

After a brief awkward silence, his words rushed out. He was still uncomfortable at being caught off guard. "Haria has taken care of you?"

"Yes, very well. She's been telling me how good you are."

"She makes me sound very dull."

"Dull is the last word I would use to describe you, *monsieur*." She laughed.

"Now I am intrigued." His eyes lit up at once. "Now I must ask you what you really think of me."

She decided to say nothing in response, but only smiled, while in return he gave her the full power of his indecipherable gaze while he led her towards a comfortable armchair.

He waited till she had seated herself, then he threw himself down on the settee opposite, curling his legs underneath in the Indian fashion. He was dressed for the house in a white muslin *kurta* and baggy linen pants narrowing at the ankle, where a thin gold bangle hung over one of his naked feet. When he saw her glance at his foot, he tucked it hastily away under his *dhoti*, aware that a bare foot was not an appropriate sight for an English lady. He covered his discomfort by playing with a long strand of sandalwood beads he wore around his neck, while he watched her through half-closed lids.

"You are looking very well, better than when I saw you last. Pondi must be agreeing with you."

"Yes, I'm very much better. I don't know why, but I seem always to be ill in Madras. Perhaps it's the bad air."

"You are always ill?"

"It must be a passing thing, as I feel wonderful now," she reassured him with a laugh.

He listened to all she said, though his face gave away nothing of his true thoughts. He pulled out a cigarette from a silver filigree box on the table and waved it before her. "Do you mind?"

She shook her head and the delicious aroma of smoke mixed with spices crept towards her. The aroma was so seductive, for a moment she had a desire to try one herself. He took a long draw and leaned back on the cushions, lazily blowing the smoke in the air.

"I have been with my Guru this morning; there are many things pressing on my mind. It is a great comfort to me to receive spiritual guidance, but I suppose you think Indian mysticism is a lot of nonsense, as you English say."

"How could I, after what I've experienced since I've been in India? I'll keep an open mind on the subject."

He shrugged his shoulders, showing his French side once more. She was fascinated by his sudden changes in character; a few moments before he'd been Indian to the core with his talk of mysticism, but she also noticed his manner had changed towards her. He was cold and almost businesslike.

She couldn't know it, but he was angry with himself for having succumbed to her charms the last time he'd seen her. It made him feel ashamed; as he thought himself so much in love with Maya, no one could ever turn his head for a moment. He was proud of his attachment to his lover and saw his momentary slip as a weakness he would crush. He despised some men of his acquaintance who had many mistresses. He knew, as a man of power and position in India, the same was expected of him, even risking the scorn of his associates because of his devotion to one woman. But nothing could be done; when he was in love, he was in love, and he had eyes for no other woman.

And yet there was something compelling about Sara Fitzroy. He sighed in an almost despairing way, and her head lifted up to look at him. He stared at her face in the morning light, looking for imperfections. He would not be taken in by her again. She looked less tired than when he had seen her last and gone were the blue shadows under her eyes.

He admitted to very much liking the dark mole on the base of her neck and her black winged eyebrows, contrasting against the mass of dark auburn hair, even her almost too slim body, usually considered so unattractive by Indian standards, he admired for her elegance, but he said to himself she was nothing special after all, despite her cool charm.

Sara couldn't help but be aware of his close scrutiny and she began to fidget with her gloves again. "I couldn't come before now. Lady Palmer doesn't look kindly upon you so, as you know, my visit must remain a secret. It seems you have made some enemies."

He shrugged his shoulders again. "So be it."

"Is that what those fierce-looking men outside are for, to protect you?"

His mouth twitched very slightly at the corners and his eyes showed he was not pleased by her remark.

"They are some of my polo team. When we are not practising, they guard my house. It gives them something to do."

This time she couldn't help but laugh out loud. "You play polo with these men?"

"They are the best, and they are fearless. They will play to the death."

She began to fidget with her hands; she didn't want to be reminded of that day on the polo field. "Even so, they are very unpleasant men. They frightened me."

"They frightened you?" His head jerked up at once. Suddenly his eyes were hard.

"They were horrible to the poor man who brought me here and, I think, insolent with me."

"They dared to be insolent with you?"

"I think so; perhaps I was imagining it."

He rose at once. "Would you care for some refreshments?" he asked in a very formal way.

"Yes, I suppose so." She felt a faint dissatisfaction with him. He could at least apologise.

"Will you excuse me for one moment?"

"Of course."

While he was gone, she thought about Lady Palmer and Cynthia, and how she hoped she could lie convincingly when they asked her about her day. She would say the driver had refused to stop and insisted on taking her to a silk merchant where he could make a commission. She made a mental note to stop and buy something to throw them off her scent. It would never do to return empty-handed.

She looked around, smitten again by the beauty of the house, admiring the high marble arches supported by their delicate pillars and the wide terrace overlooking the sea.

She watched a young man who was employed as a *punka wallah* to keep the house cool. He lay on his back on the terrace, the string of a giant fan tied to his ankle. He waved his leg back and forth as he sang a song to himself. She tried not to think about how Charles would have reacted to the sight in her own home.

Sabran came back into the room and sat before her. "I have ordered something I think you will like." He was so severe she wondered what could have upset him.

"Then I'm sure I will." His cool manner was making her nervous, and she longed for the sight of Prema to change the mood.

"Prema will join us for tea?"

"She is being bathed."

"Of course ..." The distance between them was almost unbearable.

"Oh, before I forget ..." She reached into her purse and held out a thick handful of notes.

"I want to give you something for her upkeep. I feel she is really much more my responsibility than yours. You can't think how guilty I feel."

He looked at the money as though she had offered him poison. "Please, do not insult me."

244

"But that's ridiculous. I want to help."

"I will not take it." He spoke with such conviction she put the money away at once, lest the sight of it offend him further. In a way she was grateful for his determination not to take the money. It had cost her a lot to save it, snatching a few coins here and there from the housekeeping, and secreting it away in her underwear drawer. She had discovered something else about Charles since her marriage she didn't like. He was mean with money; that was, he was mean with her. She was supposed to account for every note while his gambling had increased with his marriage, though his losses were shrugged off as something men did as a matter of course.

She searched her mind for something to say while Sabran continued to watch her through the curling smoke of his cigarette. If he was uncomfortable in her presence, he showed no sign of it.

To cover her own confusion, she turned to the pattern on the richly embroidered cushions of the settee. "How lovely!" she said without really seeing it.

"Yes, the Moguls had a fascination with love." He smiled almost dreamily. "I'm told those embroideries are three hundred years old ... I found them in Rajasthan."

She held up a cushion to examine it more closely. What she had thought was a conventional design was an illustration of ardent lovers, their intertwined limbs forming an abstract pattern.

"Oh!" she said, dropping the cushion as though it burnt her hand.

He was reminded of the time he'd watched her at the

forbidden sculptures on the beach, and he changed the subject to save her embarrassment.

"Now, what is that letter you have clutched in your hand? Is it for me?"

"No, well, yes, it is, but now, as I ..." She put the letter away in her purse. "It was an explanation, the reason why I want your house, and also a request."

"You cannot take Prema back. Maya has become very fond of her, she treats her with special favour, and I too believe the child has brought me luck. It's true that charity brings its own rewards, but business has never been better."

"How cynical you are, but I suspect you're trying to hide a soft heart."

"Then, madam, you do not know me very well." He fixed his strange grey eyes on hers and she felt a shiver run down her back. "Everything I do with a benefit in mind, though my Guru says that taking Prema into my home will bring mixed blessings."

His face darkened as his brows shot together with an unpleasant thought.

"He says she is a messenger from the gods, who brings great changes." He changed his position in his seat. "Deep happiness, but also great suffering." When he said the words Sara could see he was shaken by the prophecy, even though he spoke as though unconcerned.

"Surely you are not as superstitious as all that? She's just a little girl. She has no power over the future."

"Perhaps, but what can I do? It is fate. Ah! Here she is."

A young woman appeared, leading the child by the hand.

Her baby face showed pride in her faltering steps as she looked around for approval. He laughed and waved a hand in her direction, almost a proud father.

"What do you think? She is very pretty, no? Who would have thought it, under all that dirt?"

"She is very pretty. Yes."

It was almost as though she was seeing a different child. Now the head wobbling on her little shoulders seemed in proportion to the body, the skin plump with health. Even the expression in her eyes, once vacant with hunger, glowed with a new life and intelligence. As usual when she was deeply moved, Sara couldn't find the words and she cursed herself for not thinking of something profound enough to express her thanks. She swallowed hard and stared at the floor but could only say, "To see her like this ..."

He didn't appear to mind her incompetence and seemed to understand.

Sara bent down to take her in her arms, but the child turned away and began to cry.

"Come, come," he said. "I must prove to Mrs Fitzroy that I'm a suitable guardian, once and for all."

He took the child and cooed a few soothing words. She stopped crying at once and began to laugh, putting out a tiny plump hand and grabbing at his hair and pulling hard. After releasing her grip, he turned to Sara. "As you see, I am more in danger of being ill-treated than she is ... Here, take her."

He handed her back to the nurse. "That's enough. I have to admit to being bored very quickly with people who cannot speak. Bring her back in an hour. She can eat with us, as a special favour."

They both watched her being led away and laughed when she forgot how to walk and sat down heavily on her little bottom.

When she thought he wasn't looking, Sara turned her gaze to study Sabran for a moment. Here was a puzzling thought. She wondered how such a man, who appeared to be so harsh and uncompromising, could find pleasure in the antics of a little child. She knew men hid their softer side under a hard outer shell. It was a simple answer, but she knew Sabran was more complicated than that. She felt, no matter how well she might know him, she would never truly know him, as she knew she would never know India and all her numerous mysteries.

He turned to find her eyes still fixed on him and gave her a strange twisted half smile, almost as though he had triumphed over her in some way, and that smile made her wary of him once more.

"Now, what is this request you ask of me?"

Sara found it difficult to speak at first, then the words tumbled out in a rush. "I lived in your house in Madras as a child. It belonged to my parents ..."

"Your parents lived in my home?" He stared at her with something like horror in his eyes. "That is most strange."

"Yes, very. A strange coincidence."

"You say a coincidence? I don't think so. We are connected by fate in yet another way."

He seemed deeply concerned and distracted by the thought

and returned to playing with his sandalwood beads while he watched her, with more interest now than before.

"You see, the graves in your garden belong to my parents. I'd like very much to be near them ..." Tears were pricking her eyes and making it difficult to speak.

He took pity on her and tried to make it easier. "The graves say Radcliffe. But I heard you were a Miss Archer."

She wondered for a moment how he knew that, then realised he must have been talking to Lucy.

"Yes, but my father changed his name to Radcliffe, for what reason I can't tell."

"Yet another mystery. And the child buried with them?"

"My sister ..."

"I've often wondered about them ... I'm very sorry."

For a second she imagined him, a stranger standing by her family's grave. Somehow, it made their resting place seem less lonely.

"You lost everyone ..."

"Not quite everyone. Malika, your servant ... who cares for the house ..."

He sat upright again, his interest aroused. "Malika? Ah! She is a character, no?"

"Yes! She was my ayah as a child ... from the day I was born."

"Your ayah? That is remarkable, *non*?" Again, his face changed and his voice was almost inaudible when he spoke. "It is indeed fate that has brought you back to India ..."

He leaped to his feet and walked around the room, excited now. "The other servants laugh at her because she talks of your family as though they are still alive ... and you want her back with you, of course ..."

"You may find this hard to understand, but she was closer to me than my own mother."

"No, I don't. As you can see ..." He placed both hands on his heart. "My own mother was Indian." His dark eyes watched her for any sign of contempt, but she showed no sign of it. Her eyes held his steadily.

"Then you'll let her visit me sometimes?"

"If that is what she desires, of course, but I don't think she will leave the house for long, not even for you, and, as I said, I will never sell my house to your husband, even if he would agree to buy it, which I very much doubt. Forgive me, but I have my reasons. If it were you alone, perhaps I would consider it."

"Then there is nothing I can say to change your mind?"

"Not while you are the wife of Charles Fitzroy, and I'm sure that situation is unlikely to change."

This time she became angry and rose to leave. "What do you want me to do? Leave my husband? You want me to throw away my marriage, just like that!" She snapped her fingers. Tears of frustration formed in her eyes. "What is the alternative for me ... to live as an outcast? In that respect Englishwomen are no different from Indian women!"

She stopped, feeling she had gone too far and acutely aware of how he watched her, his eyes more intense than ever. She looked for signs of sarcasm but saw none. Instead he took her hand and kissed it very gently, only saying, "Forgive me. Please, don't go."

He made her sit while she composed herself, only muttering, "I'm sorry. I must be tired."

There was a long painful silence till Haria came into the room and stood before them both. "Everything is ready. Prema will join you in the garden."

He rose from the couch and took her by the elbow.

"Before we do, I have a matter I want to clear up." He led her down a long hallway, out into a wide courtyard at the back of the house.

As she stepped outside, she saw before her, at the foot of the steps, almost naked and wrapped only in the loincloths worn by beggars, prostrate in the burning sun, on their stomachs with arms outstretched and heads bowed, every one of the proud guards who had dared to treat her with disrespect. There was not a sound or movement. They lay as though dead.

He walked amongst the prostrate bodies with a look of deep contempt on his face. "What do you want me to do with them?"

"You go too far." She stared at him in disbelief. He stood like a lord before them, his black eyebrows knitted together and his arms crossed over his chest. This again was another facet of the man. He was nothing more than a barbarian.

"Their behaviour was inexcusable. They will stay like that till tomorrow if you request it, without food or water!" he shouted.

"I do not request it. Please, *monsieur*, let them rise at once."

"You can tell them yourself. It will hurt them more to take an order from a woman." He spat the bitter words over their heads and one or two of the men flinched.

"I'll spare them that indignity. I want no part of it." She turned and hurried inside to calm her agitated feelings. She swore she could never like such a man. She heard the short sharp sound of his hands clapping, then, moments later, he joined her to stand beside her in the darkened hall, near enough to feel the still powerful charge of anger emanating from his body.

"You think I'm nothing more than an uncivilised monster, don't you?"

He was so close she could feel the little gasps of warm air from his mouth on the back of her neck.

"Yes. There's something cruel about you, and harsh. You frighten me." She shivered, afraid to turn to look into his eyes.

"I have my reasons." His voice flowed over her like honey now, soothing and reassuring. He took a step closer still; surely his lips were now only an inch from her throat.

"India is a dangerous place. I must have absolute control over my men and total obedience from them."

She turned suddenly to confront him. "What is it you do, Monsieur Sabran, that is so dangerous you need to keep a private army?"

The question shocked him at first, but he recovered quickly. "A private army?" he scoffed as he took her arm in his. "I play polo, madam, and, as you know, I always play to win."

Chapter 21

When Sara returned in the early evening, after lingering too long in Ravi Sabran's seductive garden, the hotel felt curiously silent and empty, and for this she was grateful, as she'd hoped to be able to slip back to her room without being seen. Then a door slammed when she was halfway up the stairs and the distraught manager burst out of his office wringing his hands, almost in tears.

"They have all gone, madam ..." he cried. "The ladies have gone ... because of the typhoid!"

It seemed that, despite his pleas, Lady Palmer and her daughter, their faces covered in handkerchiefs soaked in lavender oil and the carriage piled high with purchases from the French merchants, had left for Madras at noon, after hearing of an outbreak of typhoid in the town.

"They have left you a note, madam," he said as he handed it to her, unable to look in her eyes for fear of what her reaction might be.

He need not have worried. Instead of the anger he'd expected, Sara burst into wild derisive laughter as she read Lady Palmer's note.

"I cannot risk my daughter's health by waiting for you any longer. In any case, after seeing you in town in a native rickshaw, exposed to God knows what disease, for whatever foolish reason you may have, I have no choice but to leave you to find your own way back to Madras."

"There is something else, madam." The manager was encouraged by Sara's reaction to the letter to break the news without fear. "Our hotel is now in quarantine and you cannot leave. The doctor has just left. One of the servants is ill. You cannot leave, madam."

At breakfast a few days later, Sara found two letters waiting for her on her plate. One was from Charles. He spoke of his concern for her health, then, further down the page, a lecture for not having been at the hotel when Lady Palmer had decided to decamp.

"It seems you have been rightly punished for your continuing insistence on some absurd form of independence. Lady Palmer has also informed me of your encounter with Sabran, and frankly I am seriously displeased you chose to dance with him in a public place knowing how I would disapprove. My only consolation is knowing you are in quarantine and cannot receive visitors ..."

She didn't bother to read further but, in a wild, childish fit of anger, tore the letter to tiny pieces with trembling hands, all the while telling herself there must be a way, somehow, to be independent from him. The thought was momentous though, and she needed time.

Later, when she'd calmed down a little, she opened the other letter and found it to be from Ravi Sabran, telling her of his intention to visit her later that day, having just discovered she'd been left behind at the hotel. She smiled to herself. It was a constant source of wonderment how well informed he seemed to be about even the smallest piece of news.

"I blame myself entirely. If I hadn't persuaded you to stay longer, you would have left with the other ladies, and it is my duty now to entertain you."

She considered writing to tell him he would probably not be admitted to the hotel, then she realised Ravi Sabran was a law unto himself, and a mere matter of quarantine would not stop him visiting her if he wanted to.

When he found her later that evening, she was wandering alone through the lush hotel garden, pausing now and then to admire a bloom or to trail her fingers in the fountain. He stood back a while to watch her, knowing she was unconscious of his presence. Despite the stifling heat, he had never seen anyone so coolly unaffected, dressed as she was in a white silk gown gathered in a soft bow at her throat, though showing a hint of her slim arms and shoulders through the fine fabric.

For a moment he was struck by how absurdly English she appeared, but also so charmingly feminine. A wide black band decorated with a cluster of mauve velvet violets trimmed her small waist, and he remembered she was wearing a similar dress when he had seen her for the first time.

Though, with a sure instinct, he knew as he watched her straighten the delicate petals between her long slim fingers, she'd dressed then to please her husband, but now she'd dressed to please him.

That knowledge made him want to go to her and take her in his arms and tell her how lovely she was. He took a step towards her, then stopped when she looked up, her face in shade under her parasol so he couldn't see her expression.

She welcomed him with a finger on her lips, motioning him to be quiet. "You shouldn't be here, *monsieur*," she said in a severe voice. "Someone might see you, and it could be dangerous for you to come near me.

"Yes, it could be most dangerous for me if I go near you," he said, his voice softening. Then he added, "So I will keep my distance, for both our sakes."

She turned away from him, thrown into confusion by his words. "Well, since you're here, you might as well stay and amuse me."

She let herself relax back into a garden chair while she waved a painted silk fan before her flushed face. "I've been thinking how little I know about you, Monsieur Sabran. Tell me about yourself. Tell me about your family while we wait for tea."

He was silent as he admired the curve of her slim wrist as she gently flicked the fan through the still, humid air.

Then he dragged a chair as close to her as thought proper,

ignoring the warnings of contamination. He lit one of his fragrant cigarettes.

"Are you sure it would not bore you too much?"

"Boredom is not a word that springs to mind when I think of you, *monsieur*." She laughed.

It was on the tip of his tongue to ask her if she thought of him often, but instead he returned to the subject of his family. "My father has retired to the French countryside, where he has a vineyard; his poor health would not allow him to stay here any longer."

"Your mother is not with him?"

"My mother died when I was ten years old." His voice faltered as he changed position in his chair, while inhaling deeply of his cigarette, as though he wanted to crush an unpleasant thought.

"I'm sorry." She was shocked to see how affected he obviously still was at the mention of his mother.

"Her death is something I don't like to reflect upon." Then he turned to Sara, his eyes darker than ever. "You see ... she killed herself."

"Oh!" she gasped out loud and, without thinking, put out a hand to comfort him.

He leaped to his feet and began to pace before her, running his fingers through his long dark hair, his hypnotic eyes dark with pain. "Forgive me. I should not have told you."

"We are friends, are we not?"

"It is my place to amuse you, not burden you with my own demons."

"Please, continue."

He spoke as though wanting to get the unpleasantness over with as quickly as possible. "I was sent to the English school in Madras to be educated, and she couldn't bear to be parted from me. My father wanted me to become a gentleman, and he felt the British would do that. Even though he was French he admired them very much, mostly for their apparent self-control. I was a wild little boy and he wanted me to learn self-discipline.

It was while my father was in France she tried to see me at the school but they refused her. She waited outside the gates for days, till at last they drove her away with a beating. They wouldn't believe she was my mother, as she didn't speak English well. She went home and poisoned herself. I think the shame of the beating was too great for her, especially as she was from an aristocratic family. That, and knowing in her heart she could never be accepted by the society she found herself in."

"I'm so sorry." A slow stray tear ran down her cheek. "Your poor mother ... This country seems to encourage the most bitter of tragedies." She was so upset by his story she had great difficulty in maintaining control over her emotions, and only succeeded by twisting her handkerchief into knots.

They sat together without speaking for a few moments, then he rose to leave. "I'll come again tomorrow, if you'll let me."

"Yes, of course. I'll be free around five."

He raised a questioning eyebrow. "Free? I did not know there was anyone left in the hotel to socialise with, unless you count that rather dull parson who seems to be marooned

258

here with you as well." He nodded over his shoulder to where a middle-aged man was reading a newspaper under the shade of a mango tree, at the same time keeping a watchful eye on Sara and her guest.

She couldn't be certain, but she sensed a sudden alertness in Sabran's manner. Perhaps even a slight hint of jealousy.

"The poor man is not the least bit dull, and I'm very happy he's here with me. No, it's not a person who takes up my time, but an occupation. I have my writing to keep me busy."

"And may I ask what you are writing?"

"A series of stories about life in India. I thought, perhaps, as I find this country so fascinating, someone else may as well. You might find this odd, but I have a desire to be financially independent."

Her words were so wistful and her expression so darkened by a troubling thought, he knew now for certain there was a hidden strain on her marriage.

"I don't find it strange at all. You don't strike me as the type of woman who would be satisfied with the usual accepted pursuits of the English lady. There is something unawakened and restless about you. Perhaps writing is the answer."

As usual, his words prompted a sense of uneasiness in her, but she replied with her customary light, safe banter. "Be careful, *monsieur*. I may even write about you, with all the added flourishes that will make you irresistible to female readers."

"Added flourishes? I am insulted. Am I not enough as I am?" He held his arms out wide and smiled in a wry self-deprecating way.

"As to that, *monsieur*, it's not my place to say," she replied with the same wry manner, then laughed with an unguarded delight that illuminated her face. For a moment she looked into his eyes and held him, entranced by her own, till she seemed to rouse herself before looking away in confusion.

He was shaken by this fresh expression of her beauty, and for a moment he struggled to control his desire to cross the boundaries holding them apart and place himself in danger by declaring his admiration for her.

Just in time the waiter appeared with the tea tray, and this simple act of mundane activity dampened any lingering threat to his self-control.

All at once he leaped to his feet, his face grim. Then he bowed in her direction and began to walk away at an almost furious pace.

She called out, "But you haven't had your tea!"

Without looking back, he answered her over his shoulder. "I must go. Forgive me."

It seemed very lonely in the garden once he'd gone, till the parson, seeing she was alone, joined her and made polite conversation while she poured the tea, all the while wondering what had made Ravi Sabran leave so suddenly.

Chapter 22

He came the next evening at the same time, dressed as usual for his forays into the European world in an immaculate cream linen suit and fine straw hat. After an hour or so of light banter, where he was careful to keep the conversation in safe waters, he brought up the subject of her writing.

"I thought I might be of help to you, and it might amuse me also if you would read your work to me."

"I'm touched by your interest," she said, laughing, as she picked up the pages of her manuscript, "and I'll do my best to amuse you."

Her face softened into a smile as she ran her fingers over the cover. "Shall I begin?"

He nodded and leaned back in his chair, half closing his eyes so he could concentrate on the sound of her voice, but at the same time watching her attentively.

She began calmly as she spoke about the *rangoli*, the pretty patterns the Indian women made afresh each morning out of varicoloured dried lentils and grains or, when very poor, fine sand and pebbles, to place before their doorways in the hope of scaring off evil spirits and bringing good luck to the house. The women competed with each other to produce patterns of such intricate beauty it seemed sacrilegious to erase them every day ...

She looked up, not sure if he was listening or not, but even in repose he seemed alert, like a great cat feigning sleep but always on the watch for unwary prey.

Then she read on, her tone growing cynical.

"Sometimes it is difficult to be proud of being British, especially when faced with some of the antiquated codes of behaviour one is forced to endure as a member of this marooned race. The rules for women especially have been fixed at a time one hundred years ago and have been frozen in time since, though the rest of the modern world has moved on. In our little community we are presided over by the undisputed doyenne of Madras society, who dispenses judgements with the careless unconcern of an empress.

Her body is large though her brain is small, much like a mindless predator who greedily consumes everything in its path as its blundering right, then spits out the remains after not really having tasted anything ..."

She had to stop reading as Sabran was laughing so much.

"You must be careful," he said. "If I can identify her, others must, and she might do you some damage."

"Personally, I don't care but ..." Here she halted. Even now, after all the pain Charles had inflicted on her, she found it difficult to hurt him. "I suppose I must remain anonymous. That is, as long as I can rely on your discretion."

"Of course; it will be our secret."

She read on, trying to ignore Sabran's lazy smile and perplexing gaze, and at the same time wondering why she trusted him at all.

"... though there are many here who devote their time to helping the sick and homeless in any way they can. There are, however, the type of Englishmen who seem to take pleasure in acts of deliberate cruelty towards the natives. I know of someone who kicked his servant in the stomach with such force the man had to be taken to hospital, where he later died in agony ... It seems his spleen had ruptured. The courts found the servant to be insolent and only fined his master one thousand rupees, to be paid to the man's widow."

Her voice had begun to tremble at this point. She knew the man in question well; it was her husband's friend, George Perry, and her own husband had intervened personally in the case, as he'd said his friend had only acted in self-defence.

Sabran's eyes opened wide, alert to her words. He too knew of the case, and also of the public outrage at the court's decision.

"This is not quite what I expected ..."

"What did you expect?" she almost snapped at him. "That I would write about the difficulties of growing daisies in a

263

hot climate? Perhaps you might suggest I stick to more lady-like topics."

He was unused to people challenging him. And the fire in her eyes aroused him more than he liked, but now there was admiration of her intellect to add to the list of her charms.

Her presence began to seriously trouble him, and he made a pact that he would stay away from her. He would seek his revenge on Charles Fitzroy in a different way, a less complicated way.

But he couldn't stay away.

He always came at the same time and after an hour or so where they each cleverly avoided any topic which might ignite any intimacy, she would pick up her manuscript and continue from where she'd left off the day before.

He always listened with care to the words, though every now and then he halted her to make a comment on the eccentricities of the English language or exclaimed out loud in outraged French at the injustices being endured by the characters in her stories. Sometimes it was difficult for her not to laugh at him, so involved had he become in the story, though every now and then she caught him not listening to her words but looking at her through half closed eyes with a curious expression on his face.

It never failed to unnerve her and she would stumble over the lines, or suddenly snap the pages shut as a sign she had read enough.

Later, alone in her room at night, she would reproach herself for enjoying his company too much. It was impossible to think ill of him while he was so kind to her, telling herself that surely all the gossip about him was a lie. There was no sign of the cruelty she'd seen fire up in his eyes on the day she'd visited him and he'd exacted revenge on his guards for their contempt of her.

Though there was a side to him that was a mystery to her. Once, while she was reading to him, a messenger came hurrying into the hotel garden to whisper in his ear. He stood and excused himself at once, saying he would not return the next day.

When he did appear after a few days he was more silent than usual, his face strained and almost grim, and though he tried to hide it with his usual gallantries, it seemed his concentration was elsewhere.

Later, when at last the fear of contamination was over, he came to say goodbye before she returned to Madras.

She stood before him in her travelling clothes, torn between feeling relief at the prospect of being freed from the sphere of his charm and regret at leaving her oasis of peace.

"Well, then," she said as she struggled to keep her voice under control, "will you write to me about Prema? Perhaps this time to the post office, so I can pick up the letters myself and there's no danger of them being lost."

"Of course, madam."

He seemed unable to look in her eyes, then, as she was about to climb into the carriage to take her to the train station, he moved close to her for the first time in weeks, as though with her leaving there would be no chance of her touch igniting what he hoped was a past desire.

"Thank you ... Thank you, for a most peaceful interlude. It is as though I have been in an *ashram*." Then he took her hand and kissed it and, did she imagine it, as he held it to his lips, then quickly brush his warm cheek upon it?

She snatched her hand away and stood back from him, rubbing her hand behind her back at the spot where he'd kissed it, as though to neutralise the effect it had upon her.

She hurried away, trying to ignore the almost painful sensation in her chest. She was angry with him, but even angrier with herself.

'A peaceful interlude', was how he thought of their time together. It seemed she was the only one who'd found their shared experience both pleasurable and unsettling.

She told herself what a fool she'd been. In a way she was glad of his indifference, it made it so much easier for her to return to Madras, and to her husband, despite her unwillingness to do so.

Chapter 23

At first she thought about telling Charles everything, then she decided there would be no point. He was still angry with her for having danced with Sabran in a public place while deliberately defying Lady Palmer, when she must have known he would object. In any case, she didn't really believe it was any of her husband's business. She told herself she had committed no crime and had a clear conscience, despite a faint nagging twinge of guilt.

She was relieved to find, though, his questions about her trip were brief and distracted, freeing her of the pressure to have to lie, as lie she must, but it seemed he had more important matters on his mind.

A week had passed since her return, and it appeared her marriage was entering an almost happy phase; he had missed her, and some of his former charm had returned, making her believe there was hope for their marriage after all. He agreed to let Malika come and stay for short visits and had even welcomed the old woman kindly when she was finally coaxed away from Sabran's house for a day or two. He seemed determined to do what he could to please his wife and for those small mercies Sara was pleased.

She had even begun to think she could safely tell him about her visit to Sabran's home without any serious consequences.

Most of all she wanted to be truthful with him, so when they were having lunch she began, taking a deep breath, "Charles ... while I was in Pondi ..."

He didn't hear her; he was staring straight ahead, deep in thought, though every now and again he turned his attention back to his plate, attacking his food, sawing at it with unnecessary ferocity. Before she could finish, he interrupted her with a curse, threw down his fork with such violence it bounced off the table then landed on the floor where Shakur, who was standing behind his master's chair, hurried to retrieve it.

"If only I can prove it's him ... but so far he's managed to keep one step ahead of us."

"Is something wrong?"

"That half-caste mongrel, Sabran, of course ..."

A thin shiver of hate towards her husband ran down her back. "I wish you wouldn't speak that way about him, or any human being, for that matter."

He shook his head as though she needed to be humoured. "You know nothing about this man ... and what he's capable of."

With extra caution Shakur placed a clean fork on the table, then hurried away to watch the unfolding scene from behind the door.

"He's behind this armed opposition to tax collecting, I'm

sure of it. So far, there've been no casualties, but I won't tolerate it."

"But surely, it's not the time to be pressing people to pay taxes ... what with the famine ..."

"And this is not the time to be forcing your rather revolutionary notions on me. This is the last straw, though. It was enough that I forgave you over the dancing business. You can never visit that child again and I'll consider it an act of treachery if you do."

"And I have no say in the matter?"

"Not in this ... no."

She hardly heard him when he spoke again. "By the way, we're expected for dinner tonight at Lady Palmer's."

Sara pushed her plate away, her appetite gone. "I don't want to go. Perhaps it isn't safe for me to go out in society yet."

He was unmoved. "I've been looking forward to it."

"I don't feel very well. It's better I stay home."

It was true; she wasn't feeling as well as she had when she was in Pondicherry. The old feelings of faint nausea and headache had returned, leaving grey shadows under her eyes and a new pallor to her skin.

"If Lady Palmer wants us to attend, we must; there's an end to it."

"Really, Charles, is it so very important? Tell them I have a headache."

"I'll do no such thing. You'll enjoy it when you get there."

"I won't. I loathe their parties."

He softened then, seeing her pale, almost pinched face. "Please, darling, do this one thing for me. It's important. I'm sorry I spoke to you that way. Forgive me. I'm under a lot of pressure at the moment ... And wear something pretty, darling, something bright to give you a bit of colour. You know, a wife can work wonders for her husband when it comes to promotion. You can employ your many charms on Lord Palmer, as you do me."

He threw down his napkin and went to her, kissing her almost tenderly.

"It's time you got to know one another."

"What if he doesn't like me? The rest of his family don't."

"Don't be silly, they love you, and of course he'll like you; make him like you. It's the least you can do for me."

Charles's words were of no use. She didn't care if Lord Palmer liked her or not. She had rarely met a more unpleasant man. Even so, she made the customary polite effort to be civil.

"How long have you lived in Madras, Lord Palmer?"

He was a small man, at least two inches shorter than his wife, though he pushed his barrel chest out aggressively in an effort to make himself appear bigger. Sara had found herself alone with him and had made an effort to open the conversation. He'd shown no signs of doing so and the silence was painful, at least for her. He seemed content to stare ahead and grunt every now and then while taking large gulps from his brandy balloon.

"Thirty years this monsoon and, if you ask me, that's thirty years too long." He threw back his brandy while rocking back and forth on his rather small feet.

"Oh! Then you might remember my parents ... I've been longing to talk to someone about them. You see, I've only just discovered the name he used here ... My father was William Radcliffe."

"Radcliffe?" He stared at her for a moment with his mouth hanging open.

"Radcliffe? Of course, I remember now ... died in the typhoid epidemic of sixty-five ... or was it sixty-six? Bad business that. You're not his daughter, are you?"

His face had turned bright red, and he coughed two or three times as he played with his necktie.

"It appears so," she said, shaken by his manner.

"I thought your maiden name was Archer?"

"Well, yes, it was. That is, my father was an Archer as well ... but he changed his name to Radcliffe, for reasons I can't say."

"Radcliffe? Radcliffe's daughter?" He examined her features once more. Then a look of pure distaste came into his eyes. The intense scrutiny was crudely done and without any concern for her feelings.

At last he gave her a stiff little bow and stepped back a little, just a little, but enough for her to feel uncomfortable.

"Of course, I didn't get the connection when Cynthia said Charles had married a Miss Archer."

This time there was no escaping his change of attitude towards her. Sara felt a rising discomfort.

He scanned her features again, his small eyes narrowing. "Yes ... you are very like him. I remember him quite well ..." His voice was cold now.

"You knew my father? How wonderful!" She couldn't hide her delight, despite his manner. "Oh, please tell me something about them ... anything ... you see, I was sent away when they died ..."

"Yes, yes of course."

He had decided he didn't like her, and she knew it was because of her father. She could see that clearly now, though she would not be put off and she persisted. "It would mean so much to me."

"Perhaps I'm not the right person to talk to. You see, often we didn't see eye to eye about things ..."

"Oh ..."

"Your father was a very unusual man ... He took a keen interest in the community, especially the Indian community." He spoke the word "Indian" with a tinge of contempt. "He stirred up feelings a bit around here, and not everyone agreed with all that he said and did. Set him apart a bit, talked a lot of nonsense."

Sara faltered. "What nonsense?"

"He was of the old school, from the days when relations with the Indians was actually encouraged ... Soft on intermarriage ... That's all done with these days, thank God. We got nothing for it but a lot of half-caste brats ... and in the end he paid for it too, with his life."

"I don't know what you mean." She too drew herself away a little, her anger rising.

"All those cursed Indians he had visiting the house ... He probably caught the disease off them ..."

He pulled his watch out of his pocket and glanced at it, before looking around the room, making it clear he wished to be elsewhere.

Sara didn't care; she hated him now and wanted nothing more than to be as far away from him as possible. Even so, she asked one more question.

"And my mother; do you remember her?"

"We didn't really move in the same circles. Never met her, I'm afraid. Now, if you'll excuse me." He gave her another stiff little bow and hurried away.

She watched him as he joined Cynthia and Charles on the terrace. He welcomed his daughter with an affectionate smile and Charles with a friendly pat on the back. It made a pleasant family scene, though he looked at Charles for a moment before glancing back at Sara, his face showing an odd mixture of pained displeasure and curiosity, then he turned away, leaving her feeling abandoned and alone amongst Lady Palmer's many guests.

"Whatever did you say to Lord Palmer?" Charles asked when they arrived back home at last.

She flung herself, exhausted, in a chair and kicked off her shoes.

"What do you mean?"

"Well, he wanted to know all about you, where we met and all that ... who was your aunt et cetera ... Of course, I assured him your background was impeccable."

While gritting her teeth she tore the pins from her hair, longing to throw them across the room. She was preoccupied with what Lord Palmer had said about her parents. What had they done to make him react in such a way?

"What a snob you are, Charles. What would you do if you discovered my background wasn't so impeccable? Throw me out in the street to beg?"

"Well, I know it is, so the occasion will never arise." He laughed as he kissed her on the back of her neck.

There was a discreet knock on the bedroom door and Malika's gentle voice called out, "Madame do you need help with your gown?"

His face changed colour at once. He fixed his gaze hard on the back of the door, his eyes bulging. "No, she does not! Go away!" he shouted, almost trembling with rage.

"Please, Charles, everyone will hear." Sara opened the door a crack and saw the old woman crouching in the hallway, unsure what to do.

"Go to bed, Malika," she whispered, "I don't need you tonight."

He came up behind her and shut the door with a loud bang. "Whatever possessed you to bring her here? Her eyes are everywhere."

"Because you said she may come. She will only stay a day or two."

"That's a mercy at least. Send her back as soon as you can. I can't bear her creeping about.

"'Well, she will be 'creeping about', as you put it, every now and then. I've been banned from visiting her because you don't trust me outside of my home so she must come here. Or have you forgotten?"

For a moment it seemed he might flare into anger again, then he calmed himself a little. "All right, there's no need to make a fuss!"

Then, still glaring at the door as if it might suddenly burst open, he mixed himself another nightcap from the sideboard and drank it down fast, before turning to Sara to unlace her corset. She could tell by the look in his eyes he wanted her, and she hurried to hide her nakedness with her dressing gown.

In a sudden rush, he pushed her back on the bed and pressed his wet, whisky-smelling mouth on hers. She froze at once, turning her face away and wiping her mouth with the back of her hand.

"Really, Charles, I wish you wouldn't drink so much; it turns you into a beast."

He stood up, angry with her now. "I've been meaning to ask why you don't show any signs of having a child yet. You are all right, aren't you?"

She didn't look up at first but rubbed at an ugly imprint of his fingers he'd left on her arm. She wouldn't be able to wear short sleeves till it faded.

"I don't think it's unusual."

"Well, if it doesn't happen soon, you'd better see a doctor."

He began to take his clothes off to get into bed with her, and her stomach revolted at the thought of it.

Her voice came muffled from the pillow where she'd turned away from him.

"I want to sleep alone tonight. You hurt me, and I don't want you here."

At first it seemed he might fly into a rage, but his words were cold and calculated as he stood over her. "You know I could divorce you for that!"

She lay still till she heard the door slam behind her, then she jumped up and turned the key in the lock, relieved to be alone at last.

After sleeping late, she woke to find he'd left a letter saying he'd decided to join his friends from the club on a tiger shoot and would be away for at least a week. A wild uncontrolled thought came into her head.

She had a sudden urge to flee, anywhere, as long as she could escape him. She rushed to the secret cash box she kept in her drawer and found it empty of everything but a note.

"Try not to leave money about, my dear. You know what thieves the servants are."

Chapter 24

It was while Charles was away that she met with Ravi Sabran again. She'd been wandering through the maze of little shops and silk warehouses lining the narrow, forbidden laneways of Blacktown and had been lured inside her favourite store by the owner, Mr Chandran, who promised her a refreshing tea and the sight of a special bale of rich green silk newly arrived from Pakistan.

"To suit your beautiful hair, madam," he said in his high sing-song voice. "The silk was woven with you in mind."

An Indian lady had taken a long chestnut strand out of its chignon to match the colour against the fabric when Ravi Sabran came into the warehouse, as usual surrounded by his gang of courtiers.

"Mrs Fitzroy, I beg your pardon." He clapped his hands and his men scattered. It was almost as though he'd broken into a harem, so strong was the reaction. Then she realised it was the sight of her hair unbound before strange men that was considered to be so improper.

She began to feel it was improper herself and hurried to push the vagrant strand back into her neat chignon. Then she looked up to face him but couldn't meet his gaze, and he too seemed shaken by their encounter.

When he found his tongue at last, his voice was more than usually husky, as though the words were sticking in his throat. "You must buy the silk. It is as Mr Chandran says, and woven with you in mind."

"I think perhaps the weaver had someone in mind with more money than I." She laughed, fighting desperately to regain her composure.

"Even so, you must have it."

He ran his fingers over the silk, then frowned and dropped it, as though being reminded of something unpleasant.

The ritual of the pouring of the tea stemmed the flow of conversation till Chandran broke the uneasy silence. "Ah, *monsieur*! Your suit is ready." He snapped his fingers at his assistant. "Go and get Mr Sabran's suit."

Chandran grinned as he looked from one to the other, quickly assessing the tension in the air and smiling to himself. It was unusual to see the great Ravi Sabran thrown into confusion.

"Ah! *Monsieur*, you know our most charming Mrs Fitzroy?"

Sabran made an effort, though his voice was soft and almost hoarse.

"Yes, we have met before, many times."

She knew instinctively he was affected by her presence after all, and that knowledge made her heart jump in a peculiar way. She avoided his eyes; it was too dangerous.

When she found her voice again it was light and careless. She returned to the safety of more conventional topics. "And how do you find this weather, *monsieur*? I thought you said nothing would make you return to Madras."

"Unfortunately, despite the fact that all the tailors in Pondicherry are French, I cannot find anyone I admire nearly as much as my old friend Chandran, and since I consider a well-tailored suit one of the chief necessities of life, I sacrifice my discomfort in favour of style."

He shrugged his shoulders in a very French way and smiled.

"I don't believe you." She laughed. "I know you're not quite as frivolous as you like to pretend."

"I have business in Madras, of course, but there is something else pressing." He turned and captured her with his dark gaze. She felt herself being drawn towards him, unable to pull away. He smiled very briefly, a strange smile, difficult to read. She thought perhaps he might be laughing at her, and it was enough to break the spell.

"I really should go." She rose to her feet, her heart pounding. His presence was too unsettling, and she wanted to be alone to steady her thoughts. "I've been here too long already."

He put a hand up to halt her. "No, stay for a moment. There's something I want to discuss with you."

She sat down again, almost grateful to put off her leaving, and waited while he took a mouthful of tea.

"It concerns the child."

"Prema? Is she ill?"

"No, no, not ill. As I said, Maya is most affected by the child, seeing her as an omen of sorts, and she has insisted I consult my astrologer regarding her. He has chosen the eighteenth of this month as an auspicious day for a birthday celebration. Does this suit you? Can you come to the house?"

She looked at him, her eyes wide. "The eighteenth? This is May is it not?"

"It is."

"Then, as usual, *monsieur*, you have managed to astound me. The eighteenth of May is my birthday also."

A cloud of concern crossed his face. "It cannot be."

After his first reaction his tone was fatalistic. It was almost as though he was thinking aloud. He ran his fingers through his black hair, at the same time pressing his forehead hard with the palm of his hand as though he was trying to crush an unwanted thought.

"We must accept it. I have consulted the Brahmins and that is the date they chose. It is most strange."

She laughed at this. "Why are you so concerned? It's only a coincidence, unusual, yes, but still only a coincidence."

"Because now it is clear to me, once and for all, that Prema is an omen. She was meant to cross your path and mine, for good or ill. Now you must come to her birthday. You are meant to come."

She watched him for a moment before replying. "It may not be possible."

She thought of Charles and his words of warning: "You know nothing about this man ... and what he's capable of," and, worst of all, "You can never visit that child again and I'll consider it an act of treachery if you do."

She looked up and saw his eyes contemplating her. There was nothing in his expression that spoke of pity, but she felt, somehow, he knew what it would cost her to agree.

She rose to leave. "I will see you on the eighteenth."

Even as she said the words she knew the repercussions of openly defying Charles, but at the same time she felt it was fundamentally unfair of him to impose such a sanction upon her. It struck her how trivial his demands were, compared to carrying out a dying man's wish, and she would stand up to him and take the consequences of her actions willingly, even if it meant the end of her marriage. A shadow of emotion swept over her then as she now realised how much she longed for her marriage to be over. Up to that moment she hadn't really dared to seriously consider such an event could actually happen.

"Madam?" Sabran was watching her, puzzled by her silence as well as the expression on her face.

"Forgive me, *monsieur*. I was deep in thought."

He kissed her hand and, as he did so, he looked up at her with veiled eyes and, as usual, his look was inscrutable.

Chapter 25

She was alone in the wooded grove sheltering the tombstones of her family, as Sabran, seeing the flowers she'd brought to place on the graves, had retreated on some pretext of business inside the house.

Slipping into the past once more, she saw herself as a child on birthdays long ago, when she would wake earlier than usual, to be bathed and dressed in her best white muslin in readiness for the unique favour granted her only twice a year, at Christmas and on her birthday. Her parents climbed the nursery stairs and joined her in her special breakfast of banana pancakes sprinkled with sugar.

How different was her life now; it seemed there was so little laughter, so few moments of happiness.

A chorus of frenzied screeching from the tamarind tree above her head snapped her back into consciousness. A chattering group of wild monkeys were watching her with hard red eyes, swinging on the branches with what seemed like menacing intent. She knew they were waiting to snatch the offerings of bananas and rice Malika had left at the little shrine of Shiva she had placed before the headstones.

She stood rigid with fear, knowing they could be rabid and their bite fatal. But in an instant one of the larger monkeys swung down before her and crouched a few feet away with bared teeth. She remained completely still, not knowing what to do, but the small timid act of moving one foot backwards enraged the rest of the tribe into action. They hung suspended from the branches, gibbering or leaping to the ground, surrounding her, stamping on the spot or making crazed threatening forays to where her dress swept the ground, snatching at her hem with long spider-like fingers before retreating a safe distance to jeer.

She was reminded of the irony of her situation. It was rare to find herself alone in India, and yet when she longed for the comforting presence of another human being she waited in vain. There was silence in the garden and, except for a soft chattering coming from the house, not another soul was in sight.

A loud screech from the monkey before her made her jump. There was something strange about its behaviour and Sara panicked, thinking perhaps it did have rabies and had gone mad. The rest of the tribe fell silent and moved away to watch from a distance. Then she saw the creature was nursing the ragged corpse of her dead baby. Every now and then the mother groomed the little rotting body and pieces of matted fur came off in her hands. She seemed to be puzzling over this great tragedy while looking up at Sara with eyes mad from grief. Sara shivered in the heat. It was as though the creature could see through to her soul.

A faint noise behind her broke the spell, and with wild screams of outrage the monkeys fled.

She turned her head to see a girl standing alone on the terrace steps. At first Sara thought she was an illusion, her nerves were so tested by her encounter with the monkeys. The girl wore a gold sari, the silk so fine it floated around her exquisite form in the gentle breeze from the sea. Above her glistening almond eyes, strands of fine pearls and precious stones hung over her forehead and around her perfect creamy neck.

She was a living, breathing statue of the goddess Parvati, a fitting consort to Shiva, god of love.

The appearance of Sabran on the terrace brought the moment back to earth. The apparition smiled as he held out a hand towards her, and he in turn gazed enraptured at the face before him. He led the goddess down the steps and, as the girl came closer, Sara saw she had pale green eyes, in India a sign of the highest beauty, and in a well born girl more valued than white skin. The girl dropped to her knees, while holding both of her hands to her forehead. "Welcome, madam."

"No, please don't." Sara put out a hand to raise her.

"You are Maya, are you not? I've seen you once before, and have never forgotten how lovely you are."

The girl shook her head and laughed, showing her perfect teeth. She spoke in halting broken English, as though she had practised for some time.

"You are very beautiful, madam ..."

Sabran smiled. "It seems you please each other."

He escorted them both to a bower under a tree, adorned with a rich Turkish carpet and scattered silken cushions, where Sara was asked to take her seat in a carved wooden chair that had once been her mother's favourite. She ran her fingers over the wood; there was a carving of a rose, with the tendrils creeping up the arms of the chair. She smiled when she remembered her own childish fingers tracing the pattern when her mother was alive. For a moment she was almost overwhelmed with sadness for what she had lost, and a large tear escaped down her cheek. She wiped it away, hoping no one had seen her, then, looking up, she caught him watching her.

She was determined not to ruin the day with sorrow, so she smiled almost gaily at him through her tears. "How beautiful they have made it, how very beautiful!"

He smiled in return, relieved, and took his place next to her, while Maya, rejecting a western chair with a girlish laugh, curled up by his side.

He clapped his hands to signal the beginning of the proceedings and at once the musicians began their intoxicating plaintive sound, spinning a web around the senses and banishing any remaining ghosts of the past.

Champagne appeared before them, offered by a servant dressed in the whitest of linens adorned with a scarlet sash and turban.

"This is from my father's winery. It's very good, I think. You will share a bottle with me?"

She laughed. "I feel I must."

Maya waved it away with a flutter of her tiny hand, but

she made encouraging signs to Sara to accept. She whispered in Sabran's ear and he translated her words.

"'Your pleasure will be my pleasure'." Then he took the girl's hand and kissed her fingers. His eyes only briefly glanced into hers, but Sara could see the understanding between them. She had to turn away, so intense was their passion. Her heart twisted within her, and a pang very like jealousy threatened to ruin her happiness.

Sabran turned to Sara and raised his glass. "To everything you wish for on this happy day, and for every day of your life!"

It was a generous toast and she was grateful for it, and it made her birthday special. She realised too the lavish arrangements were more for her than for Prema, and because of that she was thrown into confusion. It was plain he wanted to impress her, but for what reason? He had introduced her to his lover, and had shown her by his every deed how much he loved Maya, so he clearly was not carrying a secret passion for her. It was all very confusing.

The champagne held the perfume of violets from the south of France, and after drinking the first glass it was as if she was in a dream.

The sea beyond the garden wall rolled over the stony beach, making a sound like a deep sigh, and unconsciously she sighed aloud with it. Sabran turned to stare at her and gave her a look so searching she felt as though her every thought was exposed to him. For a brief dazzling moment nothing else existed; it was as though she had found herself in a magical land that could disappear in an instant.

Then the sharp clap of hands brought her back to reality. An ayah appeared and placed Prema beside her with strict instructions to be on her best behaviour.

Sara picked up the child and placed her on her lap, whispering, "Perhaps Monsieur Sabran is right, and your life will be as lucky as he says he is." The child smiled up at her, completely fearless now.

Servants appeared as silent as wraiths, carrying dishes of every kind: delicious breads stuffed with freshly made cottage cheese, fruit and nuts, plates of saffron rice piled high, bowls of *dhal*, fish in a rich spicy coconut sauce, each one more fantastic than the last. Maya watched as each dish was placed before them, scanning the plates, her eyes sharp now, on the watch for any flaw in the perfection.

Sabran ate with his fingers in the Indian manner, feeling the food sensuously and spooning it into his mouth with obvious enjoyment.

Sara watched, fascinated, longing to do the same but unable to do so. She felt almost silly having to use the dainty silver fork placed before her. After the mostly bland flavours from her own kitchen she ate almost with abandon.

Sabran watched her as she piled more food on her plate. "I have never seen an English lady enjoy our food so much."

"You forget." She spoke with her mouth full. "I was weaned on this food. You don't know how much I've missed it."

"What is wrong with your cook?" he asked. "If he is no good you can have one of mine."

She laughed at the simplicity of his solution. For a moment

she thought he was joking, then realised that he was perfectly sincere.

"Oh, it's not Mutu, he's a very good cook, that is, as long as it's Indian food, but it disagrees with my husband's stomach," she lied, and she could see at once by his look, he knew it.

A plate of small golden puffs of pastry accompanied by a fragrant sauce was placed before them with particular deference.

"Ah!" he said. "This is special!"

With a deft gesture he pushed his thumb into the pastry and ladled a spoonful of the fragrant sauce into it.

Maya moved closer to Sabran, tilting back her beautiful head in a swanlike movement and parting her lips while he dropped the morsel in her mouth. Sara watched, fascinated, but then wished she hadn't. It was as though she was spying on a couple making love. His hand lingered for a moment on the creamy throat as with great tenderness he brushed a stray strand of hair away. It was just a moment, but it spoke a thousand words. Sara again experienced a deep bolt of pain, a sensation so strong her head swam. She knew she would never experience that passion with Charles, and she couldn't bear it.

Maya clapped her hands and out of nowhere a group of dancers sprang before them, though they danced only for Sabran; his presence seemed to command nothing less. They encircled him, seducing him with the movements of their long golden fingers, their jewelled feet beating the hard ground in time with the drums, sensuous hips encircled with garlands of flowers, their movements compelling and intoxicating.

He received their acclaim as his due, showing hardly a trace of emotion or pleasure, just a contented half smile and a faint flicker of interest from his heavy-lidded eyes.

The music took on a life of its own, with both the dancers and the musicians in a trance, imbuing the very air with the deep and primitive pulse of life. When it seemed the feverish pitch couldn't be maintained a moment longer, the music halted, giving the cue for the dancers to throw handfuls of white flowers into the air. The flowers hung suspended for a brief moment, then fell to the ground in a white fragrant carpet.

Sabran looked at Sara and smiled, transporting her back to the night in Pondicherry when they had danced in each other's arms. She could tell by the expression in his eyes he too was thinking of that night, and he turned away hastily after glancing in Maya's direction.

At the sound of strange voices from the outer courtyard, Maya leapt to her feet, covering her beautiful face with her sari before bowing briefly at Sara and retreating. She flew through the garden as fragile as a butterfly, in a cloud of golden silk. Only the lingering fragrance of her perfume remained as evidence she had not been conjured from a dream.

Sabran tore his eyes away from the vision and turned to Sara, his voice matter-of-fact now, as though determined to keep her at arm's length.

"We have visitors. The Brahmins will give a blessing."

Sara rose to leave, anxious not to be seen before strangers, but Sabran raised a hand to stop her. "I want you to stay."

He was so insistent she remained beside him, despite her misgivings.

"I want you to know what kind of man I am. I want you to see me as my world sees me, and not as the British see me. I know it's rumoured I'm a corrupt man, but it's not true; they say that because they are jealous of my wealth. They think it should be theirs and would like very much to take it off me."

A crowd of men, richly dressed, stood in a silent group and one by one came forward to fall on the ground prostrate before him. Sabran's hand, held out like an emperor, was clutched in a fervent blessing, then held briefly to the forehead, before each man was raised to his feet and blessed in return.

Costly gifts were laid at his feet, while lengths of cashmere and woven gold were thrown over his shoulders, then swept away almost at once to make room for another. An enormous pile of shawls of varying beauty and richness grew at his feet, then, at the snap of his fingers, they were carried away out of sight.

Sara whispered to him, "Why do they do this?"

He shrugged his shoulders. "They are representatives of my various charities. They do this as a sign of respect to me."

He lifted his chin with great pride. He was a powerful man and he knew it. He also knew to show any sign of humble gratitude would be misconstrued as weakness.

His expression took on the quality of an idol, impenetrable

and remote, way above the concerns of ordinary mortals, making Sara feel very small, ordinary and colourless.

There was a distance between them she felt she could never hope to cross and, despite all her resolutions not to be affected by him, the thought depressed her. A cold feeling of isolation overtook her despite the heat, and the ever-present curious eyes began to oppress her. She was aware, too, of being watched from the upstairs windows.

She caught sight of Maya, looking down at her from behind a silk curtain, before retreating into the shadows of her self-imposed prison. It was only a brief glance, but enough to see Maya regarded her as a threat. Her look, though, was not of jealousy or hatred, but of sad resignation. As though, whatever the relationship was between Sara and Sabran, she was power-less to do anything about it.

When it came time for her to leave, Maya appeared to be as charming as ever, though the deep sadness behind her lovely eyes remained. She blessed Sara with tears in her eyes before floating from the room in her cloud of golden silk. An intense feeling of reproach flooded Sara's consciousness as she realised with startling clarity how delicate the girl was, and how she must be protected from pain at all cost.

Some of Maya's mood had filtered through to Sabran as well, and his eyes followed her with a marked anxiety.

When he turned to Sara he was almost grim, his manner more removed than ever. He was treating her differently, remote but very polite. "You must come to visit us again ..." He held her hand while he scanned her face with his dark impenetrable gaze. "It's pleasant for me to talk with an educated woman who is familiar with my European side ... You know you are my only English friend."

He clapped his hands and a servant rushed forward carrying a huge package.

"I want you to take this small gift. You will see how small it is."

"I can't ... No, it's impossible. You have given me so much already."

"You're being English again." He laughed. "You don't understand what a pleasure it is for me to give presents and, anyway, it's an insult to refuse me."

"It seems to me, *monsieur*, that being from two cultures has advantages; you can plead custom at whim."

He clapped his hands. The servant tore off the wrapping and threw down before her a long bale of the green silk she had so admired. He flicked the end so a great length of it rose high into the air and floated for a moment on the breeze.

She was blinded by the beauty of the moment, but managed to find her voice at last. "I can't take it. You must know a lady would never accept a present from a gentleman who is not her husband."

"In our culture a gift of silk is something a brother may give to a sister; it is impossible for you to refuse."

She felt the material as though in a dream. The lovely green silk was a present from a brother to a sister. Why, then, when she looked into his eyes, she didn't believe him?

Chapter 26

She left the house like a child leaving a party, tired, but glutted with conflicting sensations, unwilling to let the day die.

When she returned at last to her little mock Tudor house, she decided to order a special meal, even venturing into the kitchen to see to the preparations, knowing she was breaking all the rules by invading the servants' special domain. But she braved Mutu's sulky looks and the curious stares of Lakshmi. Nothing could crush the party atmosphere of her day, wanting it to linger so she could share what was left of it with Charles.

Since returning from his tiger shoot, he had again been very contrite, saying he'd missed her desperately and would be careful not to drink so much in future. He'd again turned back into the charming young man she had at first become engaged to, at least on the surface.

But always there was a tension, as though at any time he might give way to one of his frightening outbursts and destroy what gains they had made in their relationship.

She sat in the shade of the veranda to wait for him, wearing the thick gold bracelet he had given her that morning for her birthday. She had decided once and for all to tell him of her day with Prema. It wasn't in her nature to be dishonest, and she was suffering from a faint feeling of guilt for not having told him her plans before he'd left for the day. But they had had such a happy morning celebrating her birthday together, she was unwilling to ruin it with the sure threat of an argument.

It was the bewitching hour, the time before sunset when the birds settled after a final flurry of bickering before the evening light faded.

All in the house and garden were calm and the servants were taking a short nap before serving the evening meal. Everyone except Malika was asleep, but the old woman found it hard to give up her daily tasks, even though Sara encouraged her to rest as often as possible.

Malika's visits had become more frequent now, and she often only returned to her old home for a day or so to dust the rooms and put fresh flowers on the graves. She knew she was for some in the house unwelcome, but in her mind Sara was still the little girl who had been torn from her arms long ago and who now needed protection, from who or what it was unclear. But, with the instinct of a mother, she sensed something in the house that threatened the happiness of the child she saw as her own and she would do her best to guard her from it.

Now she moved through the garden, enjoying the close of the day while sprinkling handfuls of water over the dust, her red and gold sari a glorious splash of colour against the green of the plants. The pungent smell of damp earth mingled with the scent of flowers, rising up and catching Sara in the back of the throat. Sara watched as a bright blue kingfisher hovered on a pawpaw tree heavily burdened with ripe orange fruit, dripping with juice. The bird's iridescent wings gleamed like the silk hidden in her bottom drawer and, even though she felt a flash of guilt, she knew she could never tell Charles where it came from.

She wanted the rest of her birthday to be unmarred by argument. She hugged herself. Why was she so joyous? She felt almost like a child again. Her heart went out to the beauty of the world around her and she felt she could spend the rest of her life in India, gorgeous, wild and absurd India.

When at last Charles opened the gate in the little picket fence and came up the path she rose to her feet, an eager smile on her lips.

"You're home at last …"

"Yes."

Her smile died on her face as he strode past her into the house, making straight for the brandy cabinet. He took a glass and was about to pour a drink when he noticed a faint smear around the rim. He called angrily to Shakur.

Shakur came into the room at a snail's pace, his face fixed into a stiff, unhappy grin as he smoothed his clothes and tidied his hair. Sara felt for him as he stood with his head bowed. He knew he was in for a storm and he stood as limp as the flowers on the lawn outside the window, preparing to weather it, only hoping the inevitable tongue-lashing would not be too severe.

There was something sad and touching about his appearance. He was wearing one of his master's cast-off shirts and the sleeves were too long as well as being frayed about the cuffs and collar. He loved the shirt so much and had it washed so often it was almost in tatters.

"What is your job in this house, Shakur?" Charles asked coldly.

"To look after you, *sahib*"

"Do you think giving me a dirty glass is part of that job?"

Shakur stared at his feet. "No, *sahib*."

"I should have you thrown out to beg ... There are plenty of others who would be only too glad to take your place ..."

Charles paced back and forth, holding the glass up to the light, savouring his words and enjoying their full impact.

Shakur fell to floor, lying prostrate, his voice muffled with fear.

"Oh, please, sir ..."

Sara could only watch and wonder at the change in the person she'd once thought she loved. The blue eyes she had once thought so attractive now seemed mean and cold, and even cruel.

"Shakur has been very busy today; he's been doing some things for me ..."

Charles turned on her, his face white and pinched. She realised then, his anger was not for Shakur but for herself.

"Is something the matter?" She raised her chin, hoping to stare him down.

"Is something the matter?" he echoed. Then, remembering Shakur on the floor at his feet, he spat, "Get out!"

Charles watched, unbending, as Shakur almost crawled out of the room and shut the door. Then he turned his cold wrath towards Sara.

"And how was your day?"

"I went into town."

"You did nothing else?" His face was close to hers, threatening and ugly, so close she could see the little beads of perspiration on his upper lip and smell the brandy on his breath.

At first she thought of lying to protect herself from his wrath, then her rebellious spirit surged within her as she was overwhelmed with the injustice of her situation. She glared back. "Yes, I went to see Prema as it was her birthday! I was going to tell you, and I would have this morning if you weren't so unreasonable!"

The skin around his throat turned a deep red as his temper rose. "So, your interest in an Indian brat was enough for you to throw all sense of decorum to the winds ... to defy all I've said about you visiting that man ...?"

"Why should it matter? I wasn't alone with him ... and even if I was alone with him ... what would it matter?" She busied herself with tidying the books on the piano, hoping such an everyday action would somehow calm him and herself.

"Do you want to know how I found out? Well ... do you?" he asked, not giving her time to answer. "I found out from Lady Palmer." He savoured the words and spoke them slowly.

"She saw you riding out of his driveway. His driveway! How do you think it makes me feel? My wife! Associating with that ... that ... half-caste! And that's not all. Riding through the streets of Madras alone! Do you imagine you are invisible?"

"I wouldn't have gone behind your back if you didn't make such a fuss of it ... What harm is there in me visiting a child I have an interest in?"

She was shouting now, and beside herself with anger, but it was more than that; all of her restrained resentment began to spill over.

"What you want from me is impossible! You want me to be nothing but a simple adornment to your life! Well, I want a life too!" Tears ran down her cheeks, more from frustration than anything else. She began to feel sick and sat down, still trembling.

"For God's sake, calm yourself. The servants can hear everything."

"I don't care! You're a tyrant! And I can't love you! I can't love you! Not as you are! If our marriage is to survive, you will have to treat me with respect! I visit Prema because I want to! And I will continue to do so, regardless of what you say!"

"Is the brat the only reason you visit?"

"How dare you? I have never been anything other than faithful to you! If only you would trust me!" She spat the words, though at the same time guilt surged within her.

Then, in a brief reflective moment, she saw clearly that it was Charles's behaviour driving her towards Sabran, as well as Sabran himself, who seemed to value her and her opinions more than her own husband. It was no wonder she wanted to be close to his world and to bask in the warmth of his admiration, for she was sure he admired her, even if he didn't desire her. But, more than anything, it was being with Sabran that made her realise there was more to love than what passed for love in her own home.

She was quieter now, and could even speak calmly. "If you're really so unhappy with me and I with you, perhaps we should think about a divorce."

He spun around to face her. "So you can make a fool of me? No! Don't ever speak of it again."

"Is that the only reason you won't let me go?"

He put his arms around her, hoping to soften her mood, but his touch only gave her a feeling of revulsion.

"No, I do love you, you know, but do you have to be so damned unreasonable?"

"Love!" She gave a kind of grim laugh. "If you loved me you would allow me some freedom."

A soft knocking made them both swing around and stare at the door.

"What do you want?" he shouted.

The sweet voice of Lakshmi came from beyond the door. "*Sahib* ... I have a note for *sahib*."

"Well, bring it in."

Lakshmi entered the room as she always did, her eyes cast down, smiling her usual puzzling half smile, but her flashing eyes missing nothing. Sara had the feeling she'd been standing outside the door for some time before knocking. She handed him the note, at the same time bestowing on him one of her lovely smiles.

He smiled in return as he watched her back out of the room, her body bent almost double as she gave blessings, while Sara wondered what she could do to have the same look of approval applied to herself.

"I have to meet a fellow," he said, dismissing her after reading the note. "We'll discuss this when I get home."

Later, when Charles had retreated to his club, Sara called Shakur to her. "Why didn't you bring the letter yourself? Why did you send Lakshmi to do your job?"

Shakur answered with an innocent smile. "Because, madam, when the *sahib* is angry we always send Lakshmi. He is never angry with her."

Sara scanned his face for signs of sarcasm but there was none. He was simply stating a fact and, for the first time, she began to seriously suspect there might be more to her husband's relationship with Lakshmi than he was willing to admit.

Chapter 27

After a bitter, almost sleepless night, Sara woke the next morning determined at all cost she would leave the house and never return, but the old weakening illness had come back, this time worse than before.

"My dear Mrs Fitzroy ..." Her doctor fussed over her, straightening the pillow while making reassuring noises. "You are suffering from the same malady as many other Englishwomen who come to live in India and find themselves unsuited to the climate. I'll give you a month or two more and if you don't improve I recommend you leave India at once for a long period abroad."

His words came almost as a relief to her, despite her love of India. She was a jasmine wife after all, and she felt a deep sense of failure, but a trip back to England due to poor health would at least be a way out of her hateful marriage. But it seemed impossible she could leave now, when there was so much to keep her in Madras. Malika had regained a firm hold in her heart, but there was Prema too and, much to her help-less shame, Ravi Sabran held her there also. She had no right, but the thought of never seeing him again brought on a kind of panic that in her illness tortured her with wild thoughts. Did she really desire him as Charles implied or, even worse, did she love him? These tormenting thoughts revisited her over and over, though she was too weak to try to resolve them with any rational plan, so the days passed in a blur, so hot even the birds were stilled in the air. The leaden silence was broken by the rhythmic sound of buckets of cold water hitting the grass curtains outside the darkened windows in what seemed to be a vain effort to cool the house.

With nerve-racking regularity the water hit the window with a dull splash, though the sound seemed amplified a hundred times over, making her want to hide her head under the damp sheets.

Charles was more than usually attentive, spending an hour or two by her bedside each day, encouraging her to eat the thin meat broths recommended by the doctor to build up her strength. He seemed to have forgotten the ugly scene over her visit to Sabran and seemed genuinely anxious for her.

"Mutu has made a special soup for you, darling. You must try to eat it." He took the bowl from Lakshmi, who had crept into the room almost unnoticed and placed it before him on the bedside table.

Before leaving, she gave Malika, who was crouching in the corner of the room, a look of deep resentment and hatred.

He held the spoonful of soup to Sara's lips, his expression so concerned and gentle it seemed unkind not to oblige him, despite it tasting so unpleasant.

"Well, perhaps just a little ..." She tried to smile, though she was wary of him still and secretly longed for the time when he would leave her alone. She swallowed and made a face.

He laughed. "It isn't that bad. I know, I tasted it myself."

Malika sat silently in the corner of the room, ready to take over, her eyes downcast under her sari shawl. She only looked up when Charles spoke to her before he left for the day, and it shocked Sara to see the naked fear written so clearly there.

He stood over the woman, his legs apart as she knelt at his feet.

"Make sure madam finishes the soup! You want to see her well, don't you?"

"Yes, *sahib*."

"Well, see that you do."

He gave her a final look of absolute contempt, then left the house at last, with a great deal of banging and shouting orders as he did so. Sara listened to the sounds of his retreating boots on the pavement outside, then all was quiet and she fell into a deep exhausted sleep.

The soup stood cold on the bedside table till Malika crept forward to take it away, careful not to wake her mistress. She lifted the bowl to her nose, inhaled deeply, then crossed to the window and threw it into the garden, before waiting by the bed till Sara awoke.

Later, while she was brushing Sara's hair, she began, with difficulty, to speak. "I will look after you till you are well. Here in this room. Remember when you were a child? I took care of you. It was I who made you better. I will again. But only I can cook for you."

"Mutu will be unhappy."

"Let him send his food. I will decide if you can eat it."

She was so determined Sara agreed. She was too ill to do anything else.

The woman smiled, satisfied at last. Then she frowned as a dark thought flew across her face. "I do not like Lakshmi ..."

"She's a little jealous because I would rather have you with me. That's all."

"I do not trust her; she thinks she is mistress here."

This time Malika drew blood, and again Sara was concerned. It was true the girl used her beauty to control the men. She'd seen it herself with her own husband, and at times she thought it might be possible that Charles had a secret desire for her, but still it seemed unlikely that Lakshmi could have any real power over Charles. Too often she'd heard him on the subject of Indian women. "Too dirty for my taste" and "as black as boot polish". Horrible words that made her cringe with dislike for him.

Even so, she would take Malika's advice. "When I'm well, I'll find a new place for her."

Malika smiled, then looked around the room as though someone might be hiding there, before lowering her voice to a whisper. "A letter has come for you. It is on the hall table."

"A letter for me?" Sara brightened a little. "Can you bring it to me?"

"I cannot ... It would make Shakur very angry."

"Then ask Shakur to bring it to me."

"He will not ... The master ..." Again, her eyes avoided Sara's.

"What do you mean? What about the master?"

This time Malika found the courage to look into Sara's eyes. "The master does not like you to have letters. Shakur must first give all your letters to him. He decides which ones you can have."

Sara stared, and for a moment was unable to speak. Then she berated herself for being a fool, though she had never suspected Charles would ever stoop so low.

"Will you bring me the letter?"

"I cannot. Shakur will tell the master and then he will not let me see you. He said I must do as he says or he will have me thrown into the street."

Sara tried to sit up, stirred into life by her anger, but fell back onto the pillows. "Get the letter for me. Nothing will happen to you and, anyway, Monsieur Sabran will take care of you always. I promise."

Malika hurried out into the hall, returning a minute later with the letter hidden beneath her sari.

It was from Ravi Sabran and she clung to it like a lifeline from the outside world.

"Dear Mrs Fitzroy, I know you have been ill ..."

She managed a small weak laugh as she wondered how he knew.

"I will be in town on business and I have the child with me. It would be pleasant to receive you again in your father's home, but of course I will understand if it is impossible for you ..."

She would go, of course. Her promise to Charles meant nothing now. If anything, it would breathe new life into her. It would be wonderful to sit in her mother's cool garden again. After experimenting with raising her head from the pillow, the dizziness was so acute she fell back, tears of frustration burning her hot eyes. She reached for her writing pad and in her misery wrote a letter without the usual formalities. It was as though she was writing to a dear friend, her only lifeline to the outside world.

> "I'm so ill I'm afraid I may not live. If that should be so, promise me you'll always take care of Prema and Malika? Forgive me for my morbid thoughts, but this has been weighing on my mind."

"Take this ... and give it to Monsieur Sabran, but don't let anyone see you."

The woman hurried away, the letter hidden under her sari, while Sara fell back into bed, a prisoner of her illness, over-whelmed with the thought that her dreams of freedom and happiness had come to nothing.

Chapter 28

The sickness passed and for the first time in two weeks Sara was strong enough for a walk in the morning air. She'd eaten nothing but what had been cooked by Malika, or what Malika had deemed fit to eat from the kitchen, mixed with a daily dose of mysterious herbs drawn out of a secret hiding place in her sari.

Sara was certain she owed her life to this concoction, though her doctor still said her symptoms had been nothing unusual in Englishwomen in Madras.

"You're looking better," Charles said as he walked into the room and placed a letter before her on her dressing table.

"I have my beautiful girl back again." He leaned over and placed his hand where her negligee had fallen open to expose her breast.

She flinched at his touch and crushed the now familiar rising sense of revulsion, then reached for the letter, though her pleasure was mingled with concern that it might be from Ravi Sabran. She'd waited for his reply and had to admit to being disappointed and a little angry she hadn't yet heard from him.

"A letter? For me?" Her smile faded when she saw it had already been opened.

He beamed back at her. "It's from your friend the Maharaja; he asks you to visit at his palace. You'll have to go."

"You've read it?"

"Of course. Married people have nothing to hide from each other."

She threw the letter down on the dressing table. "Then why did you hide letters for me from Monsieur Sabran?"

He showed only the faintest sign of concern at her words. His smile faded and for a moment he seemed to struggle with his emotions. "I did that for your own good. I am protecting you from a relationship that could hurt you very much."

"What do you mean, 'hurt me'?"

She tore at her hair with her brush, her eyes flashing angry lights, trying to release some of her fury.

"Apart from his dubious political associations, Sabran has a reputation with women: an unsavoury reputation. There have been many rumours, often more than rumours. I would tell you but it's unfit for a decent woman's ears."

She bristled. "It sounds like gossip to me. You've been listening to Lady Palmer. He's never behaved in any way at all other than as a gentleman, and it doesn't excuse you keeping correspondence from me."

"I did it for your own good; in some ways you're very naïve."

"I consider that an insult."

"Well, then, I'm sorry."

To her surprise, he leaned over to kiss her on her bare shoulder, then sat in a chair next to her dressing table, crossed his legs and lit a cigarette, smiling at her all the while. She felt her anger rise, despite his good humour.

He kissed her again, this time on the base of her neck. "It was wrong, I admit it. Forgive me?"

He flashed his most contrite smile but as she turned away from him she felt her heart harden; she would never forgive him.

"You seem very pleased about me going to the palace," she said, while watching his reflection in the mirror.

"The pearls are nothing compared to what you might have if you play your cards right. Don't refuse him or we'll miss our chance and he might not ask you again."

"Really, Charles, you sound almost greedy."

This time his good humour faded, his voice was cold now. "I'll write to tell him to expect you at once."

He left the room without waiting for her answer, and Sara realised that she was unable to bear him now. The very sight of his handsome face made her uneasy.

There were so many reasons to hate him: his constant criticism, his neglect of her. But, most of all, it was his threatening behaviour towards Malika that left her feeling so repulsed, and she began to count the hours till she could be apart from him from that moment on.

Chapter 29

As the train left the coast and climbed higher the choking yellow dust from the plains gradually vanished, to be replaced by dark green foliage so thick it crept to the very edge of the tracks and, in parts, tangled amongst the rails themselves.

Sara found herself laughing out loud for the first time in months when an elephant wandered onto the tracks and, paralysed by the sight of the steam engine, refused to move till finally coaxed away by the engineer with a bunch of bananas.

They stopped at busy little stations crowded with children selling fresh fruit and tea, clamouring at the open windows of the train, pushing their thin arms and sticky, fly-covered wares into Sara's face, while Malika tried unsuccessfully to shoo them away, though Sara, uneasy at the sight of so much desperation, bought things she didn't really want to distribute amongst the other passengers.

Charles had kissed her goodbye with more warmth than usual and, despite everything, she felt a pang of regret at parting from him. Regret for her unhappy marriage and her lost dreams of mutual love. She had no plans beyond her stay in the palace, though in her present state of mind she felt it would be impossible to return to him.

She wondered if he would miss her very much but, even as he waved goodbye from the front steps and before she was out of sight, he'd turned back towards the house and smartly ran up the steps and disappeared inside. He had already begun to think of more important things.

Late the next afternoon the train halted at a tiny village at the base of a low mountain range. For a moment she experienced a sense of isolation so acute she almost wished she hadn't come. Malika was tired and fretful after the long journey and there was no one to greet them except a group of curious villagers, who gathered about her with looks of such awe she was overwhelmed with sudden shyness.

After a few minutes of anxious waiting in a tiny dusty room attached to the station, a richly dressed servant wearing a blue turban appeared, hot and breathless, before her. He threw himself down at her feet and it was only with much encouragement he was persuaded to rise. "Forgive me, madam. He is coming ... He is coming ...."

A few minutes later strange sounds could be heard in the distance, a discordant mixture of trumpets and drums mingled with the sounds of many voices.

"Come, come ..." The servant ran ahead, urging her forward. "Come, madam."

Sara hurried to the open door, then stopped, her mouth open. An elephant, heavily decorated with colourful embroideries dotted with semi-precious stones, waited patiently outside the station amongst a crowd of musicians and servants.

And there, sitting in a palanquin under a fringed umbrella atop the elephant, sat Ravi Sabran.

The elephant dropped to its knees and Sabran swung down from the palanquin with the ease of a circus performer. He took off his hat and bowed low. "My dear Mrs Fitzroy, welcome to Chittupur."

"Monsieur Sabran!" She was too shocked to be angry at first. "What on earth are you doing here?"

"Forgive me for being late. Unlike a horse, it is difficult to persuade an elephant to go faster and, as I am a complete coward in such matters, I did not care to argue with it."

"If I'd known you would be here I wouldn't have come." She lapsed into silence, almost overcome with conflicting emotions. Being alone with him would expose her to all kinds of speculation if anyone should find out. But it was more than that; she was secretly pleased to see him. In fact she had longed to see him for some time, but he had also exposed her to danger, and that danger was mostly from herself.

"I was sent by the Maharaja himself." He laughed, hoping to soften her look. "He would have come, but he's too fat to fit in the palanquin."

She ignored his attempt at humour and turned away, determined to go home on the next train. She began to march towards the waiting room.

There was a touch of mischief in his voice when he spoke. "If you are thinking of returning to Madras, my dear Mrs

Fitzroy, there is no train till the day after tomorrow. You have no choice."

Then, without a word and too tired to argue, she stormed back to where he stood, his arms folded over his chest and with an amused smile on his lips, and reluctantly allowed him to help her into the palanquin.

He watched her face out of the corner of his eye, then shrugged his shoulders in a very French way, deciding it would be best to hold his tongue.

The elephant rose to its feet and her heart almost failed her when she saw how far it was above the ground. She wanted to clutch his arm and hang on, but on no account would she give in to her fears except for a small involuntary squeal.

"It is not too uncomfortable, I hope?" he said at last.

She would not look at him but kept her face averted, all the while clutching the sides of the swaying palanquin while looking down at the beast below her as they crashed along the jungle path.

He tried again. "I can see you are angry with me."

After a moment she turned to him, her face flushed under the shadow of her hat. "So you were behind the Maharaja's invitation."

"You said you were ill, so naturally I thought perhaps a change of scene would be good for you."

"So you did receive my letter?"

"Of course ... and I decided to help you, and get you away from Madras as soon as I could."

"Forgive me. I was perhaps a little melodramatic."

"I don't think so. Madras can be a very dangerous place."

He watched her intently with his shrewd grey eyes, but she did not see the anxiety written so clearly there.

"Yes, that is true. It's well known as an unhealthy spot, but my doctor assures me my condition is a common one for Englishwomen and, as you can see, I'm well now." She smiled as if to prove her point. "And I suppose happy to be here." She gripped the side of the palanquin at a sudden lurch. "Despite you being here as well."

"Well, thank you for your kind words." He laughed. "But if it will please you, I'll do my best to stay out of your way."

He was silent for a while. Sara took a furtive glance at his averted face. She could see he was sulking.

The jungle had retreated, making the path wider, and it was bordered on one side now with crops growing in rich soil beside a muddy river. Little grass huts had begun to spring up amongst the crops, and women in bright saris carrying baskets on their heads passed them by, calling out greetings or stopping to stare wide-eyed at the unusual sight of an English lady on top of an elephant.

Without warning, the palanquin swayed sharply again as the elephant flinched at the sight of a team of oxen coming towards them.

Sara made a frantic grab at Sabran's arm to steady herself, blushing as she did so. "Forgive me ... If someone should see us ... together ..."

"Who will see us here?"

"It's just that you don't seem to understand how this might affect my reputation."

314

He shrugged his shoulders and spread his hands wide. "I have no reputation at all, and I forget anyone else does."

She tried to frown but it was no use; her defences were down at last and she laughed. "I should be angry with you, *monsieur*, but I'm very grateful to you for being kind enough to have the Maharaja invite me here."

"We are still friends, no?"

"Yes, we're friends. Now," she said, beginning to feel almost light-headed with freedom, "can we talk about something else? I don't want to think about Madras or my life there." A shadow fell over her face as she thought about her husband and how she didn't love him any more, but her present world was so beautiful, so exciting, she threw off her cares with a laugh. "I just want to enjoy myself. Can we change the subject?"

"And I have the very subject. Again, you wear one of your lovely absurd hats."

She turned again to look at him, her face glowing in the almost iridescent light. The hat was her favourite, a very wide brim of fine pale straw, decorated with a mauve ribbon tied in a large bow under her chin. It threw a shadow over her face, giving her a mysterious charm.

"It flatters your eyes to perfection."

"How French you are, *monsieur*. It's almost as though we're in a drawing room in Paris."

His eyes darkened, then he gave her a look that warned her to be careful. His eyes flickered over her face and body with an expert appraisal. Her recent illness had given her a pale and delicate charm he found oddly alluring. He had great difficulty destroying an image of gathering her up in his arms and crushing her slight body against his own, her creamy throat falling back as he kissed her. The image was so intense he felt almost dizzy with it.

"Look! We are here at last." He swallowed hard and with a huge effort forced his thoughts back to hard reality.

From a distance the palace seemed rundown, almost crumbling where it stood on a rise overlooking a river. Families of black crows had made homes in the minarets of the pale pink stone turrets. They flew in their hundreds, circling and crying mournfully, their ragged shapes giving the place a desolate air of neglect.

Though, as they came closer, the elegant lines of the building became more evident and carved archways could be seen amongst the crumbling walls, decorated with broken pieces of faded lapis lazuli, amber and turquoise.

"How very beautiful!" She wiped a small tear away before it fell. "I'm glad I came after all."

He saw her tears and was impressed to see her so moved by beauty. That one small tear also moved him another step closer to her, even though she would never know it.

"It was built by Shah Jahan as a hunting lodge, the same fellow who built the Taj Mahal. No one could build like the Moguls."

At their arrival the palace became instantly alive. Servants came from everywhere, bringing necklaces of fragrant jasmine to drape around their necks, and to strew the ground with petals where they walked.

The head man, wearing the colours of the household, bowed before her. "The Maharaja begs you to rest. I will send refreshments to your rooms at once."

Sabran also parted with her. "Will we meet later, or would you prefer I stay in my room in case your reputation is ruined?" He was deliberately flippant, though his eyes scanned hers with a look that made her heart race with something like joy. She crushed the feeling at once, even despising herself for what she saw as a vain and silly thought. She straightened up to meet his eyes head-on.

"I'm not afraid of you, *monsieur*." She smiled, but it was a lie; she was afraid of him but she would do her best to hide it, though even now her legs trembled slightly just being near him.

"I'll see you this evening, of course." He bowed and kissed her hand then hurried away.

As soon as he left her side a depression began to take over her spirits once more. She didn't want to be there after all, a stranger alone in the vast palace. How would she ever get through it?

She was shown to a suite of rooms at the end of a long corridor adjoining the apartments of the Zenana, where the women and the children of the palace lived in seclusion.

Set high into the corridor walls, filigree windows as delicate as lace screened the women from view, but allowed anyone looking out to watch unseen on whoever happened to pass below. Sara was aware of moving shadows and the sighs of soft laughter, then, when turning to catch sight of the source of the mysterious sounds, all fell silent as curious eyes gazed out above veiled faces, before darting back behind the screens.

After a fragrant bath in a small pool set into the floor of her private courtyard, a girl came with a tray of food and drink. She ate everything put before her, and almost at once fell back on the huge bed set under a domed ceiling and slept till the late afternoon, awakening to the sound of a sitar playing in a far-off room. She lay for a long time, unable to move, her head heavy on the pillow. It was as though she had been drugged with an intoxicating mixture of anticipation, scents and an atmosphere steeped with romance.

Tears sprang to her eyes without warning. Romantic the place undoubtedly was, but for her all romance was over. It belonged in the past with the girl she had once been. Now she must find comfort in other things.

Chapter 30

Before leaving her room, she paused before the gilded mirror to tidy her hair and to scrutinize her reflection. Her finely embroidered silk gown flattered her skin and matched the lustre of the creamy pearls she wore as a compliment to the Maharaja.

She made a final adjustment to the knot of white tuberoses she wore in her smooth chignon, straightened her back and took a deep breath, before going into what she saw as the usual emotional battle with Ravi Sabran.

Echoes of muffled whispers could be heard as Sara walked down the corridor towards the dining room. It was unnerving to see no one except an old man half-asleep outside the door. He hauled himself to his feet and bowed as low as he was able to, hindered as he was by stiff limbs. "Welcome, madam," he squealed, his voice curiously high and feminine. She realised with a wrench of pity that he was a eunuch, one of the last survivors of a cruel practice from a darker age. Her heart almost broke for him as he ran ahead of her, every now and then looking over his shoulder at her, as excited as if Queen Victoria herself had suddenly appeared before him.

She was shown to a large room with marble archways opening onto a wide stone terrace. There was a great deal of frantic activity. Servants ran back and forth carrying trays, lighting candles against the failing light and setting a long mahogany table for dinner. All of them stopped and stared with great curiosity when she entered the room, including two women who were seated on the floor in a corner of the room.

"Ah, you have come. You are very welcome, my dear Mrs Fitzroy."

The Maharani was seated on a *gaddi*, an embroidered cushion of state, placed on a raised dais. The other woman sat at her feet and stared at Sara shamelessly as she walked towards them.

They had been playing the Indian game of Ganjifa, and exquisitely carved ivory cards set with precious stones lay scattered around her bare feet amongst piles of coins.

The Maharani had been a great beauty in her youth and there were signs of it still in her magnificent kohl rimmed eyes and thick raven-black hair. She sat cross–legged, her hair and body covered with a fine silk sari elaborately embroidered with gold thread. Her ears and neck were hung with enormous rough-cut rubies and she wore a pair of loose silk trousers bound with a jewelled belt. Every now and then she took a puff of a strong-smelling tobacco from an elegant hookah that wound about her body like a cobra. The trousers gave her the air of an independent woman even though she clung to the old traditions and chose to rarely leave the confines of the Zenana.

The other woman whispered in the Maharani's ear, all the while scrutinizing Sara.

"My sister was wondering what English ladies wear under their skirts," the Maharani said as Sara bowed before her. At Sara's bewildered expression, she laughed. "I am only joking, of course. How lovely you are. As fresh as a daisy is the English expression, I think.

Sara managed to control her nerves enough to reply. "It's all so unsuitable to the climate really, and not nearly as elegant as your own."

The Maharani looked at her with narrowed shrewd eyes. "You are not saying this to please me?"

"No, but if you are pleased then I'm glad." Sara bowed her head and curtsied and the Maharani was charmed.

The Maharani's sister gave a sly smile. "I sometimes think some of the English ladies look as though they are trussed like chickens on the way to market."

Sara laughed. "I think our style of clothing proves that we English are not as sensible as we might think."

The Maharani leaned back on her cushion and inhaled deeply of her cigarette. "We should ask the gentlemen what they prefer, but I think Monsieur Sabran will favour the European style, no matter what he says or does."

Sara didn't know what to say, or if it was even allowed to contradict royalty, but speculation had to be stopped, no matter what the consequences.

"I don't know Monsieur Sabran well enough to know his personal likes or dislikes. We hardly know one another."

"Ah! You are being very English and are putting me in my box."

"No, no, not at all. It's just that ..." Sara floundered for a while, not knowing what to say in reply, and was relieved when she heard voices behind her.

It was hard to tell if the Maharani was offended or not, her smile was so inscrutable, but she became almost girlish when the men came into the room.

"Ah! Here are the gentlemen, and I won't be able now to invent romances that do not exist."

Sabran wore an elegant black dinner suit of European cut, in honour of Sara's visit. He again kissed Sara's hand while both the Maharani and her sister giggled and nudged each other.

He seemed edgy, even nervous. She could tell by the way he kept running the fingers of one hand through his black hair, his eyes looking everywhere but at her, and again she wished she hadn't come.

The Maharaja entered the room with great care and deliberation, as if in a moment he might topple over and never get up again. He was not burdened with as many jewels as when Sara had last seen him, being dressed in a long muslin shirt and baggy silk trousers. Even so, he managed to give the impression of a magnificent stateliness.

His face lit up when he saw her. "What a pleasure it is to look upon you." He bowed graciously at Sara as he leant upon Sabran's arm. "But please, no waiting for me; let us dispense with the formalities. I get so very sick of it. This is my country place; this is where I relax."

Sara smiled to herself. To be surrounded by fifty servants instead of a hundred was a strange notion of relaxation.

"My wife and her sister have broken with tradition tonight and have decided to join us for dinner. I like to think of myself as a progressive man and ours was a love match ..." he waved airily towards his wife "... and she is my only wife. One is enough!" he added, rolling his eyes with mock despair.

The Maharani laughed. "He knows I would kill any other woman who would try to take my place."

The Maharani's eyes flashed with such ferocity Sara almost believed she wasn't joking, though the Maharaja was unmoved by her obvious passion.

"Once I would have been expected to have a hundred wives, but I have been civilised by your British ways. The Zenana is now only for show; instead of wives it is full of my poor relations." He laughed heartily, as though his responsibilities were a joy to him.

He took Sara's arm and led her towards the dining table, saving her from having to reply to such a delicate statement.

After much manoeuvring of chairs and a great deal of help from his servants, the Maharaja was at last seated at the head of the dining table. He indicated that Sara should be placed at his right and Sabran at his left.

"So he can gaze at your lovely face," said the Maharaja with great gallantry. "It is a bad combination, to be both French and Indian, the two races most obsessed with love."

"All races are obsessed with love, even the British." Sara spoke without thinking and all eyes were upon her, especially Ravi Sabran's, who gazed at her with a thoughtful intensity that unnerved her.

"But you are not British through and through, my dear

Mrs Fitzroy, not with your exotic looks," the Maharaja insisted. "You are Spanish perhaps, or Italian. I have seen Italian ladies who look very like you."

"I'm not really sure about my background; my aunt said my mother had Spanish blood, but I have never met any other relations."

The Maharani was horrified. "Only one relation! You can have some of mine. I am drowning in them!"

There was a burst of laughter from around the table and Sara smiled, beginning to feel at home amongst them.

"My parents died when I was six years old. It's most strange ... Did you know Monsieur Sabran owns their old house ... the same house I lived in as a child? My parents are buried there."

The Maharaja looked at her and then at his wife, who seemed to sway ever so slightly in her seat. When she spoke, her voice seemed to shake a little.

"But Monsieur Ravi owns the Radcliffe house. Surely you aren't William Radcliffe's child?"

For an instant Sara wavered between fear of what they would reveal about her parents and a desire to know more. Her voice almost trembled when she spoke. "You knew my father?"

The Maharaja nodded, silent now, still staring at her with his mouth open.

"How strange ... Yes, I'm his daughter, but in England I was brought up as an Archer. I don't know why, but I fear my family were hiding a dreadful secret." She laughed again, but with increasing discomfort.

"Your mother's name was Lillian?" The Maharani was almost standing, with her hand held over her heart as though she was in pain.

"Then you are Sarianna? Little Sarianna! Yes, you are she, I can tell by your hair; hers was lighter, but it is the same hair!"

Sara was alarmed now. "Yes, that was my name. Malika is the only person who calls me by that name. Did you know my mother?"

Sabran too was alert to the events unfolding before him, following the conversation with his eyes. "Sarianna?" He almost breathed the name, rolling the word on his tongue. "It suits you."

The Maharani stared at Sara more closely now. "Yes, I can see the resemblance." She seemed to pull herself together with a great effort then settled back into her seat. "Yes, I knew your mother. Not well, but she was most charming."

She looked across at her husband, who sat with his fork halfway to his open mouth, and something seemed to pass between them.

"Yes, she was most charming," he murmured, as though to himself. "It was a great tragedy when they died."

"Then there's nothing you can say about them?" Sara frowned. "Is there something you're not telling me?"

Again there was silence, while looks passed between them all.

"There is nothing I can tell you about them," the Maharaja said at last, "except they were more in love with each other than anyone I have ever known, and we were most upset when we heard about their deaths. Perhaps that is why I liked you at once. I could see the resemblance without realising it."

He waved a hand at no one in particular, then changed the subject, though it seemed to Sara he was more attentive and courteous to her than before, and in some curious way there seemed less distance between them.

The conversation turned to lighter things and the Maharani seemed to recover her spirits as the night wore on, though she looked at Sara often with a sad frown on her brow. Once she was heard to mutter, almost inaudibly, "Poor child, poor orphan child ..."

Sabran was mostly silent all evening, allowing the Maharaja to talk without interruption, though Sara could feel his eyes upon her even though his face was in shadow. The first evening in the palace was an uncomfortable one and Sara was glad to retire early, pleading exhaustion as an excuse, though she slept badly, haunted till dawn with wild uneasy thoughts.

Living in the little palace in the jungle was as though living on an island where her every desire was fulfilled. It was so easy to forget her life with Charles outside the walls and it was almost as though her marriage hadn't happened. Sometimes, just for a brief moment, she would remember, then she would throw the memories off and immerse herself in the much more agreeable present.

Her mornings were spent writing about the daily life of the palace and she felt, of all her stories, they were perhaps the best. So far she had heard nothing from the English publisher, and had almost given up hope of a reply, but she sent the latest stories with a flimsy confidence, hoping they were worthy of notice.

Her afternoons were spent with the Maharani and her entourage in the privacy of the Zenana, where they indulged in hours of lazy gossip, and where she wore the sari and went barefoot, luxuriating in the feel of her toes against the cool marble floors. Though in the evenings she reverted to western dress once more and, as though adopting armour, she put on the layers of silk petticoats and chiffon and piled her hair into the current style of the English fashion magazines. In this way, suitably equipped, she felt fortified once more against Ravi Sabran's mysterious charm.

The Maharani made it more difficult for her by speaking often of Sabran with admiration. "He is a good man, even though he tries very hard to make us all believe he is not. Even his love for Maya is based on his kindness. He could not bear to see her treated the way she was by her brute of a husband, so he convinced her to run away with him. She is safe while she is protected by Monsieur Ravi, but her husband will stop at nothing to get her back, not because he loves her but because she belongs to him."

"Monsieur Sabran must love her very much."

"She is as beautiful as a flower, but for him I think it is not her beauty that draws him to her, it is pity, and love came afterwards. But for her it is a passion so deep it will only die with her death. That, I am sure of!" She emphasised her point by striking the fingers of one hand into the palm of the other. "Sometimes I wish they had never met; it is an impossible situation."

"You might find she's perhaps not so dependent on Monsieur Sabran's love as you think. People do not die of broken hearts."

"My dear Mrs Fitzroy, you have a lot to learn about love. That is clear."

At this point Sara was silent; words had failed her. It was true; she knew nothing about love. Her unhappiness was proof of it.

Sabran announced his intention to leave almost without notice.

There was business in Pondicherry he must attend to at once, and he would leave as soon as possible.

There was a chorus of protests from everyone except Sara, who couldn't help but be a little relieved to be free of his unsettling presence at last.

Champagne was called for to celebrate their final evening together, and as the evening wore on the Maharaja became more sentimental.

"If it hadn't been for Monsieur Ravi, we would never have met," he said, patting Sara gently on the hand. "'You must ask this lady to your garden party', he said. 'She will interest you.'"

Sara looked at Sabran, who raised his glass to her and smiled, though she could see he was embarrassed by this revelation.

"And I shocked dear Mrs Fitzroy by telling her a great fib about a tiger and how my father used widows as tiger bait." He laughed. "I can see her face now as she went pale with horror, but nonetheless remained the perfect lady."

Sara laughed. "Then it was only a story after all! Thank heavens! I often worried about it. I didn't like to think of your father as being cruel."

"And we talked about my fondness for some English customs. The English manner of dancing is charming to me, and if I wasn't so fat I would love to dance with our dear Mrs Fitzroy. But alas, it is not to be." He patted his huge belly with his jewelled fingers. "But Monsieur Ravi, would you ask Mrs Fitzroy to dance so I can watch? I can pretend it is I."

"Dance with Monsieur Sabran?" She was about to refuse when the Maharaja clapped his hands, warming to the idea.

"Yes, yes, a dance, if you would oblige me, my dear Mrs Fitzroy. I have a desire to see you dance. A waltz! I do love a waltz."

Sara rose to her feet. It was not possible to refuse him now. The Maharani hurried to the piano. "I had an English governess for a long time, a Miss Leach; she was very strict with me. Every time I put a note wrong she hit my knuckles with a ruler. But I have never forgotten."

She began to play, thumping the notes with great enthusiasm even though the instrument was badly out of tune.

"Play the Strauss, play the Strauss." The Maharaja was already tapping his sandalled feet.

"May I?" Sabran stood before her, his arms held out, his dark eyes watching her.

There was a moment of confusion and little shocked gasps from the Maharani's sister when he put his arm around her waist and drew her to him. He took her free hand and held it in his own. At once, a powerful tingling sensation seemed to shoot from his body into hers, and she had to steady herself. She looked around, sure everyone must have noticed her discomfort. The Maharaja seemed unaware, and only smiled and clapped loudly in time to the music, though the Maharani and her sister, who had joined her at the piano, both stared and whispered enough to unnerve her.

She kept her eyes fixed on her own hand as it rested on his shoulder, determined not to be captured again by his hypnotic gaze.

"My secret is out," he whispered as he held her close, causing a shiver to run down her back. "I confess to wanting to know more about you. Is that so very bad?"

He waited for her answer, watching her with his heavy-lidded eyes, his face almost touching hers, but she was determined to remain silent.

She straightened her back and bit her lip. It was dangerous to be so close to him. She must put a stop to it at once. "If you will excuse me, I think we have amused their Majesties enough."

He removed his hand from her waist, though his eyes were still fixed upon hers with a burning gaze.

The Maharaja sat, unaware of the drama unfolding around him, still tapping his foot in time to the piano. The Maharani exhausted herself at last and creaked to a halt.

Sara curtsied before them both. "Will you forgive me if I retire to my room early tonight? I'm very tired."

"Of course, my dear Mrs Fitzroy. You have had enough of our nonsense, I'm sure." The Maharaja tried to rise to his feet but gave up almost at once.

"Not at all ... Monsieur Sabran, I won't see you before you leave in the morning, but thank you ..." She could think of nothing more to say.

Sabran kissed her hand while bestowing on her a look, unsmiling but intent. She hurried away, cursing herself for her awkwardness and lack of composure.

Chapter 31

In the privacy of her room she paced back and forth, oblivious to everything except her thoughts pounding at her brain. Over and over again they taunted her. Was it obvious to everyone he had a disturbing influence over her? Why did she have to make such a fool of herself by leaving the room in such a way? Why did she flush with colour every time he looked at her? He must think her a complete fool. She tugged at the tight stays of her dress. Malika was nowhere to be found. It was impossible to rest after such a day. She hurried outside to continue her pacing by the fountain in the courtyard. She was beginning to think she might be ill again.

"Malika!" she called out, pulling at the back of her dress. She saw the courtyard door was open onto the terrace.

There was a figure, standing alone, watching the going down of the sun. She could see at once it was Sabran but, before she could hurry away, he turned and saw her.

"*Monsieur*, excuse me. I was looking for Malika." She made a move to leave. It was impossible she could be alone with him. He unnerved her too much. She was afraid her shaking voice had already given her away.

"Don't go. It's such a beautiful evening. It's almost as bright as day." His voice was natural and calm. Perhaps he was unaware after all.

Malika appeared on the terrace and stood between them, her eyes watchful. It was plain she disapproved of her mistress being alone with a man other than her husband. Sara knew she liked Sabran and there was no danger of gossip but, even so, she was instantly on her guard.

"I must speak to you about something of great importance, but it must be private. There is a place I go to meditate, if you would do me the honour to accompany me."

"We are alone here; please speak freely."

"It is a very sensitive subject ..." His intense grey eyes flashed about, as though someone might hear them, and, even though she was afraid to be alone with him, her curiosity grew.

She nodded, for a moment not being able to speak.

He led her through a gate in the palace wall and she followed him in silence, puzzled as to why he was so secretive, through a high walled garden thick with the fragrance of a strange jasmine that was known to only bloom at night. The little bunches of waxy, trumpet-shaped flowers seemed to glow in the moonlight, sending out their heavy scent in perfumed waves to intoxicate and ensnare any creature foolish enough to succumb to their spell.

Every now and then he would stop to wait for her till she caught up with him. Once he held out his hand to help her, but she refused to take it, knowing it was dangerous to do so. They came at last to a small bungalow set apart from the main buildings of the palace, where candlelight flickered through the wide-open windows and cast a beckoning glow on the veranda surrounding the house. Here the scent of jasmine was almost overwhelming.

"Come." He gestured towards the open door.

She hesitated at first. His eyes were so intense, so penetrating, she began to tremble all over. Then a feeling of carelessness took over and she told herself there was nothing wrong with being alone with him, and she stepped inside.

A wide divan covered in cushions and surrounded by muslin curtains stood in one corner of the room. A book lay half open on its front where he had left it. She turned her head away. She wouldn't be able to bear being in this place; it was too intimate. It was almost indecent for her to be there.

An unreasonable anger crept over her. It was unfair of him to compromise her in this way. She took a look at him out of the corner of her eye but he seemed unmoved by the situation, only watching her with an eager expression on his face, happy to be showing off this beautiful place to someone, anyone.

She relaxed a little but kept her eyes towards the other end of the room. Bowls of fragrant white flowers stood on every surface and the seductive perfume of jasmine filled the room. A fine ivory statue of the dancing Shiva stood alone on an exquisite antique table in the centre of the room.

"Charming, *non*?" he said, opening his arms wide and grinning.

"Very." She laughed, but it sounded awkward and almost shrill.

He gestured towards two low divans facing each other near the open window, then clapped his hands and a servant appeared.

"Will you have chai?" She nodded her reply, then the woman disappeared as quickly as she had come.

Sara stared down at her hands twisted in her lap and was overcome by shyness. Her whole being seemed electrified and her head swam. Even normal sounds were amplified, and the clatter of the servant in the background as she made the tea seemed deafening, straining her nerves to breaking point. When she felt she couldn't stand the tension any longer the woman reappeared, for a moment cutting the current running between them.

She placed the tray on a table between the divans, then, after taking a sly look at Sara, she left them alone.

"Shall I?" Sara asked, relieved to have something to do with her hands, though they trembled as she reached for the teapot and her voice came out a husky squeak.

"Please do." His voice was calm, but he too seemed to find it difficult to relax. He crossed and uncrossed his legs several times while watching her as she struggled with pouring the tea. He darted forward to take the cup before it crashed to the floor.

He held the cup with both hands before settling back on the settee. He took a deep breath and began. "You are aware of a series of events that have linked us together?"

"Yes, I have noticed a strange string of coincidences."

"They are not coincidences. Something else has occurred and it has made me uneasy."

Sara put down her teaspoon with great care, for fear of drawing attention to her shaking hand. "You won't tell me what it is?"

"No, I can't. You'll find out when the time is right. It is not for me to tell you."

"This is very mysterious, *monsieur*. Then what have you brought me here for?"

He frowned and gave a deep sigh, then ran his fingers through his hair as though he could drive the troublesome thought away. "To tell you ..." he hesitated, unsure about continuing "... to tell you that, despite everything and everyone else in our lives, we must be together. There is nothing anyone can do about it, because it is fated. All the signs point that way."

"Oh!" She could say nothing else, though she felt a rush of joy so intense she was sure she would faint. She stared at him, breathless, while he gave an exasperated sigh, then his words poured out in a rush.

"I also wanted to tell you I love you, and to ask you if there is any chance you might return my love."

She stood to face him, her knees trembling, with her hand on the back of the divan supporting her. "Do you love me only because it is fated that it must be so? It seems the idea of loving me is distasteful to you. I don't understand."

He too seemed shaken. He stood opposite her, flexing his hands and biting his lip. "I don't understand it myself," he said. He added bitterly, "This is not something I wished for."

"Then I won't stay to hear any more!"

She turned to leave, almost distraught, then she felt an

overwhelming compulsion to look at him one last time and her hesitation, and something in her expression, caused him to spring forward and take her in his arms.

"No, please ... Let me go ... I must go ..."

He held her gaze with his own and she found herself unable to look away. "The barrier separating us is almost gone," he whispered.

She didn't reply. It would be contemptible to reprove him for something she longed to hear.

She felt him shiver; the tremor passed through his body into hers, then her head fell back as he pressed his warm lips on the nape of her neck. "I've wanted to do that for so long," he murmured. "That little mark is so tempting."

She found the courage to turn to him, terrified she would succumb to her own almost blinding desire, and the first time she allowed herself a long luxurious moment to appreciate his exotic charm. She smiled at the heavily lashed grey eyes filled with passion and longing.

"You give me no time. I need time." Her face was extremely pale, and her eyes glittered as though she had a fever.

"Sarianna, this was meant to be. There is nothing either of us can do about it." His voice was hypnotic and she was mesmerised. Then he lifted a strand of her hair from where it lay around her throat and put it to his lips. A shiver ran down her back and she began to tremble. He kissed her very gently at first, playing with her top lip, luxuriating in antici-pated passion till her lips opened. His kiss was deep and crushing and filled her with warmth.

They both let out a deep sigh and clung together, amazed

and thrilled at finding themselves so alive to each other. They were unable to still their bodies, frantic for the touch they both craved but feeling as though their desire could never be fulfilled.

"My darling, I can't help it," he murmured, then, taking both her hands he pulled her towards the divan.

They fell back under the muslin canopy and allowed themselves to be enveloped further into their own world. Her mouth tore at his, all the while rejoicing in the feel of his hard body pressing into hers. This was what she had wanted from Charles but would never have.

She whispered, panic in her voice, "Ravi ... Ravi ..."

"What is it, my darling?" His voice came out of the mist as he played with her long hair.

"Is this love?"

He laughed and raised his face to look at her. "It is for me, and I hope it is for you."

He kissed her again and again. Deep, soft and all-consuming, till she felt she would faint from pleasure.

Then he pulled back, wanting to enjoy her at his leisure. He lifted her dress, smiling to see so many petticoats. He felt the delicate white lace between his fingers. "So many clothes ..." He laughed. "How charming, how erotic all this can be ... It's driving me mad."

She struggled to hold the skirt down, but he took both her hands and kissed them and said firmly, "*Non!*"

She sighed and gave herself up to the moment. Her eyes closed as she lay back on the cushions, her cheeks flushed, watching him, mesmerised.

"So lovely ..." he murmured. "So lovely."

She moaned aloud, then thrust her fist into her mouth, feeling a sudden shame at her pleasure. He took her hands again and pressed them down into the pillow above her head, before kissing her once more and crushing her with his body; feeling the strength and power of him she knew she had only just tasted.

The moon filled the room with light, illuminating their bodies on the bed. He said nothing but he moved his hand to the place where the top of her stocking met the flesh of her thigh, feeling the soft skin. He pressed his face into her thigh, biting playfully and licking, moving his mouth to where the curve of her thigh met the lace of her silk panties. He laughed as he slowly untied the thin black ribbon around her waist. "So feminine, so pretty," he murmured as he pressed his mouth against her warm belly. His warm hand on her thigh thrilled her beyond anything she had ever felt before.

"If you want me to stop, you must say so now. In a moment it will be too late." His long black hair fell forward around his face. He pushed it back, impatient, his eyes burning, waiting for her answer.

She answered him with her lips, soft and yielding, and in an instant he had pulled her body towards his, his hands tearing at her silk panties. She cried out as he entered her, and he covered her mouth with his, whispering, "You are too small for me ... Open a little wider ..." She let her trembling legs fall further apart and he moved deeper inside her. "More," he whispered as he ran his forefinger gently around her sex. She'd never been touched in such a way before and she rejoiced at her rising pleasure. He pushed harder, at the same time enveloping her in his arms, almost hurting her now as he took his pleasure, not holding back till sweat glistened on his golden skin, while she lay prone, unable to move from his weight, her lips apart, dazed with joy.

"So innocent, so pure ..." he laughed, his face like a satyr "... but not so pure."

She was almost a rag doll till he pulled her up to straddle him, her long petticoats falling around them both, her breasts half exposed by her open chemise and her long red hair in a tangled mass down her back. She tried to push his hands away as they explored her body further, ashamed to be so nakedly vulnerable, but he held both her hands in his. "Don't take away my pleasure ..." he was insistent, almost angry "... and yours." Then almost at once his mood darkened and he gripped her hips, pressing her against him, intent and urgent. Her body too was overtaken by a powerful force, rhythmic and strong, till the climax burst from both of them, delirious and wild and joyous.

"*Mon Dieu!*" he murmured, panting, then, laughing softly, he turned her gently on her back so he could look at her and kiss her once more.

"Such pleasure, I feel like a young man again."

She was too dazed to reply at once, then almost humbly she asked, "This has never happened to me before. Is this how it's meant to be?"

"Only for the lucky ones." He laughed.

He kissed her again, murmuring as he nuzzled into her neck, "I was a beast, and careless. I'm sorry, but now I will take more care ... I want our pleasure to last all night."

"I must go back. Malika will notice I'm not in my room and come looking for me."

"How can I let you go now? You must be mad."

She let him kiss her again, knowing she was lost.

Sometimes throughout the too-short night they slept, curled up in each other's arms till his urgent desire took over once more. She gave herself up utterly, shocking herself with the wildness of her abandonment, letting him do what he wanted to her, till the early morning light fell on their exhausted and bruised bodies.

They awoke together, their faces touching as their eyes flickered open before falling into a warm lingering kiss.

"Such happiness," he whispered, "such pleasure." Her fingers traced the outline of his firm lips, bruised and swollen with the savage love-making of the night before. Her heart was too full to do anything but smile.

"So blooms the lotus at last," he said. "I have never seen you so beautiful. Your eyes are full of peace."

"You make me so. You've transformed me." She took his hand and kissed his fingers, her eyes filling with tears.

He abandoned his plans to leave and they met secretly every night, she almost running through the candlelit garden to where he waited for her, and, after a day spent constrained in the company of others, unable to touch except for the brief electrifying brush of a hand, they fell into each other's arms as though they had been apart for weeks instead of just a few hours.

He was frightening in his eagerness to have her, his heavy shoulders and arms enveloping her, capturing her, so she fluttered like a butterfly against his body as he lifted her to carry her to the bed, his mouth pressed against her breast.

At other times, after pacing the room like a wild thing, he met her with only an intense gaze and a few mumbled hot words, snatching at her wrist as she entered the room, she breathless from running, her eyes shining and eager, before he pulled her to him, lifting her gown to ravage her against the wall or where she stood, covering her mouth with his, stifling her moans of pleasure till he released her, her legs trembling and her body burning from his onslaught.

Then, afterwards, his tenderness as he murmured his love for her, the finely carved lids of his eyes heavy with a gentle delight as he kissed her mouth and body over and over.

He told her of the mysteries of the *Kama Sutra* and how together they could experience even greater joy. "But a little at a time, like a drop of rare and precious oil," he said, so the pleasure could last the rest of their lives.

At the mention of the future, though, she would feel a stab of pain in her heart that sometimes threatened to destroy her present happiness.

They never spoke of it, both of them unwilling to break the spell of their perfect time together. It was as though they were enchanted. They went through the days like children, living only for the moment, and within the walls of their own little palace they could pretend, almost successfully, there was no other world outside.

Others, though, were not blind to their passion for each other. The Maharani watched them together and she was filled with a sense of doom. She noticed how Ravi had removed Maya's ring, and how his eyes followed the lovely Mrs Fitzroy everywhere.

He was clearly in a kind of delirium, and the Maharani was reminded of a leopard basking in the sun, sated and contented, lazily licking its paws after a kill.

They both knew it couldn't last, but when their dream ended it still came as a shock. She had been applying kohl to her eyes, as she often did now; apart from the added allure it gave to her eyes, she felt the smoky magical potion marked the transformation she had undergone, both in her body and soul.

He was watching her from the bed as she sat before the mirror, still in her chemise, her long red hair tumbling down her back while lit by the molten gold of the sun as it flared like a halo around her head. They had lingered too long together and the bright day was already shining through the white muslin curtains. They usually left their little palace at dawn, before the rest of the household awoke, but he had insisted on having breakfast with her alone and had risked their being discovered.

As he watched her brushing her hair, the fine silk of her

chemise slipped off her shoulder, exposing the creamy skin of her back, and filling him with a sudden desire to have her once more, before their day of pretence began.

He came up behind her, his lithe step silent but swift. His fingers wound in her hair and around her breast and he kissed her neck while whispering in her ear, "Come back to bed ..." She only smiled at him in the mirror, and let her head fall back against his shoulder. They were used to each other's long tender silences.

Taking the brush out of her hand, he pulled her towards the bed, murmuring, "I want to make you ask for more ... and more ..."

Then a voice called out, jolting them both out of their dream, "Sarianna! Mistress!"

He pulled back, his eyes blazing. "What is that woman doing here? She guards you like a terrier."

She pushed away his arms and slid off the bed, winding her hair back into some kind of order.

"Sarianna!" Malika's voice called out again, this time with more urgency. "A messenger has come, from Mr Charles! Mr Charles is coming here! He comes tonight ..."

"Charles!" Just speaking his name brought terror. "He'll kill you if he finds you here."

"It is very unlikely." Sabran's voice was a cold sneer as he reached for a cigarette, and he blew the smoke into the air. "But we must talk. Send Malika away."

Sara's voice shook as she spoke. "Go back to the house, Malika. I'll be there soon."

They both waited till footsteps were heard leaving the

344

terrace, then he encircled her in his arms before kissing her very gently where the base of her shoulder met her throat.

He whispered into her neck, "We can go away together. We can leave at once."

"Oh, if only we could. If only it were that simple." She closed her eyes and tried to imagine what it would be like to have him with her always, to eat with him, to walk with him, and to sleep in the same bed every night. But there, at the edge of her dream, was Maya, weeping and distraught, pleading with outstretched arms, and Charles, who she knew would never agree to a divorce, especially if he discovered her love for Ravi Sabran. A torrent of pain and retribution would be unleashed over both their heads, and it would be relentless and pitiless, a struggle so violent and full of hate she was afraid it might even end in death.

"It's impossible." Tears formed in her eyes as she realised the terrible truth of her words.

He sat up, alert now. "We can be away from here in a moment! It's obvious you don't love your husband."

She sat up, trying to cast off the temptation to fall back into his arms.

"You must help me dress." She stood with her back to him, her stays held in place over her breasts.

"I will, if you promise to come with me now."

"Please, Ravi ..."

He scowled, but then, with almost childish reluctance, he helped to pull the silk ribbons of her corset around her waist.

"They must be tighter or I won't be able to get into my dress."

He pulled the ribbons making the circle of her waist smaller. "How can I bear it?" He kissed her bare back in a lingering way while cupping her breasts in his hands. "You tease me till I go mad."

Then, in a burst of desperation, he pulled her around to face him, hypnotising her with his eyes. "You will stay with me. You will come to Pondicherry with me now, at once."

He kissed her again, pressing her back into the pillows, willing her to succumb to his desire, even though he knew she had hardened her resolve.

It was only when she held his face in her hands and looked into his eyes, did the truth begin to dawn on him.

"Charles will find us and kill you ... or have you killed." She spoke with great care, willing him to hear her. "He won't rest till he does. I know him. I know what he's capable of."

He took her hands away from his face and held them behind her back.

"I'm not afraid of him, and I won't let you go. Not till I want to."

Her voice was choked with tears when she spoke. "Why do you make it so hard for me? Especially when we both know we can never meet again ..."

"What do you mean? Why must we part?" He held her tighter still, but she could see a little doubt begin to show in his eyes.

"We haven't thought ... We forgot everything and everyone ..." She threw off his restraining arms and began to dress, snatching up pieces of discarded clothing from where they lay around the room.

He watched her as he smoked, his expression becoming darker, even though his words were full of hope. "Yes, yes, at first things will be painful and difficult, and people will suffer because of it, but it will be worth it. As I said, it is fated. And I love you ..." he added, his voice strong and unshakable, as though that mere fact was enough to overcome all obstacles.

For a moment she felt a surge of hope, and almost believed it might be possible they could be happy together. Then the bliss faded, leaving cold reality.

"Charles will never let me go, and he'll never divorce me."

"What is he, compared to how we feel about each other?"

Her feelings were so strong, words were almost useless, but she roused herself to reason with him. "Have you forgotten Maya? Will you cast her off? She can never go home to her family. You know she'll be made to live the rest of her life in shame. Where will she go? Not back to her husband. He'll kill her; you know he will. Or will she live in a house set up by you, the same as me? Is that fated too?"

This time her words hit their mark and the expression in his eyes gave her the answer she was looking for.

"I didn't think of her. I didn't want to. She would be helpless without my protection." His dark eyes took on a look of acute pain. "How cruel I am." This time he turned away from her as he pushed his long black hair back from his face. He was frowning now and tearing at his bottom lip with his teeth.

"I must go, Ravi."

He tried again to persuade her; he accused her of caring too much what people thought, and then at last, when he saw she was unmoved, he became desperate. "I'll find a beautiful house for you. You'll have everything you want ... anything, jewels, I'm a rich man, much richer than you could imagine ... We'll go to France, or come to Pondi with me. Promise me you'll come to me there. I can't leave you here with that man. I can't bear to think of him touching you. He won't have you!"

She saw him involuntarily clench his hands, as though imagining them tightening around Charles's throat.

"I will confront him with the truth of our love, then he'll have to give you a divorce. The shame will be too much for him." He smiled, as though he had the answer at last.

"You forget about Maya. She'll stand between us like a ghost forever. Forever! You know that to be true! I can't hurt her, knowing what her future would be, even though I want you!"

He stood there for a long moment, filled with a mixture of rage and helplessness. "I'll leave this place for your sake, but I won't say goodbye to you. I can't, even if I wanted to. You forget. The gods have willed we must be together."

"Oh Ravi," she said as she wiped the tears from her eyes, "we can't forsake Maya, even if the gods have."

Chapter 32

The Maharani and her ladies watched her with curious eyes. Sara was sure they suspected something, and the feeling made her anxious and guilty.

The Maharani was the first to speak. "Monsieur Sabran has gone. What will we ladies do for amusement now?"

If there had been any colour left in Sara's face it would have rushed up to her cheeks at that moment, but she turned to the Maharani and, after a faltering start, found the courage to ask her not to mention Sabran's visit.

"You see, my husband has an unreasonable dislike of Monsieur Sabran ... and it could be uncomfortable for me ... and for him." Saying the words out loud only made her feel more miserable, and a slow tear escaped and ran down her cheek.

"Of course, my dear Mrs Fitzroy, his name will not be mentioned. I understand completely." The woman's shrewd eyes, though, couldn't conceal what she really thought. Even so, she patted Sara's arm kindly.

"You must rest. You must look pretty for when your husband arrives."

Charles had written that he would be taking her to the nearby hill town of Ootacamund, where they would meet up with Cynthia and Lady Palmer. There would be no question of her not accompanying him.

"Snooty Ooty", as the Maharani laughingly called it, where the British community of Madras went to escape the heat of the plains for the worst of the summer months.

"I hope having my husband here will not inconvenience you too much."

"It is an honour, of course. He will be made most welcome." She was gracious as always, but Sara could sense a slight tone of sarcasm in the woman's voice.

Sara left her to find refuge in her lovely rooms, made all the more dear to her now, as they would be hers alone for the last time. She spent a restless day reliving the nights of passion in the arms of Ravi Sabran, in between helpless bouts of tears and the dread of Charles's reaction to her request for a separation. For a separation she must have now. It would be impossible for her to ever endure his touch again.

She thought about Ravi's suggestion of a house in Pondicherry. She could easily bear the infamy and gossip that would inevitably follow if she decided to take up his offer; the thought of a future without him seemed by far much worse. But again it was Maya who dominated her thoughts. There was no refuge for her apart from Ravi Sabran. Even if he established her safely in a different house, it was impossible he would never see her again, and it was equally impossible Sara could share him with another woman.

From the moment Charles arrived, the mood in the palace changed from one of relaxed friendliness to a formal, almost ceremonial round of duties.

The Maharaja didn't like him but made a huge effort to hide the fact for Sara's sake. She sat next to her husband, maintaining a polite and almost distant conversation, while Charles ate the dishes placed before him, made especially plain by the bemused kitchen staff.

Charles seemed undeterred by the chilliness of the table but kept up a constant barrage of talk in between mouthfuls of food. Sara was reminded of spasmodic bouts of rifle fire, so strict he seemed after the amusing idle chatter of the past weeks.

The talk was of the small rebellions springing up all over the country and the need to crush them at once if order was to be maintained.

"I expect your help, sir ..." he turned to the Maharaja, who sat with a tightly controlled dignity at the head of the table "... especially with the local people here. There's talk of them being whipped up by Sabran and his men. Do you know anything of this?"

The Maharaja laughed and spread his arms wide apart, as if to show he had nothing to hide. "How would I know anything, when I haven't seen Monsieur Sabran for months? He is like a phantom; he appears and disappears at will."

Sara looked up from where she'd been staring down at her plate of uneaten food and caught a sly wink from the Maharaja. She looked around, alarmed. Surely Charles would be able to tell it was a lie, but he kept his eyes fixed on his own plate as he ate.

"Well, if you hear of him could you let me know at once? I confess it is difficult to prove, and the devil is, as you say, very slippery. He's a powerful man and has a lot of friends in high places. We will get him eventually though, make no mistake. And when we do ... I'll make him pay."

Sara looked around the table, pale and alarmed, unable to speak. There was silence till the whisky and cigars arrived, then a half-hearted attempt at conversation for a respectable number of minutes.

But the Maharaja had the royal prerogative to please himself and made an attempt to rise. In a moment his retainers and the Maharani were at his side to haul him to his feet. He nodded towards Charles, who was clearly put out by the Maharaja leaving so soon. "Forgive me, but here I keep early hours."

Sara knew he was leaving because he couldn't bear her husband's company a moment longer. She almost didn't care. Charles's words had crushed any other thought.

She rose and curtsied as the Maharaja began to make his very slow and dignified exit. The Maharani too chose that moment to make her excuses. "I go where my husband goes." Her face was impassive, but Sara could see she too was deeply offended.

"Make him pay". The words spun around and around in

Sara's head. She was almost blind with fear, and all she could think of was Ravi being dragged before Charles for questioning, and how humiliating it would be for him. He would be sure to react and give Charles a reason to have him imprisoned. She had to get out of the room and away from Charles or it would be impossible to hide her feelings from him any longer.

"If you'll excuse me, I must speak to the Maharani about something ..." Charles had risen to kiss her on the cheek and she caught the expression in his eyes she dreaded. He would try to make love to her and she wouldn't be able to bear it. She would have to lie about being indisposed. The mere mention of her menstrual cycle was enough to make him blanch in horror and hurry away to the narrow bed in his dressing room.

A few minutes later she joined the Maharani in her private apartments.

She stood at the open doorway, unsure now if she would be welcome.

"I must apologise for my husband. He seems to have an irrational hatred for Monsieur Sabran, and it doesn't seem fair you have to lie to hide your association with him."

The Maharani picked up on her bitterness and smiled in a way that showed she understood. "I would say anything to protect Monsieur Ravi ... and perhaps your husband has another reason for hating him so much."

Sara blushed. "I've never given my husband a reason for jealousy ... that is not till ..." She stared down at the floor and bit her lip.

"There's no point hiding your love for him from me. It's written on your face for all to see when you look at him."

"Please don't say such things, because, even if it's true, it can never be." Saying the words out loud added a finality she'd never really considered before. Deep in her heart she had hoped there would be a chance all obstacles could be overcome, but even a few hours in the company of Charles had been enough to convince her how desperate her situation was.

The Maharani beckoned her to sit beside her on the settee, before taking Sara's hand in her own. "Before I met my husband I was deeply in love with a young man who was not of my caste. I thought I would die if I could not have him. But, as you see, I did not die. Neither will you."

Sara turned her face away; she had broken down at last and was sobbing into her hands. "I would rather die ... I hope I die."

"Don't be unhappy, my dear. You're so young, and there's so much ahead of you yet."

"If that's true, then why do I feel my life is over?" she wailed like a woman bereaved. "My husband will never allow me to leave him, and I can never love him again."

The image of Ravi when she saw him last rose up before her, taunting her, causing her to writhe as though in pain. Though, even in the midst of her torment, she tried to tell herself she had been seduced by his exotic charm as if she had been entranced by a character from the *Arabian Nights*. He was a mere figure from a picture book; she would soon forget him, she must forget him. In her agony she pounded the cushions with her fists and sobbed, crying his name aloud, not caring now what the Maharani thought of her.

"It can never be." The Maharani was firm now. "You must stay with your husband. He would never give you up to Monsieur Ravi. Your husband will have him thrown into prison for the rest of his life, or worse. You must think of him, and you must think of Maya. She will kill herself if he ever leaves her, I'm sure of it. The gods will punish you both."

"The gods won't have to punish me," she sobbed. "I'm suffering enough already. I'll never see him again, never!"

She allowed herself only a few more moments of grief, then she wiped her eyes and made a decision. She would never look back. It was far too painful. His name would never be mentioned again, either spoken aloud or whispered to herself in her moments of longing.

The night before she was due to leave, Sara visited the Maharani and the Maharaja again in their private apartments. She was filled with apprehension, knowing she might be offered a parting gift and she had nothing of value to give in return except a silver tobacco case that had once belonged to her father. It had taken a great deal to think about giving it up, so dear it was to her, and her hand trembled at the thought of parting with it.

The Maharaja looked at the tobacco case for some time without saying a word, giving Sara the impression she'd made a dreadful mistake. She chewed on her bottom lip and waited. The gift was too poor for a man of such importance.

After a while she felt compelled to say something in her

defence. "The case belonged to my father; it isn't valuable, but you can see the pattern is very interesting." She traced the design with her finger, wishing he would speak and put her out of her misery. "I believe it's very old ..."

At last he looked up. She was amazed to see signs of tears in his eyes.

"I know this cigarette case. I have seen him use it in past times." He turned to the Maharani, though she only gave him a cautious warning look in return.

Sara picked up on their signals at once. "Why won't you speak to me about my parents? Forgive me, but if there's something I should know ..."

The Maharaja looked at his wife. "We must tell her."

"Tell me what? Please, don't keep me in suspense."

"We wanted to tell you, my dear Mrs Fitzroy, from the first night you were here, but we were afraid you would be angry. Monsieur Ravi said we must tell you the truth for your own sake."

"What does Monsieur Ravi know that I don't?" She was frightened now and finding it difficult to remain calm.

The Maharani made herself comfortable on the settee beside her, crossing her legs and taking out one of her strong cigarettes. She took a deep breath and blew out the smoke with a great sigh. "Did anyone ever tell you anything about your mother's family?"

"No, not even my aunt had any idea where she came from, she often became angry when I asked questions about her."

"I do know ..." The Maharani hesitated for a moment, as though what she was about to say would cost her a great deal of pain. "I know everything about her. You see, your grandmother was my aunt. She was a very great princess from Hyderabad." As she spoke she seemed to grow in stature, her pride was so evident. "That means you are a princess also."

"A princess? Surely not ... You must be mistaken ..." She began to tremble and had to support herself on the arm of the chair.

Ravi Sabran's words filled her brain, soft and echoing. "It is indeed fate that has brought you back to India."

The Maharani took her hand and held her eyes with her own, and for the first time Sara felt she was looking at a true reflection of herself.

"There was a terrible scene when your grandmother Lilita married an officer from the English army, a Major George. My family spoke of it often, how she was an outcast from both the British and the Indian community. She defied her own parents to marry this Englishman."

Sara shook her head in disbelief. "Is this true? How can you be sure?"

The Maharaja took her arm and placed it in his own. She was glad of it, as her legs still shook oddly. "I will show you the proof, come with me."

There, on the wall above their bed and adorned by a wreath of marigolds, the Maharani pointed to a small painting of two people from a time many years before; it showed a lovely girl in wedding attire, almost weighed down with precious jewels, seated next to a tall, smiling, blond English officer. Sara examined the portrait and, real or imagined, could see something of herself there. It was barely noticeable, but surely there was something about the shape of her eyebrows, almost exactly the same as her own, and the shape of the mouth ...

"They were in love and would not listen to reason. They had one daughter only before your grandmother died in childbirth barely a year after. That child was your mother Lillian, named after her dear mother, but of course her name was the safe English version of Lilita."

"It must be true then, it must be true."

"Yes, yes, it is true, and her family have never forgiven Major George for taking her away, only to die. Then he married again to an English lady, and Lillian was brought up as an English child. She was very like her father Major George, except she had hair the colour of a raven. This picture was returned to our family by Major George's new English wife; she wanted no reminder of Lillian's mother. Lillian in turn married a charming Englishman, Radcliffe, and moved to Madras, is that not so?"

"Yes, that is so, but why didn't they say that my mother had an Indian family? It was wrong of them not to tell me. My aunt must have lied about my mother having Spanish blood."

"She lied to protect you. She knew how you would suffer, like your poor mother, even though her skin was as white as yours and it was never actually known by the English community she had an Indian mother. There were rumours, and it seemed that was enough for some members of the English community to treat them as outcasts."

"But it's such a small thing ... so unimportant ... I will

never understand why ... and yet my mother, my beautiful sweet mother, was an outcast. Yes, I saw it in Lord Palmer's eyes."

"Your own father's family disowned him also because he married an Anglo-Indian girl. It made no difference to him at all. He was proud of it, and even wrote to your grandmother to say so. It seems your grandmother wrote back to him and said if he married your mother she would have nothing more to do with him. I know it broke his heart.

"My poor father ... He must have suffered terribly, to be cast out from his own family because of a stupid prejudice, then to die so young ..."

"Now you can understand why they kept your background a secret.

It was to protect you, but I believe if your parents had lived they would have told you. Do you mind very much? Are you ashamed to be one of us?" The Maharani watched Sara's face for a sign that might betray any hidden feelings, but there was none. There was only joy and relief.

She threw her arms around the Maharani and kissed her. "I'm proud, very proud. I've found my family. I had no one and now ..."

She thought back to all those years of silent rejection. Her uncle's suspicious stares when he thought she wasn't looking. Her aunt's strict manner, and her defence of her when Sara was accused of all kinds of misdemeanours from laziness to lying. How often had she heard her fellow Englishmen on the subject of the Indian race? "You can't trust them, a lying, thieving lot on the whole. An Englishman's honour is everything to him. They could never hope to understand that."

She wiped the tears from her eyes. "So much is clear to me now, so clear." Though, even as she said the words, she knew she would be forced to make a painful decision. She looked to the Maharani for the answer, searching her eyes.

The Maharani answered at once. "You must never tell a soul, least of all your husband." She spoke the words "your husband" with an undeniable contempt. "He will not take this news well, I think."

"I'm not sure if it will matter much any more what my husband thinks. I don't plan to stay with him any longer than I have to. You must have suspected we are not happy."

"Are you sure, my dear child? It is a big step you are planning."

"Even so, there seems to be no choice."

Sara's problems seemed insurmountable now and, of course, if she told Charles the truth of her parentage the result would be terrible and immediate. She needed time to think and absorb such momentous news, and she needed money, to start life afresh. For the moment, the lies and secrecy must continue.

Chapter 33

Sara was dressing for dinner in her room at the Royal Hotel in Ooty, enjoying a pleasant moment alone with Malika as she brushed her mistress's hair before containing it in its usual heavy chignon. They were talking of a shared memory of the past when Charles burst in and they both flinched, as though guilty of some offence. At first it seemed as though he might be angry at finding them behaving in such an informal way with each other. They both knew he disapproved of familiarity and expected an outburst of anger, though his eyes went at once to the emeralds lying on the dressing table.

"Sara, my dear ..." He waved Malika away and she fled, dropping the hairbrush as she ran. She stopped and glanced at it lying on the floor, thinking he would abuse her for her clumsiness. But he stooped to pick it up and went to Sara, smiling as he did so.

"Clever little minx," he said as he helped fasten the earrings in her ears, then raised her face to the light to admire the way they emphasised the green lights in her eyes. "They must be worth a fortune. It's as though they were designed for you." Sara crushed a desire to laugh, and to blurt out that they'd been designed for someone very like her. The earrings had been impossible to refuse, having been worn by her own grandmother on her wedding day.

"I'm glad I please you at last, Charles."

"You do please me, very much." He cleared his throat as though embarrassed. "Listen, I want to be a better husband to you. I feel I've let you down and I intend to make up for it."

For a moment he looked at her with such intensity it was almost possible to believe him. "There's something else ... I don't like it about myself ... but ..." It took him some time to blurt the words out. "I admit I've been terribly jealous of your friendship with Sabran ... terribly jealous. It may have made me dislike him more. But can you blame me? You seemed so damned impressed by him." He took her hand and held it, his eyes downcast. "Try to forgive me."

She couldn't look at him, her heart was so heavy with guilt, but it was all too late now.

"You should have trusted me. I wanted to love you."

"You make it sound as though you don't any more."

"And do you still love me? I never seem to make you happy."

"I do love you. I love you madly."

"Even if you should discover something about me you may not like?"

His face clouded over for an instant, but he spoke with absolute certainty. "You could never do anything wrong, I know that much."

But Sara persisted, burning at that moment to tell him of her mother.

"Charles …"

He didn't hear her, so engrossed he was in his plans for their future.

"From now on everything will be different. Oh, and when we return home," he added, almost as an afterthought, "you'll be pleased to find Lakshmi gone."

"Lakshmi's gone?"

"Oh, she was a bit difficult, I'll admit." He poured himself a brandy from the decanter on the side table and swallowed it in a gulp.

"Don't worry, darling. I found her a good place."

"But Charles, couldn't it have waited till we got back? I would've liked to say goodbye at least, and to make absolutely sure she's happy."

"She had to go. She caused too much trouble amongst the men. You were right after all, but I felt we had to keep her because of Lady Palmer. You know what she can be like."

"Yes, I do."

He took her in his arms and kissed her with more than usual passion, then pulled back to smile at her. His blue eyes were clear and unclouded by guilt.

The seed of suspicion had proved to be unfounded after all. She was convinced at last he could never have had anything to do with Lakshmi.

"I've got you someone else." He smiled. "She's a quiet little thing. You'll like her. What's her name again? Nagma."

Sara felt her anger rising. She was beginning to hate him again. "I don't want anyone else. Malika's enough for me. She's all I want."

"Malika's getting old; you need someone younger."

"I wish you'd asked me first."

"You were away, and the girl was looking for a place. She'll make an excellent ayah when you have a son. Which, my darling, I hope will be soon." He took her arm, but she resisted.

"Surely it's up to me who I choose as a servant?"

"Well, this was a favour to George. She wasn't getting on with his household. You know how these things work."

"No, I don't."

"Well, it's nothing to get upset about. If it means that much to you, I'll ask George to take her back, and you can get someone else. Now, come on, I'm hungry!"

He was already thinking of something else, but for Sara none of this mattered now. She had laid her plans and would leave as soon as she returned to Madras. She would take her jewels and sell them and set up a house somewhere on her own. It would be too scandalous for Charles to endure, and then he'd have to give her a divorce.

Cynthia was waiting at the dining table when they came downstairs. She could barely contain her excitement. She whispered through clenched teeth, "There's that Sabran person over there by the window. Who does he think he is?"

Charles glared across the room, instantly on the alert but saying nothing.

Sara's hand flew to her throat. Surely he hadn't come to see her. She felt her head swim as the colour drained from her face.

Cynthia prattled on regardless, unaware of the pain she

was causing. "He's behaving as though he has a perfect right to be here ... in a hotel meant for us English alone. God knows it's the only time we get away from them."

Sara looked up and caught Sabran's glance from the other side of the room. His eyes were full of meaning. He sat with one arm over the back of his chair while he smoked a fragrant cigarette, surveying the room through his half-closed eyes. When their eyes met, he gave her a glance that meant he wanted to speak to her and she knew if she didn't he would come to her, and the consequences would be disastrous for them both.

"I must go and speak to him, if only to be polite."

"I would prefer you didn't, my dear." Charles made his meaning quite clear; he would be angry if she did.

It was impossible not to be aware of Sabran's presence in the room. Sara knew he was watching her. She could feel him in every nerve of her body. She cast him another hasty look. He seemed tired; she could tell by the bluish smudges under his eyes, but somehow it pleased her that he might not be sleeping well, hoping she might be the cause of his sleepless-ness.

As soon as she glanced back at him he sent her another questioning look.

The tension at the table was becoming unbearable.

"I must speak to him. It's terribly rude not to."

She rose to leave the table, but Charles pulled her down almost at once.

"I said, I would prefer you didn't."

Sara rose once more. "Charles, you're hurting me!"

He released his grip on her arm and, before he could stop her, she hurried across the room and stood before Sabran's table. He smiled up at her, showing a faint flash of his white teeth. She was so overcome with nerves she put one hand on the table to steady herself.

In the background the clinking of the cutlery against plates seemed amplified. Even the servants waiting at table were hushed at their tasks and moved around the room as though treading on eggshells.

He stood at once and bowed his head.

She spoke in almost a whisper. "How did you know I was here?"

"I went back to the palace and they said you were here. I was going to have it out with your husband once and for all. I felt like a coward, leaving you there to face him alone." He was clearly agitated and could barely remain in his seat. "I want you to come with me ... tonight ..." his voice purred as he reached out for her hand.

She pulled it away as though it burned. "Please, someone will see."

She turned around to look at Charles. Even though he seemed deeply engrossed in conversation with Cynthia she knew he was enraged by her behaviour. She could tell by the red flush on the back on his neck.

"Please, by persisting you put us both in danger."

"If you hadn't come to me I would have come to you. Then I would have forced the issue once and for all. Your husband could never have stood me approaching you at his table." He spoke with such bitterness Sara shivered.

"He senses there's something between us; you can hardly blame him for his attitude."

His mouth twisted into a nasty half smile. "I want him to know. I want him to know what it's like to lose something he loves."

A chill ran down her back. "What do you mean?"

A loud scraping noise of a chair being moved caused her to look around. Charles stood glaring at them both from across the room, holding his napkin in his hand, ready to spring.

"I must go. Promise me you won't tell him ... Please promise me?"

"You ask me to forfeit my honour ..."

"Promise me?"

"For the moment, yes, I agree, but soon I will confront him with the truth."

She gave him one last despairing look, then hurried back to her table and tried to resume her meal, despite the cold air of disapproval.

"There," she said, trying to smile at her husband's furious face, "I've spoken to him, and good manners have been observed. It wasn't so terrible, was it?"

She could see Charles wanted to unleash his anger on her but, being in a public place, he struggled to overcome it. Instead he took out his fury on a waiter who had delivered a meal not to his liking.

He leaned over his plate with a look of disgust. The waiter began to tremble, knowing he was in for a storm of abuse.

"Take this back to the kitchen at once! When will you ignorant fools learn to do the simplest of tasks?"

"Charles, please! Does it matter so much?"

"Well, of course it matters. This might seem a small thing but it's a symbol of how useless these people are." He spat the words bitterly, and loud enough for Sabran to hear on the other side of the room.

Sara glanced up and caught Sabran's contemptuous smile. His face was dark with loathing. He could barely control the contortion of his mouth. Sara realised then just how much he hated Charles; it was dangerous and all-consuming, and unlikely ever to be resolved.

Charles fell to eating his meal with relish, while Sara looked on, fighting her disgust.

"Of all places to run into Sabran, just as well I'm on holiday and in a good mood, otherwise I might be tempted to bring him in for questioning. Though it's more nuisance than it's worth, and besides I haven't a scrap of proof and his lawyers are notoriously accomplished about their work, but the fellow really is causing me a lot of trouble at the moment ..."

"What do you mean?" Sara could barely speak.

"I don't want to discuss it, not in front of decent women ..."

"Oh, please, Charles, a little bit of gossip is just what we need."

Cynthia tossed him one of her slavish smiles, and Sara noticed for the first time how much she resembled a little sharp-toothed fox.

"Well ..." he laughed "... you ladies must have your gossip ... It's about the woman he lives with. You know her husband wants me to intervene in some way and make her go back to him. I told him there was nothing I could do and it's the truth. But I suggested he use force if need be. I won't stand in his way ... By the way, this isn't half bad," he said, indicating with his fork at the roast beef.

Sara started, shocked to the core. "Charles! How could you suggest such a thing?"

He looked at her with genuine surprise. "You know nothing about it, and I don't believe Sabran really cares about the girl. With his money he could buy fifty of the most beautiful girls in Madras. He only keeps her to irritate me. I believe he'd do anything to get back at me ..."

His words rang in Sara's ears and a horrible doubt began to creep over her. Surely, surely Ravi hadn't made love to her in order to get back at Charles? Was the love-making, the passion, the words of love, only to get back at Charles? No, she was sure that wasn't so. He loved her ... He must love her ...

"The man is capable of anything." Cynthia's voice broke into her thoughts, though the words came muted and far away, in the form of an echo. "You remember, Charles, that vulgar affair with the wife of that fool, Harry Tyler. They were carrying on behind the poor devil's back for months, and everyone knew he was only doing it because Harry had spoken out against preventing half-castes from joining the tennis club in Sabran's hearing ... Just the sort of disgusting revenge that cad would go in for ..."

"Yes, and I believe he'd murder me without a moment's hesitation if he thought he'd get away with it. Though he's cunning enough to find other ways to hurt me without getting caught."

"Do anything to get back at me ..." The words seemed to pound in Sara's ears.

"I want him to know what it's like to lose something he loves."

"Cunning enough to find other ways ..."

She'd been warned over and over about him, right from the very beginning, by almost everyone of her acquaintance, yet she had chosen to ignore them all. Even when it was obvious he hated her husband with a passion. She was a fool! A naive fool!

Sara glanced up at Ravi and, catching him off guard, saw his smile of sneering hatred as he watched Charles. How could she have ever imagined he could be interested in her, when he had Maya, beautiful Maya, the loveliest, most desirable of women?

He had made love to her for revenge. She was sure of it now. How could she be so stupid? Without realising it, her face took on a look of absolute horror.

"Are you quite well, my dear?" Charles asked, though Sara could do nothing but stare down at her plate.

Cynthia's voice chattered on. "Of course, the Tyler woman had to leave town; no one would have anything to do with her once the whole thing was discovered. Her husband was sent to Cairo, I believe; he could never hold up his head in Madras again. Sabran just laughed, of course, as publicly as possible, as he always does when he sticks his knife into one of us. And that's not all ... There are so many rumours. It seems even that Turnbull woman was having an affair with him as well ..."

Sara rose from the table, summoning all her strength to

appear to be normal and unconcerned. "Charles, would you mind? I think I'll take my dinner in my room. I'm feeling a little unwell …"

"My dear, you are looking a little pale." He stood to help her, and she swayed a little. He put an arm around her waist to steady her.

From the other side of the room, Sara heard the sudden noise of a coffee cup hitting the saucer, and she knew Sabran was watching her.

Cynthia's sharp eyes crossed from one to the other and Sara caught the look in her eyes. It was barely perceptible but there all the same. She suspected something.

Sara stayed in her room feigning sickness and spent the whole of the next day pacing the floor, condemning herself for her own foolish behaviour, and blushing with shame at her willingness to fall into Sabran's arms when he must have been laughing at her the entire time.

She waited till Charles went downstairs for dinner before leaving her room, only venturing out into the cool of the hotel garden when darkness fell, and she felt safe from prying eyes. But again she paced, wearing herself out with recriminations, till at last she threw herself down on a garden chair and wept with frustration.

A sudden movement from the depth of the garden made her look up, at first in alarm, to see the dark figure of a man silhouetted against the light of the full moon.

"Who's there?"

A figure stepped out of the darkness.

"It's Ravi ... I've been waiting for you. I thought you must leave your room some time."

"Monsieur Sabran," she said coldly.

He sat down beside her and tried to take her hand, but she snatched it away.

"Please, if Charles should ..."

"I have something to tell you. It cannot wait, my darling ..."

She squeezed her eyes shut and shook her head from side to side. If she looked into his eyes or even listened to his words she would weaken.

"I told you. I don't want to see you again, ever!"

"That's impossible. Too much has happened."

As he came closer to her she drew back, recoiling from what she saw as his false charm. "Nothing has happened ... If you are referring to my disgusting behaviour, please don't. I'm terribly ashamed of it. I was lonely and feeling sorry for myself ..."

She stood to leave; the moonlight lit up the expression on her face. Her eyes were so cold he stepped back. His smile faded; he understood at last. "Disgusting? You call what passed between us disgusting?"

She thought back to those joyous weeks, weeks she had once held sacred as a beloved memory. A memory she'd turned to, to sustain her as she had lain unhappily beside her husband.

"Why are you talking to me like this? What have I done except confess my love for you? You know we're meant for each other, even more so now."

"If you mean because you've discovered I have Indian

blood?" she sneered. "I don't see what possible difference that could make."

She drew on everything she had to repel him. She raised her chin to look down on him with a cold disdainful stare. "I don't want to discuss it. If you were a gentleman you would forget the whole thing. Can't you see how your presence here is offensive to me?"

This time his anger was palpable, and he chose his words for maximum impact. "Disgusted and offensive! You didn't seem so disgusted and offended at the time."

She put her hands over her ears as though his words gave her pain, but he was pitiless in his scorn.

"So an affair is acceptable as long as no one finds out, and then you crawl back to your husband."

"Is that what Harry Tyler's wife did to you?" She snapped around to face him, her eyes black with fury.

He almost laughed out loud. "What do you know about this?"

"Enough."

"Enough to condemn me forever, on what seems to me to be very thin evidence."

"I'm told your behaviour was dishonourable in every way."

"Dishonourable! Maryanne was a lonely woman whom I liked very much, as it happens, but it was long ago and I was alone; we both knew it was never serious. It's unfortunate she was discovered, that's all, and she was made to pay dearly for her indiscretion. Yes, part of me wanted to get back at her husband. He offended me, and I was ruthless in getting my revenge and I didn't care who I hurt. But it's different with you ..."

Ruthless! The word taunted her. Yes, he was ruthless; she had seen it herself when he had commanded his men to lie prone before her. Well, she could be ruthless too. Her face when she turned to him was almost contorted with emotion.

"There is something you should know, and it might help you to understand once and for all. I love my husband! I always have. I was bored, that's all! And for a moment or two you filled that boredom!" Her voice shook as her eyes filled with tears. "But your presence is now hateful to me, despite what the gods have ordained!"

Her rage had sustained her, but now everything seemed flat and listless.

He looked at her closely, as though trying to read her mind. Then he smiled, very cool and very calm. "As you wish, madam. You will never see me again."

Then he stepped back into the darkness of the night, his footsteps echoing on the flagstone path as he stormed away, without once looking back.

Chapter 34

Barely a month later, Sara looked out of the window of her house in Madras to see, with the coming of the rains, the scarlet sunbirds had returned to her garden once more.

To be back was almost a relief after all, despite the time of year and the unsettling monsoon season. She loved the sudden storms and flooding rains, which seemed with their downpour to act on her own emotions and somehow relieve the pent-up pain and anger she still felt over her final scene with Ravi.

Life was relatively calm now, at least on the surface. The atmosphere in the house had altered, especially since Lakshmi had left, and it seemed she had taken some of the tension with her. Sara could almost convince herself she liked the little house now, but she knew it was really because she was about to leave it forever. It was hard, though, to turn her back on the life around her. She had lingered only because she'd become so fond of all the people in the house, and they too looked to her as a stabilising influence over Charles. His wild and unpredictable moods frightened them, as they had once frightened her, but now, as she was about to put all of it behind her, she felt like a traitor for their sakes.

She wondered at the wild episode with Ravi and put it down to a type of temporary madness. The image of Ravi's face, once so strong, had now begun to fade, as the tiger lilies in her garden faded after being exposed to too much sun.

At times, when she felt the old burning desire to be near him again, she quickly crushed the sensation, reminding herself over and over again of how he'd tricked her, and how he had used her, and it became easier as time passed to convince herself she felt nothing for him.

Though sometimes her agony became unbearable, and the wild deep sobs that followed left her with not only swollen eyes and a bleak heart but also with just enough courage to carry on a seemingly normal life.

She had managed to persuade Charles not to return Maya to her husband, and her conscience was soothed by the thought that the girl would be safe at last. That one concession by Charles had helped her to forgive him some of his other faults and had made it more bearable for her to live with him till she could leave. There were no pangs of regret, only that she hadn't left him sooner, and a deep, all-consuming sadness.

There was pity for him, as in a way she felt he was a victim too, of a society that trampled and twisted its people into a hard, unfeeling mass of repressed emotions. He had been trained well and she knew, deep in her heart, he was unlikely to ever change.

Her main regret was that she would never be able to see Prema again, though she consoled herself with the knowledge that the little girl was well taken care of, and better off with her own people, even though she felt she had not really fulfilled her promise to the old man.

Though, even as she said the reassuring words to herself, she crushed a feeling of longing. The episode in her life where she'd felt the most fulfilled, the most truly herself, was over with, along with the storms and colour and the burning passion. It had been too consuming after all, and, she told herself, it was a relief to be safe from feeling too much.

At times she thought she might go to Europe to live, Italy perhaps.

The climate was much healthier than India and, as her past sickness had returned more frequently than ever, she began to think it was the best plan after all. But it was all so painful to think about: to leave India, her parents' home, and Malika as well, when she had only just discovered them.

However, her real reason to consider leaving India, even though she dared not admit it, even to herself, was because the pain of her memories was at times too much after all, and if she was ever to have real peace of mind she needed to forget she had ever once loved Ravi Sabran.

Her bag was packed and hidden under her bed. All that remained now was to tell Malika, and they could leave before Charles returned.

She couldn't go to Lucy's, as Charles would be sure to go there. Also, it was very possible she might run into Ravi, and that would be disastrous. The Maharani would take her in, but she and the Maharaja had left for Ceylon to wait out the dry season in their little province and it would be several months before they returned to India.

Then she remembered the small hotel next to Chandran, the silk merchant. It was a respectable place, mainly for ladies from the country who came to Madras to buy wedding saris for their daughters. There, no one would ever be likely to discover her.

Her precious jewels had been wrapped in a silk nightgown and pushed to the back of her underwear drawer. But as soon as she opened the drawer she knew something was wrong. Her various silks and linens lay scattered about in wild disorder when they were usually folded neatly. Malika would never leave her things in such a state. She made a frantic scrabble at the corners of the drawer, but she already knew it was hopeless. The mother-of-pearl box had gone, along with her self-control. She lunged at a fine lawn nightgown in frustration, tearing at it with her teeth, till it lay a tattered rag at her feet. Of course he'd taken her jewels, to make sure she was enslaved to him forever.

There was nothing she could do but wait till he came home. But even then she must be cunning and show no sign of her intention to leave. She would ask about the jewels and find out where he'd hidden them, and somehow she would get them back.

Meanwhile she sipped a glass of brandy and water while

she waited; it was something she rarely did, but the warm smooth fluid settled her stomach and her nerves.

Soon the drink did its work and she began to relax as she watched the play of golden light on the arbour of flowering vines that formed a type of tunnel leading from the front fence to the back garden.

There was a sudden flash of bright pink fabric crouching low, moving through the foliage. It was puzzling as all the garden staff had finished their work long ago and had left for the day.

Nagma, her new maid, would never wear such a bright colour. She was always shy and modest, being quite religious, and hurried around the house with her huge shy eyes downcast and her hair hidden by a sari shawl. Sara was overcome with sudden anxiety and called for Malika. "Who's that in the garden? I think I saw someone."

"It could be Mutu's wife; she comes to visit him sometimes."

But Malika left the room in a hurry, and Sara's suspicions were aroused. Malika was not behaving in her usual way, and there was something furtive about her movements.

Sara followed her into the back garden and down the path, and there, waiting by the fountain where she'd often sung while she combed her lovely hair, was Lakshmi. Not the Lakshmi she remembered, proud and beautiful, but a tired and ragged girl with a pale unhealthy colour. Malika had handed her a bowl and the girl was eating like someone who hadn't eaten for a while. At the sound of her footsteps they both turned around with guilty expressions. Lakshmi stood for a moment on the alert, then hurried away like a beaten animal, the bowl still in her hands.

All of Sara's faint distrust of the girl evaporated. She was filled with pity. "Stay, please stay!" She smiled as kindly as she knew how to calm the girl, who stared back at her with wild feverish eyes.

Lakshmi halted and eyed her with suspicion, but at Sara's kind tone she relaxed a little and gave a small blessing.

"Lakshmi, come, sit down and rest." A strange tenderness overtook her, knowing that Lakshmi was broken and without hope. "Why have you come here to beg, my dear? Is there no food in your new house?"

The girl stared down at her feet, unwilling to speak, but looked up every now and then with haunted eyes.

Neither of them said anything, then, after a moment, Malika spoke up.

"Lakshmi has no job."

"But I thought she had a good job, with friends of Mr Charles."

Lakshmi looked at Malika, who also stared down at her feet.

"What is it? What is it you're not telling me?"

There was an uneasy silence till Malika spoke again. "Lakshmi has run away."

"You were not happy in your new place?"

Again, the women stared at each other, unwilling to speak.

"It is nothing."

"If it's nothing, why does she have to beg?"

380

Malika disguised her words by speaking Tamil, knowing that she spoke too fast to follow. Now Sara knew for certain there was something they were hiding from her.

"Malika, tell me."

This time Lakshmi turned on her with something of her old fire in her eyes. "I would not sleep with Mr Charles's friend!"

"What? Sleep with ... who?"

"Mr George. He makes me sleep with him, like Mr Charles, but I hate him! He beats me!"

Sara stood, dazed. "Sleep with Mr Charles?"

"Do not listen, madam. Lakshmi is not well. Here ..." Malika pushed some money into the girl's palm. "Go!"

"No! Come inside and eat some more. I want to know everything."

"I cannot."

"Don't you trust me, Lakshmi? Have I ever been unkind to you?"

The girl stared at her for a long moment, then she fell to her knees, sobbing as though her heart would break. "It is I who has been unkind, I who have been cruel. I did not want you to have a baby, so I gave you herbs to eat and make you sick. I was afraid if you had a baby Mr Charles would send me away."

She grasped both of Sara's hands in her own and kissed them over and over again. "Forgive me, madam ... forgive me ..."

There was something odd about the girl's manner, as though she was losing her mind. Then she leapt to her feet, almost crazed now, her skin glistening with beads of sweat, her eyes staring. "Mr Charles send me away, he send me away." She spoke as though she could not believe it. "He send me away. And he take Nagma instead! Nagma is not as pretty as me! She's not as pretty as me!"

Then she turned and fled before Sara had a chance to realise she'd gone.

"Nagma!" Sara almost fell with the shock. Her voice came back to her, a faint echo of disbelief. "But she's just a child!"

The summer house had always been his domain, and up till that moment she'd only ever been inside it for brief visits. He'd always discouraged her from invading what he called his 'masculine retreat', and she always respected his need for privacy while working.

Now a burning curiosity drove her to open the carved wooden door onto his private world. His divan bed, heaped high with embroidered cushions, lay against the wall next to a desk piled with papers. The room was strongly impregnated with the smell of musk incense, a fragrance he'd always claimed to hate. It clung to everything, cloying and overwhelming. She sat down on the bed to think. Then her eyes noticed a small, almost tattered book poking out from under the pillows. She opened it, at first flicking idly through the pages without really seeing. Then she realised what she was looking at, and the illustrations shocked her to the core. It wasn't so much the lurid positions of the lovers; they were crudely drawn and almost too technical to be erotic. It was the thought of herself, in bed with him, and her revulsion at what he expected of her, and how he had selfishly tried to deny her pleasure for his own sake.

"Hypocrite!" she spat through clenched teeth. "Hypocrite!"

By the time Charles came home that night she had composed herself. There had been no wild crying with rage at her husband's betrayal, only an icy calm and a new strength to face what was ahead of her. Now, all she wanted was to get away from him as soon as possible.

He came into the drawing room at his usual time, calling for Shakur as he did so. "Where are you, you lazy dog? Get me my drink."

He was in a good mood and looking forward to telling Sara his daily news.

"Sara!"

"I'm here, Charles."

"There you are ... what's the matter? Are you ill?"

"No, I'm not ill."

"Then what are you doing, sitting there in the dark?"

"Is it dark? I hadn't noticed." She dragged herself to her feet. "Charles, I saw Lakshmi today."

A vein on his forehead twitched, and he straightened his back as he always did when he was displeased about something. Then he swallowed hard and regained his self-control. "What did she want?"

Despite her attempts to appear composed, her voice shook when she spoke.

"How could you? To throw Lakshmi out when you grew tired of her, and then hand her over to another man, as though she's nothing ..."

His eyes opened wide in genuine surprise. "Is that what this is about? Is that all?" He seemed relieved, even summoning up a faint laugh.

"Listen, my dear, there are things you don't know about men and certain women; it's not for pure women like you to understand."

"Pure?"

She felt a sudden urge to tell him how pure she really was, though, despite her fury at Ravi, she didn't want him to suffer for it.

"Did you know she's in love with you?"

"In love? Is that what you call it? Well, I knew the girl had a bit of a thing for me, I suppose. That was her trouble; she was too jealous. You noticed it yourself. Listen, what does it matter; you wanted to be rid of her, and George is a good fellow. She'd be as happy with him as with me. Happier! George's not so damn bad-tempered ..." He gave a faint echo of a laugh while he brushed his blond hair out of his eyes. "Listen, Sara, I'm sorry about this but all the men have a girl. I tried to get rid of her before you came, but she begged me to keep her. I know I shouldn't have listened to her ..."

"Then Nagma is somehow different in your eyes?"

For a moment he couldn't answer, and the room fell quiet except for the sound of Mutu banging the pots and pans in the kitchen.

"No wonder the servants laugh at me behind my back. Well, they won't be able to for much longer. I'm leaving you."

At first he was puzzled, staring at her blankly and not realising she meant what she said, then, in a sudden rage, he rushed to the door and screamed down the hall, "Quiet! Or I'll come and make you!"

Instantly there was a tense silence and, feeling better, he softened his tone. "You're not serious, my dear, over some Indian girl? Why, if every woman left her husband over this, there wouldn't be a married couple left in Madras. But of course I'll get rid of her at once."

"I was going to leave you anyway, Charles. Right from the beginning, our marriage has been a mistake. I don't blame you, really ... I blame myself the most. I want my dowry returned to me, at least what's left of it, so I can support myself till we get a divorce ..."

At first it seemed he might plead with her, then he chose anger instead.

"Don't be a fool! You're not leaving this house ... Anyway," he added, "your dowry belongs to me now."

He'd played his trump card. Whenever he wanted to assert his authority over her, he could remind her of her dependence on him.

"My jewels then. Where are they?"

"They're locked in my office safe, and there they'll stay. But they're not really your jewels, are they? It's only because of my position here that you have them at all. They belong to me, as does everything else in this marriage. You can never leave me ... ever! If you think I'll stand by and let you humiliate me, you're mistaken!"

Then he changed his tone, taking her hand in his to reason with her.

"Listen, can we talk about this later? I must go. I'm sorry, I really am. We'll talk about this when I come back."

It was useless to argue with him, she could see that, so she nodded a silent agreement. It was best he leave her, allowing her time to make her escape.

There was no alternative; she must go now, penniless or not.

The sound of his footsteps echoed on the stones running down the front path. The gate of the picket fence was closed with a furious bang, then all was silent.

She hadn't moved since he'd left the room, being too drained of emotion to do anything except fix her eyes on the spot where he'd last stood.

The silence of the night was so deafening she felt she could hear her own blood pounding in her ears. At last she dragged herself to her room to retrieve her packed suitcase hidden under the bed.

After counting the money in her purse, she found that with strict economy there was just enough to last till her small monthly allowance arrived from the lawyers.

Then she told Malika of her plan, and the woman fell to her knees and wept with relief.

Later, when she was dressed in one of Malika's plain cotton saris, Malika stood back to view the effect.

"I cannot bear to see you dressed this way ... If someone should see you they will blame me for not looking after you."

Sara laughed, but it was brief and bitter. "It doesn't matter what anyone thinks any more. From now on I do as I like."

She took a final sip of tea from the china tea service that had come with her from England as part of her dowry, for a moment feeling a faint pang of pain at having to leave behind all her precious belongings, especially to a man who was now a stranger to her, and for whom she now felt nothing but hatred.

Chapter 35

Madras at night was almost as busy as day, but nobody noticed two poor women, their faces hidden by their saris, in a shabby carriage pulled by a small thin pony. Sara thought of her beautiful Pansy, and how she had to leave her behind for the moment at least, but knew she would be well taken care of by the little boy who fed her every day, till she could take her back somehow. They passed rows of sleeping figures, women with small children wrapped up in their saris, old men as thin as sticks, more dead than alive, and ragged children curled together for protection against the terrors of the night. For once, Sara felt truly at one with this band of refugees and her heart wept for their plight, but she at least could pay to have a roof over her head.

Their room was at the back of the hotel, high above a busy courtyard, where she could sit on her latticed wooden balcony and look down on life below without being seen. A wide wooden bed hung with mosquito netting sat in the centre of the room, covered with a cheap but clean cotton mattress and a striped woven bedspread. Despite the simplicity of her surroundings, she felt at last she was at least being true to herself. No more would she have to endure the sight and touch of the man she knew now for certain she could never return to.

Though, knowing she should be making a plan for the future, she felt curiously unable to motivate herself to action. She spent many hours sitting on her balcony and listening to the sounds of strange, incoherent talking and singing rising up from the courtyard below, while turning her thoughts over and over in her head.

If she sold her aunt's gold earrings which, thankfully, she'd been wearing when he had taken her jewel box, she might have enough money to keep herself and Malika for the few months till the Maharaja came home, providing she could find somewhere cheap enough to live. She was too proud to rely solely on the Maharaja. But where would she sell her small handful of valuables? Who would buy them? Somehow the problem seemed unsurmountable.

In this way the days passed, till one morning she could hardly find the strength to rise from her bed. The heat inside the room was unbearable and not being able to go outside in the heat of the day was beginning to play on her nerves. She stumbled wearily around the room all day or sat watching small naked children play in the muddy courtyard through the closed shutters. She knew she would have to make a move soon, but everything seemed so difficult. She was overcome with an almost constant nausea now, and everything she ate she almost instantly vomited up.

A day later Sara awoke too sick to leave her bed, only being able to watch, her eyes listless and vacant, as Malika boiled some tea on a small stove in the corner of the room.

"We must leave this place," Malika said as she watched Sara swallow the tea she had prepared. "I have seen Mr Chandran and he asked me why I am here."

"You didn't tell him, did you?"

"I had to; he will not say anything. He promised to help."

"No, he'll tell Mr Charles ..."

She sighed and fell back on the bed, weighed down by her problems. If only she didn't feel so ill. If only she had the strength to make a decision.

Later in the evening she fell into a listless state and was only just aware of being carried outside into the night air. Someone placed her with great care into the back of a carriage, and in a brief moment of consciousness she caught sight of Chandran's kind anxious face as he looked down at her.

"Do not worry, my dear Mrs Fitzroy, do not worry ..."

When she woke much later she found herself in a wide cool room, the shutters thrown open to let in the night air and the sweet fragrance of frangipani and the salty tang of the nearby sea. The soft light of a candle burned on a small table by the bed, casting a warm comforting glow on the room. Even so, she let out a small groan of despair as she remembered the past, and with a sob rolled over to press her face into the pillow.

A figure was bending over the bed and whispering as she held one of Sara's hands. "Shh ... you're safe now ... go back to sleep ... The doctor has given you something." She tried to raise herself but fell back on the pillow as Lucy's voice came out of the mist. "You are in your mother's house. Mr Chadran went to Monsieur Ravi and he told me to bring you here. Ravi will take care of you."

"Not Ravi ... I must not see him, I must not see him ..."

Lucy took her hand again to soothe her. "Ravi is going away to France and he's not coming back. He will be gone from India in a few days ... so don't worry any more."

"Ravi is leaving Madras?" Sara could barely speak his name as for so long he'd become a faint memory to blush over and reproach herself with, though, later in the depth of her dream, she felt his firm hand around her waist when they had danced on the night of the ball in Pondicherry. Then, all at once, the music stopped. He bent to kiss her hand, then left her.

The sweet night fragrances washed over her. It was a room for dreaming and there she lay floating, in a state of suspended animation, wanting to move but not feeling strong enough to make such a small resolve.

She lay in a posture of hopeless fatigue, too tired to think, her head pressed into the pillows. What a relief it was to sink into oblivion, to sink deeper into the gentle blackness of night.

She felt a cool hand on her forehead and Malika's voice. "Sleep now ... Sarianna ... sleep."

Later, much later, when Lucy pulled open the shutters to let in the light, the morning was black with a monsoon storm, while gusts of cool wind blew into the room, laden with the smell of damp earth. It was a scent Sara loved and, still not fully awake, she smiled, for a while not realising where she was. When she could focus, she became aware of a painting on the wall opposite, of a vividly painted scene of a street in Paris, the trees fresh with blossom and the sky a happy blue.

The painting cheered her for a moment, then she felt a deep pang of misery in the pit of her stomach. She stared vacantly around her but smiled when she saw a bowl of frangipanis on the table beside her bed; their fresh beauty comforted her, as flowers always could. Then she shifted her tired body, feeling weak and depressed. Something had happened: something she couldn't remember.

Hearing her sigh, Lucy came towards her. "You are awake?"

"I feel so strange ... What time is it? I feel as though I've been lying here for such a long time ... What is that painting on the wall? I feel I've seen it before somewhere."

"Monsieur Ravi put it there so you will see it when you wake."

Sara remembered with a sudden jolt. "Of course, he brought me here."

"I'm glad he did. You were in quite a state."

"What's wrong with me? Am I ill?"

Lucy smiled and took her hand in her own. "You had some sort of breakdown ... but the doctor asked if you may be with child also ... because of the vomiting in the morning. Is there a chance he may be right?"

Sara's hands flew to her stomach. "A child! No, it's not possible; it couldn't be. No, there's no child, I'm sure of it."

Then, gradually, the truth dawned on her. Her breasts had been sore and swollen lately. Because of the shock of the discovery about Lakshmi she hadn't thought about it too much, but she had missed her monthly cycle. She must be pregnant! That was why she'd been so ill, and there was no doubt in her mind the child was the result of those passionate weeks with Ravi Sabran.

Charles had not been in her bed for months, and he hadn't insisted, which was unlike him. Then she realised with a wave of bitterness it was probably because of little Nagma.

The irony of her situation was not lost on her, and she laughed out loud, a hollow, sour laugh. After all the times Charles had forced himself on her she hadn't conceived a child, and now she was pregnant after only a couple of weeks in Ravi Sabran's arms.

There would be more secrets: secrets that would go on and on for generations, as her own family's secret had.

A horrible thought overwhelmed her. Could it be that Ravi had planned to make her pregnant so she would have to bear the humiliation of giving birth to a child that would so clearly not be her husband's? Surely that would be an unthinkable revenge. But, even as she thought it, she dismissed the idea. He might have used her, but in her heart she knew he wasn't capable of that depth of cruelty.

Even so, a silent despair overtook her as doubt crept in, taunting her, till even her more passionate emotions shut down, leaving only a cold detachment.

She was sure she would die in childbirth, as her grand-mother had, and she told herself it might be best after all.

Later that same evening Ravi Sabran came to the house.

He watched her from the open door of the bedroom, his

face dark with anxiety, though, despite her illness, in his eyes she had never appeared more beautiful. The dark red waves of her hair lay spread out on the pillow to relieve some of the heat from her aching head, and when she called out his name in her sleep her voice was so low and full of pain he could hardly hear her.

He longed to go to her and take her in his arms one more time, to comfort her, to tell her how he loved her, how she was wrong about him, but he held back, knowing it was useless to prolong their inevitable parting. He could never leave Maya, knowing it would be certain death for her if she was ever left unprotected. He was afraid too of her killing herself if she ever knew of his love for another woman. He knew she loved him with an unusual passion, mixed as it was with gratitude and an almost childlike devotion.

It was his own fault, and this was his punishment; he was a prisoner of his own making.

While he watched, Sara cried out as faces from her past began to crowd in on her. An old man pleading with his eyes as he drowned; Cynthia's eyes with an expression of vacant dislike; Charles, when she first saw him in the garden back home in England with the sun shining on his golden hair. A stray thought reached her subconscious. Where was home now? She had no home.

Then the fragrance of sandalwood half revived her. What did it remind her of? Of course, it was Ravi.

She dreamt of Ravi's dark eyes when they came close to her own, and the deep impenetrable gaze she struggled to understand. Then she felt the touch of his hand on her cheek and the gentle pressure of his lips on her eyelids, her forehead, and on her lips.

She moved in her sleep and reached out her arms to him. "Ravi ..." She sighed his name.

Then his voice flowed over her, far away now, coming out of the mist of her dream. "*Au revoir ... au revoir,* my love, my only love, Sarianna ..."

Chapter 36

When she woke the next day, the room was half shuttered against the sun and she had no idea of the time
or how long she'd slept. She lay for some time, too tired to
move. She could only just recall that something momentous
had happened, something that unsettled her but thrilled her
at the same time.

Then she had a recollection of a dream she'd had, or was
it a dream? Was the feel of his warm breath on her cheek
real? Did he really whisper the words "My only love
Sarianna"?

Then she shook her head; it was a dream after all. Ravi
had left for France. She would never see him again.

In the background she heard a door slam, shaking her out
of her dream, then an angry male voice was raised against
the silence and she was plunged into a dark fear.

"No, sir ... Please, madam is very sick still ... You come
back another time, please, sir."

"Get out of the way! If I want to see my wife, I will ..."

"But the doctor say ..."

"I don't give a damn what some doctor said! How dare you try to stop me? Get out of my way!"

The door swung open and Charles stood before her, shaking with anger, his riding whip in his hand. "What are you doing here? In that man's house! Get up at once!"

At first she thought he might use the whip against her, but she roused herself to face him and he stepped back, giving time for her fear to dissolve and leaving only a kind of revulsion.

"How did you find me?"

"I had that McKenzie woman followed; she was cunning, but not cunning enough. You must have known you can never hide from me."

It was true; she could never escape him. He would make her life miserable to the end if she let him.

She pulled on her dressing gown and stood to face him. "I want you to leave. This is my house now. Monsieur Sabran has let this house to me."

"I told you! We can never rent from an Indian! You must know how it would appear, you being here! Have you lost your senses?"

She stared straight ahead, not even bothering to turn to look at him.

"I'm not married to you any more, Charles. I can do as I like. So, if you don't mind, kindly leave."

"Don't be a fool! You're coming home with me!"

He tried to drag her out of the room, but Malika threw herself between them. "Sir, sir, the doctor is here! Dr Shankar is here! He will explain it to you." She made little frantic movements at the air near his legs, afraid to touch him.

He stood back to stare at her, as though the feel of her hands would defile him. "Dr Shankar?" It was as though he'd been hit in the face.

"You had an Indian doctor attend you? You didn't have the decency to call an Englishman?"

She turned to look at him now, unleashing all her resentment at his bigotry and injustice with an icy calm. "Why shouldn't I have an Indian doctor attend me? After all, my own grandmother was Indian!" She faced him, proud and fearless, and hugely empowered.

There, she'd said it; there was no going back, and she was glad of it.

He laughed at first, then he opened his mouth, said nothing, and closed it.

There was a long silence while he stared at her, unable to collect his thoughts.

"What are you talking about? Don't be ridiculous! You don't even look Indian. You're making it up!"

"I told you. My grandmother was Indian. And I'm related to the Maharani; we are second cousins, but closely related nonetheless."

"Why didn't you tell me this before?"

"You mean before I married you? I didn't know myself till recently."

His expression conveyed his full horror on hearing her words. He almost lost his balance and for a moment she thought he might faint.

"It's true then?"

"Yes, it's true."

"That explains everything."

He paced the room, unable to stand still, as though looking for an answer, then, wanting to unleash his anger on someone, he turned to where Malika stood, crouched against the wall.

"Who told you to bring her here?"

Sara roused herself. "Leave her alone! She's afraid of you!"

"She has good reason to be afraid of me, now more than ever."

His voice terrified her, but somehow Malika found the courage to speak up. "I tell Monsieur Sabran! He said to bring Madam Sarianna here!"

"Sarianna! You dare to call her by that name?"

He stared at the woman, who by now had fallen to her knees and pulled her sari shawl over her face. For a moment Sara thought he would kill her on the spot, but with a great effort of will he turned away and made his way to the door. He stopped for a moment and turned to Sara, though the faraway expression in his eyes made it seem as though he was really talking to himself. "I'll make him wish he'd never been born."

When she heard his footsteps fade away at last, taking her past life with him, she consoled herself with the thought that at least Ravi was safe from Charles at last. He would be far away now, on his way to France with Maya.

Chapter 37

Sara sat in the summer house, turning over the pages of a book; she had given up trying to concentrate and instead sat mesmerised, watching a bronze lizard basking on a rock in the last rays of the late afternoon sun. Peace held sway for the moment, though it was an uneasy calm. She was well again, at least physically, well enough to wander in the garden and even to take up her pen and write. Now, hidden away from disapproving eyes, she had taken to wearing a sari to both hide the swelling of her stomach and to glory in the freedom of the light fabric.

She was a fragile shell still, but had now begun to try to plan her future, despite being almost overwhelmed with a feeling of impending doom. It was as though she was waiting for something to happen, something to change the course of her destiny. Her eyes closed and her head fell back in her chair, allowing the evening sounds to wash over her. The mynah birds were shrieking as usual, fighting over some scrap or other, but she liked their noise; it was friendly somehow.

Then her ears became attuned to another sound. Lucy had

come to visit and had left her for a moment to meet someone who had come with a message.

Lucy's soft tones were mingling with the excited, strident sounds of someone she didn't know.

After a moment she heard Lucy cry out, then silence.

Sara was instantly alert and, despite the warmth of the afternoon, she felt a shiver pass over her.

A few moments later Lucy stood before her, clutching a damp handkerchief. She stared down at the ground as though unwilling to look Sara in the face.

"Lucy! What is it?"

"Something has happened."

A cold knot of fear clutched at Sara's stomach. The nameless dread she had been expecting was upon her and her mouth was dry when she spoke.

"Tell me ..." The cup of tea she was holding began to shake wildly.

"It's Maya ... I'm afraid she has killed herself ..."

Sara froze. "Killed herself?"

The image of Maya appeared before her, the fairy-like beauty, the innocence of her glance, her sweetness. She felt a sob rise in her throat.

"But why? How? Are you sure?"

"She must have found some poison ... poor child ... Ravi is beside himself with grief."

"But he was supposed to be in France. I don't understand."

"He changed his mind. At the last minute he left the ship for no reason whatsoever. Then somehow your husband found out he hadn't sailed and ordered Maya be returned to her husband using whatever means they could. Ravi was in Madras when they attacked his Pondicherry house ..."

"Charles ordered this?" A wave of fresh hatred swept over her. So this was his revenge. She remembered his words when she'd last seen him.

"I'll make him wish he'd never been born."

"Some of Ravi's men were killed trying to protect Maya, and she was dragged away screaming. He swears to get his revenge on your husband, but he must not. Forgive me, but I've heard that your husband has laid a trap for Ravi ..."

With great difficulty Sara found the strength to speak. Her words came out choked with emotion. "If he had sailed like he was supposed to, then she would be alive now ... alive now ..." The words swam around and around in her head and the panic that had been held at bay swept over her in a sickening rush.

Later, in an agony of despair, she struggled to find the courage to write to him but, unwilling to remind him of her existence or of the evil of her own husband, she tore up page after page and didn't send a letter at all, though after a week of torment she received a letter from him that made her heart grow cold.

"Madam", the letter began, and his icy tone wounded her far deeper than she was prepared for.

"There is much I must say to you. I intend to go away from India forever. I don't care to be here any longer. Everything reminds me of Maya and my own treachery."

It was right he should address her in such remote terms, but to know he was going away forever somehow seemed unbearable. It was also impossible now to tell him about the baby she was carrying.

"She didn't deserve to die like that. She was only a girl still. It took a long time, you know, she was still alive when they brought her home to her mother ... the acid had burned her poor mouth ... she couldn't even say goodbye to me. Despite what you think, I'm not a savage. I could never kill anyone, but I have made it known to your husband that I intend to have him cut into a thousand pieces when he least expects it ... It could happen any time ... when he is in court or on the street or even when he is in his own home ... He will never be safe, and for not one second of the rest of his dog's life will he have an easy moment. He'll live in fear of my revenge till he dies of fear, then perhaps you will be released from the marriage you say is so hateful to you.

My Guru says I must not go down the path of revenge, as it will end with more pain, but I'm full of hate now and I must go away before I lose control and kill him myself. I must be a free man, not a murderer in a cage. If I had loved her better, taken better care of her ... She gave up everything for me, and I failed her.

Do you remember? I said to you that people would suffer because of the love I had for you, but in the end it would be worth it ... I didn't know what I was saying ... I couldn't imagine pain like this ...

Take care of the house for me, I owe this to you, but if by chance you ever return to your husband, promise me he will never live there.

There is one more thing. I want you to believe I did not feel about you as I did those other women. I admit at first I wanted to hurt your husband by making love to you, but it was I who was hurt in the end. I truly loved you then. Now I am nothing. I am unable to feel.

I will have the child Prema restored to you. I believe she was always meant to be yours.

Ravi Sabran."

There were no words of endearment she could take comfort in, only that he had once truly loved her, and somehow that hurt her even more.

There was a final reminder of his mysterious presence in her life when, a few days later, Pansy was returned to her by the little boy who fed her and attached to the saddle was a large parcel wrapped in silk.

Inside was the mother-of-pearl jewel box containing her necklace and the emerald earrings. There was no note accompanying the box, or any explanation of how the jewels were reclaimed; the boy who was paid to deliver the horse spoke only of a servant, dressed in clean white muslin and wearing a red turban, who'd given him the parcel to bring to her.

The red turbans were worn by Ravi's household, and then she knew for certain it was because of Ravi she had her jewels back.

The jewels were precious to her, but more precious still

was the thought that he had cared enough for her, in the midst of his pain, to think of her.

A week later, in the Madras newspaper was an account of how property of the Honourable Charles Fitzroy had been stolen from his office in the Department of Justice; the authorities were baffled as to how the intruder had managed to enter and leave the building unseen.

Chapter 38

For a month Sara had no news from her husband, till one day a letter arrived from him. Her first thought was to burn it; nothing he had to say could interest her at all. In her mind now it was as though he'd never existed, except when she was suddenly struck with the thought that she was, after all, still a married woman and would one day have to be confronted with the fact. Till then she lived from day to day, if not happily, her life was at least without acute misery. Living once more in her parents' home was her great consolation, and there it was easy to hide away from the unwelcome society of her former life.

She opened the letter with shaking fingers, disinterested at first, then with growing amazement. There was no sign of his former empty endearments, only her name at the top of the page.

"Sara,

As you know, I don't believe in divorce, and until now nothing would have driven me to commit such an act. However, Lady Palmer has convinced me the matter can be arranged without too much of a scandal.

Lord Palmer acknowledges our marriage is over, and that intermarriage between the races cannot be condoned. He knows how you tricked me into the marriage, and how you have never been a good wife to me.

He's also aware of how you flaunted your behaviour by living in the home of a well-known enemy of the English government.

Therefore, he's agreed to use his considerable influence to hurry the divorce through.

I don't expect to hear from you ever again."

According to Charles, the divorce would be finalised within a few months, as long as she didn't stand in his way. He didn't want the real reason to be made public, and as long as she kept quiet about it no one need be any the wiser.

"Cynthia and her parents are the only people aware of the true reason for my divorcing you, and I may as well tell you now, as you'll find out sooner or later. Cynthia and I will marry as soon as our divorce is final. We intend to leave for England as soon as possible, and from there I'll travel to Egypt to take up a more profitable position arranged by Cynthia's father. I'm tired of India and don't care if I never lay eyes on it again, or anyone in it ..."

Sara laughed out loud. "Coward!" she shouted, and relieved some of her emotions at least. She knew the real reason he was so anxious to be gone from India. He wanted to escape the ever-present fear of Ravi Sabran's revenge.

Within the week, Sara read again in the Madras Times:

> "Lord and Lady Palmer are to return to England after thirty years of service. They are to be accompanied by their daughter, Miss Cynthia Palmer, a popular local beauty who will be sadly missed by the entire English community".

There was no mention of Charles having left on the same boat. It was as though their marriage had never happened.

Chapter 39

Somehow, news of Sara's Indian blood had become common knowledge and, to some of the English community at least, she was now a social outcast and, even though she tried not to mind too much, she knew she would never get used to people turning away from her whenever they met her in the street. Although, before her swelling body had become obvious and still able to take her morning rides, she noticed the men looked at her with curiosity and even a new insolence, appraising her face and figure with a slow pleasure that was plainly insulting.

It was safer and more enjoyable to stay at home and create a world that was both harmonious for herself and her unborn child. Soon she began to take pleasure in her pregnancy, and drifted into a pleasant dreamlike, semi-happiness, tinged as it was with deep sadness.

It wasn't long before Lucy guessed the secret of her pregnancy, but she seemed to have a sixth sense as well as an innate delicacy and there was no need for explanations.

Sara's need for privacy was accepted without question, and the two women became closer than ever, bound by the mutual love and admiration of the man whose name could never be mentioned.

Lucy had sworn never to reveal to Ravi that Sara was carrying his child, even though she was tempted at times to enlighten him. Her comfort lay in her belief in fate, absolving her from a feeling of responsibility.

"If it is meant to happen, it will," Lucy said to herself when she sometimes felt a desire to take matters into her own hands.

"The gods will decide."

At times Lucy received a letter from him. At first they were brief and imbued with a sense of his despair, though, as time wore on, his mood seemed to lighten as he talked about the life he'd made for himself.

He'd bought a vineyard in the south of France, close to where his father lived. He liked it there and found the French way of life appealed to him and, as his father was getting old and needed him now, there was no question of him returning to India for a long time. Lucy sensed, despite the overall sad tone of his letters, he had begun to find some kind of peace within himself at last.

Sara's baby girl was born at the end of the monsoon season and was christened Lilita in honour of her grandmother. She was so beautiful Sara couldn't tear her eyes away from her, but lay with her in her arms while stroking her pale golden skin and black hair for hours on end, unable to believe she was really hers.

On the morning of the following day she received a letter from a London publisher telling her they had decided to print

The Diary of an English Lady in Madras in the form of a book and included an offer of what seemed to be generous terms, and a request for further instalments.

She was elated by the news, it seemed almost insignificant now compared to the birth of her baby girl. All at once there was happiness enough to sustain her, even despite her conflicted thoughts and the more pressing demands of daily life.

She longed to tell Ravi of the existence of his daughter, but till she felt the time was right she was determined the child must remain a secret to everyone but Lucy and the immediate household.

Malika loved the child with a passion, hardly allowing anyone else to go near her except her mother. She was the comfort and joy of her old age and gave the last months of her life a deep happiness. She firmly believed her beloved mistress had been returned to her at last in the form of this new baby and, because of this, the child was blessed, and a gift from the gods.

By now Sara's household had swollen to six people, and she was in constant fear of being unable to support them, though with a moderately generous monthly cheque from the sale of her book, and her own private allowance, she could manage to feed and clothe them all.

There was Prema and her ayah, and Mutu and Shakur as well, as Charles had turned them both out to fend for themselves when he'd closed down his own household.

With the mysterious workings of the gossip of Madras, they

had somehow found their way to her doorstep, and she could not bear to send them away. The sight of Shakur in the tattered remains of his former master's shirt, and the once plump body of Mutu, now reduced to that of a beggar, made it impossible to send them away.

Sara encouraged Malika to rest, and to enjoy her days in retirement with the baby, but the labour of decades was not easy for her to give up, and she seemed to take pleasure in her role as maid to her beloved mistress.

Though the day came when she didn't appear as usual to help brush Sara's hair, and it was clear at once there was something wrong.

The doctor confirmed Malika had suffered a stroke, and that there was nothing he could do. For a brief moment Malika opened her eyes and seemed to be very alert and in full command of her senses. She put out a hand and touched Sara's face, speaking with a deep tenderness. "I will see your mother again, and I will tell her of her granddaughter."

She slipped away without a struggle, seeming to almost welcome death, and, to Sara's great comfort, she was without pain to the last. She'd often spoken of her desire to be buried in the garden next to the grave of Sara's mother, and this was done. Now there were four graves, side by side under the giant tamarind trees.

The coming of the wet season brought on a listlessness that threatened to drag Sara's spirits down as heavily as the afternoon downpour. Every evening she wandered through the garden, which was fragrant in the moonlight and cool after the day's rain. But, instead of being comforted by the beauty of the night, she was tortured by thoughts that refused to go away. She thought of the failure of her marriage and of her fatherless child.

She fretted over her love for Ravi, and her desire for him, a desire that seemed to grow stronger every day, despite not having seen him for over a year. She tortured herself with the thought that one day she must make a decision about her future, and many times she took up a pen to write to Ravi and tell him about the child.

But afterwards, after staring blankly at the page for some time, she would tear it up and return to pacing her room once more.

She sometimes visited her cousin the Maharani, but had to leave her daughter behind in case they should tell Ravi, and even though the old couple would beg her to make her home with them, she refused, despite her loneliness. Apart from her secret child, it was Tamarind House that held her. The house had a hold on her emotions impossible to break, and every time she returned, even after a short visit to the outside world, it seemed the spirits of her long-dead parents were waiting to greet her, and envelop her once more with a sense of peace.

Then came a powerful change in her spirits and, even though there was no apparent reason, she began to bathe and dress with extra care, even changing into a fresh gown every evening before slipping the Maharaja's pearls around her neck and the emeralds in her ears. There was expectation in the air, even though the hot inky-blue nights were sure to be the same as any other.

Before beginning her nocturnal wanderings in the garden, she would scrutinise her reflection in the mirror above the sideboard. Her eyes seemed larger in her face, and there was a new understanding in her eyes, a maturity gained through suffering. As a final touch she always applied kohl, making her eyes larger still, but darkened now with an air of exotic mystery. Then she would recall, with vivid clarity, how she had always worn it for Ravi, and how they had made love in the Maharaja's palace; it seemed so long ago.

As usual, before retiring for the night, she lingered in the summer house as her mother had done, leaning back in the old cane chair, her eyes closed, listening to the sounds of the birds settling in the trees and the sweet baby laughter of Lilita coming from the open nursery window.

It was as though she was waiting for something, but for what she had no idea. She had almost despaired of ever seeing Ravi Sabran again, till that night, just as evening had fallen, a new noise, the sound of urgent footsteps, separated itself from the others.

She leapt to her feet, her hand to her heart, straining to recognise the shadow standing in the doorway. The faint lingering scent of sandalwood came first, and then she was sure.

At first both of them were hesitant. He approached her, almost with stealth, as though drawn inevitably towards the soft glow of her now radiant face, lit as it was by candlelight. His own eyes remained fixed on hers, as though she might all of a sudden take fright and leap away like a startled animal.

But she was mesmerised by his strange light grey eyes and unable to move, and she remembered how in the past he had always brought something with him, something indefinable and magical. On her part her senses were so intensified it felt as though she was almost disembodied and floated in a shimmering silvery haze, enveloping both him and her. Only once before had she experienced such a sensation, and she remembered it was the night when they had made love for the first time in the Maharaja's palace.

The impact of his sudden presence was almost as overwhelming as the day they had first met: the day of her arrival in India. The straight black hair that once hung to his shoulders was trimmed almost to the point of being civilised, though even the European cut and French tailoring of his cream linen suit couldn't disguise the strange, mystical and complex man he was underneath. She was struck afresh by his power, the leopard-like movements, the sense he kept his body and soul only just contained in the outward trappings of a sophisticated man. It struck her she would always be a little in awe of him and that was dangerous, but she was alive again, her flesh was warm again, and she was willing to take any chance just to be with him.

Then the light caught his face and she could see him clearly. He was only a man after all, a man who had suffered and come through the storm with signs of that struggle in clearly etched lines around his mouth and a new painful understanding in his eyes. It seemed his old cynical arrogance had been replaced with something else. He was proud still and the regal manner was there, but there was compassion now to moderate that pride.

She put out a hand to steady herself and to clear her head, finding hard reality in the feel of her book, placed only moments before on the little garden table. She had dreamt of this moment for so long and now she found it difficult to utter a word.

He spoke first and, for the first time since she had known him, he seemed a little unsure. "You are looking very beautiful this evening ... Why are you dressed so? You're not waiting for anyone, are you?"

"Well, yes I am ..." she murmured, then turned away to hide her faint smile, her face hidden in shadow, while his eyes followed the glint of the emeralds as they danced in the candlelight.

His black eyebrows drew together in a frown. It was plain he was confused. "But I heard ... Lucy said ... You and your husband ..."

"Yes, all that is over now ... over forever ..."

He took several steps closer, only a few inches away from the creamy skin on the back of her neck, so close he could breathe in her fragrance. The bulk of his shoulders overshadowed her, and again she experienced the prickling rush of his warm breath on her skin as he whispered, "There is no one else?"

"No ... no ... of course not."

She felt him let out a sigh of relief, then a hurried stream of words.

"I couldn't come to you any sooner, not until I had lost the desire for revenge. Do you understand? I couldn't come till I had found peace. I had to wait ... till Maya ..." There he hesitated, then placed his hands on her shoulders, turning her to face him, to look into her luminous, almost pleading eyes, while emphasising his words.

"She will always be with me, but not as it was. I know you will not mind that ... but now life has returned to me. Now I have seen you, we must never be parted again, never. I know now I am nothing without you."

In a moment she was in his arms, her head against his chest as he kissed her hair and told her over and over how he loved her.

There was so much she wanted to ask him. Why hadn't he written to her? Had he missed her? Was he tortured by thoughts she might be suffering without him? Was he tortured by thoughts of her? But all of that seemed unimportant now. There was time for that later, sweet endless time.

She knew in her heart they were always meant to be together. He talked of finding peace and she understood, for she had found peace too, now that he was there before her.

"Forgive me, Ravi," she murmured, in between kissing his face, his mouth, his hands, "for everything I once said to you ... I have always loved only you ... I have been waiting for so long ... Forgive me ... forgive me ..."

It took some time to tell him about their baby; she had made several starts, but somehow no words seemed enough to speak of such a momentous event, then when all was quiet in the house she took him by the hand and led him upstairs to the nursery.

Lilita slept in the middle of the room under a mosquito net in a cot that had once been her own. He didn't ask why she had led him there.

It needed no explanation, he understood at once, and some of the pain and guilt still written on his face fell away as he picked up the child with an exclamation of wild joy, before turning to her to cover her with kisses.

They married under a bower of jasmine in the garden of her family home, on a clear and fragrant morning, amongst the lilting sounds of birdsong, and she became the most radiant and happiest of wives, Madame Sarianna Sabran.

The air was filled with the ghosts of the past, but it seemed they were at peace now and unlikely to haunt her, except with thoughts of what might have been.

The scent of Attar of Roses, her mother's favourite perfume, filled the air around her, startling her at first, then, looking around at the bright morning, she felt sure the fragrance must be coming from an earth-bound soul.

A little shiver ran down her back as she thought of Maya, the beautiful fairy-like Maya. She had always been a wraith-like soul, but would she torment them forever with her tragic death? Then she stole a glance at her beloved Ravi, holding his exquisite daughter, a tiny fragile thing in his powerful arms. The baby, who wore a garland of tuberose around her head, began a happy gurgle as she played with her toes, causing

Ravi to laugh too, and Sara felt a surge of hope, knowing life, as ever renewing and certain as the seasons, would overcome what had gone before.

For her marriage, as a sign of love and gratitude, she wore the Maharaja's pearls, as the Maharaja himself proudly gave her away in front of a crowd of loyal friends.

Standing alongside with her ayah and Lucy was little Prema in her white muslin gown and bouquet of flowers, who had indeed been an omen for the future, but, like the meaning of her name, an omen for love.

Her grandmother's emerald earrings she wore for tradition and family, and as she slipped the green stones into her ears she felt a curious and instant connection with her once secret past; it was a powerful sensation and it gave her a renewed strength to know that they were worn now with a certainty that her own future would be different.

There would be no more secrets and no more lies; she could face what lay before her with pride in her family, and absolute belief in her love for the man by her side. Their love had been tried in the cruellest of ways, but had survived to be stronger than before, and more precious for what they had endured.